For Harlan Ellison –
The Dangerous Vision that got away . . .

Born in New York City in 1940, Norman Spinrad has travelled extensively throughout America and abroad to Europe and the Far East. He has been a sandal maker, a literary agent, a critic and columnist, and a radio talk-show host. His novels and short stories, including *Bug Jack Barron*, *Child of Fortune* and *The Void Captain's Tale*, have been translated into a dozen languages and nominated for many major awards, including the National Book Award. He is also the author of *Stayin' Alive: A Writer's Guide*. He currently lives in Los Angeles.

By the same author

NORMAN SPINRAD

The Men in the Jungle

GRAFTON BOOKS

A Division of the Collins Publishing Group

LONDON GLASGOW
TORONTO SYDNEY AUCKLAND

Grafton Books
A Division of the Collins Publishing Group
8 Grafton Street, London W1X 3LA

Published by Grafton Books 1989

First published in Great Britain by
Sphere Books Ltd 1972

Copyright © Norman Spinrad 1967

ISBN 0-586-20420-2

Printed and bound in Great Britain by
Collins, Glasgow

Set in Times

Chapter 1

Bart Fraden sat loosely on the edge of the desk, a strange mixture of tension and repose, like a hunting cat at rest. What the hell, he thought, biting off another savoury piece of pheasant leg, you can't expect to ride the same gravy train forever.

He dropped the pheasant leg casually back on to the tooled silver tray which rested on the heavily waxed walnut desk top, picked up the half-full bottle of chilled Rhine wine, and washed down the bit of fowl with a small swallow. The wine was good, it was damned good – and it had better be, considering that each bottle of the stuff set the Belt Free State back thirty Confedollars.

The pheasant, on the other hand, was kind of dry and overdone. But after all, Fraden thought indulgently, Ah Ming must be having a hard time concentrating on his cooking with the good old Belt Free State falling in around our ears.

Ah Ming, after all, as personal chef to the President of the BFS, had a nice little thing going here on Ceres, and, Fraden knew, strictly from outside observation, the average cat pretty much goes ape when the bird in his hand suddenly begins to take wing.

It was an attitude that Bart Fraden found utterly alien. After all, a cat with a given talent just had to stick his nose in the air and sniff out the proper arena for his particular line of evil. When one flower runs dry of nectar, the bee goes on to the next. A chef as good as Ah Ming could carve himself out a nice little niche anywhere from Earth to Antares. He could do something superlatively that most men couldn't do at all. That, after all, was the only security any man, chef or politician, could ever really have.

Fraden reached across his desk and took a big Havana cigar out of the hand-carved ivory desk-humidor. He sniffed at it appreciatively for a moment then stuck it in his mouth and lit it. He sucked rich smoke and stared for one wistful moment around the office – at the teak-panelled walls, the red wool wall-to-wall carpeting, the Picasso, the Calder, the Mallinstein, the wall bar stocked with the best booze, every drop of it imported all the way from Earth, the constant-humitemp closet filled with cases of cigars . . .

Quite a layout for the Asteroid Belt. This room alone must've cost something like ten thousand Belt Dollars. There was nothing like the Presidential Dome this side of Mars – wood, food, cigars, whiskey . . . And every bit of it imported directly from Earth at enormous expense to the BFS treasury. The first and last President of the Belt Free State lived in high style.

Fraden sighed wistfully, but the wistfulness did nothing to soften his hard, angular face, handsome in its own stark way. Fraden's face was all flat planes, sharp angles, and hard shadows playing up his deep-set dark brown eyes and sharp though well-proportioned nose. With his hard, live face, his large-boned but wiry body, his thick crest of black hair, Fraden looked every inch the predator that he was.

Bart Fraden caught his own moment of wistfulness and forced a sharp, mocking laugh. 'Hey, man,' he said aloud, perhaps trying to convince himself, 'the Asteroid Belt ain't the only catfish in the sea! Easy come, easy go!'

He turned to the communicator on the stand next to his desk. It was really time to make sure things were ready to go; in fact, it was about time to split, if only that damned

Valdez would show up already. If the Confederal blockade kept him from getting through . . .

That was an eventuality that Bart Fraden did not care to consider. Things were bad enough as they were, without ringing in theoretical disasters. The so-called rebels – actually nothing more than regular troops of the newly organized Confederated States of Terra in drag – already held just about every rock in what had been the Belt Free State except the capital worldlet of Ceres and a few surrounding asteroids. Most important, they had already captured every last one of the Uranium Bodies, those chunks of nearly pure pitchblende which were the real reason for the so-called revolution in the first place. Sure, the official flack was that the Oppressed People of the Asteroids were rebelling against the despot Fraden so that they could join with their Terrestrial comrades in the newly formed CST, et cetera, ad infinitum, ad nauseum. But the truth of course, as every microcephalic idiot in the solar system over the age of two knew, was that the new amalgam of the Atlantic Union, the Greater Soviet Union and Great China was feeling its collective cheerios and had decided that it was tired of paying Bart Fraden good hard cash for the Belt's uranium and that grabbing the Belt for its very own would be cheaper in the long run. *Sic transit gloria mundi.*

Fraden pressed one of the large cluster of buttons and spoke into the communicator. 'Ling? Fraden here. The starship, I trust, is loaded and ready? Good. Keep it primed for lift-off. Remember, Captain, my Swisstate bank has orders to transfer a hundred thousand Confedollars to your numbered account the moment we're safely beyond Pluto. Spotted Valdez's ship yet? Well, call me the moment you do. And transfer the cargo pronto, the moment he lands. Right. Out.'

Fraden sighed and puffed on his cigar for comfort.

Anyway, he thought, no one can say that Bart Fraden can't read the handwriting on the wall.

Said handwriting had been clearly visible to Bart Fraden for the better part of two years. The first letters had appeared when the GSU, the AU, and Great China, scared witless by a near-miss at a three-way thermonuclear war over some trifle that was already an obscure footnote to history, had banded together in mutual terror to form the Confederated States of Terra. To anyone smart enough to come in out of the rain, the message was all too clear. With the System's Big Boys at last banded together into one clutching cabal, the days of the System's myriad little independent states – the Martian Commonwealth, the Jovian Hegemony, the Trans-Saturnian Dominion, the Belt Free State, and all the rest – were numbered. The only questions were who would be grabbed first and how soon.

Fortunately, the Confederation had been nice enough to tip its hand by doubling its purchases of uranium from the BFS. Clearly it was stockpiling the stuff, which meant that it expected the supply to be temporarily interrupted, which was a dead giveaway that the BFS was first on its Christmas shopping list.

So even before the phony revolution started, Fraden had reached deep into his large Swisstate numbered bank account and bought himself a small but by no means cheap starship. Once a behemoth like the Confederation had eyes for the Belt, there was nothing to be done about it but to prepare an exit, an exit to the stars, where there were still scores of independent planets, at least one of which should have the proper revolutionary potential for a man who knew where it was at to knock over and set himself up a planetary government that would keep him in goodies for centuries, or at least for the rest of his life. With skill, and cunning, and a little insurance.

If only the damned blockade didn't stop that insurance, all one hundred million Confedollars worth, from coming through.

Fraden shrugged. Might as well hear the latest disaster report, he thought. Nothing else to do till Valdez shows.

'Have General Vanderling come to my office pronto,' he said into the communicator.

Willem Vanderling, a squat, bald bullet of a man, bustled through the corridor connecting the main Ceres Dome with Fraden's self-contained little mansion, scowling and shaking his head.

The military situation was, to be conservative about it, hopeless. Ceres was already enclosed in all but the Plutowards direction, and it was only a matter of time before the Con-men completed the englobement. And not a hell of a lot of time at that, Vanderling thought. Bart'll have to give up his cosy little nest in less than a standard day if he expects to get off with a whole skin. The thought gave Vanderling a certain grim satisfaction.

Thing was, Bart seemed more bugged at the way Ah Ming's cooking had deteriorated than at the prospect of losing the Belt Free State. The bastard always acted as if he had four aces hidden up his goddamned hand-tailored sleeve. Even now, with the BFS being chewed to bits around him.

The hell of it was that Bart Fraden always did seem to end up pulling an ace or two out of his sleeve. The man was always five steps ahead of every political and economic bump in the road – even the ones that Vanderling didn't feel when he went over 'em. Damn good thing Bart doesn't know a lasecannon from a snipgun. If he knew as much as I do about running a war, I'd be out on my ear in the vacuum, Vanderling thought. This way, at least, neither of us knows one word about the other's line of

11

evil. No chance of a double-cross either way – we need each other, we're a team.

Fraden and Vanderling had risen from a mutual gutter to rule the Belt Free State together, Fraden had hit the Belt more or less fleeing Earth after his first and only term as governor of Great New York Province in the Atlantic Union, a term distinguished by a record for graft and corruption impressive even for that infamous den of political backscratching and bakering. Vanderling had been born in the Belt, of grandparents who had made the New Voortrek and was the leader of a nice-sized band of hijackers that stayed one step ahead of the New South African militia only by dint of his inborn tactical genius.

Apart, they were a small-time pirate and a has-been politician grubbing among the Asteroids, then ruled by the New Voortrekkers as New South Africa. But when they came together in the catalytic atmosphere of the fetid dictatorship that was New South Africa, they were suddenly transformed into a revolutionary force, and they had replaced New South Africa with their own Belt Free State in two intensive years of high-powered demagogy and low-key guerrilla warfare.

Of course, as Fraden had contended from the first, it was true that New South Africa was more than over-ripe for revolution. The Asteroids had been originally settled by Boer refugees from the Great African Pogrom who hoped to establish a new Boer state in the Asteroids, with their rumoured mineral wealth. Two years after the founding of New South Africa, the Uranium Bodies were discovered, and the Great Uranium Rush began as thousands upon thousands of hopefuls from Earth's poorer areas hocked their worldly goods to buy one-way passages to the Belt, confident of striking it rich.

But of course when they got there, the Geiger Guys found that the Boer government had staked out each and every Body for itself and that they were back on the bottom of the heap without a ladder. Since most of the flood of Asians, Africans, and Latin Americans had arrived stone broke, history repeated itself with a vengeance, and New South Africa became the new South Africa indeed, with a Boer oligarchy lording it over darker-skinned masses all over again.

In short, as Fraden had quickly convinced Vanderling, an ideal pushover for a good guerrilla leader and a smart politician who knew which end was up.

'Easy come, easy go,' Vanderling muttered to himself, trying to draw some reflected solace from Fraden's easy indifference and not at all succeeding. Fleeing the Solar System for parts and planets unknown was not exactly Vanderling's vision of the Good Life.

When Vanderling stormed through Fraden's outer office and into the inner sanctum, unannounced as was his prerogative, he saw that Sophia O'Hara was sitting in the big chair, with Fraden leaning against the desk. This is all I need to make my day complete, Vanderling thought sourly.

Sophia was a girl who had attached herself to Fraden somewhere near the end of the revolution. She was short, lithe, well-stacked, dark-skinned, fine-featured with deep green eyes; flaming red hair fell down to her shoulders, and she oozed sex appeal. Vanderling hated her guts, and the feeling was quite mutual.

Sophia smiled at him with sweet sarcasm and said, 'Here's our bullethead come to tell us, no doubt, that he's saved the day, surrounded the Con-men, and we'll all live happily ever after. You can tell by the cheery smile on his noble Neanderthal puss.'

Vanderling, as usual, totally ignored her. 'It's bad, Bart,' he said. 'It's very bad. They're about twelve hours from completing the englobement, which means with luck we can hold Ceres for another thirty hours. *Maybe*. If we're gonna get out at all, we damn well better get out now.'

'Cigar, Willem?' Fraden said, with an infuriating smile. Damn him, he enjoyed watching that chick of his bad-mouth people. But in spite of his irritation, Vanderling took a cigar from the proffered ivory humidor, lit it with Fraden's gold table lighter, and inhaled the rich Havana smoke. Fraden's taste in tobacco was as good as his taste in women was lousy. You had to give him that.

'How soon is "now"?' Fraden asked, lighting himself a fresh cigar.

'How long will it take to get the ship loaded and ready?' Vanderling said.

'Except for one small item, we could leave now,' Fraden said.

'Then I suggest that you and me and Little Miss Sunshine get aboard right now and get the hell out of here. Thirty hours is the optimistic figure, it might well be under a standard day. And once they've englobed Ceres a Martian sandflea couldn't sneak past the blockade on his hands and knees.'

'We can't leave yet,' Fraden insisted.

'What the hell's the matter with you?' Vanderling snapped. 'The ship's loaded and ready to go, the Conmen are practically knocking on the door, and you can't leave yet! What in blazes are you waiting for, a brass band to drum you out of the System playing "Hearts and Flowers"?'

'The small item we're waiting for,' Fraden said, 'is one of those big things that come in little packages. Valdez is running it through the blockade all the way from Earth, and I'm shelling out a hundred thousand Confedollars for the service. We've got to wait for it as long as we possibly can. It's our insurance.'

14

Here it comes, Vanderling thought with a mixture of annoyance and admiration. 'What kind of insurance?' he said dully.

'Use that naked head of yours,' Fraden said. 'We board the ship and split the Solar System for some outback planet. With no money, and the Confederation anxious for a little chat. So what happens then?'

'So you tell me, genius,' Vanderling said wearily.

'We're grabbed and held for Confederal extradition, that's what happens. No two-bit planetary government out there is about to play footsie with the Confederation for the sake of three paupers.'

'*Paupers?*' shouted Vanderling. 'You flipped? We've got better than a hundred million Confedollars in the Swisstate account!'

'Which,' said Fraden, 'anywhere outside the Solar System, we might as well use to line garbage cans. You're forgetting that there's no galactic monetary system. Each planet prints its own paper, and no other planet considers it money. That goes in spades for Confedollars. Only a few things are valuable everywhere – radioactives, manufactured stuff, Earthside gourmet food, tobacco, and booze. And we'd need a whole fleet of ships to carry a hundred million worth of any of 'em.'

'So?'

'So,' said Fraden, 'I've used our little clandestine bank account to buy a hundred million Confedollars' worth of commodities which *are* universally valuable, which do have small enough mass to be carried in the ship, and which will be worth ten times what they're worth on Earth in the outback. That's what Valdez's ship is carrying, and that's why we've got to take the chance and wait for it.'

Vanderling snorted. 'And just what in the blue blazes is this – ?' The buzz of the communicator cut him off. Fraden turned the volume up and Vanderling could hear

15

a voice that he recognized as that of Captain Ling, the officer in charge of the main port facilities.

'. . . Valdez is coming in now, but he's being chased by three Confederal cruisers . . .'

'Well, cover him, man! Give him cover!' Fraden shouted. 'Fifty thousand to every man on the gun crews if Valdez lands safely. And get that cargo transferred the moment he touches down.'

Already halfway to the door, Fraden said over his shoulder, 'Come on! This is it! Whether he makes it or not, we leave immediately, one way or the other.'

With Sophia and Vanderling trailing behind him, Fraden burst through the safety lock and into the Port Control Dome. For a vertiginous moment, he had the sensation of standing under the naked stars – for the dome was clear plexsteel and the sharp bright stars of Ceres' black sky were all around him, seemed close enough to touch . . .

But this was hardly the time to enjoy the view. As he half-ran to the control console in the centre of the small dome, where Ling and several other officers were tracking the incoming ships on the screens, he noted that the four lasecannon turrets which bracketed the concrete-floored landing area outside the dome were already sweeping their deadly red beams in intricate patterns among the multicoloured stars.

Reaching the control console, Fraden stared up along the beams, trying to spot the four moving points of light that were Valdez and the three blockade ships, among the unwinking stars of the Belt firmament.

'Over there, sir . . .' said Ling, a slight, balding half-oriental. He pointed low on the horizon, well below the angle of the lasecannon pattern. 'We're trying to get the beams between Valdez and the blockade ships. I think he's got the idea; he's dropping fast.'

16

Fraden sighted along Ling's finger and saw a tiny dot of light dropping towards the jagged and nearby Cerean horizon. Above it, three similar dots were following it down, but now the deadly red pencils of laser light interposed themselves above Valdez's ship, a gridwork of red death between the Confederal ships and Valdez.

Valdez's ship waxed as he watched it; now it was a clearly visible silver needle, streaking low, almost parallel to the jagged surface, headed straight for the landing field. Above, leery of the lasecannon at this range, the Confederal ships were veering off, giving up.

He's making it! Fraden thought. By damn, he's got it made! Valdez's ship was over the field now, nosing up and settling to the concrete surface on a thick orange tail of retrorocket fire . . .

'Look! Look!' Vanderling suddenly shouted, grabbing his arm and pointing wildly with his free hand. 'We've got one of the buggers!'

Out of the corner of his eye, Fraden saw one of the Confederal ships burst into flame as a laser beam hit its power plant and begin to spiral crazily down beyond the horizon out of control. But he kept his eye on that which mattered: Valdez's ship, the rockets now guttering as it touched down.

'*Bully* for our side, Chrome-dome!' he heard Sophia say sardonically. He understood, this time. What was it with Willem that he gave a damn for one very minor victory in a war already irrevocably lost?

As the two remaining Confederal ships turned tail, space-suited men were already wheeling towards Valdez's ship on powered dollies to transfer the precious cargo to the starship, which sat, a comparatively large silver ovoid, at the other end of the field. Home free! Fraden thought.

'Come on,' he said. 'Let's get to the airlock. We can

leave now. Say goodbye to the Belt Free State. It was a good thing while it lasted.'

'So is a mescbinge,' said Sophia O'Hara. 'But oh, what a morning after!'

Bart Fraden leaned forward in the copilot's seat of the small starship, stared at the maze of gauges, screens, dials, and controls before him, and said, 'Damn good thing these newer models virtually fly themselves.'

Willem Vanderling looked up from the check-out panel of the computopilot, a board of amber lights that one by one were turning green as the computopilot went through its check-out cycle, each light announcing, as it went green, that the air supply, or the auxiliary rockets, or the stasis-drive generator, or any one of the 178 other factors necessary for a safe lift-off and voyage had been automatically checked out and were go.

Vanderling looked at Fraden narrowly. 'I can con this thing manually, without the computopilot, if I have to,' he said. 'Thinking of ditching me somewheres, Bart?'

That's Willem, Fraden thought, still doesn't trust me an inch. I wonder if *I* have any business trusting him . . . But then, who trusts anyone? The only real trust is when you've got something the other cat needs. So I *can* trust him.

'You're not thinking again, Willem,' Fraden said. 'If I wanted to dump you, I could do it right here on Ceres without lifting more than my little finger. I need you, and you need me. Once we pick us a planet and get a revolution going, we'll – '

'And just how in hell do you expect to finance another revolution?' Vanderling said, turning back to the check-out panel. 'At least when we started in the Belt, we had my two ships, twenty men and all that loot you had from your term as governor of Great New York. Now all we

18

have is our brains, this ship, and a big-mouthed chick with expensive tastes.'

'You're forgetting the crates from Valdez's ship. The crates that cost a hundred million Confedollars . . .'

'Yeah, I sure am,' Vanderling said surlily. 'Ten damn crates that couldn't weigh more than a couple hundred pounds, and you risked our necks for 'em. Suppose you tell me what's in those crates that's worth about four hundred thousand a pound.'

'Three hundred pounds of assorted drugs,' Fraden said smugly. 'LSD, Omnidrene, herogyn, opium, hashish, huxleyon . . . you name it, we got it.'

'*What?*' Vanderling roared. 'You blow a hundred million on a load of drugs? I know you got expensive vices, man, but this is too much!'

'For crying out loud, Willem, even you can't really be that dense! We've got more drugs in the hold than have ever left Earth in one lump before. Don't forget, most of 'em are dependent on ingredients like opium or peyote that won't grow on any other planet. Which means that any other planet in the Galaxy that wants these drugs has to import them from Earth, which is, of course, strictly *verboten*. Those drugs are money, Willem. They're better than money because they're worth money anywhere. Can you think of anything else that's universally valuable that we could carry a hundred million Confedollars worth of in this crummy little ship?'

'No . . .' Vanderling muttered dubiously. 'But we'll be awfully hot wherever we try to peddle the stuff. What are you going to do about that? We escape the Solar System and get grabbed for pushing drugs. That doesn't make one hell of a lot of sense.'

'You're learning, Willem, you're learning,' Fraden said. 'You have just pointed out the reason why we're going to

19

pick a planet where our first and best customer will be the planetary government itself.'

'That makes sense,' Vanderling admitted. 'You know a planet like that?'

'Nope,' said Fraden. 'But I'm sure the computopilot does.'

Chapter 2

As the ship drifted dead in space, somewhere beyond Pluto, Bart Fraden sat in the Spartan ship's mess, glumly watching Sophia O'Hara wolf down great quantities of eggs, bacon, coffee, and toast with real cow butter.

Still intent on the food, Sophia, without looking up, said: 'Just how long do we sit here in the tag-end of nowhere playing with ourselves?'

Fraden winced, not at what she said, but at the rate she was consuming the ship's meagre store of decent, Earth-grown food. 'Soph,' he said, 'if you keep eating like there's no tomorrow, we'll be out of the good stuff and on S-rations within a week.' Ugh! The thought of eating the wretched synthetic glop that passed for Space-Rations did something to Fraden that losing the Belt Free State could not. That damned computopilot had better complete the program quick!

'I see you've managed to avoid answering my question,' Sophia reminded him, swabbing up egg yolk with a piece of toast – her fourth of the meal. 'And for your information, I'm doing us a big favour by gobbling up the goodies. The sooner we run out, the sooner your delicate gut will start to rumble, and the sooner you'll pick us a planet and get us the hell out of here, you miserable, degenerate, lazy – '

'So if I'm such a lout,' Fraden said with a smile, 'why didn't you head for Earth instead of tagging along? The Confederation couldn't care less about *you*. The party was over, and you could – '

'Oh, shut up, idiot! You're the only man I've ever met

21

who thought with something besides his stomach and his crotch, albeit at distressingly infrequent intervals. You've almost got a brain, Bart Fraden. I intend to stick tight to you, whether you like it or not, and see to it that you use it.'

Fraden looked across the table and his gaze met Sophia's green eyes. Her face softened for a moment, and she leaned across the table and kissed him on the lips, touching him lightly on the ear with a fingertip, and Bart Fraden was reminded once again that this was the only human being in the universe who really cared whether he lived or died.

Then the moment passed. Sophia went back to her food and said, 'Why don't we just head for the nearest inhabited planet? If we stay cooped up in this sardine can with Bullethead Vanderling much longer, I'm afraid I'll contract hydrophobia.'

'Aw, come on, Willem is no prize, but he's not *that* bad.'

'Isn't he? He's a shaved ape, a thug who bathes regularly, or at least I assume he does. The man has no vices. He risks his life, but not because he likes to eat well or take expensive drugs or keep a high-priced item like me around. A man who fights hard without supporting expensive tastes is doing it just for kicks. He's a latent sadist. I just do not have eyes for being confined in the same ship with him when he stops being *latent*. Therefore, I suggest we make tracks for the nearest glob of mud that calls itself an inhabited planet.'

'It's not as simple as all that,' Fraden said. 'We've got very specific and rather hard-to-fill requirements. That's what I spent the last three hours working on. I set up a program for Willem to feed into the computopilot. We need an inhabited planet that's out of the way, preferably one that doesn't get visitors. The population shouldn't be too large. The local government should be such that they'll be interested in the drugs. Most important, it must be a planet with a high revolutionary potential.'

'Now wait a minute! I can dimly understand that that mechanical moron can come up with a list of planets of a given size or population or even form of government. Are you trying to tell me that it's a mechanical Machiavelli that can measure "revolutionary potential", whatever that may be?'

'Hardly,' Fraden said. 'The computopilot has data on every inhabited planet in the Galaxy, strictly objective data. But there are certain objective criteria of revolutionary potential – dictatorial government, economic set-up, rigid class lines with high social tension, and about a hundred others. I simply constructed a schema listing the factors. Willem programs the schema into the computopilot, the computer cross-correlates the factors with the data in its memory unit and prints out a list of planets in order of degree of correlation. I do the thinking. The computopilot just looks things up like a coolie librarian.'

'Science marches on!' Sophia said dubiously.

'Think I'll go see how far it's marched by now,' Fraden said. 'Care to join me?'

'Wouldn't miss it for the world.'

When they reached the control room, Vanderling was fumbling with a long ribbon of print-out paper.

'That the list?' Fraden asked. 'It looks awfully long.'

'Well, you had me program the thing to give us the revolutionary potential of every planet in the damn Galaxy, whether you realized it or not,' Vanderling said. 'However, seems like there's only four planets in the whole Galaxy with potentials better than fifty per cent.'

Fraden shrugged. It was about as he had expected. But

23

after all, one planet would be quite sufficient. 'Let's have a data print-out on those four,' he said.

Vanderling fiddled with the computopilot console. In about a minute, the printer rattled off about two feet worth of data. Vanderling tore off the paper and handed it to Fraden.

Fraden scanned the list. Sundown, Yisroel, Sangre, Cheeringboda. Never heard of any of 'em, Fraden thought. Which means hardly anyone else has either. So far, so good. Hmmm . . . Sundown looked good: .8967 Earth-normal, population ten million, mixed Sino-Russian population . . . Uh, oh. Population about evenly divided between both groups. Good revolutionary potential either way you played it. Which meant that you'd have a chronic revolutionary situation that you could never eliminate. An easy planet to conquer, but impossible to hold. Scratch Sundown!

Yisroel . . . . 9083 Earth-normal. Population, nine million. First settled by ultra-orthodox Jews in '94. Later generally Jewish migration. Now ruled by Chief Rabbi. Rumours of unrest by descendants of later migrants . . . Hmmm . . . looks promising. *Huh?* Standard English unknown on planet. Classical Hebrew official and only language . . . Two down!

'Well?' said Sophia. 'By the look of your face, it's not so good.'

'Too bad none of us speaks Hebrew . . .' Fraden muttered, still scanning the data sheet.

'*Hebrew?* Have you been hitting the drugs in the hold?'

'Hey, wait a minute!' Fraden exclaimed, his face brightening. 'I think we've hit the jackpot! Listen to this. Sangre: .9321 Earth-normal . . . population, fifteen million humans, indeterminate number of semi-intelligent natives . . . *Semi*-intelligent? That sounds impossible.'

24

'Some of my best friends are semi-intelligent,' Sophia observed.

'Yeah, sure . . .' Fraden muttered abstractedly. '. . . originally settled three hundred years ago by religious splinter-group known as the Brotherhood of Pain ejected from the Tau Ceti system on charges of murder and ritual torture which were never proved . . . Believed to have taken slaves from the Lost Colony of Eureka, which was found gutted fifty years later . . . Hey, dig this! No officially verified off-worlder touch-downs on Sangre for 220 years. Last suspected contact in 2308 when looted ship was found on trajectory that would've brought it within a light-year of Sangre. Ship believed to have contained illicit shipment of herogyn for Balder . . . and that's all that's pointed out on Sangre. That and two asterisks. What in hell does that mean, Willem?'

'One asterisk means that a planet should only be touched down on in case of dire emergency,' Vanderling said. 'Two, I guess means the same thing, only in spades.'

'It sounds like the Black Hole of Calcutta,' Sophia said.

'Exactly!' replied Fraden. 'In other words, it sounds great! Sounds like there's a nice tight little oligarchy of nuts running the place, maybe even with a slave-population. Couldn't ask for a better revolutionary situation if I designed it myself. And a good indication that the people who're running the show have a more than passing interest in drugs. Sangre it is!'

'You're the boss,' Vanderling said, without much enthusiasm. 'Just wish we knew something more about the place.'

'I can tell you one more little piece of gossip,' Sophia said. 'Sangre is the Old Spanish word for blood.'

The stasis-drive, by encysting the ship in a bubble of subjective time independent of the objective time of the outside universe, enabled it to reach the vicinity of Sangre in three weeks, instead of an Einsteinian ninety-three years. There were times during the voyage, though, when Bart Fraden was certain that the drive was out and that they wouldn't get to Sangre in centuries. One of those times was when the real food ran out, ten days out of Earth, and they were reduced to living off the loathsome S-rations. And any time when he was in the same room with Sophia and Vanderling together, minutes seemed like hours. If Vanderling wasn't bitching about Sophia's appetite, Sophia was bitching about Vanderling's supposed sadistic personality, or his stupidity, or if she had nothing better to grouse about, the unsightliness of his shining 'chromedome.'

Thus, by the time they made orbit around Sangre, Fraden didn't care what the planet was like – Sangre was *it*. Another week of this, he told himself, as they gathered in the control room, and I'll be chewing on the nearest rug.

'Welcome to Mudball, Jewel of the Galaxy,' Sophia said, eyeing the planet in the ship's main viewscreen with a sour sneer. 'And what can you tell us about this planetary paradise that we don't already know?'

Vanderling studiously buried his face in the series of aerial photos that the ship's drone missiles had taken during the twelve hours they had been in orbit around Sangre.

'Not one hell of a lot,' Fraden admitted. 'Only the eastern half of one continent seems inhabited. Nothing strange about that on a planet with only fifteen million people. Mostly a lot of very small towns, or farms with a central complex of buildings every hundred square miles or so. Hard to tell which. One big city, couple hundred thousand or so, which seems to have something that looks like a spaceport. And that's about all we can reasonably expect to learn about Sangre from orbit.'

'So what now, Peerless Leader?' Sophia said.

'Now,' said Bart Fraden, 'we've done all the planning we can for a while. Now we play it by the seat of our pants. Willem, see if you can raise that spaceport on the radio.'

Vanderling fiddled with the radio while Fraden sucked at a tooth in a peculiar fashion.

'Something stuck in your teeth?' Sophia asked.

'Might say so,' Fraden replied. 'I've replaced a filling with a microminitransmitter. Clever little jobbie, works off body electricity and bone conduction. A little piece of insurance, as you'll see once we – '

'We're getting something, Bart,' Vanderling said. 'Wait a minute . . .' There was a series of hisses, whines, and crackles as Vanderling adjusted the radio, and then, abruptly, a voice came in loud and clear.

'. . . unidentified ship. Calling unidentified ship. You will give co-ordinates at once, or be destroyed. Calling unidentified ship. You will give your co-ordinates at once or be destroyed . . .'

There was a peculiar quality to the voice, a kind of manic assurance, paradoxically mixed with what sounded like laconic indifference.

'Now there's a nice cheery welcome,' said Sophia.

'There's a nice pure bluff,' said Bart Fraden. 'If they had the hardware to destroy us, they'd certainly have the gear to track our signal back to the ship. They certainly wouldn't be asking us for our co-ordinates and thereby admitting that they can't locate us themselves. Two points for our side.'

Fraden took the microphone. 'This is Bart Fraden, President in exile of the Belt Free State. This is the President of the Belt Free State Government-in-Exile.

27

We formally request political asylum. Put me in touch with your head of government or chief of state immediately.'

There was a long pause. Apparently, Fraden thought, these bozos never heard of a government-in-exile. All the better . . .

Finally the Sangran voice said blandly, with that same weirdly laconic ferocity, 'Report your co-ordinates at once, or leave the system. You are ordered to report your co-ordinates at once or leave the system.'

Progress of a sort, Fraden mused. 'Willem,' he asked, 'could you rig one of the lifeboats to explode and make like a missile, if you had to?'

'I suppose so. They have atomic power plants of course, and I could rig a delayed timer to pull the rods. But it wouldn't be very accurate.'

'Wouldn't have to be,' Fraden said. He picked up the microphone. 'Listen, sonny,' he said, 'this is President Fraden again, and I'm not accustomed to dealing with flunkies. You get your ruler on this radio, and you do it in five minutes, or we'll put a nice medium-sized A-bomb right in the middle of your crummy little burg. Minus five minutes and counting.'

The response was totally unexpected. Fraden heard a few moments of what sounded like very heavy breathing, then suddenly the voice on the radio was screaming, 'Kill! Kill! Kill! Kill!'

'What in the blue – ?'

There was a click, a moment of silence, then another voice, strangely like the first, said, 'You will state your business with the Prophet of Pain.'

'If this Prophet is your ruler, then you can give your buddy his rabies shot and tell the big cheese that I want to talk to him pronto and that if I don't have him on the radio in three minutes and sixteen seconds, he'll have an

28

A-bomb in his lap. Three minutes three seconds and counting.'

A minute passed, then another. 'Looks like we may have to put on a fireworks display to convince the natives,' Vanderling said. He did not seem exactly dismayed at the prospect.

'This is Moro, Prophet of Pain,' a deep, resonant voice said.

'Pity to spoil old Bullethead's jollies,' Sophia said.

Fraden shot her a quick and definitive shut-up look.

'This is Moro, Prophet of Pain, calling President Fraden of the Belt Free State Government-in-Exile, whatever in Hitler's name that may be. State your business and state it speedily. My patience is non-existent.'

'This is President Fraden. We request political asylum on Sangre under interstellar law.'

A heavy, oily laugh came over the radio. 'There is only one universal law,' the man called Moro said. 'The strong kill and the weak die. We want no refugees on Sangre – unless, of course, you care to die in the arena.'

'That's not exactly a hospitable way to talk to a man who just may bounce an A-bomb off your head if he gets bugged,' Fraden said. 'It's also no way to talk to a man who's offering you paradise at bargain-basement prices.'

'Paradise?'

'You've heard of Omnidrene?' Fraden asked.

'Omnidrene? What is Omnidrene?'

'I have it from an inhumanly reliable source that you know all about herogyn,' Fraden said. 'Well, multiply the pleasures of herogyn by ten, subtract its addictive properties, and you've got Omnidrene. Or I should say, *I've* got Omnidrene. A couple centuries' supply. I'm selling if you're buying. Of course, if you're not interested, I can always go on to – '

'Wait!' said Moro. 'This Omnidrene . . . Yes, I am very

29

much interested. You will land at the spaceport. I will send my personal car for you and we will discuss this matter face to face.'

'Fine,' said Fraden. 'It's obvious you're a man of taste and reason. And being a reasonable man, you must realize that I'm not about to land a shipful of Omnidrene until certain arrangements have been made. I'll bring some samples in a lifeboat. My associates will remain on the ship. I hate to be crude, but of course if anything should happen to me, there would no longer be any reason for my associates to refrain from bombing your city . . .'

'To be sure,' said Moro smoothly. 'Believe me, you can trust me. I'll be expecting you shortly. Out.'

'Bart, you're crazy!' Sophia said. 'The minute that thug has you in his hot little hand, he'll force you to order the ship down. He knows you're bluffing. Even a cretin would know you're bluffing.'

'Two points for his side,' Fraden replied. He tapped his tooth. 'But five points for ours. I know that he knows. Insurance, remember? Willem, you'll stay here and monitor what goes on on the microminitransmitter in my tooth. Don't make a move until I tell you to.'

'I insist on going with you!' Sophia said, balling her hands into fists. 'If you're going to jump into the frying pan, you'll need someone with a modicum of intelligence to pick you up when you fall flat on your face. Besides, I've no intention of staying cooped up in this tin coffin with old Bullethead while you get to breathe fresh air.'

Fraden looked at her, with her green eyes blazing, her body tension-stiff, and he realized again how much she really loved him. But love was something neither of them would ever admit to the other.

'Since you insist,' he said, 'I suppose I have no choice. You can come with.'

30

Secretly, he admitted that he would've found some excuse to take her along anyway. Sophia had more guts and glands than any three men and for reasons he scarcely admitted even to himself, he wanted her by his side – but seen, and not heard!

'Just one thing,' he said. 'I do the talking. *All* the talking. You're beautiful, brilliant, passionate, and the love of my life, but a diplomat, Sophia O'Hara, you are not!'

The air of Sangre was hot and sultry as Bart Fraden led Sophia O'Hara out of the lifeboat's airlock and on to the concrete, such as it was, of the spaceport landing area. It was obvious that the Sangrans had not been using the spaceport for decades, possibly longer. The concrete landing apron was deeply pitted and cracked. Thick yellowish weeds grew tall in every crack; even a small tree here and there thrust its way up through the ruined concrete. The windows of the control tower were broken, nothing had much paint left on it, and four rusty, ancient ships rotted at one end of the field. A top team of engineers just might be able to put together one ship capable of lifting off by cannibalizing the others, Fraden thought. I was right; they can't touch our ship.

'That monstrosity must be our welcoming committee,' Sophia said, crooking a finger towards a large black groundcar that was bouncing across the field towards them on honest-to-god antique rubber-tyred wheels instead of modern aircushions. Although the design was ancient, the car's black paint and brass bright-work gleamed richly in the reddish Sangran sun, and as it screeched to a halt in front of them, Fraden could hear that its turbine was humming smoothly.

Two tall men in black uniforms and black forage caps got out of the rear section of the car, and Fraden noticed that there were two more of them in the front seat with the driver, a cadaverous hunched-up little man wearing some kind of black livery.

The uniformed men approached them. They carried obsolete but obviously well-cared-for projectile rifles. Strange-looking weapons dangled from grab-away holsters on their Sam Browne belts – two-foot steel bars ending in a heavy-looking steel ball, the ball covered like a porcupine with scores of tiny sharp blades. Fraden recognized it as a grisly modification of the ancient Terrestrial morningstar.

But the really disconcerting thing was the soldiers themselves. Both were tall, lean, and very hard-looking. Both had thin, receding brown hair, out-thrust chins, thin noses, and small, sunken, almost colourless blue eyes. Perhaps they were brothers. For some subliminal reason, though, Fraden was sure they were not.

'You are Bart Fraden,' the lead one said. It was not a question, but a statement in that same peculiarly laconic-yet-tense tone of voice that the Sangran on the radio had had – before he exploded in that insane burst of rage.

'I'm President Bart Fraden of the Belt – '

'You will come with us, Bart Fraden,' the soldier said, motioning towards the open door of the groundcar with the barrel of his rifle. Fraden suddenly noticed that the man's teeth were filed to sharp points.

'You are ordered to the presence of the Prophet,' the other soldier said, in virtually the same tone of voice. His teeth were filed to points too. 'You will move quickly now. You will take your female slave with you.'

'Slave!' howled Sophia. 'Why you hydrocephalic, cretaceous, worm-eaten son of a – '

Fraden winced, kicked her in the ankle, and dragged her bodily towards the groundcar. 'Damn it it, Soph,' he muttered *sotto voce*, 'take a good look at these characters and keep your big mouth shut!'

Fraden found himself and Sophia wedged into the back seat of the groundcar between the two soldiers who sat, ramrod-stiff and silent, as the car bounced off the concrete of the field and on to the far-better-maintained surface of what seemed like a main avenue.

The driver, under the watchful eye of the soldiers in the front seat, drove like a lunatic, or, Fraden thought, like a man who does not have to worry about rules or accidents. The car was moving very fast, and the soldier to the left of him partially blocked his view, so what he saw was sketchy and blurred.

It was also damned unsettling. The low buildings lining the avenue were spotless and beautifully faced with synth-marble, polished metal and wood, but he was sure that he had caught glimpses of fetid hovels behind them and on the cross-streets. There were no sidewalks as such, only general areas at the edges of the street that seemed reserved for what paltry foot traffic there was.

It seemed as if this area of the city was restricted territory of some kind – the street was nearly deserted. At one intersection, the driver had to swerve to avoid piling into a line of beautiful women. The women were naked, they were all slim redheads, and they were strung together by a chain connecting the steel collars around their necks. At either end of the line was a black-clad soldier, tall, lean, hard-looking, with receding brown hair, out-thrust chin, thin nose, small, sunken eyes.

There were few other pedestrians – here and there a few of the strangely similar-looking soldiers apparently guarding richly dressed men, a line of scrawny, pathetic-looking men carrying bundles, a group of about twenty fat, naked little boys no older than five or six being herded along by more soldiers, a similar group of pretty little girls . . .

'There is something mighty peculiar about this planet,' Sophia muttered, as the car swung off the avenue and on to a long driveway that led up a bare grassy hill towards a large walled compound.

'I'm glad you noticed,' Fraden muttered, glancing at the soldiers, who seemed totally indifferent to the conversation.

'I mean there's a pattern here,' Sophia said. 'Sure you expect a strange planet to feel weird, but there's something about this place that I can't quite put my finger on . . .'

'Well, we'll soon see,' Fraden said. 'Looks like we've arrived.'

The drive led to a heavy steel gate in the concrete wall. Atop the wall at regular intervals were a series of small towers. In each tower was what looked like a heavy-calibre projectile weapon manned by two soldiers. Four armed soldiers stood to either side of the gate. By the time the car reached the gate, it was sliding open, and with hardly a slack in speed, the car passed through the gate and into a large courtyard.

There were a score of small buildings in the interior of the compound, but the vast, square, enclosed area was dominated by a sprawling two-story concrete building with black-veined synthmarble steps, entranceway, and facing, and a large black-painted stadium which loomed behind it.

The car screeched to a sloppy halt in front of the main building, and Fraden and Sophia were hustled out of the car, up the synthmarble steps, through the heavily guarded arched entranceway, down a maze of wood-panelled hallways lit by old-fashioned fluorescents, and were finally brought to a halt in front of an ornate gilded

34

door. Two of the tall, hard-looking soldiers stood at attention in front of the door.

'You will inform the Prophet that Bart Fraden and his slave are outside his office,' one of the two soldiers with Fraden and Sophia said.

One of the guards spoke into a microphone grid cunningly concealed in the ornate design of the door: 'Bart Fraden has been brought to your presence, Master.'

'He will come in,' boomed a resonant voice from a similarly concealed speaker.

A guard opened the door, practically shoved them through it, and closed it behind them.

Fraden saw that they were in a small, opulently appointed room. The floor was covered with a deep black carpet. Three walls were panelled with some rich dark-burgundy wood, the ceiling was covered with gold leaf. The entire fourth wall was an enormous television screen.

In the centre of the room, a grossly fat man sat behind a large heavy table. On the table was some kind of small control console and a huge golden platter on which a half-eaten roast about the size of a large suckling pig sat in a bed of something that looked like rice. Fraden eyed the roast hopefully – it wasn't a pig, though it did look strangely familiar, but after two weeks of S-rations, any real meat looked like ambrosia.

Two guards flanked the fat man, who was dressed in a plain black robe. Although his body was obscenely fat, the man's face seemed hard, cruel, and intelligent: small, shining, dark eyes, a large, strangely thin-lipped mouth, oily black hair, a tiny beak of a nose, almost hidden in great pads of oleaginous flesh.

'Welcome to the sacred planet Sangre,' the fat man said. His voice was deep, resonant, somehow sinister. 'I am Moro, Prophet of Pain. We will talk of this Omnidrene, Fraden. While we talk, some diversion.'

He did something with the control console, and the huge television screen came to life. The screen showed a view down into a dirt-floored pit. In the pit were two beautiful redhaired women who looked like twins. They were naked except for cruel steel spurs, like those of a fighting cock, strapped to their wrists and ankles. Suddenly, they flew at each other in a terrible rage, ripping flesh with the spurs, biting, gouging, writhing in the dirt, a horrid, tortured knot of bleeding, tearing, murderous humanity. Mercifully, there was no audio.

Fraden stared at the terrible spectacle in horrified fascination, mesmerized by the hideous, unbelievable carnage. What kind of planet is this? he thought. What kind of man would – ?

'Yes . . .' Moro said sibilantly. 'Not a bad exhibition. Not bad at all . . .' Then with an abrupt change of tone: 'This entertainment is for my amusement, not yours, Fraden. You will keep your attention on the matter at hand. The matter at hand is this drug, Omnidrene. You have a sample with you?'

Gratefully, Fraden snapped his eyes and attention away from the horror on the television screen. He reached into a pocket and withdrew a small polybag of white powder. Of all the drugs in his huge cache, Omnidrene was the best one to peddle to the rulers of Sangre. One dose was five hours of paradise, a bliss that no external displeasure – even mortal pain – could penetrate. It was not physically addictive, there were no withdrawal symptoms, but anyone who used it for prolonged periods developed gradually a psychic dependence on the drug, a reluctance to face the vicissitudes of the real world that was so slow, so insidious that the victim never realized that he was an addict. An oligarchy addicted to Omnidrene would eventually simply come to not give a damn.

'This is the stuff, Moro,' Fraden said, holding out the

polybag. 'About the most powerful narcotic known to man. One dose is five hours of paradise, it's non-addictive and there are no physiological side effects. You can snort it, eat it, or inject it – injection is fastest, of course, and if you'd like to try it now, I brought a syringe with me . . .'

Moro's boar-eyes gleamed greedily. He reached out a fat hand for the polybag, hesitated, then pulled it back.

'Not so fast,' he said, eyeing Fraden narrowly. 'You didn't trust me and I see no reason to trust you. It could, after all, be poison.'

'What percentage would there be for me in poisoning you?' Fraden said.

'None,' Moro admitted. 'But for all I know your ideas of pleasure may be . . . *exotic*. You will take the drug first.'

Fraden swallowed hard. One shot wouldn't addict him by a long shot, he knew, but bargaining under the influence of Omnidrene was a good way to go home in a barrel. Occasionally, he thought, honesty really is the best policy.

He smiled knowingly. 'Very clever,' he said. 'We're on your home ground, and now you expect me to bargain while I'm bombed on Omnidrene. One shot of Omnidrene, and any lousy offer you make will look great to me. No, sir, if you want me to take it, you've got to take it at the same time. Then we'll at least be even.'

Moro's swarthy face contorted in a spasm of fury that was gone almost as soon as it came. 'You realize I could simply force you to take it,' he said, shrugging. 'But then, why bother arguing when there are plenty of useless slaves fit only for the Public Larder around?' He pressed a button on the control console. 'Slave!' he ordered. 'At once! An old one!'

'While we wait,' Moro said, 'you might as well eat.' He gestured negligently at the roast animal on the table.

'Don't mind if I do,' Fraden said. 'Soph?'

'Whatever it is, at least it isn't those filthy S-rations. I'm dying for real food, Bart. Cut me a slice too.'

Fraden carved two large slices of the roast with the knife beside the platter, handed one to Sophia. As he carved, he saw from the leer on Moro's face that the fat man had gone back to watching the horror on the television screen. He carefully avoided the sight of the carnage as he lifted the meat to his mouth. It smelled sweet and savoury. He took a bite. It had a texture something like lamb, was pleasantly pungent like pork, though a bit salty. Altogether not bad at all, he thought. Too bad Ah Ming isn't here. He could do some nice things with this.

He finished the slice and was about to carve another when a guard led in an emaciated, stooped, wizened old man, dressed only in a loincloth. The man's body was a mass of scars. Fraden lost his appetite, and he noticed that Sophia wasn't eating any more either.

'Give him a shot,' Moro ordered.

Fraden dissolved some of the Omnidrene in a vial of distilled water that he took from a pocket, filled a syringe and injected the drug into a prominent vein in the left arm of the stolidly unprotesting old man.

Almost instantly, the man's face softened into a mask of utter bliss. He grinned foolishly, went so limp that the guard had to hold him up. The old man looked around at the guards, at the television screen and beamed and beamed and beamed.

Moro studied him like an insect. 'So you're happy, eh?' he said.

The old man collapsed into low liquid giggling for a moment, then finally managed to mutter, 'Yes, Master . . . happy . . . happy . . . happy . . .' He began to giggle again uncontrollably.

'We shall see,' Moro said. 'Beat him!'

The guard holding the old man pinned his arms behind him. The soldier to the left of Moro stepped forward and began to beat the old man, in the stomach, in the neck, in the face, punch after punch after savage punch. The old man's lip split, blood dribbled down his chin, ran out of his nose. He giggled and giggled and giggled and kept grinning as the soldier beat him to a bloody pulp.

Moro smiled, obviously quite satisfied with things. 'Enough!' he finally said. 'Remove him!'

The guard dragged the blood-spattered, broken old man from the room. Even as he was dragged, the pitiful hulk kept giggling, continued to grin as he choked on his own blood.

'So,' said Moro, 'a pleasure-drug indeed. Seize him!'

One of the soldiers grabbed Fraden, who did not struggle. He had been expecting this.

'The slave too!'

The other soldier pinned Sophia's arms behind her. '*Slave?*' she screamed. 'You leprous mound of hairy whale-blubber! Your mother – '

'Shut up!' Fraden roared.

'For a man who was a President, you're not very bright, Fraden,' Moro gloated. 'Did you really think I would do anything but take the drug from you? The strong kill and the weak die. You will now order the ship to land. If you're quick about it and give no trouble, I promise you a relatively quick death. If not . . .' He shrugged and grinned wolfishly.

'You're not exactly Einstein yourself, Moro,' Fraden said. 'My crew has orders to A-bomb the city within the hour unless I say otherwise.'

'You will be taken to a transmitter and you will rescind those orders immediately!'

'Not a chance, man! No percentage in my doing that.'

'Very well,' Moro said diffidently. 'After a few minutes of the proper torture, you'll do anything I say. It will enliven a rather tedious day.'

'Strike three!' Fraden said, opening his mouth wide and touching his tongue to a molar. 'This is a transmitter in my tooth. The entire conversation has been monitored on my ship. You'll play it straight, or you'll be radioactive dust in five minutes. I'm tired of playing silly games.'

'You're bluffing!' Moro said instantly. 'An A-bomb would kill you too.'

'For a change you're right,' Fraden said. 'But the catch is that I've nothing to lose. You're going to kill me anyway, remember? You, on the other hand, have everything to lose. Want to call my bluff? Go right ahead. If you win, why then you've got yourself a nice corpse. If you lose, you're a dead man. Seems to me those are pretty one-sided stakes, no matter what the odds. But then, I never was a gambling man.'

Moro's eyes blazed. He clenched his fists. Then once again, he shrugged. 'Neither am I,' he said. 'Fortunately, this is a game I can well afford to lose. Very well. I want that drug. State your terms.'

'Now you're talking good sense! I'll sell you the drug, a modest quantity each month. I'll keep the stockpile in orbit in my ship, just in case you get any more fancy ideas. We can dicker about price once I clue myself in on what the local currency is worth.'

'Currency?' Moro said, frowning. 'What's *currency*?'

'Money,' said Fraden. He laughed. 'Surely you've heard of money?'

'Money . . . ? Ah yes, symbolic tokens of exchange! There is no monetary system on Sangre – no need for one. I own the planet, the Brotherhood, the peasants, and the Killers. The Brothers own their slaves and meat herds and Killers of their own. The peasants own the

Bugs. The strong take what they need from those weaker than they are. No need for tokens of exchange.'

'Then would you mind telling me how you expect to pay for the drug?'

Moro toyed with his heavy jowls. 'Hmmmm . . .' he mumbled. 'Well, why not, you're better than most of the fools! You will be initiated into the Brotherhood of Pain. As long as you continue to supply the drug, you'll be a full-fledged Brother.'

'I've got all the honorary titles I need,' Fraden said. 'Just what does that entitle me to?'

'Why, everything Sangre has to offer, of course!' Moro said. 'Your own Killers. Any slaves you care to take from those Animals not owned by anyone else. Your own herd of Meatanimals. Absolute power over everyone on Sangre, save me, other Brothers and our property. A seat in the Pavilion at the Pain Day Pageant. Land, if you want it.'

Fraden smiled. It was a far better opening wedge than he could've hoped for – a piece of the action, in effect.

'You've got yourself a deal,' he said. 'But I'll pass on the land. I'm a city boy, myself.'

'Good,' said Moro. 'Tomorrow we will hold the Initiation. You will be shown to your quarters now. Go. I wish to view the conclusion of this contest in private.'

And as one of the soldiers led them out, Fraden saw that Moro's attention was already riveted on the television screen again. He was careful not to look. Enjoy yourself while you can, lardbucket! he thought. Comes the Revolution!

Chapter 3

'The female slave will remain in your quarters.'

It had been a long night for Bart Fraden, a night full of second thoughts and not much sleep. He and Sophia, after looking over their rather sumptuous quarters, had spent the rest of the day poking around the large walled compound, trying to get the lie of the land.

The soldiers, Fraden found, were all over the place and seemed to be in charge. There were hundreds of them, possibly thousands, within the compound, and all of them had the same receding hairlines, lean hard bodies, prominent chins, small sunken eyes. If men were a species like dogs, then the soldiers were a breed, like Dobermans. The soldiers would answer simple, innocuous, strictly factual questions – they were known as Killers, the city was called Sade, the Sangran natives, who were nowhere to be seen, were known as the Bugs and were some kind of hive organism. But any really probing questions were turned away with blank stares.

Similarly, they were permitted to wander about the open courtyard almost at will, but arbitrary limits seemed to have been set on their freedom. When Fraden had tried to enter a small low building where fat, naked little boys entered in a long line at one end and didn't come out at the other, he was turned back at gunpoint. On the other hand, no one stopped him from watching a single Killer drilling a squad of older boys dressed in miniatures of the Killer uniform, carrying real-looking rifles and morningstars, and looking very much like the young of this separate breed, down to the teeth filed to sharp

42

points. But when he tried to follow a line of the most perfect little girls he had ever seen into a building where he had caught glimpses of older and equally perfect naked adolescent girls, he was again turned back at gunpoint. And the few men he saw dressed in black robes totally ignored him, as if he were an animal.

Later, after they had eaten a rather tasty dinner of the same pungent, salty meat that Moro had served, and were alone in the bedroom of their quarters, Sophia had said: 'Bart, let's get into that lifeboat and get out of here. I don't like this place. I don't like it at all.'

Fraden sat down next to her on the bed and kissed her. Her lips were limp beneath his. She pulled away from him. 'I'm not exactly in the mood,' she said, screwing her face into a sour expression that was half-disgust, half-fear. 'This stinking mudball is a lunatic asylum! That filthy thing old Whale-blubber was watching, getting his jollies out of watching women tear each other to pieces . . . And those horrid little boys with the filed teeth and the guns . . . And all those beautiful little girls that look so much alike . . . Bart, they breed *people* here! They breed people like animals! It's obvious – those Killers all look alike, and the young Killers look like some separate species . . . It's monstrous! We're no angels, but we're not monsters either. It's a cesspool! We've got to get out!'

'Sure it's a cesspool, Soph,' Fraden said. 'But remember what New South Africa was like? That wasn't paradise either. This planet is over-ripe for revolution. I can smell it. The worse it is for the people, the better it is for us. I know what I'm doing. In a year, this'll be *our* planet. Then I'll put a stop to the really bad stuff, I promise. Give it a year, Soph. If I can't take over a hellhole like this in a year, it's time to hang up.'

'All right, all right. But you're not going to that damned

Initiation Ceremony alone tomorrow! I'm coming with you.'

She put her hands on his shoulders, looked into his eyes, smiled wanly and said, 'You may be a swine, Bart Fraden, but you're the only swine I've got. I'm not about to lose you.'

He looked down at her, at her wild red hair, her tense, determined jaw. 'If that's the way you feel about it, you come with,' he said. 'I know I have lousy taste in women, but I could do worse than you. Beneath that crummy exterior, I sometimes detect the heart of a little girl.'

'Cut out the maudlin crap and let's go to bed,' she said. 'All of a sudden, I'm in the mood. Besides there's not a hell of a lot else to do.'

And now the Killer who had awakened them insisted: 'The female slave will remain in your quarters.'

'But she wants to see the Initiation Ceremony,' Fraden said. 'Despite her foul temper, she's my favourite slave and I like to please her.'

'Only Brothers may witness the Initiation,' the Killer said in a laconic monotone. 'Even Killers may not attend. You will come at once.'

Fraden shrugged. 'You heard the man, Soph.'

'I don't like the idea of your being alone,' Sophia insisted.

Fraden sucked at a tooth. 'Won't be *exactly* alone,' he muttered.

'You mean you've had that damned thing on all night? Bullethead heard everything that . . . ? Bart Fraden, you're a filthy, crud-minded, degenerate –'

'Just no way to turn it off,' Fraden said. He turned to the Killer. 'Come on, man,' he said, 'what're we waiting for? As I believe I've mentioned, this slave has an impossible temper!'

And he led the Killer out into the hall, just ahead of a long string of highly improbable obscenities.

The Killer led him to a small door painted dull black, opened it, thrust him through it, and slammed the door behind him.

Fraden found himself alone in a strange, medium-sized room that gave him an eerie feeling of being cut off from the world, of being thrust back into the womb. The ceiling, the walls, were draped in heavy black velvet, giving the room an uncanny feeling of indistinctness. The only light in the room was a large open fire burning in a great brass brazier, casting ominous shifting shadows in the heavily folded drapery. In front of the brazier was a rude, waist-high wooden altar, its surface stained and scratched. On the altar rested a small sharp axe and a long, thin sword. Fraden did not like it. He did not like it at all.

The draperies to one side of the brazier parted, and a great fat figure dressed in a long black robe, with a hood covering his head entered the room – Moro. Ten similarly clad figures followed the Prophet of Pain into the room, one carrying a black robe, another a white one. The last of them pushed the heavy drapes back into place.

Moro took the white robe, waddled over to Fraden, handed the robe to him, and said, 'The Prospective Brother will don the Robe of Innocence. Let the Prospective Brother know that to speak during the Initiation under any and all circumstances means instant death.'

Uneasily, Fraden put on the white robe. Play along with this idiocy, he told himself. No matter what, play along. He wondered what Vanderling, listening on the microminitransmitter was making of all this mumbo-jumbo. Probably appeals to his over-developed sense of the primitive, he thought dourly.

Moro stepped behind the altar in front of the fire,

rested his heavy hands on its scarred surface. The other men arranged themselves in a shallow semicircle, five to either side of the Prophet, cowls drawn low on their faces.

Moro stared straight at Fraden, his gross face, with its pig-eyes, tiny beak-nose, drawing a mad brand of insane dignity from the flickering orange firelight.

'The universe is dead,' Moro droned solemnly. 'It is a place of cold and fire and random death. The universe has no meaning. The universe has no will.'

'Only man has meaning,' the Brothers chanted contrapuntally. 'Only man has will.'

'Only in opposites is there meaning,' Moro droned on. 'Only between opposites may there be Choice. Only in Choice can there be Meaning. Only in Meaning can there be Existence.'

'And the measure of Existence is man,' the Brothers chanted.

Fraden shuffled his feet nervously. There was something deeply disturbing about this stupid, inane ritual . . . Then he realized what it was – Moro and the Brothers were dead serious. They hung on every word of it! It wasn't just a crock to impress the yokels; these men were fanatics.

'To live without Existence is not to live at all. Animals live, men Exist. One must choose. One must be an Animal or a man. There is only one real Choice: the Choice between doing and being done to, between taking Pleasure and receiving Pain. Pain and Pleasure are the Great Opposites. The giving of either means the receiving of the opposite. Animals receive Pain and thereby give Pleasure. Men give Pain and thereby receive Pleasure. One must choose.'

'Choose!' the Brothers chanted. 'Man or Animal? Choose! Choose!'

'The Brotherhood consists of humans who have

46

chosen,' Moro intoned. 'The Brotherhood of Pain is a brotherhood of humans who have chosen to be men. The Brotherhood of Pain consists of men who have chosen to give Pain and receive Pleasure. Brothers kill so that they may truly live. This ceremony is the ceremony of the Great Choice.'

'Brother or Animal?' the hooded men chanted. 'Pleasure or Pain! Life or death? Kill or be killed? Choose! Choose!'

Moro's glowing pig-eyes met Fraden's, held them like a cobra's hold a rat's. 'The moment of the Great Choice is at hand, Prospective Brother,' he said. 'Into this room, Brothers and Animals come, those who have chosen, and those who are to choose. To witness this ceremony is to choose between joining the Brotherhood as a man, or dying as an Animal. Only those who choose to kill leave this room alive.'

From beneath the folds of their robes, the Brothers drew long, sharp knives.

'The Great Choice!' cried Moro. 'Kill or be killed! The moment of decision is now! Bring forth the human animal!'

One of the ten Brothers sheathed his knife, and stepped behind the drapery. He emerged a moment later bearing a burden that turned Fraden's blood to ice, his knees to rubber. No! No! No! No! his mind screamed as he balled his hands into fists, felt his nails bite into the soft flesh of his palms.

For the object cradled in the arms of the black-robed Brother was a naked human baby.

The Brother passed the infant to Moro, who placed it face upward on the stained, scarred wooden altar. Now Fraden realized that the scratches were blade marks, the dark stains were dried human blood.

Moro read the expression on Fraden's face accurately.

He picked the hand axe up off the altar, thrust it in Fraden's limp palm and said, 'The moment of choice. Do not utter a sound or you die. By the death of this Animal, become a Brother, or by sparing it, die. The Great Choice is yours, Prospective Brother. Make it now, or it will be made for you.'

With that, Moro took the sword from the altar, placed its sharp tip against Fraden's Adam's apple. The Brothers encircled him, knives drawn, eyes eager.

Fraden stared woodenly down at the bland, motionless little face of the apparently drugged baby. He couldn't move, he couldn't speak. The axe in his hand seemed to quiver like a thing alive. He looked up, saw the Brothers tense with anticipation, saw Moro position every ounce of his ponderous bulk behind the blade at his throat, ready, eager, to ram it home.

He shut his eyes tight against the unseeable. To think of the Choice as monstrous was a mere inanity. To kill a . . . No! No! It was better to die, better to remove the impossible decision from his own power, better to . . .

'Now!' Moro ordered savagely. 'Choose now or die now! Kill or be killed. Now!'

Eyes still shut, Fraden felt the sword point move forward fractionally, felt the increased pressure behind it, felt the tight skin of his Adam's apple split minutely, felt a tiny trickle of blood wet his throat . . .

The moment hung suspended, extended its echoes backward and forward in time. Bart Fraden, who had led a revolution, who had fought against a counter-revolution, who planned another bloody uprising, had never killed by his own hand. Bart Fraden had never faced a moment like this, had never been so forced to delve into his own being. Kill or be killed. It was no longer an abstract problem in moral philosophy; it was an axe in his hand and a sword at his throat. He saw the next moment in his mind's eye, the bloody little body, the severed head, the blood, the blood, the blood . . . He couldn't! *He wouldn't!*

But the vision reversed itself. He saw himself with the sword thrust through his neck, pieces of blood-soaked flesh and cartilage hanging from both ends of the hole, felt the searing, terrible pain, the lazy, easy blackness closing in as his oxygen-starved brain expired . . . In that terrible moment, Bart Fraden saw himself die, and from the depths of his soul, his muscles, his heart, his guts, came a monumental spasm of refusal, denial – No! No! Not *me*!

The spasm ran through his guts, shot along his nervous system. The muscles in his arm contracted savagely, the axe in his hand came down in a heavy arc. There was a tiny, shrill scream, a hideous thunk that was felt, not heard, a soft moment of resistance; then a powerful shock that ran up his arm into his shoulders as the axe buried itself in the wood beneath the flesh.

Fraden went limp; only the muscles in his eyelids remained contracted, keeping his eyes tight shut. In the awful dark silence that followed, Bart Fraden held to sanity by a single thread that gave, stretched, then hardened to an iron, savage resolve that pulled him back from the brink. They would die! They would all die! The Brotherhood that had forced him to do this thing to himself would perish in a bath of blood. There would be no surrender for Moro or his monstrous Brotherhood when the Revolution was won. They would be exterminated like the rabid dogs they were! I'll kill them all! Kill . . . kill . . . kill . . .

A smell of scorching flesh, and a sharp slap across the face forced his eyes open. Moro grabbed him by the chin with one hand, thrust a tiny morsel of cooked meat into his mouth with the other.

Numbly, stupidly, he chewed upon it as the Brothers threatened him with their knives – and he tasted the pungent salty flavour of human flesh – the flavour he had unthinkingly relished less than a day before.

And as they stripped the white robe from him, and dressed him in the black garment of the Brotherhood, he held back the vomit in his throat only with the iron fury of his hate. There was no turning back now, no place for mercy or weakness or disgust. He could not live with himself until the Brotherhood of Pain was a nameless memory in an unmarked grave. I'll kill you all! he swore. I'll exterminate you so thoroughly that no one will remember you or your names! Or what happened in this dark place . . .

'Welcome, Brother,' the hooded men chanted. 'Welcome to the Brotherhood of Pain!'

Chapter 4

'Brother or Animal? Pleasure or Pain? Life or death? Kill or be killed? Choose! Choose!' The words filled the small cabin of the starship, loud, resonant, but somewhat tinny, filtered, remote, as Willem Vanderling sat in the pilot's seat, his face blank, his eyes unfocused, all his attention channelled through his ears as he listened, fascinated, to the event taking place on the planet far below him.

'. . . Into this room, Brothers and Animals come, those who have chosen and those who are to choose . . .'

Mo-*ther*! Vanderling thought. What kind of a planet has Bart picked out for us anyway? These yokums are out of their skulls!

He wished that it had somehow been possible to install a video pickup in Fraden's tooth-transmitter. It was pretty obvious that they were putting Bart through some kind of mumbo-jumbo ceremony, some kind of religion jazz. Great Choice . . . Pleasure . . . Pain . . . It sounded pretty screwy. Wonder how Bart's managing to keep from laughing his head off? Vanderling thought.

The voice on the radio become a shrill, threatening cry: '. . . Kill or be killed! The moment of decision is now! Bring forth the human animal!'

'Human animal!' Vanderling grunted aloud. '*Christ* – '

'. . . By the death of this Animal, become a Brother, or by sparing it, die . . .'

It was! It was! A sacrifice, a *human* sacrifice! There goes the whole Revolution up the flue! Bart's never killed a thing in his life. He wouldn't have the guts. Of all the . . .

'. . . Choose or die now! Kill or be killed. Now!'

'Jeez, they'll kill him!' Vanderling muttered. 'Where in hell does that leave me?' Damn you, Bart! he thought. Damn your chicken liver! You can't go and get yourself killed.

There was a long, ominous silence . . . Then a thunk! and a shrill scream all at once.

'Bart!' Vanderling cried. Christ, they've killed him! They've –

Then Vanderling heard the deep, wild chanting: 'Welcome, Brother. Welcome to the Brotherhood of Pain!'

Vanderling's jaw fell for a moment. Then a strange smile came to his lips, a wry smile, a knowing smile, a smile of sardonic satisfaction.

He did it! Vanderling thought. Son of a bitch, he did it! Bart killed. All by himself! These Sangrans must have *something* on the ball, after all. Kill or be killed, yeah, that was where it was at, all right. And now Bart's finally found out. Kill or be killed – no room for a cop-out there!

Vanderling laughed, a harsh, staccato laugh like the sound of an automatic weapon. Let's see Bart dish out some of his sanctimonious holier-than-thou crap now! he thought. Bart Fraden, *killer*. Now ain't *that* a kick in the head!

Vanderling felt a peculiar glow of satisfaction. He had gained something, some kind of edge, somehow. Welcome to the club, Bart, he thought. Welcome to where it's at.

Vanderling stood by the airlock door, his face a carefully composed blank, as the door slid open and Bart Fraden, trailed by Sophia O'Hara, stepped through into the ship proper. Fraden stepped briskly, shoulders squared jauntily. He smiled, nodded confidently. Christ, Vanderling thought disappointedly, it's the same damned old Bart!

52

'Well, we've got our big feet inside the door,' Fraden said. 'You're looking at a bona fide member of the Brotherhood of Pain, the local government, priesthood, mafia, and Tammany Hall all gift-wrapped in the same neat little bundle.

'No . . . ah . . . *trouble*, Bart?' Vanderling asked, hoping rather wanly to get at least some small rise out of Fraden, at least a momentary acknowledgement of what had really happened.

'Piece of cake,' Fraden said with infuriating cavalierness. 'If it had been a poker game, our mark Moro would've gone home in a barrel.'

Fraden walked towards the ship's mess as he spoke, and Vanderling trailed sourly behind him. Goddamn phony! Vanderling thought to himself. But he could not help feeling a certain grudging admiration. He noted that at least Sophia was keeping her big mouth shut for the moment. In fact, it seemed that she was studying Bart kind of peculiarly behind his back. Had he told her?

When they reached the ship's mess, Fraden plopped himself down in a chair, took a cigar from the box on the table, lit it as Vanderling and Sophia sat down flanking him.

Fraden blew a cloud of smoke into the air and sighed. 'Last box,' he said, 'and it's half-empty. Have to check and see if we can grow tobacco on this mudball.'

Damn him! Vanderling thought. Him and his cigars and food and big-mouthed chick. 'You think you can stop worrying about your taste buds long enough to tell me what's coming off?' he said. 'I'm tired of being cooped up in this tin can. When do I get some action? After three weeks in this damned thing, even a hick planet like Sangre'll look good.'

'You haven't seen our little Garden of Eden yet,

53

Chrome-dome,' Sophia said. 'When you do, you just may opt for the ship for the duration.'

'When I want *your* opinion,' Vanderling snapped, 'I'll send you a special-delivery lasergram – *collect*. What's happening, Bart? When do we start to move?'

'We're off and running already,' Fraden said. 'We'll play Mr Inside and Mr Outside for openers, and I'm already set up as Mr Inside: Brother Bart, member in good standing of the Brotherhood of Pain as long as I keep the Omnidrene coming. Supposedly, I came up here for the first month's shipment. I'll take lifeboat number one back to Sade – that's the name of the big burg, by the way, after the Marquis of the same name, which will give you a rough idea of where this Brotherhood is at. I'll work within the Brotherhood for the time being, hook 'em on Omnidrene and otherwise stir up the pot. You take number two and start playing Mr Outside in the outback. Build up a guerrilla force – I think I can leave the details of that up to you. The revolutionary potential's sky-high here, highest I've ever seen. The Brotherhood owns the whole planet and everyone else has all the legal rights of an Animal, so they should fall all over themselves to join up.'

'And what about weapons?' Vanderling grunted sourly. 'With a setup like that, you can't expect the yokums to have a single popgun.'

Fraden smiled. 'The best the opposition has is old-fashioned projectile stuff. Not so much as a lasegun. You should have no trouble making do with captured weapons once you get started.

'And just how do I go about capturing all these weapons without some weapons to begin with? With my bare hands?'

'Trust your good old Uncle Bart,' Fraden said. 'In 'boat

number two, you'll find, among other goodies, a couple cases of snipguns. How's that for an opening wedge?'

Vanderling shook his head in grudging admiration. Bart was one step ahead of the game again, damn him. The snipgun, the Sub-Nuclear Interference Projector, also known as the Edgeless Knife and the Big Slice was *the* perfect guerrilla weapon. By means of some gadgetry that about a hundred men in the Galaxy really understood, it projected an angstrom-thin beam of tortured energy that interfered with the interatomic bonds of any matter within fifty yards of the muzzle. The effect was that of a huge, infinitely sharp, infinitely strong and invisible bladeless knife, a 'knife' that cut through rock, steel, flesh, or anything else as if it were so much warm cream cheese. It was totally silent, had no muzzle-flash to betray its position, and as such was the ideal ambush weapon. Fifteen points for Bart Fraden, Vanderling thought.

'What else did you bring me for Christmas, Santa Claus?' Vanderling said. 'When do we start?'

'No time like the present,' Fraden said. 'I'll head for the city and you for the jungle. We can keep tabs on each other by using the direction-finders in the 'boats.''

'Good hunting, Chrome-dome,' Sophia said. 'I've got a feeling that Sangre is going to turn out to be just your kind of playpen. Fun and games, old bulletheaded buddy, fun and games!'

Sweat pouring down his bald skull, soaking his eyebrows, Willem Vanderling pushed his way through the heavy, tangled underbrush, past the gnarled, ringed boles of the thickly clustered trees that covered the small near slope of the little hill.

He crested the hill, emerged from the jungle, and stared down at a rolling stretch of empty plain, covered with neck-high, long-bladed, blue-green grass. A narrow concrete-paved road wound across the plain, passed close by the foot of the hill on which he stood. The high grass provided good cover clear up to the shoulder of the road.

This looked like the place.

Vanderling closed his eyes against the hot red Sangran sun, called to mind the view of the general area he had got from the 'boat. To the west was the big range of mountains that divided the inhabited area of the continent from the wild, useless western portion. To the east by a couple hundred miles or more was the city of Sade, sitting in the middle of a level, grassy plain. The bulk of the inhabited section of Sangre which lay between was a checkerboard country of rolling hills, small valleys, here jungle, there open plain. Scattered throughout this fertile country were hundreds of walled compounds, the centres of scattered groups of small hamlets, connected to the capital by a more or less radial system of roads.

Vanderling had put the 'boat down in a small clearing in the heavy jungle that backed up against the foot of the mountains – a likely place for a guerrilla camp. From there, it was a long, hot trek on foot, through jungle, across the tall-grass-covered open areas, in the sweltering heat of the reddish Sangran sun.

But this looked like the end of the line. There was a compound maybe twenty or thirty miles up the road, the road led towards Sade, so he could reasonably expect something to come along in a few hours. And when it did . . .

Vanderling fondled the weapon that hung loosely from a shoulderstrap, unshipped it. It was small – less than two feet from the pistolgrip at one end to the small lens opening that was its muzzle. Although it weighed a mere three pounds and had no recoil at all, the snipgun was provided with an auxiliary grip like that of an ancient

Tommy gun down near the muzzle end for precision's sake.

Vanderling grinned, brought the dull black plastic snipgun up into firing position, turned to face the jungle behind him. He pressed the trigger, swivelled the gun minutely, using the auxiliary grip as a pivot-point.

There was no sound. There was no kick, no muzzleflash. For an instant, nothing seemed to happen. Then cracks and creaks and thumps as a rain of branches and leaves fell to the forest floor. Vanderling stared along a thin crack of emptiness that sliced arrowstraight through the heavy foliage. Along the line of the cut, he could see branch stubs sliced through clean and even, leaves cut neatly in half. It was as if he had taken a swipe with a huge, sharp, irresistible machete. The snipgun would do the same to rock or steel . . . or flesh.

Vanderling scrambled about three-quarters of the way down the hill, took up a seated position about thirty yards off the shoulder of the road, the snipgun cradled across his knees, and prepared to wait.

The tall grass that hid him from sight was alive with insects, tiny mites, beetles, things nearly nine inches long with eight hairy legs and two staring, non-compound eyes. He wiped sweat from his brow and grunted. The whole damn planet was swarming with bugs! In fact, on the whole long hike, he hadn't seen a moving thing that wasn't some kind of lousy insect, one or two of 'em had been nearly the size of dogs. Evolution, or whoever makes planets, must've had bugs on the brain when it cooked up this mudball.

And the damned heat – it was near sunset and it still must be over a hundred . . . Vanderling checked himself. It had been a long hot walk, but not *that* long. Sunset was hours away. It was the damned reddish sun that did it; the stupid thing looked like it was perpetually setting. The grass, the trees, everything was bathed in a glaring red light, as if the whole crummy planet were bleeding . . . What had Little Miss Bigmouth said, Sangre was Old Spanish for blood? It figured, it sure figured.

Vanderling waited and waited in the hot sun, working up a fine loathing for Sangre and things Sangran. About the only good thing you could say for the mudball was that the jungle and the tall grass made it an ideal battleground for a guerrilla war – from the point of view of the men in the jungle, that is. Big gnarled trees with lots of feathery, palm-type blue-green leaves, plenty of undergrowth, the tall grass in the open areas – there was good cover almost everywhere. And bugs almost everywhere too! he thought unhappily as he swiped at something small buzzing around his head.

Vanderling waited in the heat and the boredom with his little coterie of insects. The sun had moved perceptibly in the sky before he saw a vehicle coming into sight around a bend in the road north of his position.

Vanderling bolted to a crouching position, covered the stretch of road directly in front of him with his snipgun. The vehicle headed straight down the road towards him, making about forty miles an hour. As it got closer, he could see that it was a truck, an obsolete wheeled job with a closed cab and an open bed.

He knew that he would have to make a snap decision in the next moment or so. The truck was only a few hundred yards away and it would be by him shortly. He shielded his eyes from the sun with his right hand and peered at the rear of the truck. He saw tanned, near-naked figures huddled together on the open truck-bed, caught glimpses of black uniforms, a red glint of the Sangran sun on naked steel.

Well, well, well, he thought approvingly, soldiers and prisoners, looks like. Who could ask for anything more?

Vanderling rose to one knee. He aimed the snipgun at an imaginary point about nine inches above the road and waited. As the truck approached the firing point, he saw that there were two black-uniformed men in the cab, the crumbs that they called Killers, four more armed men in the open truck-bed guarding ten sorry-looking men clad only in loincloths who were chained together by steel collars around their necks.

As the front wheels of the truck passed his firing point, Vanderling pressed the trigger. '*Snip!*' he said, grinning.

The rubber tyres on their steel rims intersected the stationary snipgun beam. With a loud bang, both front tires blew. Then there was a jarring, scraping sound as the circular rims, truncated nine inches from the road by the snipgun beam, hit the concrete in a shower of sparks. Vanderling swivelled the snipgun rearward, and the rear tyres blew, the rear rims were cut through, and the back of the truck hit the road like a ton of bricks, knocking prisoners and guards alike flat on their backs. Borne by its forward momentum, the truck skidded a few yards on its belly, then ground to a halt in a pool of oil.

The moment the truck stopped sliding, the four Killers in the back leapt over the low sides, stood on the road, waving rifles around futilely, their eyes mad with rage, their jaws working convulsively.

Still hidden in the grass, Vanderling hesitated long enough to notice that the Killers were all tall, lean, hard-looking men with receding hairlines and outthrust jaws, and that they carried blade-studded steel balls on the ends of steel rods clipped to their Sam Browne belts. Then he raised the snipgun higher, to the Killers' neck level, pulled the trigger, and fanned the gun back and forth like a man watering a lawn with a hose.

Shrill screams started, ended before they had properly begun, became choked liquid burbles. Four heads teetered crazily on their necks for an instant, then toppled to the pavement. The headless bodies stood ludicrously for a few moments, fountains of bright blood spurting from the cleanly severed neck arteries. Then they crumpled and fell like ruined dolls.

By this time, the two Killers in the cab had dismounted. As they stood there staring stupidly at the headless bodies of their comrades, Vanderling cut the pair of them neatly in two at the navel. They fell to the road, their arms clutching madly at their severed torsos, screamed horribly for a few moments, then were quiet.

Vanderling patted the barrel of the snipgun approvingly, then stood up and trotted to the truck.

In the rear of the truck, he found ten sorry-looking specimens of humanity. They were filthy, their near-naked bodies were covered with old scars and their ribs showed through their deeply tanned skins. Either end of the chain that connected the collars around their necks was anchored to a bolt in the truck-bed.

Hollow-eyed, phlegmatic, they stared uncomprehendingly at him, shuffling mutely like cattle in a corral.

Vanderling leapt easily to the truck-bed, cut the chain at both ends with the snipgun, the beam slicing through the truck-bed as well, and deep down into the concrete and the earth beneath it.

The Sangrans stared at the gun woodenly, their eyes bugging wildly. Otherwise, they reacted not at all.

'Come on, damn you, up and out!' Vanderling shouted. 'You're free! Comes the Revolution! Move your asses, we don't have all day. Let's get the hell out of here!'

A tall, gaunt, redhead stared at him. 'Free . . . ?' he muttered slowly, rolling the word on his tongue as if it were a morsel of some unfamiliar food.

'What the hell's the matter with you guys?' Vanderling

snarled. 'You like being chained up or something? Move it! You're free! I'm freeing you. *Move!*'

'Y'say we're free . . .' the redhead said. 'Y'a Brother?'

'Can't be a Brother,' another said. 'Got no robe.'

'Sure ain't a Killer,' a third man said. 'Look at his teeth. Got to be an Animal.'

'Got a gun, can't be an Animal,' the redhead insisted.

'Never heard of no gun like that . . .'

'What do you think this is, a goddamned coffee klatch?' Vanderling roared. 'Get out of this truck and do it now, or I'll slice you all to dog meat!' He waved the snipgun at them menacingly.

The Sangrans shrugged collectively and climbed slowly down from the truck, still chained together at the neck. Vanderling was about to cut the chain that held them together like a string of grimy pearls, when he thought better of it. These were ten mighty weird bozos. Maybe they were morons or something, or maybe they were just plain fruitcakes. It wouldn't hurt to keep 'em safely chained up till they were away from the scene of the ambush and he could find out what in hell was with them.

'All right, now let's pick up all those nice guns that are lying around,' Vanderling ordered, leading the Sangrans around to the front of the truck and the horribly mutilated bodies. The Sangrans moaned when they saw the mangled Killers, but made no move to obey.

'Pick up those guns, you cretins!' Vanderling said. 'Don't worry, I promise you'll have the chance to use 'em on more of these creeps later. I'm your friend. Now hop to it!'

'Ain't right . . .' one of the Sangrans muttered.

''Gainst the Natural Order . . .'

'Stuff your Natural Order!' Vanderling shouted. 'Now – '

Suddenly, he heard a weak shout behind him, a dry croak that sounded something like 'Kill!' He whirled, saw that one of the Killers he had sliced in half was lying in a great pool of blood behind him, eyes glazed, jaws snapping weakly like those of a dying turtle. He saw the razor-sharp teeth flecked with blood futilely trying to nip at his leg, heard the rattling croak of the dying thing, and a spasm of loathing went through him.

Convulsively, he whipped the snipgun around, sliced the near-moribund head from the dying body. The ten Sangrans uttered shrill little surprised cries.

'Now pick up those guns, or you all get the same,' he said shrilly.

Gingerly, as if they were touching something at once dirty and holy, the Sangrans finally gathered up the guns and the morningstars. Vanderling had to stand over them all the while, brandishing the snipgun menacingly.

'Now that wasn't so bad, was it?' he said. The Sangrans said nothing, stood waiting phlegmatically, holding the weapons and shaking their heads slowly.

And Vanderling had to prod them, curse them, herd them like balky oxen carrying unfamiliar loads up the hill and into the jungle towards the base of the mountains and the lifeboat.

What yuks! Vanderling thought as the ten Sangrans stood torpidly in the little clearing in the jungle. They weren't even showing any particular curiosity about the lifeboat which sat incongruously in the low underbrush, surrounded on three sides by the dense wall of tree trunks and shrubbery that was the edge of the concealing jungle. Yet they could never have seen a lifeboat in their lives.

None of it made any sense. Look at the crumbs, Vanderling thought. Full of scars, skinny as rails, chained in the back of a truck like animals. From what he had seen, and from what Bart had told him of how the planet was run, these boys should be all full of piss and vinegar, ready to tear apart the first Brother or Killer that came along, once they had the chance. They should've been dying to get their hot little hands on some guns . . . What was wrong with 'em? Any man with anything left in his scrotum who was treated the way these creeps were should be fighting mad.

Not these crummy Sangrans, though. They carried those weapons like they were honeybuckets.

'Okay, boys,' Vanderling said, motioning with the snipgun, 'put down the weapons and rest your bones. This is base camp.'

Vanderling sank to his haunches. The Sangrans simply dropped the rifles and morningstars where they stood, folded their legs under them and sank to the ground. Sourly, Vanderling found himself wishing Fraden were there. Dealing with nuts was more Bart's line of evil. When it came to snowjobs, Bart was the pro and he was the amateur . . .

Nevertheless, Vanderling did his best to look earnest, comradely and concerned. 'I suppose you guys are wondering just what's going on here, eh?' he said. 'Well, so am I. What were you boys doing chained up in that truck? You convicts or something?'

'Convicts?' the gaunt redhead said. He seemed to be more talkative than the rest – which was not saying a hell of a lot. 'What's "convicts"? We're Animals, Brother Boris' quota this month, 'course. What're you?'

Vanderling puffed himself up in his old Belt Free State General's uniform. '*I* am . . . er, Field Marshal Willem Vanderling' (Well, why not a promotion? he thought) 'formerly Commander in Chief of the Belt Free State Armed Forces and now Commander of . . . er . . . the People's Army of Sangre. What's your name, man?'

63

'Gomez. Lamar Gomez. Got two names in my village,' he said with what was almost a trace of pride.

'Okay, Gomez. You seem to have the most on the ball here, so I'm appointing you full colonel in the People's Army of Sangre and my aide-de-camp. Rest of you guys can get in on the ground floor too. In fact, I hereby commission you all captains. Why not? Now, Colonel, suppose you brief me. Just what in hell do you mean by Brother Boris' quota?'

Gomez stared stupidly at Vanderling. 'Y'on Brother Boris' estate, 'course. Got a quota of ten Animals a month. That's us, this month. We're now slaves of the Prophet. For the arena, or the Larder, or whatever the Prophet says. He owns us now.'

'Owns you? Slaves? Arena? Larder? What the hell is a Larder?' Vanderling said.

'Y'Sadians gotta eat too,' Gomez replied. 'Y'think they get t'eat Meatanimals? Only Brothers and Killers eat y'Meatanimals. Y'Sadians, they gotta make do with old meat like us.'

'You mean to tell me that they were gonna *eat* you?' Vanderling shouted. 'Just like that?'

'All Animals're eaten sooner or later,' Gomez said laconically. 'For us, sooner. Others, later.'

'Well, if that don't – Look men, you don't have to take that kind of crap any longer! This is your chance! We'll show those crumbs what happens to creeps who think they can treat people like pigs, right? I've got guns in the 'boat, and we've got guns here. Enough guns for all. And we'll use those guns to raid the estate and get more guns and free more men and raid more estates and get more guns and more men and more and more and more and before you can say "Comes the Revolution", we're an army, and we'll know what to do then, eh?' He grinned wolfishly.

64

The Sangrans looked vastly shocked. 'Y'guns are for y'Killers,' one said. 'Y'crazy?' said another. 'What y'talking about?' said Gomez.

'What . . . ?' Vanderling grunted. 'Look, you jerks, I'm talking about Revolution! We arm ourselves and we boot the Brothers and their Killers out on their asses! I gotta draw you a picture? I know the Revolution game backwards and forwards. We'll show those crumbs a few tricks they haven't seen before, don't you worry about that! In a year, we'll wipe 'em all out to the last man. You saw what I did to those Killers. One man with one gun. Think of what ten thousand men with ten thousand guns can do!'

'That's blasphemy!' one of the Sangrans shouted. 'T'kill Brothers! T'fight Killers! 'Gainst the Natural Order!'

The rest rolled their eyes fitfully and looked scandalized.

Vanderling felt like Alice down the rabbit hole. They were all raving nuts! Slaves, *eaten*, for chrissakes, and they wouldn't fight back!

He decided to change his tack. 'Okay,' he said, 'so I'm new here. What did you guys do before you became a . . . a quota?'

'Were Brother Boris' slaves, 'course,' Gomez said. 'Herded and tended his Meatanimals, what else?'

'Meat animals? Sheep? Cattle? Pigs?'

'What're those? Only one kind of animal on Sangre – human animals. Everything else is some kind of insect or other. Can't eat 'em, they're all poison. We tend y'Meatanimals, till they're ten. Butcher 'em, dress 'em, smoke the surplus for later t'feed Brother Boris and his Killers.'

'You mean to tell me you butcher your own children?' Vanderling exclaimed.

Gomez laughed. 'Y'crazy?' he said. 'Our kids're mongrels, tough, stringy meat. Y'Meatanimals are pure-bred, fat, and tender. Y'think Brother Boris'd make do with mongrels?'

'And with all this crud going on, why won't you yokums fight? You dig being slaves? You dig being eaten?'

'Dig?' said Gomez. 'Just the Natural Order. Y'Brothers rule, y'Killers kill, y'Meatanimals're eaten, y'Animals do what we're told, y'Bugs do what we tell 'em. Natural Order.'

'Bugs? What the Sam Hill are Bugs?'

'Y'native Sangrans, 'course. Big smart insects. Each village got a Bughill. Y'Brothers give us a tame Brain, y'Keeper tells y'Bugs what to do, y'Bugs grow our food so we don't starve. Y'Brothers don't want slaves starving on 'em. Each got his place in y'Natural Order.'

'And none of you imbeciles want to change any of this?' Vanderling roared. 'You're not fed up? You don't want to kick the Brothers out on their fat asses and run things yourselves?'

''Gainst the Natural Order!' the Sangrans shouted, to a man. 'Blasphemy! Y'crazy!'

Vanderling groaned. These jokers had been so thoroughly snowed for so long even Bart couldn't talk 'em into fighting. Clean stables long enough, and you get to love horse-hockey. Some planet! Some 'high revolutionary potential!' He furrowed his brow in thought. These chickens had no guts at all, so he could probably force them into fighting. But what kind of army would that be? A bunch of zombies you couldn't turn your back on for a minute! What this mudball needed was an army of killcrazy herogyn-heads, and . . .

Wait a minute! Wait just a damned minute! Sure, we're rolling in herogyn! Pounds and pounds of the stuff. Why not?

Vanderling smiled. 'Enough palaver,' he said. 'How

about some refreshments? You guys stay right here, I'll be right back with some goodies.'

Keeping his eye on the Sangrans, Vanderling opened the 'boat's outer airlock door. The Sangrans made no move to flee as he watched them through the open airlock while he rummaged around and came out with a bottle of small blue pills.

He loped back to his prisoners, squatted, measured out ten pills, passed them around.

The Sangrans stared dubiously at the small blue pills.

'Go on, take 'em,' Vanderling ordered. 'Satisfaction guaranteed! And if you don't, I'll slice your heads off with *this*.' He brandished the snipgun.

Vanderling grinned as the Sangrans phlegmatically downed the herogyn pills. Instant army, that's what it was! Herogyn was illegal on every ball of mud that called itself a civilized planet, and for good reason. The stuff had been developed by the Jovian Hegemony during that brush with the Far Satellites. A dose of the stuff gave you about the best high there was, but then, brother, you were hooked, but good! It did permanent things to your hormone balance. Eight hours of paradise, and then you started to come down. Ten hours later, you were in deep withdrawal, a mindless, savage killing machine – so savage, so bloodthirsty, that you were useless as a soldier. But in between, ah in between, you had a fearless, homicidal soldier-fanatic utterly obedient to whoever supplied the stuff. The Jovian desertion rate had been zero. Of course once the war was over, there was the Total Wipeout, but . . .

We'll cross that bridge when we come to it, Vanderling thought as he watched the bodies of the Sangrans go limp, saw their eyes glaze, watched inane beatific smiles engrave themselves on their lips.

'That's it, boys, enjoy yourselves,' he said. 'We'll have

some work to do tomorrow, and by then, oh, how ready you'll be to do it. Relax, have fun. After you've had your kicks, I think maybe you'll start to see things more my way. In fact, I'm sure you will!'

In the red heat of the Sangran sun, two crescents of men trotted down the slope of a small hill, obscured by the gently undulating tall grass, towards the low complex of buildings surrounded by a high wooden palisade in the valley below. In the forward crescent were ten men carrying rifles, naked except for the rough green loincloths and green sweatbands around their foreheads that Vanderling had adopted as the closest practical thing to a uniform for his People's Army, under the circumstances. A similar skirmish line of twenty more men followed about fifteen yards behind the first, with Vanderling, his snipgun at the ready, sandwiched in between.

So far, so good, Vanderling thought nervously. He had few illusions about his embryonic army under these tactical circumstances. About the only thing he felt he could count on was that they would more or less fight.

The herogyn, at least, had worked perfectly. The original ten Sangrans had lain around in a euphoric stupor for most of the night. Then, around dawn, as the withdrawal set in, they had begun to squirm, fidget, mutter, snarl, bicker among each other, whine for more herogyn, their eyes reddening, growing vulpine, hungry. And then Vanderling had laid it on the line – they would have to fight for their next fix and the one after that and the one after *that*. There were no real complaints – in the early withdrawal state, they wanted herogyn and they wanted to kill, and if one brought the other, all the better. Not trusting them with snipguns, he had armed them with captured weapons and waited by the road for what would come along.

What had finally come along was a convoy of three trucks loaded with 'quotas' from other districts: eighteen Killers and a total of thirty-six Sangran prisoners. The Killers were not much trouble – Vanderling had wrecked the trucks and cut most of them down with the snipgun before the hopped-up Sangrans were sent in to mop up what was left, and in their kill-crazy state, the Sangrans had not had much trouble in killing the few survivors. (Though the Killers, decimated and dying though they were, had taken four guerrillas with them.) But the Sangrans were a bit too far into the herogyn withdrawal, and they had got the taste of blood and they had started in on the prisoners. Vanderling had had to cut down three of his own men with the snipgun to regain control.

Two other raids on isolated squads of Killers had gone better, since the guerrillas were simply required to kill everything that moved, not distinguish foe from potential friend.

But now, at least, he had thirty men and enough captured guns for all, though not one hell of a lot of ammo. But if this first really big raid went off as planned, ammo and arms would not be a problem for quite a while.

Target for today was the estate-compound of good old Brother Boris, the local poobah. Vanderling refused to kid himself – it was a mighty iffy situation.

Trouble was, so many factors were unknowns. From what he had been able to pump from the Sangrans, who just didn't seem to notice such things, the compound would be guarded by thirty to forty Killers. He had never really seen the Killers fight – the three previous actions hadn't really given the Killers a chance to do much of anything – but from what little he had seen, they were mighty good indeed. And his own troops, if you could call them that, stank on ice. All he could really expect to do with them at this point was to point them in the right direction and pray. It had to be a set-piece, a plan that required that the guerrillas be pairs of legs carrying rifles and nothing more. The word for them was *gunfodder*.

And this was the acid test. Knock out the compound and get rid of Brother Boris and Company, and the whole estate would be left hanging, and recruiting would be that much easier. Fail this early, and bye, bye, baby!

Now the forward line of men was about two hundred yards from the compound wall, well down into the valley, but still hidden by the tall grass, which was cropped only immediately in front of the single gate in the palisade.

Vanderling held up his snipgun, shouted, 'Halt!' Sloppily, the two lines stopped, and with angry gestures, he managed to close the two ranks well enough to give them their final orders without advertising their presence from here to Betelgeuse.

'Okay, *men*,' he said sourly, 'just do as you're told and it'll be a piece of cake. On the first signal, the forward line charges, firing at will and making as much noise as possible. Remember, advance to ten yards from the gate and keep firing. We want them to come out and get us; we don't have a Chinaman's chance of storming the wall.

'Second line follows the first on the second signal. I'll be right behind you with the snipgun. Remember, the second line stops fifty yards from the gate and takes fixed firing positions, and you *stay put*, no matter what. The Killers come out to attack the first line, and we cut 'em down before they can close. I don't want any infighting. Remember, we're outnumbered. Okay, got it? Now give 'em hell!'

The response was something less than reassuring. The Sangrans stood there silently, their red eyes sunken and glazed, their mouths unreadable slits, and Vanderling had no way of knowing whether one word he had said had penetrated the herogyn haze or their thick skulls.

He shrugged. Here goes nothing! he thought. He waved the snipgun over his head and somewhat sarcastically shouted, 'Geronimo!'

The forward line hesitated, then broke into a dogtrot that quickly became a ragged run, a mindless, pell-mell charge. They began to fire their rifles randomly, hopelessly into the air as they ran, and they started to scream, shrill, ululating, wordless demoniac cries, working their way up swiftly into a fine berserker frenzy. Vanderling flinched for a moment – they were further out of their heads than he had thought . . .

The forward crescent was about fifty yards away now, churning up the tall grass into an angry sea of screaming, firing men. Vanderling waved his snipgun again, and the second crescent started forward, breaking almost immediately into a dead run, screaming even louder, firing even more wildly.

So far, so good, Vanderling thought tensely as he trotted forward a safe distance behind the howling second line. Berserker stupidity had its uses, if you knew what to do with it. The first line of men were decoys; they were as good as dead. The second line would be firing right through them, and the Killers would be sure to get them if the fire from their rear didn't. Fortunately, they weren't exactly the thinking type.

Sure are making enough noise, Vanderling thought, as the shrieking, wildly running men got to within about thirty yards of the gate, their bullets tearing splinters out of the wooden palisade and the heavy wooden gate. Now if the Killers will only oblige and . . .

And here they come!

With the forward line of guerrillas less than twenty-five yards from the gate, the second line another fifty yards back, Vanderling twenty yards behind them, the gate suddenly swung open. Instantly, five, ten, twenty men, clad in the black uniform of the Killers, swarmed out into the cleared area, firing straight ahead even as they emerged, twenty-five, thirty, and still they kept coming.

The Killers formed a solid wedge, hurtled fearlessly straight at the guns of the guerrillas, and Vanderling heard a new sound, a terrible sound, a guttural yet somehow shrill rhythmic chanting like the cry of some monstrous carnivore: 'KILL! KILL! KILL! KILL! KILL! KILL!'

Chanting this horrid animal sound, the wedge of Killers charged straight into the now-hesitating guerrillas, flinging aside their rifles as they closed and unshipping the morningstars, the wicked blade-studded steel balls on the ends of rigid rods. Like a rabid wolf pack, they fell on the hapless Sangrans.

For a long, long moment, Vanderling could not think. He had seen plenty of no-quarter fighting in his day, but nothing remotely like *this*. Foam flecked the Killers' lips, turned scarlet as they gnawed their own lips in a howling rage. They tore into the guerrillas like living buzz saws, bashed heads like so many watermelons with their morningstars. They kicked, stomped with their heavily booted feet, shrieked like fiends gone mad. And there, incredibly, a Killer sunk his razor-sharp teeth into a human throat, bright blood gurgling over his face and shoulders as his hands tore gobbets of flesh from arms and torso. Another Killer clutched at a man's face with both hands, ripped features away like a bloody Halloween mask. Here a guerrilla was down, and a Killer stomped at his neck while another sunk his teeth in a leg and a third smashed the man's rib cage with his morningstar.

Vanderling went mindless for an instant as the mêlée became a senseless churning of tortured bodies, ripping limbs, flashing morningstars, a screaming pack of mindless, desperate animals tearing each other to shreds in the blood-red Sangran sun. He felt something calling to him in that writhing horror, in the ragged chanting that still went on – 'KILL! KILL! KILL!' Something that fascinated him, yet turned his blood to ice, something that beckoned, heaved within him, struggling to be born . . .

Abruptly, the fearful moment passed as he saw that his second line, instead of stopping and firing, was screaming, howling, and rushing insanely towards that hideous, lethal human meatgrinder.

'Stop, you cretins!' he yelled. 'Hold your ground and fire! Stand and fire, you morons!'

It was hopeless. Vanderling realized that he was the only man left with a working mind on the entire battlefield. It would be an utter disaster. Those crazy fiends would tear his men apart like so many grasshoppers, once they closed with them. It was no use, there was nothing . . .

Or was there?

As his second line rushed pell-mell towards annihilation, Vanderling broke into a furious run, off on a diagonal, towards the left flank of the battle. It was a race against his own men. Could he get into position in time? The guerrillas were less than thirty yards from the battle now, but now . . .

Now, his breath coming in sharp pains, Vanderling was in position, off to one side of the battle and within snipgun range, with a clear line of fire past his own second line and into the writhing, screaming mêlée of Killers and dying guerrillas.

Still panting, Vanderling dropped to one knee, raised the snipgun, pulled the trigger, kept it down, fanned the gun back and forth, back and forth, back and forth.

It was as if he were swinging a gigantic sword straight through the heart of the battle. Heads, arms, legs, seemed to leap from bodies in fountains of blood. Back and forth, back and forth. Bodies split in half, at the navel, at the chest, at the groin. Back and forth, back and forth. His knuckles went white around the snipgun grips. Like the Grim Reaper, he scythed a field of human grain with the infinitely thin, irresistible snipgun beam. Killers and guerrillas alike seemed to fly apart like shattered glass. Back and forth . . .

In the few moments before the guerrillas closed with what was left of the Killers, the battle had already been decided. Armless, legless, half-men, hardly a Killer was left whole. As the guerrillas fell upon them, those left alive fought madly and futilely on, minus limbs, minus everything but life itself and the will to kill. It seemed as if even severed heads were sinking their teeth into legs in a last paroxysm of blood-lust and hate.

Carnage unthinkable. Lacking arms, mutilated Killers kicked; lacking legs, they lashed out with their teeth, flopping about convulsively like beached and dying sharks. It was more like a battle between two schools of voracious piranhas than between men. The ground was littered with bodies, limbs, grisly gobbets of flesh, sodden with blood. Killers maimed beyond belief fought on and killed, taking guerrillas with them as they died.

But the snipgun had made the difference. The dying Killers, every ounce of their flesh imbued with blood-lust, were no match for the guerrillas; in five short minutes of horror it was over.

Piled in front of the open gate was a vast bloody garbage heap of pulped and bleeding dead flesh, great pools of blood, bodies twitching in their death throes and nothing left alive.

A pack of rabid animals, the remaining guerrillas poured into the compound, and Vanderling followed behind, dazed and numbed.

The next half-hour was a red fog, a boiling madness that Vanderling remembered afterwards only in bits and

74

snatches. Somewhere, someone found a torch, and palisade, outbuildings and main house were set ablaze. Strange, fat, vacant-eyed little children, naked little bleating things cowering in a corral were shot and slashed and torn to pieces. Slaves, women, children were dragged out of buildings and summarily butchered.

Vanderling raced around the courtyard trying to stop it, but the guerrillas had scattered on myriad gruesome errands and he could do nothing but rant and wave his snipgun.

Finally, there was a great shout, and from everywhere in the maze of carnage and burning buildings guerrillas converged on a small knot of men who had dragged a fat man dressed in a black robe out of the main house – Brother Boris.

They dragged Brother Boris, kicking and screaming, down the small flight of steps. He began to blubber as he was kicked into the churning mob of guerrillas.

Vanderling retched, tried not to look, as the guerrillas pulled the fat man down, ripped at him with scores of hands, tore chunks of living flesh from his body with their teeth. Then he disappeared in a swirl of stomping bodies, and in another moment his screaming stopped.

Vanderling ran to the mob of guerrillas, waving his snipgun. 'Enough!' he roared. 'Next man that so much as twitches, gets no more herogyn! It's over! Gather up the weapons and let's go!'

For a long, pregnant moment, the guerrillas faced him, covered with blood, their eyes blazing, hungry for one more thing to kill.

'Anyone who tries anything dies,' Vanderling said, pointing the snipgun straight at them, 'I'll kill you all if I have to.' And his voice and his eyes said he meant it.

And they knew he meant it, they had seen what the snipgun could do.

Half an hour later, Vanderling found himself trudging through the tall grass behind seventeen men heavily laden with captured arms and ammunition – all that had survived the day's slaughter. Far behind, a pillar of billowing smoke was all that reminded him of those short minutes of horror, a horror that already seemed distant and unreal.

And at that moment, with his men bearing the booty before him and the estate of Brother Boris a burning ruin far behind, Willem Vanderling smiled.

For what had happened was, after all, a victory.

Victory, Sangran style.

Chapter 5

'Ah, Brother Bart, the source of infinite pleasure,' the short, lean, hawk-faced, black-robed Brother said. 'Have some wine, nice wine, delicious wine, precious wine . . .' he lifted a brimming jug of wine from the low table before him, his hand shaking as he raised it, the pupils of his eyes abnormally full.

Bart Fraden smiled as he declined the wine with a negligent motion of his forearm. Brother Theodore was nicely swacked on Omnidrene. It was going nicely, most of the Brothers were lapping the stuff up like a cat laps milk, and some, like old Teddy here, were practically perpetually stoned.

Fraden sat down on one of the low cushions in front of the Japanese-style table, which was piled high with jugs of wine, local fruits, bread, and a ghastly centrepiece – a roasted whole human infant already half-consumed. He took a small polybag of Omnidrene out of a pocket nicely tailored to the inside of his black Brother's robe and dropped it on the table.

'That should hold you for a while,' he said.

Brother Theodore snatched up the polybag, ripped it open, took a pinch of the white powder, shoved it into his left nostril, inhaled, sneezed, giggled like a schoolgirl, and said, 'For a while, Brother Bart, for a little, little while.'

His eyes rolled, he leaned back in his nest of cushions and bellowed: 'Woman!'

Almost instantly, a tall, well-built, fine-featured young redhead appeared. She was naked. Theodore grabbed

77

one firm young buttock viciously in a clawlike hand, yanked the girl down on to his lap. 'Amuse me,' he said, 'but slowly at first.'

Obediently, totally ignoring Fraden, the naked woman reached beneath Brother Theodore's robe. Theodore smiled.

'Very accomplished, this one,' he said. 'Perhaps you'd like to try her, Brother Bart? I'd certainly like to try that slave of *yours*. She seems quite . . . exotic. You know, breeding these female creatures to our taste has one drawback – one seldom gets to enjoy the unusual, the unpredictable, the exotic. Now that slave of yours . . .'

'Er . . . a peculiar creature,' Fraden said quickly. 'I'm sure you'd find her more trouble than she's worth.' And that, he thought, has to be the understatement of the century. 'I can handle her only because I've . . . shall we say, conditioned her to obey me.' And that one had to be the lie of the millennium.

Brother Theodore laughed. '*Conditioning* the creatures is half the pleasure,' he said with an unpleasant grin. 'I wouldn't want to interfere with your . . . disciplinary programme. Increase the tempo, woman!' he ordered. He began to lick his lips and rock rhythmically back and forth. Fraden found his gorge rising, but he knew he couldn't show it. Public masturbation by slaves was the least of the Brothers' vices, and this stage of the game required that he be 'one of the boys'.

'Shall I send for a woman for you?' Theodore inquired. 'Perhaps some entertainment? A contest, yes indeed, a contest! With knives? Fists? Whips? Two males? Two females? A mixed event? Name your pleasure, Brother Bart! Anything for the purveyor of pleasure . . . Perhaps a small torture-pageant? Yes indeed, a pageant by all means!' He laughed boyishly.

'I'm afraid I must be going,' Fraden said quickly. 'Got

to give some Omnidrene to Brother Leon and Brother Joseph and . . . Busy, busy, busy . . .' he said, rising, and moving with poorly concealed haste towards the door.

But Brother Theodore was past noticing such subtleties. He was breathing heavily, and cruelly kneading the naked body of the woman. 'Too gentle!' he snarled. 'Much too gentle. More fire, woman!'

Fraden heard a series of sharp slaps of flesh on flesh as he backed out the door and into the hallway. Get it while you can, you greasy bastard! he thought. You won't be getting it forever.

The air of the open courtyard cooled Fraden off a bit, but the sights appalled him. There was no getting away from nausea in the madness of the Palace of Pain. The courtyard was a busy display of grotesqueries. Here, a Killer led a string of naked women, all young, all similarly beautiful, all bred to please, chained together by collars around their necks, towards the entrance to the Palace proper. Near the concrete wall, another Killer was drilling a squad of young cadets. The small boys were all dressed in miniature Killer outfits, down to the rifles and the morningstars and the filed teeth. Four more Killers were herding a group of the obscenely fat, semi-imbecilic children they called Meatanimals towards the slaughtering shed behind the Palace. On impulse, Fraden called one of the Killers over to him.

The Killer, like all Killers, was tall, lean, with receding brown hair and filed teeth. He wore the bars of a captain – fairly high rank in the Killer hierarchy.

He came to attention in front of Fraden. 'You require a service, Brother,' he said laconically.

'Just some information, Captain,' Fraden said. 'Those boys drilling over there – where do you get them? You recruit them, or what?'

'Recruit, Brother?' the Killer said. 'They are pure-bred Killers of course. I myself as an officer have been permitted to sire two cadets in the past year. It is a high honour, the third highest honour possible.'

'And the first two . . . ?'

The Killer looked faintly scandalized that even a new Brother should ask such a question – but then, he had never encountered an off-worlder before. 'The highest honour is of course to kill,' he said evenly. 'The second highest is to die in battle. The fourth highest is to be permitted to enjoy a female slave. I myself have been permitted this lesser pleasure ten times in the past year. I have served the Brotherhood well.'

It figured, Fraden thought grimly. A totally celibate army would figure to fight furiously, but would be kind of hot to handle. But if you made occasional sex a reward for service, you kept 'em under control and still perverted their sexual drives into battle-frenzy. Logical. If you accepted the basic premise that anyone who wasn't a Brother wasn't a human being, everything the Brotherhood did was all too logical.

'That will be all, Captain,' Fraden said. Fraden shook his head as the Killer disappeared behind the Palace. The Brotherhood was utterly ruthless and to defeat them would require an equal lack of scruples which was not really his bag at all.

'But in this case,' Fraden muttered to himself, 'I'll be happy to make an exception.' The Brotherhood of Pain did not know the meaning of mercy. They would get none from Bart Fraden.

'Bart Fraden, this just isn't like you,' Sophia O'Hara said scooping up a big mound of the rice and vegetable pilaff that was the staple of their diet on Sangre. With no Terrestrial animals on the planet and no edible native fauna, it had been a long time since either of them had tasted meat. Neither of them were quite ready to try the traditional Sangran solution to the chronic protein shortage.

Across the table in the main room of their Palace suite, Fraden washed down a mouthful of the boring stuff with a swallow of the rather rancid local wine. 'So who is it like, Soph?' he said.

'Don't play your snide little word-games with me,' she said, wrinkling her nose as she gulped down a slug of the resinous wine. 'I'm not Bullethead and I'm not that greasy oaf Moro and I'm not one of these hooded refugees from a funny farm either. I'm Sophia O'Hara, remember? Don't try to con *me*. The Belt Free State was not exactly the Model Social Democracy, and you didn't grab it by thinking Pure Thoughts and thus obtaining the Strength of Ten. But dope pushing *is* a new line of evil for you, isn't it?'

'Omnidrene isn't "dope" as you so crudely put it,' he said defensively, not meeting her eyes. 'It's physically non-addictive and has no adverse physiological effects whatever.'

'No doubt it also stimulates the flow of liver bile, cures dandruff, builds strong bones and healthy bodies, and increases sexual potency – as if these swine needed an aphrodisiac to whet their perverted appetites. Nevertheless, I notice that most of our so-called Brothers seem to be spending quite a bit of their time in wall-eyed stupefaction – which would be fine by me if it kept them off the streets. But instead, it seems to increase their jollies – like fights to the death, and torture-orgies, and other good clean fun. This mudball makes the Black Hole of Calcutta seem like a Quaker prayer meeting and you seem bent on making it that much worse.'

'Nice guys finish last,' Fraden said. 'Revolution is a

dirty line of evil and the fouler the regime you're out to do in, the less scruples you can afford. The more thoroughly hooked they are, the less killing later. Let 'em stay bombed and happy till it's too late, and it'll save lives in the long run. Or do I detect a certain softness on your part towards these filthy swine? Just remember the kind of pigs we're fighting. Moro makes Caligula and Hitler and De Sade look like little Lord Fauntleroy. So if some innocent people get hurt in the Revolution, just remember that this time the planet as a whole stands to benefit. For once, I find myself in the peculiar position of being on the Side of the Angels, and you know, it doesn't feel all that bad.'

'Come off it, Bart,' Sophia said. 'You look utterly ludicrous as a Knight in Shining Armour. A Knight in Shining Armour pushing dope, at that. It's something personal, isn't it? Just what *did* they make you do in that Initiation Ceremony?'

Fraden choked down a huge swallow of wine. What . . . what he had been forced to do during the initiation was something he had tried hard to forget, but something he knew was festering within him, and something he was determined not to let come between Sophia and himself. As far as he was concerned, with the possible exception of Willem, off in the jungle, Sophia was the only other human being on the entire planet. He longed to share the burden with her, but was deathly afraid of losing her. He was not about to make the gamble of telling her the truth.

'Told you a hundred times,' he said. 'Just a lot of stupid mumbo-jumbo.'

'You're lying to me, Bart,' she said quietly. 'Look at me and say that again.'

He met her big, neutral green eyes and tried to read what was behind them. Compassion? A willingness to understand the truth, whatever it was? Or simple female suspicion, an eagerness to condemn?

'All right, Soph,' he said slowly. 'I . . . They . . . They forced me to kill! With an axe, with my own hands! Just . . . just an animal, but I had to kill it, with my own hands. Me or it. I killed it, or they killed me.'

'You've been responsible for plenty of deaths before,' she said cynically. '*Human* deaths. So why should – ?'

'This wasn't an order, it was *me* doing it! Me, listening to the screams, seeing the blood, feeling flesh come apart under my axe!' he found himself shouting. 'I've never killed before. This wasn't war, it was . . .' He caught himself short. The word he had been about to say was 'murder'.

Her face suddenly gone tender, Sophia reached across the table, held his cheeks lightly in both hands. 'I'm sorry, Bart,' she said. 'I won't mention it again. There's a heart in there somewhere; I can feel it beating, however faintly. You're the boss, Peerless Leader.'

'Thanks Soph . . . I needed that from you. When this is over, I'll make it up . . . I'll make up a lot of things . . .'

Abruptly, he felt the sharp twinge of an emotion with no name. 'So much for today's confessional,' he said with exaggerated harshness. 'Bless me, Father, for I have sinned, three Confedollars in the collection plate and back to business as usual. It's about time I looked in on Willem. He should have something resembling a guerrilla force by now. That compound that burned down could've been an accident, but they say no one escaped alive, and that sounds like we're in business in the jungle too. Time we started coordinating. I'll be going out in the morning. Want to come with?'

'I think I can live without the stimulating company of old Chrome-dome for a while longer. Just tell him how much I miss him. I'll pass on the outing. After all, a woman's place is in the home.'

'I've seen better armies in toy boxes,' Fraden said, glancing around the guerrilla camp again and then back at the harried-looking face of Willem Vanderling. The camp was a vast disappointment. It was far smaller than he had expected it to be at this point, and it was a mess, with guns and equipment scattered all over the clearing. About thirty near-naked men sprawled torpidly around the camp, and Willem should've been able to recruit at least double that number by now. Moreover, a strange 'boat had just landed and the soldiers were lying around as if an off-worlder dropped in every other Tuesday.

'What's going on?' Fraden snapped. 'Why so few Sangrans? Why in blazes are they all sitting around playing with themselves? Where in hell are your sentries? Why –'

'Take it easy, man, for chrissakes, take it easy!' Vanderling whined. 'You don't know the half of it. This mudball is impossible! And they're all sitting around because they're all bombed on herogyn.'

'They're *what*?' Fraden roared. 'Have you completely flipped? Where in hell did they get ahold of herogyn? And why aren't you doing anything about it?'

'Because I gave it to them. I had to.'

'You . . .' It was one of those rare moments when Bart Fraden was struck speechless. Giving herogyn to partisan troops was like performing a brain operation with a shovel. When they were bombed, they couldn't beat off a squad of Space Scouts, and if they ever went all the way into withdrawal . . . *Brrrr!* You had to maintain a razor-fine balance, and if you goofed just once, you had had it.

'It would seem that you've got some explaining to do,'

Fraden said thickly. 'Some mighty fancy explaining. What's been going on while you've been on your own?'

They sat down in front of a rude hut next to Vanderling's 'boat, and Vanderling told him.

'I don't get it, Bart, I just don't get it,' Vanderling said. 'It's like there isn't a testicle on the whole planet. I never heard of anyone getting their asses as thoroughly kicked as these damned Sangrans, but they just won't fight. They won't even think about it. After I knocked over Brother Boris' joint with my gang of 'heads – and believe me, *that* was no cakewalk – I thought I had it made. I mean, with the local poobah and his hired guns out of the way, I figured every yokum in every village on this estate would be hot to join up. No dice. All the same. Go into a village, and try to get 'em to join up, and they just sit around on their fat asses in front of their stinking huts, and maybe some cretin says he wonders what the next Brother will be like or maybe the goddamned quota will be lower. When I explain that there ain't gonna be no next Brother, that we're gonna wipe 'em all out, they just start yelling about "blasphemy" and how it's "against the Natural Order" and not one of 'em'll join up. So – '

'So you figured the only way to raise an army is to make 'em herogyn-heads, eh?' Fraden said sourly.

'You got it. At least this way, they fight.'

'Willem, I've seen better heads than yours on *beers*! We need maybe ten, fifteen thousand men to take over this crummy planet. Maybe you think the herogyn will last forever at that rate? What happens when we run out? And how do we use kill-crazy 'heads for political warfare?'

'I didn't think – '

'You're telling me something I don't know?' Fraden rasped.

'So what's *your* idea, genius?'

'I want to see one of these villages. I want to talk to the people. Even nuts don't act like nuts without a reason, and when I know what that reason is, I'll be able to find a way around it.'

'Now? Our boys will be bombed out of their skulls for the next five hours.'

'Roll your damned herogyn-heads into a tight wad and stuff 'em!' Fraden snarled. 'Get me a snipgun, and we'll pay a visit to our future constituents all by our little-bitty selves!'

The Sangran village was an untidy collection of about fifty small, doorless, thatched huts clustered in a very rough circle on one bank of a stagnant little stream. Behind the village, dominating it like a monument, was a great mound of dried red clay peppered with large round holes about the size of manholes. The clay mound was a full sixty feet tall, and as Fraden emerged from the nearby jungle which followed the stream to the periphery of the village, with Vanderling trailing glumly a pace behind, he saw a huge green insect, the size of a half-grown child, with eight chitinous legs, the first two of which were carried above the body like arms, and strangely intelligent-looking small black eyes on its large head, emerge from one of the holes in the clay mound and skitter off into the cultivated fields beyond the village.

'Bug,' Vanderling muttered as they approached the circle of huts. 'Must be dozens of them in that thing, what they call a Bughill. You should see 'em in the fields, working the crops in teams. Gives me the creeps.'

Fraden grunted, wrinkled his nose as they passed inside the circle of huts. The bare earth was littered with all manner of garbage and ordure. A few dozen scrawny, naked children played torpidly about the clearing. They were unbelievably filthy. Women with drawn, empty faces and pendulous, flaccid breasts, wearing only rude skirts that were little more than loincloths, looked up from mortars where they were grinding grain or cook fires where they were baking grey, tortillalike bread with only perfunctory interest at the two armed men. Here and there, an old man stuck his head out of a hut. Children, old men, women, garbage, ordure, all stank to high heaven like some monstrous, fetid locker room.

'Where are all the men?' Fraden asked Vanderling.

'Too early in the day,' Vanderling said. 'They're all out tending the Meatanimal herds.'

'But I thought you wiped out the local Killers when you sacked the estate . . . ?'

Vanderling shrugged. 'I *told* you these yokums are idiots. They're out being good boys till the next Brother shows up.'

'Well, let's talk to one of those old geezers,' Fraden said, leading Vanderling over to one of the doorless huts and stepping inside. The inside of the windowless hut was dark, hot and dank. A wizened old man sat on a pile of straw nibbling listlessly on a piece of hard, flat bread. He looked up with hollow, rheumy eyes but said nothing.

'I'm Bart Fraden,' Fraden said. 'This is Marshal Vanderling. We're off-worlders. We're here to bring freedom to the people of Sangre. What's your name?'

'Oakly,' the old man grunted. 'What's freedom?'

Fraden shook his head. 'Freedom is when you can do what you want to, not what the Brothers tell you. Freedom is when there are no more Killers and no more Brothers to keep you in slavery.'

'No Brothers, who's t'rule?' the old man said. 'No Killers, who's t'kill?'

'You rule!' Fraden said. 'You rule yourselves. And nobody kills. You grow food for yourselves, work only for yourselves, run your own lives. That's freedom.'

The old man scowled. 'I understand,' he said. 'This "freedom", it's blasphemy, is all. Y'bring blasphemy. Don't want no blasphemy. 'Gainst the Natural Order.'

'It's the Natural Order for you to be slaves? It's the Natural Order for the Brothers to take you and torture you for their own pleasures and butcher you when they're through and feed you to the Sadians?'

'Y'understand,' the old man said. 'Natural Order. Way it is, way it'll always be. We're good Animals here. Don't listen t'no blasphemy.'

'Look at this dump!' Fraden snapped. 'Look at the slop you eat! Look at you, you're skinny as a rail! You *like* starving?'

'Don't starve. Everyone eats. Y'Brothers and y'Killers eat y'Meatanimals. Y'Sadians eat y'useless Animals. Y'Animals eat y'food that y'Bugs grow. Natural Order.'

I'm wasting my time here, Fraden thought. Maybe the local chief . . . ?

'Where's the chief?' he said. The old man stared at him blankly. 'The head man? The big cheese? The most important man in the village?'

'Y'mean y'Keeper? Keeper's hut's behind y'Bughill. Keeper's getting old. I'm second oldest, he dies, I'm Keeper. Maybe he dies soon.'

Fraden turned, stepped halfway out of the hut. 'And how old are you, old-timer?' he asked.

'Forty-seven,' the old man said.

Fraden goggled. Sangre's year was shorter than Earth's! This old hulk was not much over forty standard years. And he was the second oldest man in the village!

The Keeper's hut was on the other side of the Bughill. Fields of grain spread out before it, and Fraden saw dozens of green Bugs, the sun glinting off their chitinous bodies, moving methodically, clipping off stands of the

88

tall grain with the flexible pincers on their forward pair of limbs.

With Vanderling trailing glumly behind, he entered the hut and was nearly bowled over by the stench, a fetid, rotten odour coming from the thing in the centre of the hut: a huge, green distended sack with a small head, so gross that the eight tiny stub-legs did not reach the ground. A tiny, shrunken old man was holding up a clay jug of raw alcohol to the thing's small mouth, and the creature was lapping it up greedily. A dozen other such jugs sat on the bare earth floor.

The old man whirled, dropped the jug, sloshing the stuff on the pulsating body of the green thing. 'Y'bother me when I'm feeding the Brain!' he snapped. 'Y'bother y'Keeper! During harvest, too. Want y'Bugs t'run wild? Want t'starve?'

Then he saw the snipguns, bowed low. 'Y'Killers!' he said. 'Got guns! Forgive, masters. Y'didn't look like Killers. Meant no blasphemy.'

'We're . . . ah . . . from a long way off,' Fraden said. 'Things are different where we come from. We want to find out how things are run in this village.'

'Y'came t'the right Animal,' the old man said. 'I'm Keeper here. Not for me, whole village starves and y'Brother he don't have no one t'tend his Meatanimals. I give orders t'y'Brain here. Brain makes y'Bugs do their job.'

'You mean that thing can actually talk to the Bugs?'

The Keeper goggled. 'Y'must be from far away!' he said. 'Got no Bugs on your estate? Y'Bughill, it's like one Animal. Y'brain, it don't talk t'y'arm. Y'Bughill's got a brain too, this one here. I tell it what t'do, y'Bugs just do it. Long as y'Brain is drunk. Otherwise, y'Bugs just do for 'emselves. Y'Brothers, they take y'Brain when it's just a grub, booze it, give it t'y'village and y'Keeper keeps it

89

boozed. So y'Keeper really grows all y'food, so's y'Animals can eat and work for y'Brother. Don't y'know y'Natural Order?'

'So you're the most important man here . . .' Fraden said slowly. 'Well, what if all the rest of the village refused to tend the Meatanimals? Then *you* would really rule here.'

'Y'crazy? Y'Killers'd come here and kill y'whole village!'

'What if you had guns? What if you fought the Killers?'

'Y'talkin' blasphemy! What kinda Killers're you, t'talk blasphemy?'

'We –'

'Thir? Thir? Orders, thir?' the Brain began to croak in a creaky, metallic voice.

'Got no time t'talk now,' the Keeper said, picking up the jug and holding it up to the Brain's mouth. 'Y'Brain ain't very smart; got t'keep repeating y'orders, or y'Bugs run wild. Y'found out what y'want t'know anyway, masters. We're good Animals here, don't have no truck with blasphemy. Tell y'Brother that.' He turned, ignored them, began talking to the Brain: 'Y'finish y'south field, y'go on t'y'north field, then y' . . .'

Fraden shrugged, led Vanderling outside.

'Well, genius,' Vanderling smirked, 'there's your damned "high revolutionary potential!" How's it grab you?'

'I still say it's sky-high,' Fraden said. 'But it's locked in stasis. Things have been this bad so long that they've come to accept it. But the moment you have any change at all in a setup like this, it'll blow sky-high.'

'Yeah, and just how do you go about making things any better?'

'*Better?* You don't make things better; you make 'em

90

worse. And fortunately, we'll have some help in doing that.'

'Help? From who?'

Fraden laughed. 'From Moro,' he said. 'Who else?'

As he wandered through the corridors of the Palace of Pain in the general direction of the Throne Room, Bart Fraden was something less than confident in his ability to make things in the countryside worse. Thing was, things were about as bad as they could possibly be without making the whole system utterly unworkable and how could he snow Moro into doing *that*?'

The Bugs kept the 'Animals', as they thought of themselves, in just enough food to keep them alive to raise Meatanimals for the Brothers and the Killers and to provide a bottomless source of victims and slaves. The average Animal had little chance of ending up in the arena or as a slave or in the Public Larder – what with fifteen million Animals on the planet and only a few thousand Brothers. The old mathematics of tyranny – if the heavy hand of the ruler fell only on a comparatively small percentage of the population, the rest would sit still no matter what happened.

The trick was to get Moro to spread the terror, take ten Sangrans for a 'quota' where now he was taking one. But how? As it was, the Brotherhood satisfied every vagrant whim, took as many for the quotas as they needed. A huge new demand had to be somehow created, a demand that would make them triple, quadruple the quotas, or worse. But what conceivable . . . ?

Brother Theodore lurched by him, not even noticing him, totally bombed on Omnidrene. Good thing there was so much of the stuff in the ship; they were gobbling the stuff up at a rate he hadn't believed possible. And if the supply ever ran low, they'd be desperate for . . .

Bong!

'Of course!' Fraden cried to himself. Christ, there it was all the time! No one knew how much Omnidrene there really was on the ship; they had only his word for it. What if Moro thought it was running out? What if he told Moro . . . ?

Fraden shivered. It was a grisly idea, but it would work. If he had the stomach to do it, to plunge the planet into an orgy of torture and . . . Thousands would suffer, he told himself, but in the end, the rest would be free. Wasn't that what counted? Either do it, Bart, or hang up and leave. Break a few thousand eggs and make an omelette, or give up and let the men who had . . . who had made him a murderer have their kicks for the *next* three centuries too. That was where the revolution racket was at, after all!

He steeled himself, quickened his pace, headed for the Throne Room. Drastic situations required drastic solutions, he told himself. A surgeon amputates limbs to save the whole body; well, doesn't he? *Doesn't he?*

'Well?' Moro rumbled. 'What is it, Brother Bart? It had better be important. I don't enjoy being disturbed at my pleasures, and this exhibition is proving most entertaining.'

Moro and Fraden were alone in the room. The great television screen that formed one wall showed a hideous spectacle: ten men were chained together by their left wrists in pairs. One of each pair held a long knife in his right hand, the other a flaming torch. The men with the knives were burned all over their bodies; those with the torches were covered with bleeding gashes. The camera was looking down into some kind of pit, and as the men fought, they stumbled about in a sea of large insects, about cat-size, which seemed to form the living floor of the pit. One of the pairs fell to the floor – and jumped up screaming, covered with a score of the horrors, which clung to their flesh by sharp mandibles.

The hideous sight and the screams of the men steeled Fraden's wavering will. *Anything* was justified if it helped to destroy monsters who enjoyed this kind of filth. *Anything*. Even . . .

Fraden averted his eyes from the horror, stepped closer to the raised throne on which Moro sat, his pig-eyes gleaming, his gross body shaking with delight mixed with annoyance at the disturbance.

'It's important all right,' Fraden said. 'It's about the Omnidrene. Turn off the audio, so we can hear ourselves think.'

Frowning heavily, Moro reached out to the console before him, and the screaming stopped. 'Well?'

'The Brothers are taking the stuff like there's no tomorrow,' Fraden said. 'I've never seen so much taken so fast. They're making pigs out of themselves.'

'The pleasures of others are no concern of yours!' Moro snapped. 'You keep that ridiculous female slave of yours, the one with the tongue like a dagger, all to yourself and no one complains, although Brother Theodore . . . But it's none of his business, just as how much Omnidrene anyone takes is none of yours. Each to his own pleasures.'

'I consider my life my own business,' Fraden said. 'Correct me if I'm wrong.'

Moro stared at him stupidly for a moment. It was hard to tell when he was on Omnidrene and when he wasn't. He was cleverer than the others – or he wouldn't be Prophet for very long. He used the drug sparingly and seemed to have the addiction under some control. Right now, he seemed slightly high, which was just about the way Fraden wanted him.

'I stay alive as long as the Omnidrene keeps coming, right?' he said. 'No more Omnidrene, no more Brother Bart.'

'Exactly,' said Moro. 'But amusing as it would be to see you eaten alive, or boiled inchwise in oil, perhaps, I assure you that I much prefer to have the Omnidrene. It increases my ordinary pleasures so greatly . . . What is your point with all this foolishness?'

'My point is that I never realized that the stuff would go so fast. At this rate it won't last my lifetime – and I believe in living a long, full life. I also believe in planning ahead.'

Moro frowned. 'If it won't last your lifetime, it won't last mine!' he muttered unhappily. 'I could reserve it to myself . . . but that would cause trouble. It might be dangerous.'

So far, so good, Fraden thought. He's worried. He's ripe for leading down the primrose path.

'Would you consider that I was fulfilling my side of the bargain if I told you how to manufacture the stuff?' Fraden asked archly.

'It can be made here?' Moro blurted. Then, more slowly, 'To be sure, to be sure. That would do nicely.' His pig-eyes narrowed and he smiled slyly. An imbecile could read his so-called mind, Fraden thought. Once he had an independent supply of Omnidrene – goodbye, Brother Bart! But once this little piece of bait was taken and things got started, it would be time for Brother Bart to disappear into the outback and become President Bart Fraden of the Free Republic of Sangre. It was just a matter of some neat timing.

'It can be made here as well as anywhere else,' Fraden said. 'That is, if there are enough schizophrenics on Sangre.'

'Schizophrenics?'

Oh, brother! Fraden thought. How do I explain what a schizophrenic is to Old Lardbucket? But then, if you're going to tell a lie, tell a simple one.

'Madmen,' Fraden said. 'Surely you have madmen on Sangre?'

'Madmen . . . ? You mean those Animals who act so strangely after unusually imaginative torture? The ones that sit around like vegetables or babble nonsense languages?'

That wasn't exactly a scientific description of schizophrenia, Fraden thought, but since Omnidrene is really purely synthetic, what does it matter?

'That's it,' he said. 'Schizophrenics.'

'It happens every once in a while,' Moro said. 'Of course such Animals are useless as slaves or as interesting subjects for torture, for that matter. They're given over to the Public Larder as a matter of course. What possible use are madmen?'

'None whatever,' Fraden said. 'However, their *blood* is another matter. Omnidrene is an extract of the blood of schizophrenics. But it takes quarts and quarts of schizophrenics' blood to make even one dose. If you had enough of 'em, I mean tens of thousands, we could make the stuff. But there's no point in it, since you only have a few here and there . . .'

'Let me understand this . . .' Moro said slowly. 'Omnidrene is extracted from the blood of madmen? Drive a man mad, and his blood will yield small quantities of Omnidrene?'

Ye gods, how long will it take the fat slob to get the point? Fraden wondered. Of course, anyone stupid enough to swallow a lie like that whole might have to be led by the hand every step of the way. Still, I can't be *too* obvious.

'*Minute* quantities,' Fraden said. 'You'd have to have

95

some way of driving men mad *en masse*, and I don't see – '

Moro roared with laughter. 'But that's because you're a fool, Brother Bart!' he said. 'You have no aesthetic sense. This is perfect, it proves the basic belief of the Brotherhood of Pain: give Pain and receive Pleasure!'

'What're you getting at?' Fraden said in great mock confusion, as if it weren't his idea in the first place. 'You have a way of driving thousands mad?'

'By Hitler and De Sade!' Moro roared. 'You really don't see it? It's so beautiful, so obvious! We shall institute a campaign of torture such as Sangre has never seen! What a challenge to the art! To invent tortures subtle enough to drive Animals mad without wasting a drop of their blood!'

Moro rocked back and forth madly on his throne like a kid with a lollipop. 'We'll drive the whole planet mad!' he crowed. '*The whole planet!*'

Hook, line, and sinker! Fraden thought. Torture the whole planet to insanity and then bleed 'em to death to get Omnidrene for your jollies! Not even Sangrans will sit still for *this*. Comes the Revolution, Fat Boy, comes the Revolution!

Fraden smiled in sardonic admiration. 'Moro,' he said evenly, 'I must admit that I've never run across a mind quite like yours.'

Sitting naked on the edge of his bed in the comparatively cool Sangran night, Bart Fraden found himself sweating, a dank, heatless sweat. He remembered an old, old saying, so old that its origin had been long forgotten: 'Never look behind; *something* may be gaining on you.' He felt the breath of that something on the back of his neck.

Got a planet to knock over, Bart? Need something to

break a social stasis, stir up the Animals real good? Well, why not get the opposition to go ape, try to torture the whole population into insanity? After all, that should be enough to bug *anyone* enough to fight. Clever, Bart, a real clever gambit.

And damn it, it *was* clever. It had to work. He should feel pleased with himself. So why the cold sweat, why the knot in his stomach? Why the feeling of something breathing down his neck, and what was that something? It couldn't be *conscience*, that was just a word, a phony excuse men used for not acting. Wasn't it . . . ?

Sophia emerged from the bathroom. She was naked, and her long red hair fell down over her shoulders, and her breasts were firm and lovely, her legs taut and smooth, and she was the best damned chick in the Galaxy, first-class all the way, and she was *his*. She smiled, open-mouthed, and her eyes shone. He knew that look.

'Peerless Leader . . .' she said, draping herself across his lap, and the words were strangely devoid of sarcasm. He knew that tone. This was the other Sophia who broke through now and then, the little girl before the football hero, the cavegirl before the Great Hunter. This Sophia stirred him viscerally, but he did not understand her at all.

She kissed him, a long, lingering, open kiss. 'Wheeling and dealing,' she muttered against him. 'Peerless wheeler-dealer. *My* man. *Numero uno*. Bigger than life and twice as nasty . . .'

She kissed him again, and Fraden felt his blood beginning to pound, felt the cold breath of that *something* retreat, wither, die. It was more than mere animal heat, it was something deeper, something other than the feel of her inviting body moving against him. It was what that invitation said: I want you. I want *you*. I want you because you're a winner, because you're the best. It was the pride in her calling to the pride in him.

Touch me, feel me, have me, her body said to him. I'm the best, and you've earned me. I'm the best and I'm yours, as long as you're the best, as long as you're on top, as long as you're my Peerless Leader.

And no longer, he thought as he pulled her to him. This was where it was at. This was worth fighting for, scheming for, killing for, if need be. This was worth ten thousand lives. To be the best, Number One, the centre of the universe, and to hold the best woman there was in your arms and to know she was yours because you were the best, because you won her day by day, moment by moment, against the universe, in the arena, against all comers.

He stretched his body over hers and it made him feel ten feet tall. She enveloped him, drew him to her like a special, special prize, and he took her as she gave herself.

And her little cries and her slow movements against him were a paean to his manhood, his vaulting, hungry ego.

And his fulfilment washed away the doubts and the foolish twinges of guilt and the dank, cold breath of conscience.

To the victor, the spoils! To the loser, nothingness!

Chapter 6

'What's going on around this perverts' pigpen now?'
Sophia O'Hara asked, turning from the window as Fraden
re-entered the bedroom. The window looked out across
the open space at the back of the Palace towards the
glowering black Stadium, and for the past hour or so,
truck after truck had been arriving at the Stadium, each
one packed with chained men and women, guarded by
squads of laconic Killers. 'And what did that Killer want?'

'Looks like they're preparing for some unpleasantness,'
Fraden said. 'The Killer issued an invitation – an order,
really – that my presence would be required in Moro's
box at the Pavilion for today's pageant.'

'*Pageant?*' Sophia said with a dubious frown. 'What
does Old Greaseball mean by "pageant"?'

'Somehow I get the feeling it isn't a Maypole dance,'
Fraden said. 'I've been trying to keep a rough head count
of how many people they've herded into the Stadium.
Got to two hundred or so before the Killer interrupted,
and I see they're still coming. Wonder what it's all about?'

Actually, Fraden was all too sure just what it was
about. For the past five days, all of the Brothers in the
Palace had been tanking up on Omnidrene, working
themselves up into a fine state of slavering, red-eyed
anticipation and babbling incessantly about the great show
Moro was preparing. Moro himself wasn't talking and his
silence had the ominous quality of a schoolboy preparing
a ghastly prank. On the other hand, the Prophet of Pain
was all too eager to discuss the great pogrom of torture
he was planning, the pogrom that would drive thousands

99

mad and ensure, so he thought, a bottomless supply of Omnidrene. For the past two days, there had been the sounds of construction going on within the Stadium, and now they were trucking in hundreds of Sangrans . . . And then, this invitation.

The madness-pogrom gambit had seemed like such a brilliant idea when he had sold it to Moro. Painless, distant, removed from his ken. Once it was under way, he and Sophia would leave for Vanderling's camp, he would proclaim the Free Republic of Sangre, start a rumour, a rumour that would be backed up by fact, that the Brotherhood was going to torture the entire population to madness, then bleed them slowly to death to produce Omnidrene. The Revolution would sweep through the countryside like a firestorm . . .

But when the 'gambit' incarnated itself in the cluckings of the Brothers, like teenage girls anticipating a pyjama party, in hundreds of flesh and blood victims being trucked into the Stadium for god-knows-what, it was no longer just a clever trick. It was inescapably human lives, human pain, human madness, and it was on his head. The pogrom *would* ignite the Revolution, he knew it would, it *had* to . . . But the tinder that would be consumed was human tinder, that thought and suffered and bled and died.

And only when the Killer had brought him the grotesque 'invitation' did it hit him that he was going to have to *see* what he had wrought, smell it, hear it, taste it.

But there was no turning back now, and there was no point in telling Soph of his part in the whole sordid business. So it *was* an evil, a very real evil, but, so he told himself, an essential one and the guilt, if what he felt was guilt, was something private, something he could share with no one.

'Does your invitation include family?' Sophia said.

'I must admit to a certain morbid curiosity about the more exotic folkways of our intended fief.'

Fraden was torn by the desire to spare her the horror that surely was to come and the terrible loneliness of facing it alone. After a long moment, he opted for the less selfish choice.

''Fraid not,' he lied. 'Brothers in good standing only.'

'Goody, goody, a stag party! Replete with beer and dirty movies, no doubt.'

'Haven't seen a glass of beer since we landed, only that sour grape juice they call wine,' Fraden quipped hollowly. 'And somehow, I have the feeling that today's entertainment will be live.'

At least for openers, he thought vertiginously.

Most of the Stadium – the rude, backless wooden benches that formed the bulk of the great open bowl's circumference – was empty. A comparatively small section of the stands at the far end from where Fraden had entered was roofed over against the hot, red Sangran sun which cast deep red shadows on the empty seats and the sandy arena floor. That roofed Pavilion seemed stuffed with tiny figures as if a whole stadiumful of spectators huddled there awaiting the end of a thundershower. It made Fraden feel uncomfortably alone and exposed as he walked along the lateral aisle towards the Pavilion.

He looked down at the arena floor and saw that a strange oblong wooden structure had been set up at the far end of the arena, immediately below and parallel to the Pavilion. It was a long raised platform, uncomfortably like a mass gallows, about sixteen feet wide and a full hundred yards long. A row of steel leg irons ran along either edge of the platform, and from where Fraden stood, the open back of the thing revealed a maze of wiring beneath. A heavy cable ran from beneath the platform, snaked across the arena and disappeared into the bowels of the Stadium through a large gate.

Now what in hell could that thing be? Fraden thought. Then, still walking, he looked up at the by-now-nearby Pavilion and forgot all about the enigma on the arena floor.

At least nine hundred robed Brothers reclined on tiers of upholstered couches, and for every filled couch, five were vacant. In front of each occupied couch, a low table was set up, and on the tables sat jugs of wine, bowls of fruit, and . . . and whole roast babies. Naked women, three, four, five to each Brother, held up jugs of wine, limbs from the ghastly roasts, fruit, packets of Omni-drene, whatever their masters required. Many of the Brothers were toying with women who sat on their laps. Others were being toyed with. Armed Killers stood all around the periphery of the Pavilion. They were smiling – death's-head smiles. Fraden had never seen a Killer smile before. There was a fetid, carnival air about the Pavilion; laughing, shouting, drinking, the wolfing down of too much food. Rome in the reign of Caligula, Fraden thought, might've been a pale imitation of this.

Moro sat on a raised throne in the front and centre of the Pavilion. He spotted Fraden, waved for him to join him.

Fraden pushed his way through the laughing, back-slapping, reeling mass of Brothers and servants, their hands greased with human fat, their lips and faces reddened with splashes of wine, their eyes the eyes of maddened boars. He felt his gorge rising as they greeted him, waved to him, touched at his Brother's robe with filthy fingers. He was pale and shaking with disgust and rage as he finally made it to the foot of Moro's throne, where a huge table groaned with huge wine jugs, a great

102

platter heaped high with tiny, crisply browned human arms.

Moro motioned him to a couch beside his throne with a half-eaten arm that he waved like a sceptre. Woodenly, Fraden seated himself on the edge of the couch as a woman held up a wine jug to Moro's fat lips.

Moro wiped his mouth with the back of a gross arm 'Ah, Brother Bart . . .' he cooed, 'the source of this great challenge. Welcome, welcome to our modest pageant!' He took a pinch of Omnidrene, held it to his nostril, snorted it up, sneezed, laughed and said 'Think of it – to torture unto madness without spilling a drop of blood! I hope my first poor attempt at this noble goal will succeed. However, if not, no matter. Try, try again, eh?'

Fraden found himself unable to utter a sound. He felt certain that to open his mouth would be to vomit.

But Moro seemed to be talking mostly to hear the sound of his own voice. He took another arm from the platter, nibbled it and the first alternately as he spoke.

'Observe, observe,' he said, pointing to the platform below with a half-eaten limb. 'See how the shackles are wired? The charge has been carefully calculated to maximize pain without resulting in permanent damage.'

As he spoke, two lines of people, one of men, one of women, were led out of the arena gate by squads of Killers, across the sand, and up on to the platform.

'See there,' Moro cried shrilly. 'Those buttons?' Fraden saw two parallel lines of buttons running down the centre of the platform. As the Killers began shackling the victims to the platform, men facing women, he realized that the buttons were so placed as to be just within reach of the men and women in the shackles.

'There is genius!' Moro crowed. 'The buttons control the current. The subjects may turn the current on or off at will.'

103

'I don't get it,' Fraden grunted thickly. 'Why – ?'

'Ah, but the buttons are cross-connected, you see! See how they are paired. Each subject can control the current to the shackles of the one *opposite*, not his own. When his partner's current is on, his is off. But, and this is the master's touch, if *both* buttons are depressed, the current goes to both shackles – and if neither button is pressed, both receive shocks as well. And to increase the interest, all have been briefed in the operation of the device. *And*, as the *pièce de résistance*, the paired Animals are in fact all mates! To create madness, it is best to torture the mind as well as the body, eh?'

By now, the victims were all in place, over a hundred frightened men lying prone on the bare wood facing an equal number of naked, terrified women. Moro raised his fat right arm, a Killer threw a masterswitch beneath the platform, and . . .

A shrill, animal wail split the air as the current surged into the shackles, a monstrous tortured sound as of a huge beast in mortal agony. The bodies on the platform stiffened, began to twitch convulsively. Hands reached for buttons, and there was no masculine gallantry here. In some pairs the man was the faster, in some the woman. Half the victims continued to twitch and scream, half lay there panting and watched their mates' agony.

Behind him, Fraden heard a liquid, horrid, rippling sound, the sound of laughter, little gleeful cries, wine gurgling down throats. He dared not turn, he could only watch the obscenity in the arena below, unable to face the revelling Brothers behind him.

'Look! Look!' Moro cried, thumping him on the back with a hand that still held a tiny human arm. Fraden felt vomit rising in the back of his throat.

Now *all* the victims were screaming in agony, every

button depressed, agonized faces set in devils' masks of determination, each victim determined to outlast his partner, make him grant a moment's release in return for the unspoken promise of reciprocal self-sacrifice.

Here and there a man or woman finally gave in to the unvoiced promise, released his button, continued to twist in torment while the body opposite went limp in blessed relief from the wracking pain. But once released from agony, who would willingly return to pain? Those not in torment kept their fingers relentlessly on their buttons, for to release them was to bring on the agony that writhed opposite them on the platform. In a universe of pain, there was no honour, no love, no mercy, only the grim determination to buy a moment's rest.

The betrayed ones reached for their buttons, as much in hate as in agony. And a few of those plunged back into pain released *their* buttons, hoping for another moment of future mercy. Others only gritted their teeth harder, held the buttons down in spasms of hate . . .

On and on it went, endlessly, a thousand variations on the same gruesome contest of pain and pleading, hate and hope.

Every bit of that mass agony, every amp of current, seemed to channel itself into Fraden's mind, his guts, his being. *He* was responsible for this, personally, immediately, inescapably, ultimately responsible. He couldn't bear it. He wanted to disembowel himself on the spot, scream his dreadful guilt for the world to hear, tear himself to bloody fragments.

He whirled in his seat, unable to bear the sight a moment longer. And then he saw the Brothers tiered like a pyramid of obscene, writhing flesh behind him.

They were laughing, the hideous, raucous laughter of feeding hyenas. Fragments of human flesh dribbled from their mouths on to their black robes. Most were kneading the bodies of female slaves as if they were inanimate objects, so many beanbags, drawing blood with their fingernails, inflicting cruel purple bruises in their sadistic frenzy. Some were being kneaded themselves beneath their robes as they rolled their eyes, devoured human meat, laughed merrily at the agony in the arena.

Fraden felt acid vomit sear the back of his throat, felt soul-deep spasms roil his guts. He had to get out, if they killed him for it, if they tore him apart, he had to get out!

He bolted from the couch, holding his hand to his mouth, holding back the vomit with a mighty effort of will and throat muscles.

Moro, his face purple with pleasure, a gobbet of meat clinging crazily to a yellow tooth, glanced at him as he bolted for the aisle, grunted, 'Brother Bart . . . you'll miss the best part. Where are you – ?'

'John . . .' Fraden grunted through his fingers, his back to the Prophet of Pain. 'Gotta go to the john.'

Moro was about to say something, but Fraden was already halfway down the aisle, breaking into a run. The Prophet shrugged, returned to his pleasures, all but the spectacle before him forgotten.

Fraden ran crazily down the aisle, out of the Pavilion, through an exit, down a dank passageway, and finally found himself outside the Stadium.

The aloneness, the muffled sounds still coming from the Stadium, hit his gut like a pile driver. He leaned against the Stadium wall, retched, vomited, retched again, vomited once more, retched and retched and retched till his stomach was a pounding pain against his ribs, till after-images flashed across his retinas, till he felt as if he were puking up the whole foul planet.

And the sounds from the Stadium went on and on and on, burning away the abysmal nausea, finally, and filling him with a merciful, fiery hate.

* * *

It was a measure of how routine horror had become ten days after the madness-pogrom had begun: Bart Fraden could watch the line of trucks rumbling through the main gate of the Palace compound, across the courtyard, behind the Palace itself to the ever-full mass cells beneath the Stadium with little more than perfunctory twinges of regret, one quick spasm of self-loathing as the men huddled, naked and terrified, in one of the trucks happened to stare at him, long and hard, as the truck passed close by.

Fraden glanced about the great courtyard. Killers were herding women, slaves, Meatanimals about. A squad of the Killer cadets was being drilled near the wall. There were muffled cries from the slaughterhouse. Here and there a Brother surrounded by his retinue lurched by, heavily loaded on Omnidrene. No one seemed to pay much attention to the long line of trucks hauling their human cargo to the Stadium; it was already merely business as usual. A few hundred Brothers usually showed up to watch the day's proceedings in the Stadium, but the insane, carefully bloodless tortures were no longer being carried out in a grotesque carnival atmosphere. There was a weird, assembly-line feeling about it all, as victims were trucked into the Stadium in a steady stream, tortured, herded across the courtyard into the vast system of dungeons in the bowels of the Stadium. An assembly line for the production of madmen . . .

Fraden had been able to avoid seeing the tortures for the most part, now that they were established routine. He had also been able to avoid the dungeons below the Stadium, the mass madness they contained. When Moro pressed him to supervise the beginnings of the bleeding of the madmen, the extraction of the Omnidrene from their blood, he had been able to put him off by telling him that there was no point in beginning until a pool of at least three thousand schizophrenics existed.

And by that time, Brother Bart would be long gone. For Fraden's work in the Palace was done. The madness-pogrom was established routine. The Brotherhood was hooked on Omnidrene. When Brother Bart – and the Omnidrene supply – disappeared, one would feed the other. In their desperation for a new supply of Omnidrene, they would continue and intensify the tortures, feeding the fires of Revolution. And at the moment, the pogrom was producing an unexpected dividend: obsessed with the tortures, Moro seemed to be virtually ignoring the stories of an estate attacked here, a squad of Killers ambushed there as so many isolated and probably exaggerated incidents.

Yes, it was finally time to leave this pit of horror. The groundwork of Revolution had been laid. He had already informed Moro that it was time to make a trip to the ship to get more Omnidrene, Sophia was packing, and in an hour or so . . .

'Brother Bart, the Prophet requires your presence immediately,' a flat, laconic voice said behind him.

Fraden turned, saw the inevitable lean, sharp-toothed Killer. 'You will come with me,' the Killer said. 'Your presence is required in the dungeons.'

Fraden tensed, then relaxed somewhat as he saw that the Killer's rifle was slung over his shoulder, his morning-star clipped to his belt.

The Killer led Fraden to a small door in the side of the Palace, through it, along a short passageway, down a long flight of ill-lit stairs which ended in a small anteroom.

Three halls led off the anteroom, and in the harsh light of naked incandescent bulbs, Fraden saw that they were vast cell-blocks. The Killer led him down the centre cell-block corridor.

A passage through bedlam. On either side of the stone-floored hallway were iron-barred cells. About half the cells were filled – five or ten men and women to a single small cubicle. Some sat catatonic in their own offal on the cold stone floors. Others screeched mindlessly at him as he scuttled hurriedly by with downcast eyes. Men clawed at their own scarred bodies. Women sat mumbling the same syllable over and over again like an incantation. Killers paced the corridor, eyes cold and watching, breaking up fights here and there by sticking the muzzles of their rifles through the bars, barking irresistible, laconic orders.

Numbly, holding himself under tight control, willing himself to ignore the madness around him, Fraden followed the Killer through the cell-block, down an empty corridor, past a cross-corridor where he heard moans echoing in the far distance and finally into a small chamber, lit by a single light bulb dangling naked from the ceiling.

A man was chained to the wall by his ankles and wrists. His body was a mass of ugly, small burns – and a Killer inflicted another with an electric branding iron as Moro stood off to one side nodding in approval as the man screamed.

Fraden went tense, his mind working furiously as he heard the scream, for it was not so much a scream of pain as of mindless hate and rage. The man's eyes were hollow red pits. He tore madly at his steel bonds with splintered and bloody fingernails. As the Killer removed the electric brand, the scream became a barely intelligible moaning: 'Kkkkill . . .'

The man was in acute herogyn withdrawal. His loincloth was green. It was one of Willem's guerrillas!

Moro turned, opened his mouth to speak, but Fraden spoke first. 'I hope this won't take too long, whatever it is,' he said. 'There's no Omnidrene left, and I've got to get to the ship as soon as – '

'Yes, yes, to be sure, you must see to it at once as soon as we are through here,' Moro said distractedly. 'But since you are the . . . er, *most widely experienced* of the Brothers, I want your opinion on this peculiar creature. Strange things have been happening in the countryside lately . . . Killers attacked, two estates burned. Once in a while, a village of Animals runs amok when their Brain dies and they lose control of their Bugs and we haven't trucked a new Brain in quickly enough. It appeared that this is what had happened. But out of curiosity, I ordered that the next time any Killers were attacked, they take a prisoner and retreat – something, of course, that they are quite loath to do. Yesterday, a squad of Killers was attacked by nearly thirty armed men; they killed many, of course, but since there were only six of them they were wiped out – except for one Killer who managed to follow orders and escape with this most peculiar prisoner. Observe.'

Moro waved the Killer with the electric brand aside with one fat hand, stepped close to the prisoner, who writhed, snapped his teeth furiously at the Prophet of Pain, screamed 'Kill . . . kill . . . kill . . .' weakly.

'I am the Prophet of Pain!' Moro bellowed. 'Hear and obey, Animal! You will tell me who you are and why you commit blasphemy and murder. In the name of the Brotherhood of Pain and the Natural Order, *speak*!'

The guerrilla's eyes became burning coals of hate. He lunged against his bonds. Foam flecked his mouth, turning red as he tore at his own lips with his teeth. 'Kill!' he screamed, seeming to draw strength from a reservoir of rage. 'Kill! Destroy! Death t'y'Brotherhood! Death t'y'Killers! Kill y'Prophet! Death t'Moro! Kill! Kill!' The words trailed off into a howl of animal rage.

Moro slapped the man's head with the back of his heavy hand, slamming his head against the stone wall. The guerrilla went limp, but Fraden saw that he was still breathing easily. Moro had not done him the favour of killing him.

'You see . . . ?' Moro said conversationally. 'No Animal could possibly react like that, so totally against the Natural Order. Animals obey.' Moro frowned heavily. 'It's almost as if . . .'

'Almost as if he were a Killer,' Fraden said quickly, off the top of his head. It was as good a red herring as any. He only needed time enough to get out of this room, get Sophia and get to the lifeboat in the courtyard. Maybe twenty minutes or so. As long as the guerrilla was still in this stage of withdrawal from the herogyn, they could eat him alive and not be able to get anything intelligible out of him. But it looked as if he was about burnt out, at that stage where the rage subsided into a kind of pliant torpor, and then . . . It wouldn't take them very long to find out that he was a member of a guerrilla band led by an off-worlder. And only one off-worlder ship had come to Sangre in centuries. Moro would be able to put one and one together in no time at all . . .

'As if he were a Killer . . . ?' Moro parroted pensively.

'Look at him!' Fraden said. 'He certainly acts the way only a born and bred Killer should . . .'

'Impossible!' Moro snapped. 'A Killer is trained to obey from boyhood. A Killer's obedience is absolute.'

'Well, what if . . . uh . . . somehow a group of young Killers ended up on their own in the outback, somehow? Boys, very young ones, bred as Killers but not fully trained. Say they were being trucked from one place to another, and the truck was wrecked and all the adult

Killers killed and they were left to fend for themselves. Ten years or so in the jungle, living off the land, with incomplete conditioning, and . . .'

'It sounds most improbable,' Moro said dubiously. 'I know of no such loss. Still . . . I must admit that it's hard to think of a more plausible explanation. No Animal would – '

'Can't hurt to check,' Fraden said. 'How long could it take to go through the records, an hour or so . . . ?'

Moro laughed, eyed Fraden narrowly. 'That would be unsporting,' he said. 'It will be much more aesthetic to go on to more advanced methods of torture immediately, tortures that even a Killer can't resist. We shall know soon enough. But no sense in wasting our time with halfway measures, eh?' he said, his pig-eyes gleaming. 'No sense at all . . .'

'Er . . . I think I had better go see to the Omnidrene now,' Fraden said, starting for the door. 'I've done what I can here . . .'

'Uh . . . to be sure . . .' Moro muttered, turning to the Killer holding the electric brand, Fraden already all but forgotten. 'Bring him to!' he ordered as Fraden slipped out of the room and into the corridor.

And as he rushed through the bowels of the Palace of Pain counting every minute, Fraden heard a series of terrible, agonized screams echoing behind him. This was going to be close! Too damned close!

'Come on, Soph, move it, will you!' Bart Fraden said, as he half-dragged Sophia O'Hara at a near trot across the open courtyard towards the lifeboat waiting near the wall. 'If they break that guerrilla before we get off the ground, we've had it!' It had taken him nearly fifteen minutes to make his way back to their quarters through the labyrinth of the dungeons – he had not wanted a Killer as a guide –

and nearly another five to get Sophia moving. By now, Moro could very well have cracked the prisoner . . .

'I'm coming, I'm coming!' Sophia grunted as they passed close by a squad of Killers trooping in the general direction of the Palace. 'But let's keep this a strategic retreat, not a rout! If they see us running like burglars caught in the act, it may give 'em unpleasant ideas. Besides, track simply is *not* my sport.'

She's right, of course, Fraden thought, forcing himself to keep to a less suspicious pace. They walked briskly but calmly towards the lifeboat, past another squad of Killers, who saluted in passing at Fraden's Brother's robe.

They were only about twenty yards from the 'boat when Fraden heard a shout from the general direction of the Palace. He paused, turned, saw maybe ten or fifteen Killers coming at them at a dead run, maybe fifty yards behind and closing fast.

'Come on, Soph, the shit has hit the fan!' he shouted, pulling her forward and breaking into a run. 'Move it!'

As they ran towards the 'boat the Killers behind began to fire their rifles. Had they simply stood their ground and taken careful aim, they could have cut them down like clay pigeons at that range, but calm, cool thinking was not the Killers' forte, and so they kept running as they fired, the bullets whining high over Fraden and Sophia's heads, kicking little dust-devils up behind them or pinging harmlessly off the lifeboat hull.

Panting, dragging the stumbling Sophia by the arm, Fraden reached the lifeboat with the Killers less than thirty yards behind.

He pressed the stud unlocking the outer airlock door, and there was an agonizing few seconds' wait as the door's servomotor slid it smoothly, silently and calmly upward while the Killers, who by now had flung aside their rifles and unshipped their morningstars, bore down on them,

113

eyes blazing, lips flecked with foam, waving their weapons above their heads, shrieking their ululating battle chant: 'KILL! KILL! KILL! KILL!'

The foremost Killer was scant yards away when the airlock door finally slid upward, the gangway down. Fraden leapt up the gangway, dragging Sophia behind, ducked inside the airlock, let go her hand.

'Hit the stud!' he shouted, burst by her through the open inner airlock door and into the tiny cabin, sat down on the edge of the pilot's seat, activated the computopilot's simplified automatic lift-off cycle.

As the lights on the display panel began to go green, one by one, he turned in the seat, looked through the inner airlock door and saw . . .

Sophia had hit the airlock door button. The gangway had already slid inside, the outer airlock door was in the process of sliding shut. But it wasn't coming down fast enough. A Killer had managed to get one leg up over the inside of the sill and was pulling himself up into the airlock with one hand, brandishing his wicked-looking morningstar in the other. He saw that the Killer would be able to jam the airlock door open with his shoulders, thus causing the computopilot to automatically abort the lift-off. And there was nothing he could do about it in less than a second . . .

Suddenly, Sophia braced herself with spread-eagled arms against the frame of the airlock door and raised herself up on the toes of her left foot. The Killer got both arms through, braced himself upright, prepared to vault into the airlock.

Sophia grimaced, drew back her right foot, and kicked, a perfectly aimed, graceful kick with all her weight behind it.

The point of her shoe caught the Killer squarely on the jaw; he screamed, flopped backwards over the sill and the airlock door slid shut behind him. Bullets began to whine off the hull. The last light on the display panel went green.

Sophia lurched into the cabin, dropped down into the seat beside him just as the 'boat lifted off.

As the 'boat accelerated sharply upward, Fraden grinned at her. She grimaced, then grinned wryly back.

'Well I *told* you track wasn't my sport, didn't I?' she said. 'Football, anyone?'

Chapter 7

As he broke out of the jungle undergrowth at the crest of a small hill overlooking the next village, which nestled in the bottom of a narrow, grassy valley, Bart Fraden once again swabbed oily sweat from his forehead with the back of his hand.

The four green-sweatbanded guerrillas marching in double file before him pushed aside the tall grass with their rifle butts, and it lashed back at him in rebound as he followed them down the slope of the hill into the valley. It was hot; his head felt like it was filled with warm rice pudding. He glanced at the four guerrillas bringing up the rear: green loincloths, green sweatbands, captured rifles and hollow bloodshot eyes, trigger-tense muscles. Herogyn-heads all, with their primary loyalty to the drug itself, their secondary loyalty to Willem, who dispensed it, and not much left over for the newly self-appointed President of the as-yet-gestating Free Republic of Sangre. Still, they were under better control than when he had first joined Willem in the jungle, a week ago. The trick was to give 'em tiny, sub-critical doses of the stuff throughout the day, and get 'em high enough for a really big bring-down only before a battle. It was a king-sized pain in the ass, but at least it kept them reasonably alert and under control most of the time. But it won't be like this for long, he told himself.

The hot, red sunlight seemed to beat at him like a physical thing as they reached the bottom of the hill and started out across the valley floor towards the small cluster of huts, with the red clay Bughill towering behind it and

116

the cultivated fields that ringed it. Curiously, despite the heat and fatigue and the tension-creating presence of the eight 'heads he had been forced to live with for the past week, and even despite the rather poor results, this week in the countryside, this week of visiting dozens of the little hamlets in the area, speaking to the people, proclaiming the Republic, trying to drum up a real army seemed to have refreshed him, filled him with hope and a sense of the power of his charisma. No longer was he Brother Bart, the schemer, the infiltrator. Now, for better or worse, he was President Bart Fraden of the Free Republic of Sangre, proclaiming himself for all the world to see. Even though the recruits were only dribbling into the guerrilla camp in ones and twos, even though the herogyn-heads Willem was whipping into shape as an officer corps were still the majority of the People's Army, the mere act of stumping the countryside filled him with vigour and a feeling of potency.

Now they were approaching the outskirts of the village, and Fraden ordered the guerrillas to break ranks. They formed a casual grouping around him that looked unthreateningly random but was really an effective armed guard surrounding him. There had been more than one near-riot in a village where the primitive rumour-campaign had somehow failed to precede him.

That, of course, was to be expected at this point, before it was possible to set up a really organized rumour mill. Without a system of regular agents, the only thing he had been able to do was send a few 'heads to a few villages to start the three rumours and hope they would keep their original form as they spread spontaneously. The three rumours were necessarily general and vague as they had to be if they were to spread without any real guidance: the Brotherhood had raised the quotas to ten times the normal figures all over Sangre; the Killers were mighty

117

interested in madmen; and the jungle was becoming filled with armed guerrillas.

It was the task of the moment to speak to the villagers, connect up these seemingly spontaneous rumours, offer a plausible explanation, and transform the unrest into a Revolution.

Now they were passing through the cultivated fields surrounding the village proper. It was late in the day, but the green, eight-legged Bugs were still in the fields, clipping grain with their pincers, stacking it in neat rows, collecting the stacks, carrying them to the Bughill where they would be threshed into grain for the villagers. No matter how often he saw the huge arthropods working in organized teams, the sight invariably unnerved him, filled him with a sense of wrongness, and something else – a feeling of potentiality he could not quite put his finger on.

As they passed through the circle of huts into the open central area, naked children, women, trooped after them – and several score men, just back from tending the Meatanimals – stood in the centre of the clearing apparently waiting for them. A good sign, Fraden thought. Word must be getting around. He studied the faces of the men: sullen, phlegmatic, but also somehow expectant and curious. They seemed to know that *something* was happening, something that was somehow connected with this off-worlder and his group of armed men . . .

Fraden motioned to his men as he came to a halt facing the men of the village and they fanned out, forming a crescent flanking him on both sides. Women, children, old men, and some younger ones, dribbled around the ends of the crescent, joined the crowd facing him. Fraden stood there silently for several minutes, counting the audience – maybe eighty or so potential guerrillas and another hundred women, children, and old men – and waiting until the mutterings, the feet-shuffling, the growing intensity in the stares of the men as they studied him, told him that the curiosity of the Sangrans had reached its mediocre peak.

'Name's Bart, Bart Fraden,' he finally said, falling easily into the clipped, taciturn local speech-pattern. 'Y'don't know me, but I know you. I know y'questions. I know what y'been hearing. Y'hear that y'Killers are mighty interested in y'Animals that act crazy, eh? And y'hear that y'quotas are way up all over y'planet . . .'

A guttural murmuring swept through the crowd. Men nodded, women and children seemed to go tense, even angry.

'My man,' a young woman shouted. 'Took my man!'

'And mine!'

'Ten this month from this village,' a burly man said. 'Eight over y'quota!'

'So y'Killers have been here already,' Fraden said. 'They'll be back, promise y'that! Y'Brothers, they don't care about y'quotas any more. Y'know why?'

There was a sullen, expectant silence. 'Y'got a lot o'questions, man,' someone grunted. 'Y'got some answers?'

'Got a man who's got some answers,' Fraden said. On cue, Lamar Gomez, one of Willem's original 'heads, stepped forward. 'Go on, Gomez,' Fraden said, 'tell 'em what y'told me.'

By now, having repeated it several dozen times in the past week, Gomez finally had his little spiel down pat. He reeled it off like a recording.

'Name's Lamar Gomez,' he said. 'Y'Killers came to my village couple weeks ago, took ten of us – nine over y'quota. Took us t'Sade. Took us and put us in a big tank o'water, put a current through y'water. Thought the pain'd kill me. Kept it up for hours. Didn't kill me, didn't kill no one. But half o'us was raving nuts after couple

119

hours o'that. Finally turned off y'electricity, took us out, took y'nuts t'dungeons under y'Palace, took me and the rest wasn't nuts yet, put us in pens outside y'Palace. Heard a couple Killers talking then. Said they were gonna torture us all till we were all nuts, then take our blood f'something y'Brotherhood wanted. Y'Killers thought it was real funny. Said they was gonna torture *y'whole planet* till we was all nuts, then bleed all y'Animals dry. Well, next day they was trucking us somewhere, y'truck hit a rock, turned over, y'Killers, most of y'Animals was killed but I got away. Headed for y'jungle, met Bart here, told him what happened, and he said he was an off-worlder, knew what was happening and why they was doin' it – '

'And I do know!' Fraden shouted. 'Could be only one thing: drug they call Omnidrene – strongest drug in the Galaxy. Know how they make y'Omnidrene? Boil down the blood of y'nuts, is how! Know how many nuts y'Brotherhood'd need t'bleed t'keep 'em all in Omnidrene? 'Bout fifteen million. Know the population of Sangre? *'Bout fifteen million too!* Figure it out! They're out t'drive y'all nuts, every last one of you! And when you're all raving nuts, they're gonna bleed y't'death, they're gonna bleed y'real slow. You're all gonna die, but not fast. You're all gonna die one pint of blood at a time. Y'gonna have a long time t'think about what it's like t'be dead. Only y'won't be doin' much thinking, 'cause y'all gonna be crazy! Every goddamned last one of you! How d'y'like that? How d'y'like y'Brotherhood now?'

The Sangrans stood sullenly silent. There were one or two weak cries of 'Blasphemy', but the hard eyes and thoughtful scowls of the majority quickly squelched the ultraorthodox minority.

Fraden looked out over the sullen, confused faces. Anywhere else in the Galaxy, they'd be howling for blood by now. But this, after all, was Sangre.

'Well what're you gonna do about it?' he roared. 'Y'gonna just sit on y'asses and wait for 'em t'truck y'off and bleed you to death? Gonna stand around while they drive you nuts, torture you and kill you? Call yourselves men?'

'Animals is what we are,' an emaciated, stooped old man shouted. 'Y'Brothers rule, y'Killers kill, y'Animals do what they're told. Natural Order!' he said righteously.

'Natural Order?' Fraden sneered. 'Natural Order is t'take ten times the quota? Natural Order is t'bleed y'all t'death? Since when is that y'Natural Order? *Y'Brotherhood* don't care about Natural Order now! Why should you?'

The Sangrans grunted, shuffled their feet, did not meet his eyes. Now he was hitting 'em where they lived!

'What can Animals do?' a man asked defensively.

'Never mind what Animals can do,' Fraden said, shifting out of the local argot. 'I'll tell you what *men* would do. And you *are* men. Strip a Killer or a Brother naked and he's no different from any of you. You all know that! I'll tell you what men would do!'

He whipped a wrinkled piece of paper out of a pocket, waved it over his head like a banner. The paper was blank.

'Men would listen to what is written here and they would *fight* for it! They would fight the Brotherhood and kill the Killers and they wouldn't stop fighting until their enemies were all dead and they were free! Listen! Listen! Listen to what men all over Sangre are already listening to! Listen to why the jungle is filling with armed men! Listen to what the people of Sangre are fighting for!'

Fraden pretended to read from the soiled scrap of paper.

'For the past three centuries the people of Sangre have been tortured, murdered, eaten, owned like cattle by the

121

ruthless exploiters and sadists, the Brotherhood of Pain, aided by their inhuman, murderous lackeys, the Killers. The Sangran People have been slaves in their own land.

'Therefore, the Sangran People hereby declare that the reign of this inhuman dictatorship is ended. The Sangran People declare that from this day forward, they no longer recognize the right of the Brotherhood to rule Sangre, slaughter the people, kill them, enslave them, bleed them to death. The time for Revolution is here!

'To wage this heroic struggle against murder and dictatorship, the Sangran People do hereby establish the Free Republic of Sangre, with Bart Fraden as provisional President until such time as the struggle is won and free elections can be held. The Free Republic of Sangre is now the only government recognized by the Sangran People. The Killers, the Brotherhood, and all that aid them are hereby declared criminals against the Sangran People and under sentence of death.

'The instrument of the Sangran Revolution is the People's Army of Sangre. All able-bodied Sangrans are entitled to join the People's Army to fight the Brothers and their henchmen under expert leadership, and will be provided with guns. Guns for all! The Free Republic calls on all Sangrans to arise and destroy the Brotherhood and the Killers! Death to the Killers! Death to the Brotherhood! Long live the Free Republic!'

After giving the same speech off the top of his head about thirty times in the past week, Fraden was hardly surprised at the inevitable dull-eyed, foot-shuffling silence it received. After all, if these clowns understood a tenth of what he had said, it was a lot. Main thing was that it sounded more official than anything they had ever heard before, and that even these yokums could understand the part about guns and killing Brothers and Killers. The Noble Sangran People indeed!

'Well, there's what you can do, friends,' he said. 'Think it over. And when you've thought it over, come to the jungle near the mountains. Don't worry about finding the People's Army – the People's Army'll find *you*!'

The Sangrans watched silently as he formed his men into formation around him and marched from the village. It was always that way. Took time to sink in. But in a few days, maybe when the Killers returned and hauled away more men to Sade, a couple of them would see the light and show up in the area of the camp.

Fraden sighed as they passed by a group of Bugs hauling in grain from the fields. A week of breaking my back, he thought, and something like forty volunteers to show for it. But the situation wasn't hopeless, it couldn't be. All the ingredients for a revolution were there. It just needed a final something to ignite them.

Bart Fraden had the uncanny feeling that that something was right under his nose somewhere. He shrugged. He knew that sooner or later he would find it.

After all, he thought philosophically, Rome wasn't sacked in a day.

The camp, at least, Fraden thought, is beginning to look like it means business. He stood outside his hut, which had been built with the hull of the lifeboat forming one wall and the airlock opening directly into the interior, giving him confidential access to the 'boat. The hut had taken only a day to be knocked together and another could easily be built if he had to fly the 'boat. Willem's hut, across the clearing by the second 'boat, had no such arrangement. It was a minor point of status that Fraden insisted on. There could be only one leader, and Willem's peculiar relationship with the herogyn-heads tended to cloud that fact. The huts were by way of making it clear.

The bulk of the camp was framed by the two 'boats: a

cluster of huts near Willem's that housed the herogyn-heads, another cluster further towards Fraden's hut for the volunteers, four huts with big open doorways in the centre of camp making a big display of captured arms and ammunition (at this point better than three guns for every guerrilla) and small cookfires scattered randomly about the camp. Food was a sore point with Fraden. He wouldn't tolerate cannibalism in camp, but it was a rule that was universally unpopular, and what the guerrillas ate when they were foraging was something he did not care to contemplate.

Fraden walked towards the volunteers' huts where about seventy men were turning out in the hot morning sun. From a separate hut, four men who had been picked up by patrols in the jungle were being hustled out on to the rude parade ground formed by the semi-circle of huts by sympathetic but jaundice-eyed volunteer guards. This was another little touch: recruits and potential recruits were handled strictly by other volunteers as was any contact with the villagers. Willem's 'heads were useless, really, for anything more subtle than killing, and it would pay off in the long run to keep them isolated. Let Willem keep 'em to himself, Fraden thought. It had its dangers, but also some advantages. It kept Willem a shadowy and somehow sinister figure at the periphery of the Revolution, while Bart Fraden was the name spread by word of mouth propaganda through contacts between the volunteers and their old villages, Fraden the President, the Liberator, the Hero of the Revolution, the Man Who . . . It was never too early to protect your rear, Fraden knew from long experience.

'Morning, men,' he said as they formed up before him.

'Morning, Bart,' they answered in unison. Another subtle touch – Willem was big on titles and 'sirs', he loved

124

calling himself 'Field Marshal', so Fraden was 'Bart' to one and all, the Man of the People.

'Long live the Free Republic!' Fraden said.

'Long live the Free Republic . . .' they chanted somewhat diffidently. A wiry young man with a heavy thatch of blond hair ushered the four new men before him. He was 'Colonel' Olnay, the closest thing to a smart Sangran Fraden had yet seen, and he had plans for the kid. He needed someone to head up a propaganda and espionage section and Olnay, by sheer default, would have to be it.

'Y'four new men, Bart,' Olnay said, making it sound very formal.

'Long live the Free Republic!' the four chanted heartily. Olnay had obviously been coaching them. Two more points for Colonel Olnay.

'Long live the Free Republic,' Fraden replied perfunctorily. 'Now, before I formally induct you men into the People's Army, I want to be sure you know why you're here and what's expected of you. Suppose you tell me why you left your villages to join the Revolution?'

'T'kill Killers!' one of the men shouted.

'T'kill y'Brothers!'

'T'save m'hide,' the squat, dark one said. 'Killers took half m'village last week. Figured I might be next.' Fraden smiled. There was a man who might have something like brains!

'What's your name?' he asked the realist.

'Name's Guilder, President Bart Fraden.'

'Bart, Guilder, *Bart*. I'm leader here simply because I'm the one who knows how to lead. I'm not some superior being in your Natural Order as the Brothers pretend to be. Remember that, all of you! We're all equals here, that's one of the things we're fighting for. So happens, Guilder here is more or less right. We're fighting to save our own skins, *our own*, meaning the hides of the

125

Sangran People. That's what Revolution is all about. The Brotherhood is out to do us all in, so we're out to do them in first. But don't confuse means with ends. We're fighting for freedom. Freedom means death to all Brothers and death to all Killers, but we're not just fighting to kill the enemy, we fighting to *win*. It's not always the same thing. You'll have plenty of chances to kill Killers, but you'll be under orders at all times. That means doing what you're told, even if it seems crazy, even if it means telling lies to your own people. Once you're in, you are *in*. There's no turning back. The penalty for treason or disobedience is death. Are you with us?'

'Long live the Free Republic!' the four men shouted, if not with quite the same unrestrained enthusiasm as before. That was the whole idea – Willem's boys were strictly killers, and the less thinking they did the better, but these men had to be fully controlled partisan fighters. A guerrilla army that looted and raped and murdered indiscriminately was about as effective as a one-armed, blind spaceship pilot.

'Okay, men,' Fraden said. 'You're now soldiers of the People's Army of the Free Republic of Sangre. Colonel Olnay will issue you weapons, and you'll be expected to see to it that they don't fall apart by next week. Colonel, when you're through here, I want you over by Marshal Vanderling's hut. Got plans for you, and we might as well start in now.'

Olnay grinned greedily as he marched the new men away, and Fraden watched them with mixed feelings. With recruitment still so damned low, he was obviously getting mostly the highly motivated mavericks like Olnay and this Guilder. It was all very well getting the cream of the crop – and a mighty raunchy crop to begin with – but when things really got rolling, what kind of Sangrans would they get then, loot-hungry, fanatic killers? Well,

Fraden thought somewhat sourly, there's ways to use that kind too . . .

Fraden ambled off in the direction of Vanderling's hut. He frowned as he saw that Willem and those two 'heads of his, Gomez and Jonson, were waiting for him outside. That was another thing that was starting to bug him – Willem kept those two herogyn-heads around him like a pair of matched Dobermans. 'Colonels' Gomez and Jonson! Chiefs of staff, Willem called 'em. Willem was starting to take this Field Marshal crap a little too seriously. A Field Marshal commanding less than two hundred men . . . Why couldn't he see how ludicrous it was? Next thing you know, he'll be carving himself a swagger stick – though come to think of it, he carries that snipgun around as if it *were* a goddamned swagger stick. Fraden laughed wryly to himself. When he starts wearing a monocle, he thought, I'll have to cut him down to size!

'Well, how's the gunfodder collecting going, Bart?' Willem Vanderling said, as he, his two colonels, Fraden, and Olnay, who had just joined them, sat around the crude table in front of Vanderling's hut. Gomez and Jonson grinned like a pair of matched sycophants. Fraden saw that Olnay was scowling, measuring the two herogyn-heads with narrowed blue eyes, eyes that showed both fear and contempt.

'Let's not get into the habit of making cracks like that, even in private,' Fraden said. 'It might come out in public at the wrong time. Last I counted, we had seventy-five volunteers. Coming in at about the rate of three a day.'

'That really stinks!' Vanderling said. 'We've still got more officers than slobs . . . er, *men*.'

'Let's take a whole village,' Gomez said, his small eyes gleaming wolfishly beneath his red hair. 'Y'Animals got no weapons. Be easy. We could take hundred men, then take more o'y'villages. We could get hundreds o'soldiers like that, thousands.'

'You mean hundreds of *prisoners*,' Fraden said. 'Who needs prisoners?'

'We'll make y'Animals fight!' Jonson declared vehemently. 'They fight or we kill 'em. Kill a few, the rest will fight.'

'He's got a point,' Vanderling said, perhaps a shade too quickly for it to have all been spontaneous. 'We're getting nowhere your way.'

'The only point he's got,' Fraden snapped, 'is the one on top of his head! This is a revolution, remember? To win a revolution, you've got to get the people on your side. You can't do it by enslaving them. You can't do it by scaring them, either – especially since they're already twice as scared of the Killers than they ever could be of us. And how would you like to march in front of a bunch of armed men you've press-ganged? How long do you think you'd stay alive? You leave the recruitment problem to me. You stick to your line of evil and I'll stick to mine. I don't tell you how to fight your battles, do I?'

'But you sure as hell tell me where and when to fight,' Vanderling whined. 'They got about a hundred Killers going through the villages about twenty miles from here picking up Animals. We could hit 'em tonight, get fifty or sixty of 'em. The way you've got us working just makes no sense. Ambush five Killers here, ten there, hardly ever even hit an estate compound. What kind of a way to fight a war is that? We hit those Killers tonight, we kill more in an hour than we have all week.'

'You've got it all ass-forward, Willem,' Fraden said. 'We've got what, less than two hundred men? To have any chance against a hundred Killers, you'd have to commit 'em all, risk being totally wiped out. At this early stage, we attack for only one reason – to get weapons and to get away with 'em. To do that, you've got to completely wipe out whoever you attack, and with Killers that means you need at least a three-to-one advantage plus the surprise of an ambush. Those babies can *fight;* you know that better than I do. Less than two hundred men – we've got just a toehold here, and you want to risk losing it completely, and for what? Pointless killing!'

'So what do we do, just sit around and play with ourselves?'

Fraden sighed. What was wrong with Willem? Was the damned planet getting to him or something? The military mind . . . kill the enemy, and damn the torpedoes! Doesn't he realize that if the Brotherhood gets really stirred up at this point, they can send a couple thousand Killers in here, root us out, and finish us? If they weren't so hot to get victims for the madness-pogrom, if they weren't obsessed with getting a new source of Omnidrene, they'd probably be doing it already. Later on, when we've got thousands of guerrillas instead of a couple hundred, we can handle that. But now . . . making ourselves look like anything more than a nuisance would be sheer suicide.

'I'll tell you what you do,' Fraden said. 'They'll be breaking up into groups, trucking Animals into their main camp, right? So you take maybe thirty men and set up an ambush on one of the roads, well away from the main concentration. You knock over two, three, four trucks, one at a time, and split before the main force finds out what's happening. That way you get a few dozen guns or so, you lose only a few men, kill a couple dozen Killers, *and* you free twenty or thirty Sangrans to run back to their villages and spread stories about the irresistible guerrillas in the jungle.'

'I dunno, Bart,' Vanderling said. 'My . . . ah, officers are getting . . . uh . . . restless for some real action.'

Gomez and Jonson nodded, gritted their teeth. They were edging into herogyn-withdrawal.

'Well, I *do* know,' Fraden said. 'Don't worry, there'll be plenty of action soon enough. And if they get too restless, just give 'em a little more herogyn.' Vanderling's 'chiefs of staff' nodded again, for once agreeing with Fraden. 'You had better get started now if you want to be set up by dusk,' Fraden said. 'And don't take more than ten of your . . . *officers*, the rest should be volunteers. I don't want a single one of the Sangrans you free hurt or killed. The name of the game is Robin Hood. See that you keep it in mind.'

As Vanderling and the two herogyn-heads went off to prepare the ambush, Fraden held Olnay back. 'I've got plans for you, Colonel,' he said. 'I need a man to set up and control a rumour mill and an espionage setup, and I think you're it. Interested?'

'T'give orders?' Olnay said, his eyes lighting up with ill-concealed anticipation. 'T'tell y'Animals what t'do like a Brother? I'm interested! But what's y'rumour mill?'

Fraden grimaced inwardly. Olnay was the best he had to work with and all *he* was really interested in was playing Brother! Well, at least he had *some* ambition. It could be used.

'It's really quite simple,' Fraden said. 'You pick recruits you think you can trust. You send 'em back to their villages to do what everyone else does. The Animals shouldn't even know they're guerrillas. They report back to you and tell you what's going on and you tell me. Sometimes I'll have a story, a lie, sometimes, that I want spread. I'll tell it to you, you tell it to your agents when they report, and the agents spread it in their villages. It's all very simple, eh? But simple as it is, it'll let us spread whatever propaganda we want to every village, and the

130

villagers won't even know where the stories are coming from. Think you can run a setup like that?'

'Sure,' Olnay said unhesitatingly. 'Just tell 'em what t'do, what t'say. Easy. But why? Why bother t'tell y'Animals lies and stories?'

Fraden shook his head. Go explain the theory and practice of political warfare to a Sangran! he thought. Still, might as well give it a small try . . .

'Look,' he said, 'why did you join up in the first place?'

'Heard y'talking in m'village about killing y'Killers and y'Brothers and running things ourselves,' Olnay said. 'Couple days later, y'Killers came and took ten Animals, and only a couple weeks after they took y'quota. Remembered what y'said about y'Brothers being out t'drive us all nuts, bleed us t'death. Figured that had nothing t'do with y'Natural Order, decided that if y'Brothers didn't care about y'Natural Order, why should I? Better t'kill than t'die. So I joined y'People's Army.'

A textbook example, Fraden thought. 'So if you hadn't heard about what was really going on, you might still be in your village, or more likely nuts in Sade by now,' he said. 'I can't be everywhere – but agents can. Tell the people what you want them to hear, and you get 'em to do what you want 'em to do.'

'Without killing any o'em?' Olnay said wondrously. 'Just with y'stories? *That's* y'propaganda?'

'That's it,' Fraden said.

'So y'tell me, and I tell m'agents, and they tell y'Animals, and y'Animals do what we want 'em to? Like y'were Moro and I was y'Killers?'

That's one way of looking at it, Fraden thought sourly. *The Sangran way.* 'If you want to look at it that way,' he said. 'What do you say?'

'T'make y'Animals obey, like I was a Brother . . .' Olnay murmured abstractedly, with the hungry expression of a lifelong hermit who had just discovered sex. 'I tell and they do . . . T'rule, almost. T'be like a Brother, instead of y'Animal, change places in y'Natural Order! Sounds good, sounds real good. I'm y'Animal.'

He looked at Fraden, smiled. 'Could almost say I'm y'man,' he said, savouring the words. 'Yeah, Bart . . . I'm y'*man*!'

Bart Fraden lay awake in the middle of the night, but it was not the lumpy straw mattress which prevented him from drifting back to sleep as Sophia, warm and naked against him, had. Something was itching at his mind, percolating up from the cellars of his subconscious, demanding entrance to the living room of his mind.

He knew the feeling well. His belly was trying to talk to him. He had enough insight into himself and his line of evil to have learned long ago, back in the Belt Free State, back, even, in Greater New York, that some things you just had to wait for, wait for your belly to solve. You could call it inspiration, or the ability of the subconscious to integrate more data than the conscious – or simply your guts talking to you.

It was the difference between a technician and an artist, a cold political schemer and a charismatic figure, and Fraden considered himself very much the latter. You could fabricate the most elaborate, clever plots imaginable, but if your belly didn't talk to you when that moment for inspiration came, you were nowhere.

And the moment for inspiration was *now*. Sangre should be boiling over, but it wasn't. All the ingredients for a revolution were there – the ruthless, despotic oligarchy, the tortured, brutalized people, the prospect of something else, something better, that the Free Republic brought to the planet – but nothing was really happening. It was a tight, closed system, locked in stasis. But like all such systems, the right touch, the right little inspiration, would shatter it like crystal.

He felt his belly working on that inspiration, but he knew that there was no way to force it to the surface ahead of its time, consciously. Yet he also knew that anything could trigger the revelation – a word, a sound, a smell.

It was so goddamned frustrating, like an egg inside you dying to be laid . . .

He felt Sophia move against him. 'You awake?' he whispered.

'Uh . . .' she grunted, cuddling closer, rubbing her face on his chest. 'I am *now*,' she said bad-temperedly. 'What's with you? Why can't you go to sleep and let me get some sleep too? You just lay there making waves, thinking so hard the gears grinding in that head of yours keep me awake.'

'Would you believe that it's because the mere presence of your luscious body fills me with a lust that won't let me – ' She kneed him gently in the stomach.

'Okay, okay, so you bore me silly. Seriously, I feel on the verge . . .'

'On the verge of *what*?' she grunted tiredly.

'That,' he sighed, 'is what's keeping me awake.'

'Huh?'

'Soph, this planet is a powder keg. By now, every village in this area knows about the Revolution and the People's Army and the madness-pogrom. They should be joining up in droves, but they're not. There's some factor, some little string just dying to be pulled, and I just can't seem to find the handle . . .'

'Why don't you ask old Chrome-dome?' Sophia suggested.

'*Willem?*'

'Sure. Don't tell me you haven't noticed? Bullethead is

133

really digging this mudball. At last, he's found *his* kind of people: bloodthirsty killers, sadists, and cannibals. Sangre is like old home week for Chrome-dome. You want to know how these cruds think – assuming for the sake of argument that they *do* think – ask Bullethead. He thinks more like them every day.'

'Soph, for crying out – '

He felt her prop herself up on her elbows, saw the vague shape of her head shake slowly in the darkness. 'Bart, Bart, love of my life,' she said, 'what in hell am I going to do with you? You're the closest thing to a man that I've ever run across. One could stretch a point and say that you have a brain. You get things done, you can manipulate swine like Moro and the rest of the fetid creatures on this unlovely glob of mud for your own more or less reasonable purposes without becoming one of them. So why won't you get it through your thick skull that most men aren't like you, particularly a thug like Bullethead! I've known plenty of what you'd call strong men, and I've never stuck with one as long as I've stuck with you. Haven't you ever wondered why?'

'I thought you were wild for my body.'

'For chrissakes, Bart, I'm being serious! I've got expensive tastes, so I need a man who can get things for me, a man who can dominate, a man who can use other men to his own advantage, to be blunt about it. That's you, in spades. I'm a first-line chick and I need a first-line man. But the kicker is that most men whose line of evil is using other men end up being like the men they use. You don't see that because you're *not* that way. But the Willem Vanderlings *are*. There he is, leading a gang of kill-crazy herogyn-heads against even more bloodthirsty Killers. How can he *not* become more and more like the men he's leading and the men he's fighting – especially since that's always been his bag in the first place? You're a politician and a hedonist – you use situations like this to make life comfortable for Number One. You've got plenty of nice, healthy vices. But Bullethead's a soldier, and his only vice is *killing*. What's a war, anyway, but a long series of individual murders? And Bullethead enjoys every one of 'em. War is a means to you, but it's an end to him. Now he's got himself a whole gang of playmates who feel the same way. He doesn't have to kid himself any more. Now he can be a bloody murderer and proud of it.'

'Thank you, Dr Freud,' Fraden said. 'Pardon my stupidity, but you miss the whole point. Which is that as long as the war is a means to me and an end to him, I control Willem. Each to his own pleasures, as Moro would say. I'm not worried about Willem, what's bothering me –'

'Just what in hell *is* bugging you tonight?' she said.

'Huh? HUH? What did you say?' Fraden blurted excitedly.

'What's the matter with you? All I asked is what's bugging you . . . ?'

'That's it! That's it! What's wrong with me? Why didn't I see it before?'

'What in hell are you raving about?'

He pulled her to him, kissed her eyes, her lips, both nipples, laughing insanely all the while. 'The Bugs!' he shouted. 'The Bugs! You're brilliant! You're a genius! The Bugs! The Bugs! Sure, it's got to be the Bugs!'

'Have you completely flipped?'

He silenced her with a long, long kiss, moved his hands over her body in sheer exuberance. She wrapped her arms around his neck, and murmured, '*Vive la* insanity,' as he enveloped her. Their lovemaking was short, intense, wordless, and utterly satisfying.

And only when it was over, and they lay easily in each other's arms, did the outside world intrude, did Fraden

135

become aware of the commotion going on in the camp outside.

Pulling on his pants, he arose, stood in the open doorway of the hut. Sophia wrapped something around her, joined him, put her arm around his waist.

In the flickering orange light of half a dozen small campfires, Fraden saw that Willem and his men had returned to camp. The division in the small group of men returning to camp was all too apparent. The bulk of them, the volunteers, trooped wearily in first, laden with the captured rifles and morningstars and bandoliers of ammunition. They deposited the booty in the armoury huts and then quickly retired to their makeshift barracks.

But as Fraden watched uneasily, Willem's ten herogyn-heads, strutting, laughing harshly, twitching convulsively in herogyn-withdrawal, clustered around Willem's hut, their eyes gleaming greedily in the firelight, their lips drawn into tight, toothy grins of anticipation.

Vanderling emerged from the hut with a handful of blue pills. Fraden was disgusted at his manner. Vanderling was grinning vulpinely, his eyes – was it merely a trick of the firelight? – glowing with an animal satisfaction. As he passed out the pills, he slapped backs, laughed, was slapped in return.

The herogyn-heads gobbled the pills, sat down on the damp earth, babbling to each other like a troop of baboons after a successful day's foraging.

And Willem sat with them, nodding, grinning proprietorially like a wise old wolf supervising the division of the pack's kill. He sat with them as the herogyn was absorbed into their bloodstreams, as one by one they quieted, as their eyes began to glaze over, as they began to fall into dull-eyed, slack-jawed torpor. Only when the last of them was lying quietly unasleep on the ground, dreaming herogyn dreams, did Vanderling give them one last approving look, grin like a crocodile and retire into his hut.

Bart Fraden turned to face Sophia. She opened her mouth to say something, saw the look in his eyes, stared back, her wry green eyes, tiny fey smile, saying 'I told you so' far better than any words could.

She laughed, breaking the tension of the moment. 'Come, come, Bart,' she said. 'You look as if someone told you there was no Santa Claus. Boys will be boys! Fun and games! Fun and games!'

She took his hand and led him back to bed.

And it was only long minutes later, when the sight had finally faded from his mind's eye and he was about to fall asleep, that he remembered that now he had *the* answer, the answer that would galvanize the torpid Sangran peasantry into a revolutionary tide, a tide that would sweep the Brotherhood to oblivion and himself to victory.

Chapter 8

Willem Vanderling cocked his head, stared at Fraden quizzically. '*Killer uniforms?*' he said. 'Sure, we can pick up all the Killer uniforms we want. We're killing fifty, sixty, eighty Killers a week. It'd be no trouble to collect uniforms. But why? What in hell do you want with Killer uniforms?'

Fraden grinned, leaned back against a tree as he stood in front of Vanderling's hut, looked out across the little guerrilla camp, and saw it as it would be a few months from now, thousands of men where now there were scores, an army where now there were essentially only brigands. And it couldn't miss; it was a natural.

'Not what do *I* want,' he said, 'what *you* want, Willem. You and about twenty or so of your most trusted – if you'll pardon the expression – herogyn-heads are going to play Killer for a while . . .'

Vanderling grinned. 'Hey, that's a pretty good one!' he said. 'We dress up in Killer uniforms and infiltrate that Killer concentration I told you about, hit 'em from the inside and the outside all at once, and – '

'Nothing like that,' Fraden said. 'You're going to kill Bugs.'

'*Huh?*'

'You heard right. You're going to kill Bugs – the Brains that the villagers use to control the Bugs, to be precise.'

'I don't get it, Bart,' Vanderling said. 'We're going to kill Brains . . . What good is that going to do us? Seems like a king-sized waste of time to me.'

Fraden sighed. 'It would, Willem, it would. Look, let

me explain it to you in words of one syllable. The Bughills are hive organisms, right. It's as if all the Bugs in a hill were arms of a single body, and the Brain was the head. So what happens when you chop off an animal's head?'

'Uh . . . it dies. But the Bugs won't die, will they? I suppose they'd just run around like a buncha dumb beetles . . .'

'Very good, Willem, very good. Without a Brain a Bughill is just a collection of brainless, useless insects. Now hold your nose and consider the Sangran peasants. All the able-bodied men in the villages work a full day tending the Meatanimals, producing food for *someone else*. They work all day and don't produce so much as a morsel of food for themselves. The only reason the villagers don't starve is because the Brotherhood has it all neatly worked out: the "Animals" slave for them, and the Bugs slave for the Animals. One old man directing one Brain which controls the village Bughill grows food for the entire village, freeing the men to tend the local Brother's Meatanimals. So what happens to the villagers if their Bugs suddenly become useless?'

'*Whoo-whee!* They're up crap creek without a canoe! They keep working for the local Brother and they starve to death. They try to cut out and work their own fields – if they remember how – and the local poobah sends in his Killers to round 'em up and make 'em work. Either way, they're screwed. But I don't get it, Bart. You're always telling me how we need the yokums on our side. This is just going to make 'em hate our guts!'

'Who, little old *us*?' Fraden said with great mock innocence. 'Remember, it's the *Killers* they'll see killing their Brains. And the rumour-mill'll spread the story that it's part of the madness pogrom. Moro's out to starve 'em all so they'll flip easier. Dig?'

Vanderling shook his head in dazed admiration. 'I dig,'

he said. 'You got a mind like a rattlesnake! But won't the Brotherhood just truck in more conditioned Brains? Even the Sangrans will smell a rat if they see the Brotherhood replacing the Brains they're supposed to have killed in the first place . . .'

'Which is why we concentrate on the six nearest estates to begin with,' Fraden said. 'Round-the-clock patrols on all roads from Sade. We intercept and kill any Brains they try to truck in. Six estates, couple hundred villages, maybe ten thousand potential guerrillas. Once all the Brains in the area are dead, we'll have so many men it'd take an army of Killers just to get in here. And then we move on to the next district, and the next . . . And by that time, the Brotherhood will be so busy fighting a war, they'll forget all about trucking in Brains.'

'Yeah . . .' Vanderling muttered. 'Man, it really should work!'

'As long as we play it cool. We don't want it to backfire. So we use only twenty-five men, five teams of five. Into a village, kill the Brain, and out, bang-bang, and all at night, when they won't notice that the men in the Killer uniforms don't look like Killers. Each team should be able to hit four or five villages a night. And of course, use only 'heads – the volunteers might not . . . er, comprehend the strategic necessities. Pick five squad leaders, take 'em out the first few nights yourself, let 'em get the idea, then they lead their own squads.'

'Right,' Vanderling said. 'I'll get right on it.'

'And for chrissakes, don't take a snipgun with you! Remember, you're supposed to be a Killer. Act like one.'

'*Yeah!*' Vanderling said, with what Fraden thought was a good deal too much enthusiasm.

Willem Vanderling studied the five black-uniformed figures crouched in the clump of trees and heavy underbrush beside him. The village was a dark cluster of featureless shapes before them in the moonless Sangran night. Towering high above the huts was the huge black mound of the local Bughill. Vanderling read the faces of his five squad leaders in the starlight. Gomez, Jonson, McPhee, Ryder, Lander. They were starting to get wild; their eyes were bloodshot and sunken, their arm-muscles tight bands as they clutched their guns tightly, occasionally stroked the morningstars clipped to their belts ominously. This is it for the night, he thought. They had nearly gone ape in the last village, killing the Brain and then wanting to take on all comers. When they were this far into withdrawal, it was hard to control 'em without the snipgun, which they feared and respected. This fifth village and then back to camp and good stiff doses of herogyn to cool 'em down.

'Okay men,' he whispered. 'In we go. Last one for the night, and then those little blue pills for all, eh?'

They grinned at him, ran tongues over dry lips.

'Remember, in, make plenty of noise, kill the Brain, and then out, with no side trips. That's the pattern, and for chrissakes, let's stick to it this time! Let's go.'

Noisily, arrogantly, they tromped into the sleeping village. Vanderling led them past huts, where the sounds of awakening villagers could be dimly heard as they hurried by, booted feet pounding hard on bare earth. He led them straight to the isolated hut on the far side of the Bughill.

And there it was – you could smell that lousy Bug-stink all over the place, that and the smell of the crude booze they kept the Brains lushed on.

'Okay,' Vanderling said as they paused momentarily outside the reeking little hut. 'Remember, *guns*, not morningstars. We want to make it fast, and we want to make it noisy!'

They burst into the hut. In the far corner, a withered

old man slept on a straw pallet. Piled next to the pallet were a dozen clay jugs, open-mouthed and filled with raw alcohol. But the reek of the alcohol was utterly overpowered by the rancid odour of the thing in the centre of the hut.

The Brain lay there on its belly, pulsating, its body so bloated that its eight legs, little atrophied nubbins, did not reach the ground. Its head was dwarfed by the grotesque, sacklike body, and the face was almost invisible, a hideous doll-face, tiny black eyes, small cilia-rimmed mouth, almost buried in convoluted green flesh.

'Thirs? Thirs? Orders, thirs?' the Brain began to chitter chitinously.

Disgusting smelly mess! Vanderling thought. He raised his rifle, pointed it at the Brain, emptied five shots into its face in rapid succession. His men began firing wildly, hitting the Brain in the face, legs, body. Where dozens of bullets punctured the chitin, neat holes spouted heavy green ichor, and the room filled with the choking reek of gunpowder.

Vanderling kept firing. 'Thirs . . . ? Thirs . . . ? Orders, thirs . . . ?' the dying Brain croaked weakly. Then it tottered and fell over on its side, the eight little legs waving feebly . . .

'What – ?' Thunk! A liquid, burbling scream, a quick series of horrid little moans, more heavy thunking sounds.

Vanderling whirled, saw that the old man had risen off the pallet, had been clubbed in the face by a morningstar, his features a hideous mask of chopped and bleeding meat where the bladestudded steel ball had struck. The old man fell backwards where he stood. Gomez, Jonson, and the others clustered around his supine body, smashing it senselessly with their morningstars, kicking it savagely with their boots, uttering throaty animal noises.

Vanderling cursed, jabbed at his men with his rifle butt

and boots. 'Cut it out! Cut it out! Enough! Let's get the hell out of here! Out! Out! Out!'

With shouts, curses, and kicks, he managed to herd them out the door and into the night. As they ran through the village towards the cover of the woods, dark, shouting, gesticulating shapes erupted from the huts, bumped them, pummelled them blindly in the night.

The guerrillas began to shout, began swinging their morningstars, using them to clear a path through the villagers as casually as a man hacks his way through a jungle with a machete. Howls of pain filled the darkness, screams, curses, the sickening sound of metal on flesh.

Vanderling felt hands pummel him, claw at him. Cursing, he unshipped his morningstar, swung it in wide random arcs. He felt a shudder run up his arm as it struck flesh and bone, then another and another.

Something within him seemed to give way as he fought his way to the woods in the darkness, the anonymous darkness, where no eye watched, no man saw. As the Animals clawed blindly at him, as he felt their flesh tear and pulp beneath his morningstar, a curtain seemed to part in his mind, revealing a hot red haze, a blazing animal heat that overwhelmed him, set his blood afire, surrendered his being totally to the moment.

He screamed like an animal, swung his weapon with wild, unthinking abandon, laughed gutturally as he felt it slam home again and again and again. He swung his free arm like a club, felt flesh beneath his fist, kicked out at soft parts, and the sea of screams filling the darkness urged him on to smash and punch and kick and kill.

'Son of a bitch! Son of a bitch! Son of a bitch!' he chanted shrilly over and over again as he hacked his way through the human underbrush towards the woods.

Finally, the village, the screams and moans of the maimed and the dying, was behind him, and he stood panting in the quiet, dark woods. He took a head count as vague shapes clustered about him. One . . . three . . . five . . . They had all made it!

'The herogyn-heads were laughing, breathing languorously in the night. Vanderling found himself laughing, breathing with them, one of them. 'Okay, boys, okay!' he told them. 'A good night's work, and now back to camp for the happy stuff!'

In the knot of men, back-slapping, grinning, happy men, Willem Vanderling walked through the jungle towards the guerrilla camp, the warm aftermath of battle bathing him in contentment.

Piece of cake! he thought. A real piece of cake! And the fun, he knew, was only just beginning . . .

'Looks good. Looks pretty damned good,' Bart Fraden said. Olnay nodded, turned to glance over his shoulder at the guerrilla camp, now quieting in the twilight. Fraden watched Olnay looking the camp over, leaned back in his chair, and smiled a knowing smile.

With the campaign to destroy the Brains well under way enough by now for Willem to be out of it, with scores of Brains already dead, with the recruitment rate having nearly trippled in the past week, it was now time to test out the rumour mill that Olnay had set up.

'Okay, Colonel, you've got the agents now,' he said. 'Let's see what they can do.'

Olnay turned away from the centre of the camp, where nearly two hundred volunteers hunkered around dozens of campfires, eating the last bites of the dry, flat Sangran bread, and looked at Fraden expectantly.

'We'll see how good your boys are at spreading propaganda,' Fraden said. 'The Killers are wiping out the Brains because they figure that starving Animals can be driven crazy all the quicker. I want every villager in this district to know that by next week. And I want the story to end with "only Bart Fraden can save us". Can do?'

'Y'Killers are killing y'Brains?' Olnay said incredulously.

Fraden hesitated. There was something to be said for having Olnay know the truth . . . It would be bad news if he found out he was being lied to. On the other hand, the first rule of security was tell no one more than he had to know to do his job.

'That's not the point,' he said. 'I want the people to think that whether it's true or not. What they *think's* going on is what counts, not what really is.'

Olnay nodded. 'Y'propaganda's not truth, not a lie either? Or it's both . . .' He seemed to struggle with the concept.

'Never mind,' Fraden said. 'Too much thinking is bad for digestion. Let's just say that anything's true if you make it true. Men control truth, it doesn't control them. Now hop to it, eh?'

Olnay seemed pleased with that pragmatic definition, or at least confused enough to stop thinking about it, Fraden mused, as the Sangran went about his business.

He stood, stretched, laughed. Years ago, he had given up worrying about the essential naïveté and selfishness of the human race. The worst human traits – greed, hate, stupidity – could be useful if you simply determined to *use* them and not try to reform clods. Later, when the war was won, maybe it would be time to clean up some of the more distasteful messes. But now, he told himself, relax, dig it!! For the first time since he had landed on Sangre, he felt completely on top of things. He could feel the Revolution beginning to build up momentum, could sense events, people, whole patterns of action, the shape and feel of the Revolution itself, as part of a great web, with himself at the centre, controlling, stimulating, digging, as if the planet, the people, the Revolution were parts of his own body.

He stepped inside the hut. Sophia was lying on the bed, languid, perhaps bored. He walked over to the bed, looked down at her. A thrill went through him. How great it was to be the centre of a whole revolution, to sense men and events, a whole planetful of 'em, quickening to your own will, falling one by one into patterns that were extensions of your own self, a whole universe orienting itself around your being! To be in charge, to be Number One, the Leader, the Man Who, and to just be able to look down at your woman and to know you'll soon be able to lay a whole planet like a bauble at her feet if the spirit moves you!

She looked up at him. Her eyes widened, she smiled, a wild, wild smile.

'*Bart* . . .' she murmured. 'I've never seen you . . . You look like a bull, a big virile bull, Zeus about to rape Europa . . .'

Fraden laughed. Yeah, I feel like a god, all right! Zeus had his planet and I have mine! he thought, listened to the blood pounding in his temples. Pride, yeah, pride! What was wrong with pride? Anybody didn't dig pride, didn't dig himself. Anybody didn't dig pride deserved to have a man who did rule him. Screw humility! You are who you say you are as long as you can back it up!

He stood over the bed, looked down, anticipated her touch, yet made no move. 'I feel like a bull,' he said. 'Why not? I'm Bart Fraden and this is my planet, *mine*! Every man should feel this before he calls himself a man. If I were Tarzan and you Jane, I'd kick Cheeta out on his ass, beat my chest, and – '

'I've never seen you like this before, you goddamned arrogant bastard,' she said, but laughing with shining eyes as she said it.

'You never saw me on the bottom pushing my way up before. Scares you?'

'Does Tarzan scare Jane?' she answered touching his arm lightly. He felt the moment building between them, felt himself swelling, enlarging, felt the feeling of power feeding his manhood, felt his manhood feeding his power. He saw in her eyes that she felt it too, saw that the raw, animal maleness in him was stoking the fire of womanness in her. The heat she was giving off fed his own and the room seemed like the centre of a volcano about to explode.

'Only their chimpanzee knows for sure . . .' he said.

The inane words, like a catalyst, ignited the explosion. She reached up, pulled him down on her with surprising savage strength, uttering little piercing cries, pleading, begging, demanding. He was all over her, and clothes went somewhere, anywhere, and the intoxication, with her, with himself, with the universe, swept his mind away, and his whole being was in his body, his skin, going out to her, penetrating her, enveloping her. He felt her giving of herself as an offering, yet aggressively, proudly, and as a monarch takes homage, with pride and with grace, he took of her, and the thrust of his taking and the enfolding of her giving produced a crescendo that for a timeless instant united them, giver and taker, woman and man, as a world-filling whole.

Long minutes of silence later, she looked up at him with smoky, sparkling eyes. 'Long live . . . long live . . .' she tried to say and broke up into girlish giggles.

'Long live *what*'?

'*Long live the Free Republic!*' she roared and broke into peals of uncontrollable laughter.

Long live the Free Republic! Bart Fraden thought, half-sardonically, as he glanced behind him at the new flag of the Free Republic of Sangre – a red circle on a square of green cloth – fluttering from a pole so crude that the bark was still peeling off it.

But that flag was less presumptuous every day. Now it was being carried openly down the road in the daylight. In front of the flag. Fraden marched alone. Behind marched a hundred armed guerrillas in neat formation – volunteers all – and behind *them* came another hundred men or so from the last two villages who had joined up on the spot. Bart Fraden marched at the head of two hundred men under the hot, red Sangran sun, and to him it seemed as if he outshone it, that the heat he was giving off made that ball of hot plasma seem like a hunk of red ice. He marched, and he felt the power march with him.

What a feeling! Like being born again, coming forth from furtive scuttling in the jungle to stand shining in the light. For the first time since he had lost the Belt Free State, Fraden at last felt that the world was seeing him as the man he knew himself to be. The troops behind him marching, his flag waving in the sunlight, Sangrans falling in like little boys at a parade, and *he* was the centre, the Rome to which all roads led – Fraden the President, Fraden the Liberator, Fraden the Hero of the People. So what if the unfolding legend of Bart Fraden was a conscious creation of his own rumour mill? A hero was a man who created his own myth, crawled into it, and then pulled the hole in after him. Was a lie a lie after you turned it into the truth?

And the myth was on the verge of becoming reality. Every Brain in the area was dead. Surprisingly the Brotherhood had not tried to truck any new ones in – perhaps they too were turning propaganda into reality by actually using the newly created desperation of the villagers to feed the madness-pogrom.

The propaganda campaign to blame the deaths of the

Brains on the Killers was a total success – Willem's masqueraders had made themselves all too conspicuous, and by now any Killer that wandered into a village would be torn to pieces. The madness-pogrom had sent the sky falling in on the Sangran peasantry, and now the death of the Brains had pulled the rug out from under them as well. They had nothing left to lose. There was only one way for them to turn, and turn they did. Recruits were pouring in almost faster than they could be counted. They wanted guns now, they wanted to fight. They wanted to kill.

This tour of the countryside was less a recruiting drive than a public thumbing of Fraden's nose at the Brotherhood, a show of the flag, a show of force.

Now the road led past fields ringing the next village. In the field by the roadside a few dozen wild-eyed men were futilely trying to kill thirty or forty Bugs, who were tearing mindlessly about the field, trampling grain, ripping it up with their pincers, chittering crazily.

A great roar of rage went up from the mob of men behind the troops as they saw the rampaging Bugs. Fraden called his guerrillas to a smart halt, waved the men in the field aside. They trotted to the roadside as the guerrillas swung to their left, formed a long firing line along the shoulder of the road.

'Kill y'Bugs! Kill y'Bugs!' the villagers began to chant, and the mob of recruits picked it up, and it became a great demanding roar. Fraden dropped his right arm sharply.

The guerrillas began to fire on the Bugs, volley after volley into the huge green arthropods, again and again and again as the villagers cheered them on. 'Kill y'Bugs! Kill y'Killers! Kill y'Brothers! Long live the Free Republic!'

Bugs fell, waved their legs in the air, were still. In a few moments it was over, and the field was littered with broken green corpses, wet with dark green ichor. The men who had been fighting the Bugs joined the procession as it went forward into the village itself, shouting, 'Long live the Free Republic! Death t'y'Brotherhood! Long live Bart!'

As they passed through the circle of huts, men, women, children, their ribs showing, their stomachs bloated, their eyes mad with hate, joined the parade, and by the time they reached the open centre of the village, the entire village filled the area, screaming, 'Kill y'Brothers! Kill y'Killers! Long live the Free Republic!'

Savouring the raw animal heat, Bart Fraden made his way to the centre of the mob, mounted an old crate that someone produced from somewhere. He let the roars of his people wash over him for a heady moment, then waved his arms, gestured for silence.

Silence they gave him, and he knew that they were at last ready to give more, to give all. He could see it in their sunken, red-rimmed eyes, in the grim set of their mouths. He could all but smell it on their sweat. They were with him now, waiting to hear him tell them what they wanted to hear. Eager to fight, eager to kill. He had seen this kind of mob before, but never so savage, never so feral, never so willing to follow where they knew he would lead. The bonds had burst. The dam had busted. The shit had hit the fan.

'Long live the Free Republic!' he shouted.

'LONG LIVE THE FREE REPUBLIC!' they roared.

'They call y'Animals!' he shouted. 'They kill you, torture you, eat your flesh! Now they're out to torture and kill every Animal on the planet. But you're not Animals, you're men! Men! *Men!* You're citizens of the Free Republic now, and the Free Republic protects its

150

own. What do we do when the Killers try to make us slave for the Brotherhood while they starve us to death?'

'DEATH T'Y'KILLERS!' the Sangrans roared. 'KILL Y'BROTHERHOOD!'

'That's right, death to the Killers!' Fraden said. 'But unarmed, untrained, unled men can't defeat armed soldiers. Try to fight 'em yourselves, and they'll mow you down, eat you alive! But you've got the People's Army to fight for you. Those who want to fight, to kill Killers, join the People's Army. The rest of you, stay in your villages and grow food for yourselves and for your army. And while you're doing it, remember, do nothing to help the Killers or the Brotherhood. When the Killers come, the People's Army won't be far behind, and we'll know what to do to Killers – and to traitors, too! Soon it'll take a whole army of Killers to venture into this district – but they won't *have* a whole army for this one district, 'cause we'll be hitting them in the *next* district, and the one beyond that, and the one beyond that one, all the way to Sade itself! We'll hit 'em here and there and everywhere, all over the planet. We'll kill 'em and we'll starve 'em out, and then when the countryside is ours, we'll march into Sade with a great army and we'll take the Brothers, and we'll take the Prophet himself, and we'll – '

'DEATH T'Y'PROPHET! DEATH T'Y'BROTHERS! DEATH T'Y'KILLERS! KILL! KILL! KILL!' The Sangrans began to chant, scream, howl madly, savagely, for blood. Fraden found it impossible to stop them, or to make himself heard above the tumult. They were out of control now, they wanted killing and only the taste of blood would sate them, he knew. All right, he thought, I'll give it to 'em, kill two birds with one stone, make sure they'll never have the Bugs to slave for 'em again.

He made a megaphone with his hands, shouted at the

151

top of his lungs, 'The Bugs work for the Brotherhood! Kill the Bugs! *Kill the Bugs!*'

He signalled to his troops, stepped down from the crate, led the howling mob of villagers to the foot of the great mound of sun-dried clay that was the local Bughill. Here and there a Bug appeared at one of the many large holes which studded the 'Hill. The soldiers fired at the Bugs as they appeared at their holes. One or two were hit, tumbled crazily down the Bughill, but the rest ducked inside and stayed there.

Fraden formed his men into a ring of guns surrounding the Bughill. 'Fire!' he called to the mob behind him. 'Get torches, straw, and wood. We'll smoke 'em out!'

Minutes later, torches were carried to the holes in the Bughill, piles of wood and straw were ignited and shoved down every opening. For nearly five minutes, smoke wafted out of the holes in the 'Hill as the mob howled, screamed, brandished torches, knives, rude wooden clubs . . .

Then, suddenly, like ants scuttling madly from a smashed anthill, Bugs began to pour forth. The crowd roared, cursed, pushed at the ring of soldiers preventing them from charging up the Bughill. The soldiers began firing, and huge green insects, spurting green ichor from holes in their chitin, rolled, dying, down the steep slope of the Bughill. The Bugs went down in droves, but still they kept coming, dozens, scores, from every smoking hole, pushing burning brands and straw before them with their shiny green bodies.

The soldiers kept firing, but the Bugs were just too many and they were coming too fast. Even as chitinous corpses tumbled down the hill by the dozens, leaving rivulets of ichor in their wakes, some of the Bugs, two here, three there, managed to break through the ring of soldiers and into the mob of Sangrans at the foot of the Bughill.

Although he grimly realized that it was just what the situation called for, Fraden's stomach turned as he saw the Sangrans fall on the fleeing Bugs. Lacking Brothers to kill, lacking Killers, the mob vented its desperate fury on the hapless, dumb arthropods. The trickle of Bugs that got through the ring of soldiers disappeared from Fraden's sight into the seething, churning maelstrom of the mob, like tree limbs being fed into a buzz saw. All he saw of them after that was glimpses and broken fragments. Here a Bug was held high above the mob for a moment by dozens of green-spattered hands as more hands tore limbs from its living body, tore it down again, stomped, ripped it apart. A green head torn from a body and spouting ichor bounced about above the heads of the Sangrans like some grotesque volleyball . . . Limbs, heads, slimy slabs of broken chitin, seemed to fill the air . . . A Bug scuttled out of the periphery of the crowd for a moment, was pulled back by one of its five intact legs, stomped by a dozen naked feet, its carapace finally cracking to leak squamous, pulsating organs . . .

Turning his back on the carnage, Fraden gathered five men around him, climbed the steep slope of the Bughill, stood at the summit, looked down at the horror that boiled below him.

Lord, he thought woodenly, as he watched the Sangrans kill the last of the Bugs, dismember the bodies, rip even disconnected limbs to smaller fragments in their blind fury, it's only *Bugs*! What if it were Killers? What if it were *Brothers*?

Finally, the last Bug was dead, the last green corpse torn to pieces. The Sangrans milled about for a while hoping more Bugs would emerge from the 'Hill for them to kill, and when none came forth, and they saw Fraden standing high above them, they turned their eyes to him and began to chant:

'BART! BART! LONG LIVE BART! BART! BART! BART!'

The staccato cries echoed off the Bughill like machine-gun fire. Fraden looked down, looked down at the wildly chanting Sangrans, looked down at the soft naked earth covered with Bug ichor and littered with a thousand fragments of shiny green chitin, looked down at the smouldering fires of a dozen discarded torches, looked down at the ruined green bodies, looked down at what the sound of his voice had wrought.

'BART! BART! BART! BART! BART! BART!'

He could feel it coming up at him in pulsing, hot waves – the blood lust, the killer-urge, the will to fight, to follow *him*. Three centuries of torture, murder, unguessable drives and frustrations, released at last and bursting forth like a foaming fountain of oil tapped at last after millennia of dormancy in the dark quiet earth. And he was the torch that would ignite that gusher of blackness into a lance of fire that would sear the Brotherhood from the face of Sangre.

He had released the demon at last, the djinn from its bottle, and now he would rule that mighty creature, break it to his will, mount it and ride it to the top.

'BART! BART! BART! BART! BART! BART! BART!'

He felt the power pouring up at him, filling his mind, warming his muscles, setting his being afire. *Lead,* the chanting Sangrans seemed to be demanding, *lead and we will follow.*

Bart Fraden raised his hands high above his head.

He began to speak to his people.

Chapter 9

From the hilltop on which Bart Fraden crouched, the big column of Killers moving five abreast along the trail which snaked through the tall grass and intermittent jungle in the narrow valley below looked like a line of black army ants.

Like ants on the march, Fraden thought, you can't count 'em just by looking at 'em – though from scouting reports, he knew that there were something like three hundred and fifty Killers now moving towards the dense little clump of jungle where Willem waited in ambush with two hundred men. They were like army ants in more ways than one. Like army ants, the Killers were soldiers by birth, conditioning, and breeding. Like army ants on the march, they had to live off the countryside, and like army ants, their frantically carnivorous metabolisms required meat and plenty of it.

And meat – in this case Meatanimals – Fraden thought, is something these Killers haven't had very much of in the past two weeks. They had come to fight, and they had come to live off the countryside, and the Killers were doing precious little of either.

It was the classic beginning of the second stage of a guerrilla war. The sneaky part of the first stage, Fraden thought, is that the Ins don't realize they've got a war on their hands till it's over. Had Moro sent in a few hundred Killers before all the Bugs in this district had been killed, when the 'People's Army' consisted of a hundred or so unreliable herogyn-heads and about an equal number of dubious volunteers, he could've crushed us very cheaply

155

indeed. But of course Moro had been too busy with his madness-pogrom, and too generally complacent to get all that worked up over a mess of isolated ambushes, a few sacked estates. Even six weeks ago, after the Revolution had gained popular momentum, but before that momentum had been translated into an army of three thousand men, a district of six former estates permanently hostile to the Brotherhood and the Killers, a thousand Killers or so could've still destroyed the Revolution, or at least reduced it to a mere chronic nuisance.

But now the invading force of two thousand Killers was already too little and too late. The irony was that the only thing that had finally got Moro off his fat ass was the same thing that was making his invasion a failure: the fact that at this point, the thousand Killers who had marched into the district in three columns two weeks ago *were* invaders, not policemen. For better than a month, this small district had been *de facto* territory of the Free Republic. Killer patrols that ventured in were annihilated. Moro got neither victims nor Meatanimals from this district, with the six estates sacked, the local Brothers and their Killers dead. Moro had lost the district to the Free Republic by bits and nibbles and hundreds of ambushes, piecemeal, so that only when the district was already lost, did the Prophet of Pain face the fact that he had a revolution on his hands.

So before this expedition had arrived, stage one was already completed – the People's Army had effective control of a district, had popular support, had a stockpile of captured arms and ammunition. The Killers had arrived just in time for stage two: the beginning of the destruction of the Killer army.

Now Fraden saw that the forward salient of the Killer column was entering the woods. He tensed. As soon as half of 'em were in the woods, Willem and his boys would open fire, pick off a few, retreat, set up another ambush, kill a few more, retreat again, set up another little ambush, hit and run, run and hit, as they had been doing for the past two weeks . . .

Two weeks ago, a force of two thousand Killers had arrived at the outskirts of the district, set up a base camp, left half their numbers to guard it. Then the other thousand Killers had split up into three columns, marched into rebel territory in three roughly parallel lines. The Killers' strategy had seemed fundamentally sound, even to Willem, who had moaned and groaned and made much of the fact that a thousand Killers could easily outfight three thousand guerrillas, that any pitched battle would be an utter disaster for the People's Army.

It was a kick to read Moro's mind – he figured that he had the guerrillas in an impossible either-or bind. With the rebel district bounded on the west by the mountains, there could be no retreat. The three Killer columns would advance towards the mountains, rounding up all the Animals and Meatanimals they could along the way, living off the land and shipping the surplus back to the impregnable base camp. Either the guerrillas would retreat until they could retreat no further, then make a stand and be wiped out, or try to concentrate their forces, attack one of the columns, banking on local superiority of forces to let them wipe 'em out. At which point, the other two columns would converge on the attacked column and destroy the People's Army. Either way, the guerrillas were obviously doomed.

But Moro had been blind to the third alternative.

Now perhaps a hundred Killers had entered the patch of jungle, marched into the jaws of the ambush . . . Suddenly, there were several sharp screams from within the jungle. From atop his hill, Fraden saw three or four trees, all in a line, crash ponderously to the forest floor, pulling down a rain of leaves and branches with them. Willem had opened up with his snipgun, slicing through flesh and wood indiscriminately. Shots began to ring out – hard, tight volleys as the guerrillas blasted the Killers from their impenetrable cover, wild random fire as the Killers futilely fired back, trying to hit men they couldn't see.

Now the rear of the Killer column at the margin of the jungle broke ranks, unshipped their morningstars, began to scream, roared into the jungle like a maddened wolf pack.

More purposeful volleys rang out, more random firing. Another line of trees crashed to the forest floor. Now, muffled by the heavy foliage and the distance, like a far-off keening, the battle cry of the Killers drifted up to Fraden: 'KILL! KILL! KILL! KILL!'

Then, almost as quickly as it had begun, it was over. Fraden heard the Killers still firing sporadically, wasting more ammunition, but the guerrillas had melted away into the jungle to prepare the next ambush in the endless, harrying series.

The other two Killer columns were getting the same treatment. For two weeks, they had advanced through the countryside, fighting phantoms. Prisoners were taken, shipped back to the base camp – but they never arrived, the Killers guarding them wiped out in a score of ambushes. The Killers found themselves forced to fight a dozen little skirmishes a day bogged down by hundreds of unruly Animals. They soon stopped taking prisoners.

A scorched-earth policy frustrated the rest of the plan – the Animals herded the Meatanimals before the advancing Killers, or slaughtered and ate them on the spot. That was the only part of the whole business that gave Fraden pause – the Sangrans would not deny the Meatanimals to the Killers unless they could eat them themselves. Fraden's plan to abolish cannibalism had to be temporarily shelved . . .

But it had been worth it. It forced the Killers to call for food and ammunition from their base camp – and those convoys were easy pickings as they moved through the countryside. Now, hungry, low on ammo, living on the ragged edge of rage from the ceaseless ambushes, losing scores of men piecemeal, with nothing to fight, the Killers were getting desperate.

Fraden got up, stretched, began the long walk back to camp. It was time for the Killers to make a move. They couldn't live off the land, they couldn't get supplies through from their base, and they were too low on food and ammo to survive a long forced march back to base. Something would have to give . . .

'I don't understand you, Bart Fraden,' Sophia O'Hara said. 'I don't understand you at all. I submit that I'm not a total ignoramus. I can understand, however murkily, why you want all those Killers holed up on some grubby hilltop the way they are. I can even understand why Bullethead isn't supposed to attack them – they're just supposed to sit there and starve to death. I admit that there's a certain grisly economy in that – though you didn't seem to give much of a damn about saving the lives of our loyal constituents when you just let the Killers run wild while our folks ran and hid and starved themselves, mostly. Even that I can understand, knowing how your warped mind operates. But now, after all the trouble you went to, after all the lives it cost, getting them trapped on that hilltop without food and ammunition, you've let hundreds of Killers just loaded with food and god-knows-what get almost to where their bloodthirsty buddies are holed up. Why? Why? Why?'

Bart Fraden looked across the guerrilla camp to where

159

Willem and his twenty 'heads all armed with snipguns for the first time, were disappearing into the jungle. Giving 'em snipguns was a gamble, but the stakes were well worth it.

'Fraden's Rules of Revolution,' he said. 'Rule one: make a pig of yourself, don't settle for killing a thousand of the enemy when you can wipe out sixteen hundred. Rule two: don't give up an opportunity to grab more ammo. Rule three: sixteen hundred starving men low on ammo are weaker than a thousand men with the same inadequate supplies.'

'I'm glad you explained,' Sophia said. 'It's as clear as pea soup.'

'Look, Soph, the idea is to let the *men* in the relief column get through to their boys we've got bottled up, but not the *supplies*. Then we've got that many more of 'em trying to march a hundred miles out of here to safety, and the more men they have to spread their food and ammo out among, the easier pickings they'll be. *Comprende?*'

'In the abstract, of course,' she said. 'An idiot, I'm not. But how many of our own men is all this finessing going to cost? You said yourself that even under perfect conditions, we can't expect to kill any more Killers than the number of men we lose. That means, without taking off my shoes to count on my toes, that you expect to lose sixteen hundred of our own men. Just like that, sixteen hundred men – *blotto!*'

Fraden sighed. 'There are fifteen million Sangrans and less than thirty thousand Killers,' he said.

'*So?*'

'So? So we can lose men from today till next year at five thousand a *week* if we have to. As long as we keep winning, as long as we keep expanding our control of territory, as long as we kill Killers, we've got a bottomless supply of gunfodder. It's as simple as that.'

'As simple as . . .' She stared at him, shook her head in wonderment. 'Jesus H. Christ!' she exclaimed. 'You're talking about men, Bart, *men*! Human beings dying, not figures on some goddamned tally sheet. Human suffering, people *dying*! Men, Bart, *men*!'

What's wrong with her? Fraden thought irritably. Why can't she understand such a simple fact of life? 'I'm talking about *war*,' he said. 'What do you think war is anyway, a nice little game of chess? War is killing, Soph. You think all those guns are for show? War is killing, that's where war is at. A man who can't face that has no business in this line of evil in the first place. A man who has to delude himself that he's not *really* killing men when he sends troops into battle is a cop-out and a coward.'

'I expected that from Chrome-dome, not from you,' she said quietly.

That hurt him, a wound in a place he did not care to examine too closely. Afraid to turn inward, he lashed out.

'I expected a cop-out from Chrome-dome,' he mimicked savagely, 'not from you. Who do you think you are? Where do you get that holiness from? I came in here a few weeks ago straight from stirring up the Animals, stirring 'em up to make 'em *kill*, and I succeeded but good, and you smelled it on me. You smelled that warrior smell. Did it make you sick then? You know the answer, Soph – you practically raped me. It turned you on, it really turned you on. What's that make you? The Virgin Mary?'

She cringed, frowned, then shrugged with a wan little smile. 'I suppose it makes us a matched pair,' she said in a small voice. 'A matched pair of . . . *Touché*, Peerless Leader, *touché*.'

* * *

161

'Hah, look at 'em!' Willem Vanderling said, as he stood at the margin of the jungle staring out across the rolling stretch of open grassland leading up to the small hill on which the fortifications of the besieged Killers stood. 'Like rats in a trap! Think they're so damned smart!'

The Killers had chosen what seemed like an ideal piece of terrain for a stand-off. Something like seven hundred of 'em – all that was left of the three now consolidated columns – were dug in atop the little hill. The hill was surrounded by low, coverless grassland for a distance of at least three hundred yards in all directions. The snipguns could not reach the Killer trenches from the cover of the jungle, and they were dug in too well for long-range rifle fire to bother them. To charge the fortifications across three hundred yards of open space would be sheer suicide. And the relief column, six hundred Killers – well not six hundred any more after ten days of continual ambushes – was fast approaching from the east, loaded down with food and ammo. The Killers just had to wait a few more minutes, and they would be home free . . .

Or so they thought.

'Your men ready?' he asked Gomez, who stood hollow-eyed at his side, greedily fondling his newly issued snipgun.

'Ready t'kill, sir,' Gomez said. 'Kill twenty, fifty, two hundred. Kill 'em all. Kill – '

'Yeah, yeah. You just make damned sure they don't blow it by rushing out of cover and charging 'em. Just let 'em keep coming and hold your positions and keep swinging those snipguns. Now get back to your side of the clearing and sit tight.'

Gomez saluted and trotted across the narrow open space towards the opposing tongue of jungle which faced Vanderling's position. Knowing they were there, Vander-ling could just make out the shapes of the ten men

162

crouching behind trees across the way. Vanderling glanced at the ten men who flanked him, crouched down behind a tree himself, and patted the barrel of his own snipgun. A sweet setup, indeed!

There was only one path from the east wide enough to accommodate six hundred Killers, and it debouched into the clearing here, where the clear area sent a pseudopod about fifty yards long and fifty wide into the body of the jungle. The path ended at the tip of the projection of the open area, and the Killers would have to pass between two opposing walls of jungle. The clear corridor was only fifty yards wide, and the range of a snipgun was about fifty yards too. Vanderling had positioned ten 'heads armed with snipguns on one side of the corridor, ten more on the other. The relief column would have to run the gauntlet between them, between a crossfire of snipgun beams that blanketed the entire corridor.

Vanderling laughed as he sighted his snipgun out into the clearing. They better know how to run and run fast! he thought.

Ten, thirty, forty minutes, and then Vanderling heard the sounds of many men making their way through the bush. He motioned to his men. Snipguns zeroed in on the clearing.

Another five minutes of waiting, and then six Killers, toting heavy packs filled with food and ammunition, stepped out of the jungle and were spotlighted in bold relief by the hot red sunlight beating down on the clear corridor.

Six more followed right behind them, and another six, and another and another, and in a couple of minutes, the end of the corridor nearest the jungle was filled with heavily laden Killers. Vanderling held up his arm as the Killer column marched halfway through the corridor, close-order, till at least a hundred Killers were neatly positioned between the jaws of the ambush.

'Now!' he shouted, dropped his arm back to his snip-gun, pressed the trigger, swung the snipgun back and forth rhythmically like a man reaping grain.

Sudden howls of pain erupted, shattered the moment, as five Killers were sliced through at the navel, fell to the ground, dead and twitching, gushing bright red blood. From both sides of the clearing, the concealed herogyn-heads opened fire with their snipguns, slicing through necks, heads, torsos, limbs. Killers seemed to fly apart like burst sacs of fluid, whirled about in mindless little circles, trying to find their tormenters, trying to escape. But the crush of nearly five hundred men close-order marching into the clearing behind them pushed them forward, straight through that lethal gauntlet. The Killers milled about in massive confusion, throwing aside their packs, firing pointlessly into the jungle, a monstrous traffic jam of severed limbs, decapitated bodies, the maimed and the enraged and the dead and the dying. And still the black tide poured into the deadly corridor.

It was like shooting blind, flopping fish in a barrel. The snipguns were ominously silent; there were no muzzle-flashes. The only sound the Killers could hear was their own agonized screams, the only sight limbs, heads, drop-ping from bodies, their comrades slashed to bloody meat by the invisible assassins. It was like an explosion in a butcher shop, a convulsing whirlwind of blood and raw meat and death.

Vanderling's knuckles were bone-white as he swung his snipgun, his eyes laughing, glowing coals, his mouth a cruel scar as he sliced the black-clad men to ribbons. Son of a bitch, this was one sweet weapon! Look at those dirty mothers come apart! His arms were parts of a smoothly running killing machine as they swept the snipgun back and forth through the screaming horde of tormented Killers.

Monomaniacally, Killers kept pouring into the clearing, blocking all escape, tossing aside packs, firing madly as they came, into the air, into the jungle, into the packed ranks of their own stricken comrades. Idiotically, they tried to hold their ground against the unseen enemy, milled about in a great, immobile clot, a clot of dying, bleeding, shouting men, a ghastly mêlée ankle-deep in limbs, heads, bodies, great puddles of gore . . .

Vanderling laughed a harsh wild laugh – then suddenly dived on his face as a withering hail of bullets tore into the jungle all around him. He saw that three of his men were already hit, looked towards the fortifications on the hill, saw that hundreds of Killers had advanced to within easy rifle range of the battle, were firing furious, blind volleys into the jungle as covering fire for the relief column.

The huge skirmish line of Killers held their ground wisely out of snipgun range, continued to pour volley after volley into the jungle, wasting more of their fast-depleting ammunition. The remnants of the relief column began to run madly towards them, forgetting the vital packs of food and ammunition, forgetting their dead and dying comrades in their dash towards safety.

Under the covering fire, the survivors made for the hill, leaving hundreds of bodies and hideously maimed wounded behind on a battlefield that was a refuse heap of human rubble.

When the last of the Killers, the fleeing and their saviours, had retreated to the far safety of the hill, Willem Vanderling emerged from cover to count the bodies and the booty.

Man . . . he thought. Seven of his men had been killed by the blind fire, but look at all that lovely ammo just waiting to be picked up! As the herogyn-heads drifted out among the dead and the dying, sunken eyes still blazing with blood lust, to finish off the wounded Killers, Vanderling estimated that nearly half the relief column had been wiped out in a few minutes of unbelievable carnage. And the People's Army got the food and ammo they had been carrying, not their own boys!

Vanderling looked out over the vast heap of bodies, limbs, severed heads, their faces still locked in death's head snarls, the torn human flotsam floating in a sea of rapidly congealing blood, and smiled a wide, satisfied smile.

'Man,' he muttered aloud, 'these sonofabitching snip-guns are something else!'

'Got t'have this spread all over y'district in two days, Bart says, so y'pay attention and get it right,' Olnay said, speaking to about thirty Sangrans, all *sans* the green sweatband and loincloth of the People's Army, who stood three deep in a semicircle outside Fraden's hut. Fraden stood just inside the doorway of the hut, half out of sight, watching Olnay, making sure he was getting it straight but letting even the agents get the story first from a Sangran mouth. Further inside the hut, Sophia stood quizzically watching Fraden watching Olnay.

'Tell y'Animals this,' Olnay said slowly. 'Tell 'em that y'People's Army got all those Killers been marchin' all over y'estates just about ready for y'kill. Tell 'em Bart says y'Killers die in two days. Tell 'em Bart says y'Killers'll die in Triple Valley, two days from now. They want t'see the People's Army kill a thousand Killers, they come t'Triple Valley in two days, but they stay put in the two outside valleys, leave y'middle valley alone, and stay out of sight and real quiet. Y'middle valley's gonna be for y'big show. Tell y'Animals they want t'see the biggest battle Sangre's ever seen, thousand Killers wiped out right in front of 'em, they gather in the outside valleys o'Triple Valley two days from now, and don't get in the way of y'People's Army. Y'got all that?'

The semicircle of men nodded. 'Okay,' Olnay said, 'now move it!' The agents dispersed, began the trek back to their various villages to feed this latest story into the rumour mill. Olnay waved to Fraden, then ambled away towards the nearest cookfire.

'I wonder what Nero would've thought of your methods,' Sophia said. 'Short on bread, but long on circuses. See a thousand Killers torn to pieces! A thousand, count 'em, a thousand! See the battle of the century in living, bleeding colour! Too bad you don't have any Christians to martyr. But then, we're kind of short on lions, too.'

Fraden turned, sighed, said patiently, 'You've got it all wrong. The forthcoming battle, oh Conscience of All the World, isn't supposed to be a Roman Circus, it's a piece of propaganda. Propaganda's a big problem here. In the Belt, I used a clandestine radio and TV transmitter and an underground fax sheet. Can't do that here – the Sangrans don't have radios, they don't have TVs and most of 'em can't read. It's all got to be word of mouth. The rumour mill works pretty well, but all it can do is *tell*. The best propaganda is propaganda that *shows*. That's what I'm setting up. Let a few thousand Sangrans see the People's Army wipe out a thousand Killers before their own eyes, and in a week or so the whole planet'll get the message: the People's Army can destroy the Killers.'

'Why can't you just kill your Killers and then have the rumour mill spread the story instead of turning the whole thing into a public spectacle?' Sophia said dubiously.

'Because the Killers' biggest weapon is their mystique,' Fraden replied. 'For three centuries, they've been a legend of fear and invincibility to the Sangrans. Destroy that legend and the whole planet will begin to wonder

167

about the so-called Natural Order. You don't destroy a legend like that by telling people it's a lie. You've got to *show* 'em, give 'em a counter-legend. That's what propaganda's all about. And if you have no mass media to work with, you've got to give 'em a little live action.'

Sophia shrugged. 'Who knows?' she said. 'If Nero had read a good book on advertising, maybe we'd all still be speaking Latin.'

Triple Valley was a series of four roughly parallel ridges that formed three troughs running east-west. Bart Fraden stood at the southernmost of the two inner ridges looking down into a narrow valley. While the other two troughs of the Triple Valley system had streams running down them and thus had rather heavy undergrowth and jungle on their floors, this central valley was drier, had only scattered clumps of trees and tall grass. Not too far to the east, a couple hundred guerrillas were fleeing before the thousand Killers who were all that was left of the expeditionary force. The guerrillas were moving west at a measured pace, making sure that the Killers never lost the trail. Their job was to lead the Killers into this central valley, where the cover was nearly non-existent . . .

Fraden glanced behind him, over the crest of the ridge, down the hidden slope. A thousand guerrillas waited there, hidden from view. A thousand more waited on the hidden slope of the opposing ridge. All that Fraden could see of the rest of his forces was Willem Vanderling standing on the crest of the opposite ridge.

Behind the troops on the slopes of the ridges, down in the wooded valleys, Sangrans had been gathering all day, men, women, even children. Thousands of them. Fraden had passed among them on his way to the top of the ridge, and the atmosphere was a strange mixture of carnival and scepticism. Clearly, they were looking forward to seeing the Killers destroyed, but just as clearly they doubted the outcome of the impending battle.

Fraden could understand the disbelief. At last the Killers would get the pitched battle they had been looking for for weeks. A thousand Killers against two thousand guerrillas, and under anything like normal circumstances, that would still leave the odds heavily on the Killers' side.

But there was nothing ordinary about these conditions. The Killers were weak from semi-starvation. They couldn't have more than a few rounds per man left. And they were being led into a monstrous trap. As soon as the bait squad led the Killers into the valley, a thousand men would march up over the crests of each ridge and down into the valley, firing as they came. The Killers would be trapped in a massive crossfire; they would be thoroughly decimated before the guerrillas closed with them and it came down to the hand-to-hand stuff which was the enemy's forte.

Fraden knew that it would still be messy, costly, that many of his own men would die. It would be cheaper in terms of lives, far cheaper, to simply have the guerrillas fire from the ridgelines and wipe the Killers out without ever closing with them.

But the propaganda aspects of the battle were as important as the military ones. The Sangrans had been promised a circus, and a circus they would get. They would see a set-piece, a wordless gem of perfect propaganda: the People's Army destroying Killers on their own terms – hand-to-hand combat. That the Killers in question would be half-dead from starvation, would be virtually out of ammunition, would be decimated before they really had a chance to fight on their own terms, was beside the point. The myth of the Killers would be ended, and the myth of the People's Army would begin.

Perhaps twenty minutes passed, and then Fraden heard

the sounds of scattered gunfire coming from the eastern end of the valley . . . Now he could see a squad of guerrillas, then another squad and another and another entering the eastern mouth of the valley, loping easily, firing occasionally over their shoulders, egging the Killers on. A hundred yards into the valley the guerrillas came, a hundred and fifty. Still no Killers. Two hundred yards, and now the guerrillas began to disperse, made for the slopes of the ridges in groups of twos and threes.

Now a wedge of running black figures appeared at the eastern end of the valley, became a column of Killers, waving rifles, shooting but sporadically, as the forward salient of the Killer force entered the trap. Fraden held up his right hand, waved it high over his head at Vanderling, standing on the crest opposite. Vanderling held his hand up, waited for Fraden's signal.

Fraden and Vanderling stood silently, arms rigidly aloft as the Killers poured into the valley, raising a great cloud of dust. Fraden held his arm immobile as the valley became floored with a black carpet of Killers. Finally, he saw that the trailing edge of the Killer column at the eastern edge of the valley had begun to thin out. It became a trickle, then petered out. They were all there. They were all in the trap.

Fraden dropped his arm. Vanderling caught the signal and dropped his.

A thousand guerrillas surged over the crest of each ridge, over the top and down the slopes into the valley, converging skirmish lines one man thick, walking not running, slowly, methodically firing volley after concentrated volley as they descended the slopes, the steadily closing jaws of an immense, lethal vice.

Caught between the two jaws of the vice, scores of Killers fell in that first moment, before they had even located the source of the concentrated rifle fire that was tearing them rapidly to pieces. More fell as the guerrillas continued to march down the slopes at a slow, measured pace, firing continually as they came. Only a few Killers returned the fire – they were lower on ammunition than Fraden had dared hope. Confusedly, the Killers trapped on the valley floor hit the dirt, trying to find cover where there was none. Bullets sent up thousands of little pillars of dust all around them. The air was filled with the screams of the stricken.

Fraden stood on his ridge watching the vice jaws converge. It had been a smart move, keeping the herogyn-heads out of *this* one. Likely as not, the 'heads would've charged straight down into the Killers and been hacked to bits by morningstars before they could do any real damage. But the Sangran volunteers were none too eager for hand-to-hand combat with the Killers and as a consequence were obeying orders, marching slowly down the hill as they tore the Killers to pieces with the tremendous, converging crossfire. Had the Killers had adequate ammunition, of course, such a tactic would have been sheer suicide, but as it was, the Killers could do little but cling as close to the ground as possible and wait for the guerrillas to close with them. Charging either guerrilla line would mean that they would have to turn their backs to the other and splitting their forces would be equally futile . . .

Now the guerrilla skirmish lines were about two-thirds of the way down the slopes. An acrid haze of blue-grey gunpowder smoke hung over the valley. Fraden's ears were tinny from the continual roar of massed gunfire. Through the haze, he could see that great numbers of Killers were already slain, lying in broken heaps in the grass – perhaps three hundred or more. Here and there an almost pathetic rifle flash could be seen as the Killers

171

expended the very last of their ammunition, cutting down a guerrilla here and there ineffectually.

Fraden lifted his gaze to find Vanderling across on the opposing ridge. He saw that Vanderling had moved halfway down the slope – was the idiot thinking of getting into that mess? He looked higher, saw that the opposing ridgecrest was filling up with Sangrans, men, women, children silently watching the battle.

He turned, saw that the ridge behind him was also choked with watching Sangrans. They stood limply, jaws slack with disbelief, but their eyes were beginning to smoulder as they saw Killer after Killer go down. Here and there a dull face came alive with a twisted smile as the Sangrans saw the People's Army, the army that they were coming to think of as *their* army, marching virtually untouched down on to the valley floor. There was something in those eyes, those enigmatic smiles, that Fraden could not quite fathom, something that made him apprehensive, queasy – an unholy, hungry look that seemed strangely like lust, a wet glistening of the eyeballs, the thin edge of something dark and sinister creeping on to their countenances . . .

Almost in relief, Fraden returned his attention to the valley floor. The guerrillas had reached the bottoms of the slopes. They hesitated, stood their ground and fired round after round into the Killers boxed between them, the Killers who were now using the corpses of their fallen comrades as human barricades. The moment seemed to hang in the air. The guerrillas stood their ground pouring a murderous crossfire at virtual point-blank range into the remnants of the Killer force who huddled and died behind their human bulwarks, unwilling to close, uncertain as to what to do next. Then . . .

The remaining Killers decided for them.

Near the centre of the valley, a score or so of Killers

suddenly leapt up, heedless of the bullets filling the air around them, charged madly at the southernmost line of hesitating guerrillas, swinging their dreadful, blade-studded morningstars, howling their monomaniacal battle chant through foam-flecked lips: 'KILL! KILL! KILL! KILL! KILL!'

Panicked, the segment of the guerrilla line they charged scuttled back a few yards, then opened up. The charging Killers were smashed to the ground as if by some great metal fist.

But it was too late; they had ignited their comrades. Half-dead from starvation, mad with frustration, half their number lying dead all around them, the Killers at last erupted. As one man, they arose, all along the valley floor, flinging aside the bodies of the fallen, howling, screaming, swinging morningstars, blood-reddened foam streaming from their self-lacerated lips, charged straight at the guns of the southern line of guerrillas in a totally fearless berserker frenzy. Those too badly wounded to run hobbled. Those who could not hobble crawled forward. Those who could not move forward thrashed madly on the ground, tore at their own flesh, joined in the battle chant that had become a terrible roar: 'KILL! KILL! KILL! KILL!'

Perhaps five hundred Killers charged a thousand guerrillas, charged straight into a wall of lead as the guerrillas fired volley after desperate volley, clearly terrified despite the overwhelming odds in their favour. The second line of guerrillas trotted forward behind the backs of the charging Killers, poured concentrated fire into their unprotected rear. Twenty, fifty, a hundred, a hundred and fifty Killers fell in that mad moment, but the rest kept coming straight into the rain of bullets and finally through it, and the two or three hundred survivors fell upon a thousand guerrillas.

It was no longer a battle; it was chaos. Outnumbered three to one or worse, the Killers tore into the guerrillas with a frenzy that seemed to approach exaltation. Swinging their heavy morningstars like tennis rackets, they split skulls like mashed watermelons. They leapt bodily upon guerrillas, sank their sharp teeth into throats, clawed at faces with their fingernails, kneed groins, stomped, crushed, tore gobbets of flesh from living bodies. Stunned with terror for a frozen moment, the guerrillas finally began to fight back using their guns as clubs, using feet and hands and teeth.

Three, four, five guerrillas fell on every Killer, bashed at him with steel rifle-barrels, fists, feet. Mindless of the pain, oblivious of the mortal wounds he was receiving, each Killer would sink his teeth into the throat of one tormenter, bash a second with his bloody morningstar, kick at the groin of another, tear a face away like a bloody mask, and one by one the little knots of struggling men fell to the ground into tangles of thrashing bodies, whirling limbs and weapons, snarling, teeth-gnashing heads. Heedless of their own lives, the Killers did what they had been bred, conditioned, and trained to do – they killed.

Fraden felt spasms knot his stomach as he watched the carnage. From where he stood, the battle was a nightmare image of one great organism with a thousand bodies, thousands of limbs, tearing itself to bloody fragments in a terrible paroxysm of self-loathing.

And incredibly, unbelievably, the Killers seemed to be holding their own, fighting, tearing, killing, dying with a feral frenzy that was literally superhuman.

Then, finally, the second line of guerrillas, a thousand men strong, entered the fray. Now it was eight or nine to one. Yet still the Killers fought on as they were ripped to still-convulsing pieces by a horde of ordinary, fear-crazed men.

But the tide had at last turned decisively. Each Killer was the focus of a small savage mob of guerrillas who tore at him, kicked, clubbed as he pulled one down, split another's skull. Four, five, six more fell on him with hands, feet, captured morningstars, crushed him by the sheer weight of their bodies. The Killers were finished, but they refused to give up. The wounded, the hideously maimed, fought on, with shattered limbs, razor-sharp teeth, fingernails . . .

Suddenly . . .

Suddenly Fraden heard a terrible shout, like the cry of some immense carnivorous beast, a sound so hideous, so powerful, that it cut through the battle-sounds like a great guttural siren.

On the slope opposite him, Willem Vanderling was charging down into the battle. Behind him, the entire hillside seemed to be covered with screaming, madly gesticulating Sangrans, men, women, even children, bar-relling down the slope towards the battle behind the running figure of Vanderling.

'You imbecile!' Fraden shouted. 'You bloodthirsty cretin!'

Then a roar from behind him nearly knocked him off his feet; then he was engulfed by a tide of red-eyed, screaming Sangrans, men with faces like beasts', women, their features contorted into harpies' masks, children like savage wolf cubs, as the Animals on his own ridge surged past him down the hillside towards the battle. Fraden was knocked sprawling, was pummelled, kicked, was not able to regain his feet till the boiling cauldron of humanity was past him.

Dazed, bruised, scratched, but otherwise unhurt, he rose shakily to his feet and saw . . .

Two solid walls of Sangrans converge on the battle below.

And then the human tides enveloped all, Killers, guerrillas, the wounded and the dead and the dying in a great tortured mass of thrashing, kill-crazy Animals. He heard a sound like the sea breaking on a rocky coast, a sound compounded of shouts and screams, thousands of feet and fists pounding hundreds of bodies.

Fraden watched as the Sangrans vented generations of fear and hate and frustration on a few hundred dead and dying Killers, watched limbs ripped off and held aloft like bloody totems or brandished as makeshift clubs. Fraden watched and watched and watched, wishing he could vomit, watched till he could watch no more, then sank to his knees, covered his eyes with his arms, heard the agonizing, gut-tearing sound shear through him like a knife, a slicing, jarring pain in his ears that seemed to go on and on and on forever.

Finally, the sound seemed to change, become grotesque, almost gay, a wild, merry carnival sound that seemed to be getting louder, coming closer.

Fraden got to his feet, uncovered his eyes, saw that the mob was now surging up the hill towards him, thousands of grinning, laughing, shouting faces, bare skin glistening with blood.

He saw a figure carried aloft on the shoulders of that unholy mob. It was Willem Vanderling, his clothes torn to shreds, his bald skull spattered with gore.

Fraden had a moment to look out past the mob, time to catch a glimpse of the valley floor, a hideous red sprawl of bodies and torn meat and gore, and then the mob was upon him.

A great cheer went up, and scores of eager, bloody hands raised him up, placed him high on the massed shoulders of the mob. Fraden rode the shoulders of his people like a cork bobbing on the sea, the President, the Leader, the Hero of the Revolution . . .

Across the sea of humanity, riding a wave of shoulders about ten feet from him, he could see Vanderling, covered with the blood of his victims, the red Sangran sun casting crimson highlights off his naked skull, his eyes wide and glazed, his mouth an evil, self-satisfied sneer, oblivious of all save the glory of this moment of hideous victory, of sated blood lust . . .

And then the inchoate cries and cheers of the Sangrans began to coalesce into a regular, guttural rhythm. They were chanting his name: 'BART! BART! BART! BART! BART!'

Over and over and over again, a chant of victory, of awakening, and a chant of adulation. 'BART! BART! BART! BART! BART!'

Despite himself, despite his loathing, despite the horror of that which had given rise to the chant, Fraden found himself unable to resist its call. He felt himself riding that sea of feral adulation, felt the sheer, unadulterated, obscene glory of the moment override all else, seep into the marrow of his bones, burn away the horror he had seen in a bright blaze of animal heat. A small voice lost in the convolutions of his mind screamed a faraway protest, but it could not shout down the chanting of the people, *his* people; as they bore him above them as a talisman. He was Bart Fraden, Hero of the Revolution, lost in the mindless animal glory of the moment, enfolded in the arms of that mighty lover no man can long resist.

And he noted only in a moment that flickered from his mind in passing like a candle in a hurricane that the next time his eyes happened to fall on Vanderling, Willem's face had become a tortured mask of naked, enraged envy.

As Bart Fraden stood outside the doorway of his hut, the sounds of the camp behind him, the laughter, the slow-dying shouts of victory, the twilight murmurings of a victorious army settling itself down for the night, swirled about his shoulders like a wind-blown cloak, warmed him, caressed him, melded with the memories of other sounds, the sounds of his name being chanted by thousands of throats as he was borne on the shoulders of his people through jungle and grassland and a dozen wildly celebrating villages, finally pitched up by the great human sea like a piece of driftwood in the guerrilla camp, in the twilight.

But the sounds of the camp behind him seemed to be the not-too-distant roar of that same sea of Sangrans that had borne him through the land as their hero, and Fraden found that the exaltation, the amoral glory, the feeling of being ten feet tall, had not been left behind with the Sangrans, but still seemed to enfold him, surround him with a hot golden aura of larger-than-life charisma.

Fraden stepped through the doorway, stood inside the hut, felt his own power, charisma, manhood, light up his subjective universe, swell his sense of being to impossible proportions as Sophia, her back to him as he entered, turned, started to say something, then froze, her mouth limply open, her eyes wide with a wonder that seemed almost to be worship.

For the red twilight silhouetting his figure in the doorway surrounded him with a deep golden corona, threw his features into red and black chiaroscuro relief, and in that timeless moment, from the look in her eyes, he knew that the quirk of lighting, the animal heat he felt himself giving off, had combined in a weird alchemy that made her see him as he saw himself – triumphant, engorged, expanded, larger than life, a god, almost a god.

Wordlessly, she came to him, put her arms on his shoulders, ran her hands slowly down across his chest, sank to her knees as her hands reached and loosened his belt, slid his garments slowly, sensuously to the ground, touched his bare skin as if it were some strange substance she had never felt before.

She uttered a deep sigh of wondering, total surrender, a surrendering sigh that was also a prideful moan of ownership, possession of this man who for an instant seemed to stand astride her universe. Then, on her knees, with her arms locked around his waist, her eyes deep green pools staring up at him, she took him into her, swallowed his bursting manhood, feasted upon the mad glory that sprang from him to her, drank deep from the bottomless well of his triumph-engorged ego.

And when the moment passed and they parted, Fraden felt suddenly cold, suddenly stark sober, as if the mad magic of the whole day, the hero-ride on the shoulders of his people, the reasonless glory, had drained from him into her and at last spent itself. He looked back on the Bart Fraden who had entered the hut a moment before, and a long shudder racked his body.

'Soph . . .' he muttered, a trembling, confused sound.

Still on her knees, she looked up at him, and as he watched, the wonder drained from her eyes, and she smiled a wry, crooked smile.

'I know, Bart, I know . . .' she said. 'When I saw you there . . . like *that*, I felt it too. King of the mountain. My king, my mountain. It made me feel like . . . like queen of the mountain, the same mountain, just because I was yours. And because you belonged to me.

Fraden stared down at her and found himself unable to speak. She had always been something of a trophy to him, the most beautiful, toughest, most with-it woman he had ever known. The best woman for the best man. Like the food and the three Confedollar cigars and the imported booze, she was proof that Bart Fraden was the best, Numero Uno, the king of the mountain, the centre of his universe. It was a jolt to realize that she felt the same way about him. That just as he needed to be what he was, she needed a man who was what he needed to be.

'Soph . . .' he finally said, 'God, how much we're two of a kind! We're so alike it scares me.'

She rose to her feet, her eyes still fixed on his, eyes that laughed now, knowingly. 'We're stuck with each other,' she said. 'King and queen of the mountain. And if the mountain crumbles, we go down together. Whither thou goest . . . The best man and his best woman.' She laughed, a cool, knowing little laugh. 'And we are the best, Bart, aren't we? After all, you as much as told me so yourself, Peerless Leader.'

Fraden laughed with her. 'Conceited bitch!' he said, grinning. 'Oversexed psychopathic egomaniac!'

She tangled her hand in his thick black hair, kissed him lightly on the nose.

'Takes one to stand one,' she said drily.

Chapter 10

Bart Fraden could not help smiling at the three People's
Army volunteers who were crammed into the lifeboat's
cabin with him. Jaws clamped shut, backs pressed tight
against the bulkhead, eyes darting about everywhere,
anywhere, as long as they didn't have to look at the
viewscreens and be reminded that they were flying above
the Sangran countryside at dizzying speed and altitude. It
amused him, but it also bugged him that after five days of
this, the Sangrans were still basically unable to adapt to
the reality of flight.

It was all too symptomatic of the rank raw material he
was forced to work with. As revolutionaries, as individual
soldiers, indeed as mere human beings, the Sangran
people left much to be desired. They had no concept of
justice, freedom, common good, democracy, or anything
else that might be remotely considered a political objective or ideal. Not long ago, they had unthinkingly obeyed
the slightest whim of the Killers. Now they fought on the
side of the People's Republic against those same Killers
simply because they had been convinced by example that
the Killers could be killed, because with the Bugs in Free
Republic territory all useless, to obey the Brotherhood
and the Killers was to starve, because Fraden had been
able to build himself up into a more powerful manna-
figure than the Prophet of Pain – and finally, because they
were more afraid, at the moment, of snipguns and Willem's herogyn-heads than of the Killers or the Brotherhood. *The Noble Sangran People* . . .

The countryside reeled itself out like a map below the 'boat, an irregular checkerboard of dark green jungle, lighter grasslands and cultivated areas, here and there a village, estates at much longer intervals, linked by a spiderweb of road network with Sade squatting like a black widow at the focus. Forgetting the character of the Sangrans and looking at the Revolution schematically, like a complicated chess game, gave a much more hopeful and aesthetic picture of the war. The Sangrans, being essentially shortsighted clods, could be manipulated like the clods they were, providing one took into account and used their very lack of initiative, group identity, idealism, and virtually all other saving graces.

As the present gambit did.

It was a cold exercise in military, economic, and psychological logic. The Free Republic held one district firmly, now had an army of about eight thousand, which, by recruiting in the adjoining territory, might conceivably be increased to ten thousand, but no more under present conditions.

The Brotherhood had everything else.

Which meant a great number of such districts containing fifteen million people, who could easily be bled for enough food, slaves . . . and victims, to fulfil the needs of a mere few thousand Brothers and their supporting entourage without efficiency or tight control even becoming a consideration. They had nearly thirty thousand Killers to do the job, better than three times the forces of the Free Republic.

And that, being their strength, was also their weakness.

Thirty thousand Killers was a large *police force*, but a small *army*. After three centuries of conditioning designed to make the Sangrans react to the Killers as police, half the Killer force, or so, was enough to garrison the estates

182

with a few score Killers each, collect quotas and generally keep things under control, freeing the rest to deal with any occasional insurrection – and with the People's Army.

But if the Killers were forced into the role of an occupying *army* in a hostile countryside, instead of a police force, their numbers would suddenly become inadequate. Every Killer tied down in pacification duties was one less Killer to fight the People's Army. The key problem was how to tie down the entire Killer force guarding estates spread out over the whole inhabited area of the planet.

And the solution was the very venality of the Sangran Animals . . .

Fraden stepped out of the lifeboat's airlock a step ahead of his three-man bodyguard and stood in the centre of the village, where he had arrogantly set the 'boat down. Like every other village he had visited in the past five days, this one was far enough away from the local estate so that even if he had been spotted on the way down, he would be long gone before any Killers could get there.

And, as in the dozens of other villages, the yokums were already gathered in a curious, expectant crowd in front of the 'boat by the time he stepped out. The rumour mill had long since spread the story all over the planet that the President was going to tour villages in enemy territory, had also spread the story of the Battle of Triple Valley, as he had dubbed that revolting slaughter, and of course who but Bart Fraden, the Liberator, the Hero of the Revolution, the mighty off-worlder, could drop from the sky into the very heart of their village.

Fraden studied the crowd before him. There was a high proportion of women and children to men, which probably meant that the Killers had hit this dogpatch several times for victims for the madness-pogrom. They were lean and leathery looking, but not on the razor-edge of starvation, since the campaign to kill the Brains had not yet reached this far. But the rumour about it had, and he saw that they were plainly worried, by the rumour, by the madness-pogrom. And there was a narrow, hungry look to their eyes which told him that they knew all about the Revolution and what the People's Army was doing to the Killers. They were, in short, ripe.

'Y'know who I am,' he began. 'I'm Bart Fraden, President of the People's Republic of Sangre. Y'know about the great victory of the Sangran People at the Battle of Triple Valley – whole planet knows *that*. I'm not looking for soldiers for y'People's Army from here – *yet*. You're too far away from what we hold now, but don't y'worry, we're expanding in your direction. I don't have t'tell y'that the Killers are taking way over quota – looks like they've been here already. Y'probably know that they're starting t'kill Brains all over Sangre, and I'll bet y'already know that they're doing all this t'starve you, drive you mad so the Brotherhood can bleed the whole planet to death t'make Omnidrene for their kicks. No, I'm not wasting my time and yours, risking my life by coming here t'tell you what you already know all too well.'

Fraden paused, studied the stolid faces of the quietly waiting Sangrans, only their eyes betraying a curious impatience. They expected to hear something new, something they wanted to hear, and man, they were gonna hear it!

'I'm here t'tell you what's already happening in villages just like yours – all over Sangre! It's the simplest, most obvious thing there is: the Sangran people have begun to realize that if they want something, all they have to do is reach out and *take it*. This is *your* planet. Y'don't want

184

t'work tending y'Brother's Meatanimal herds? So *don't*! So what happens? Y'local Killers march in t'y'village and make y'work, eh? So next day, when they're all out making a couple other villages work, *you* don't. Things get a little rough for a while, you just go off into the jungle till they cool off. Live off the land! And that means y'live off whatever belongs t'y'Brother. Killers are off making a village work, y'raid the Meatanimal herds. Raid storehouses. Raid anything that's not guarded for a moment and that's not nailed down. *Take* what you want. Why work for it? How many Killers on this estate, forty, fifty, maybe sixty? And how many men in all the villages? Y'Killers just can't stop hundreds, thousands of men raiding from the jungle. Hit what's not protected, and when they rush there, you're already raiding somewhere else. Y'got it made. The Killers just can't stop y'from taking what y'want!'

Men in the crowd hooted, laughed bitterly. 'Sure!' someone shouted sarcastically. 'We do that, and y'Brother just yells f'more Killers, and trucks y'whole village t'Sade at once. We die quick insteada slow, is all!'

'No man!' Fraden shouted. ''*Cause there just ain't no more Killers t'come arunnin'!* 'Cause every other Brother on the planet is already screaming for more Killers t'stop the raids on *his* estate, raids that are already going on all over the planet! No Brother can afford to send another more Killers. And the rest of y'Killers – the ones Moro has in reserve – man, don't worry about them either. The People's Army is giving 'em all the action they can handle and then some. Remember the Battle of Triple Valley! Y'local Brother can yell for more Killers till he's blue in the face, and all he'll get is a sore throat. That's what the Sangran Revolution means to *you*, right here, right now! Now you can take what you want 'cause there's just not enough Killers on the planet t'stop you! Take what y'want. It's all yours for the grabbing, courtesy of the Free Republic of Sangre!'

Now the Sangrans were muttering among themselves, talking it over. That hit 'em where they live, all right, Fraden thought. Greedy bastards! While the cat's away . . . That's what a revolution means to your average yokum anyway – an opportunity to pillage and loot. Tell crumbs like these to do what they want to do in the first place, and they'll do it – if they weren't such total cowards. There wasn't a village he had visited that had the balls to be first. If a few villages tried it, it wouldn't work, but if they all did, they'd run the Killers ragged. What they needed was proof that everyone was doing it. Cowards hunt only in big packs. But that was being taken care of . . . yessir, it was all being taken care of!

It was a motley group indeed that passed through the fallow fields and into the Sangran village. Twenty-five men, armed only with clubs and spears, wearing only the usual loincloth, surrounded by about thirty naked, fat, moron-faced little children, their sex obscured by gross folds of flaccid flesh, on three sides herded the Meatanimals before them. Immediately behind the men herding the Meatanimals were five men in the green loincloths and sweatbands of the People's Army armed with rifles and prodding along a tied and gagged Killer who limped along on a bleeding right leg, his left arm hanging loosely in its bonds. Bringing up the rear was Willem Vanderling in his old Belt Free State General's uniform, carrying the omnipresent snipgun.

Contrary to appearances, all but the Killer and the Meatanimals were soldiers of the People's Army of the Free Republic of Sangre.

Vanderling scanned the grubby little huts as hungry-looking, filthy Sangrans erupted from them. Wasn't there something about . . .?

Vanderling laughed. Sure! What a yock! We killed the Brain in this dogpatch about a week ago! And now we bring'em eats and kicks. The People's Army giveth and the People's Army taketh away . . .

For several weeks now, the People's Army, or at least about a quarter of it, had been doing just that: giving and taking away. Hundreds of small bands like this one roamed in Brotherhood territory. They were on their own, raiding and living off the country. Each band was led by a small squad of herogyn-heads who made no bones about being members of the People's Army. The rest, the volunteers, played the parts of ordinary Sangran peasants who had taken to the jungle as freelance raiders.

By day, they raided storehouses, and, semi-contrary to Fraden's unspoken orders, Meatanimal herds, for food, taking the surplus loot into the local villages to show the yokums what they could grab for themselves if they had any guts.

By night, the herogyn-heads, dressed in captured Killer uniforms, stole into the very same villages and killed the local Brains.

Fun and games! Vanderling thought, not realizing from whom he had acquired the phrase. Man, this was the way to fight a war – loot, feast, and celebrate with the yokums! The 'heads were happy – they were getting plenty of herogyn and plenty of action. The slobs were happy – they were taking no risks, not thirty armed men against a couple of Killers who might be guarding a herd or storehouse, and for the first time in their lives they were getting plenty of meat to eat.

Vanderling grinned as he thought of that in connection

187

with Bart – poor, squeamish Bart! Bart knew that this wouldn't work unless the guerrillas ate the Meatanimals they captured – what else, after all, was there for them to eat when they were living off the land? And besides, they just wouldn't do it unless they got to eat the little critters. Try and stop'em, and you'd have a mutiny in nothing flat. Bart knew where it was at, but he just didn't have the balls to come out and say it – instead, just, 'Live off the land, boys.'

What a joke on Bart, him with his fancy foods and his Ah Ming, back in the Belt! Vanderling thought. Him living on rice and wheat and greens like a god-damned rabbit while I live high off the hog on the Meatanimals. Wasn't bad at all, kinda salty maybe, but if you washed it down with plenty of the local wine, that didn't have to bother you. What a switch, Bart the gourmet eating slop, while I get the meat!

Now the Sangran villagers encircled the herd of Meatanimals. Vanderling could see the greed in their hungry eyes, the ribs showing through their skins. He grinned.

'Okay, folks,' he said. 'We brought the eats, how about you coming up with the booze? Fair's fair, eh? We're all gonna have a nice big picnic. These boys' – he gestured towards the volunteers in mufti – 'are from the next estate, got themselves a little group living off the fat of the land. My boys and me were wandering around looking for some Killers to do in, and our kind friends here ran into us. They had all these Meatanimals that they had . . . ah, *confiscated*, and they invited us to dinner. I suggested that they should invite you to the party too, seeing as how it looked like you hadn't wised up enough yet to grab what you want for yourselves. So break out that wine, folks, and let's get these critters on the fire. I'll bet we all got nice healthy appetites, eh?'

The villagers cheered with all the enthusiasm that might be expected of starving men invited to a feast. Women began building cookfires, erecting spits. Men led the docile Meatanimals away. Old men produced clay jugs of the sour Sangran wine from the interiors of their huts.

Vanderling marched his men and the captive Killer into the centre of the village, near the cookfires. They sprawled on the ground, and all but the herogyn-heads began drinking the crude but potent local wine, watched the villagers butchering the Meatanimals with axes and scythes. The Meatanimals, bred for docility, stolidity, and near-bestial stupidity, stood quietly by as the villagers butchered their comrades, bleating and struggling for a brief moment only as their own heads went under the axe.

Vanderling leaned back, bolted down a big swallow of wine. The stuff had a kick, but it tasted like old sweat-socks. It was all a matter of technique – get it across your tastebuds and into your gut as quick as possible, and after you had enough in you, the taste didn't seem so bad anymore . . .

He watched, drinking steadily, as the Sangrans began to spit the slaughtered Meatanimals and hung the spits over roaring open fires. After a while, fat began to hiss and sputter on the burning logs, and the air became fragrant with the odour of roasting meat. Vanderling's mouth, slightly furry now from the wine, began to water. Man, roast meat over an open fire! Mmmmm! So what if the Meatanimals were kinda human? Weren't really all *that* human, after all. *Real* humans weren't so goddamned fat or so stupid . . . They were imbeciles, weren't they? They were bred that way . . . No smarter than a good chimp, at best. And nobody went around saying chimps were human . . .

By the time the food was ready, everyone concerned

was pretty well swacked, Vanderling included. A Sangran woman brought him a nicely browned haunch of Meatanimal. Vanderling bit off a big piece of the warm meat, washed it down with a swallow of wine, bit off another nice chunk. As he wolfed down the salty meat, bolted down more wine, he saw villagers and guerrillas alike similarly engaged, laughing, drinking, devouring meat greedily with greasy fingers. Nothin' like a picnic in the great outdoors to give a man an appetite! he thought, licking his fingers.

After a while, the haunch of meat was a half-bare thighbone, the jug beside him was almost empty, his belly was heavy and bloated. He burped. Man, he thought torpidly, I'm stuffed! He looked at the guerrillas. Most of 'em were just nibbling now, sipping wine, leaning back and relaxing as he was. The yokums, though, were still going strong. Each cookfire was surrounded by a knot of Sangrans, pulling off roasted limbs of already cooked Meatanimals, carving up the rest with knives, stuffing their greasy mouths like there was no tomorrow. As soon as a spit was empty, another carcass was hung out over the fire. Looks like they're gonna eat the whole batch right now! Vanderling thought.

Well, why not? Means there won't be any leftovers, and then they'll have to get on the ball and go steal their own. Man, they sure can pack it away, though! He laughed drunkenly. Guess they ain't been eatin' so well since we knocked off the Brain, he mused.

Hey . . . Something was percolating up into Vanderling's wine-sotted mind. Now where was that Killer . . .? Ah, there he is!

The captured Killer, still bound and gagged and bleeding from the wound in his leg, was propped up against a hut near the fires casually guarded by a couple of herogyn-heads.

Vanderling stared at the Killer fuzzily. Now didn't I have some reason for taking that prisoner . . .? Something that . . .? Oh yeah, sure! First dinner, then the entertainment!

Vanderling rose lazily to his feet, waddled over to the Killer, who writhed against his bonds, ground his teeth on his gag, stared up at Vanderling with eyes that were twin beacons of hate.

Vanderling shouted for attention, and in a few moments the Sangrans, still wolfing down gobbets of Meatanimal, were looking diffidently his way.

'Hey, folks!' he said. 'Look what we got here, a dirty Killer! I hear tell that some Killers knocked off your Brain a while back. Not very neighbourly, was it . . .?'

He stared down at the Killer in great mock surprise. '*Say* . . .' he said with exaggerated slowness, 'you don't suppose that this crumb was one of . . .?'

The Sangrans roared, a terrible, half-laugh, half-growl. A mad, feral look came over the feasting villagers.

Then a dozen of them, eyes blazing with wild hate, mouths greased with human fat and grinning cruelly, tossed aside jugs and chunks of meat, rushed up to the Killer, pulled him off the ground, dragged him writhing in his bonds and growling through his gag to a fire where a nearly done Meatanimal was being turned on its spit by a gaunt Sangran woman.

Looks like they *do* think so! Vanderling thought woozily, half-falling to the ground by the hut. Either that or they don't much care . . . Wonder what fun and games they have in store for the poor crud . . .?

To his horror and unbelieving fascination, Vanderling soon found out. He took a long swig of wine from a jug that lay by the hut as two Sangrans took the roasting carcass off the spit while others literally ripped every shred of clothing from the Killer's body as the entire village gathered around the fire and cheered them on.

Vanderling took another drink, found himself drifting into torpid indifference as the villagers tied the Killer, his every muscle twitching in terror, his eyes bugging wildly, to the long wooden spit.

Vanderling took yet another drink, was nearly out when they lifted the spitted Killer out on to the two forked sticks that supported the spit over the roaring fire.

The Killer began to writhe terribly as the flames licked and scorched his naked body. Vanderling could hear muffled, anguished shrieks through the gag, as his eyelids began to droop irresistibly. The gaunt woman began to turn the spit, and now the flames licked the Killer's back, now his chest, and his lank hair suddenly went up in a crown of flames . . .

Then someone ripped the gag from the Killer's mouth, and a long, shrill, terrible scream pierced the air, drowning out the howls and mad laughs of the Sangrans who clustered around the spit, slobbering chunks of meat on their bare chests distractedly as they enjoyed the enemy's agony.

After a time, the scream subsided into a kind of low, continuous moan . . . Then, after several minutes, as the fire began to pop and sizzle, the moaning became a barely audible sigh, finally stopped.

But the Sangrans continued to roast the now dead Killer.

Vanderling managed to shake his leaden head once. Gonna eat him, he thought in almost schoolteacherish disapproval.

'Can't be any good . . .' he managed to mutter drunkenly. 'Crazy bastards . . . Mother gotta be tough as 'n old boot . . .'

Then he fell into a deep, totally stupefied sleep.

Bart Fraden glumly shovelled another glob of the mealy stuff into his mouth – a bland concoction of rice, vegetables and dried weeds that passed for the local spices. Across the table, Vanderling's plate was untouched, but Sophia was still packing the slop away. Nothing seemed capable of slacking her appetite for very long. Once we've got this mudball under control, he thought, we've *got* to find some way of importing Terran animals, though what we'll use for foreign exchange . . .

'What's the big joke, Chrome-dome?' Sophia said, and Fraden saw that Vanderling was grinning an infuriatingly smug, self-satisfied grin. Willem had certainly been acting strangely on this visit back to camp – grinning at odd moments at incomprehensible things, at his herogyn-heads, at other guerrillas returning from turns at playing bandit, looking sleek, well-fed, even fat . . . And now, he's grinning at nothing at all, just a meal in my hut. What the hell's so funny about that? Screw it, we've got business to attend to!

'Time to start stage three, Willem,' he said.

'Huh . . .?' Vanderling muttered abstractedly.

'Third stage of the classic four-stage revolution,' Fraden said. 'First stage is to secure and hold a district, and we completed that months ago. Second stage is to tie down the opposition by fomenting general planetwide pillaging, looting, and banditry. That's what you've been doing for the past two months, isn't it? Okay, so now we're ready for stage three. We've got the Killers tied down in thousands of small occupation groups, and now we can hit 'em all over the planet with locally superior forces,

193

wear 'em down inch-wise, bleed 'em dry, and finally force Moro to pull back what's left of the whole kit and caboodle to an enclave in Sade. Then stage four, we wipe out the enclave and we're the only force left on the planet; we clean up the terrorism and sit back and congratulate ourselves.'

'Yeah, sure . . .' Vanderling said. 'Only your stage two needs more work. *Much* more work.' Vanderling's eyes seemed almost to be glowing. What was going on in that shiny little head of his?

'I don't get it,' Fraden said irritably. 'The reports I get from Olnay's boys say half the villages on the planet are striking. The woods are full of bandits. The Killers are running around like chickens with their heads cut off. Every Brother on the planet's screaming for more Killers by now, and we *know* they're not getting 'em because there've been no significant troop movements since Moro spread out his reserves. The Killers are spread as thin as they can be. It's time to start hitting 'em, and hitting 'em hard!'

'Jeez, we only got a couple thousand of our boys in the raiding parties,' Vanderling whined. 'We got another six thousand or better you can use against the Killers.'

'*Me?*' Fraden snapped. 'What the hell do you mean, *me*? You're the tactician, remember? Running the army in the field's your line of evil, not mine. Why do you think I took you with me when we left the Belt, for laughs? What's with you, Willem? What is all this?'

'I'm telling you, man, I'm telling you! Sure we got the Killers tied down. Sure there are raids all over the place. But damn it, our boys are making half those raids. We hit and move on and hit again, maybe two or three times in a good day, but those dumb-ass villagers, they raid and have a big feast and stuff themselves silly and they don't

194

move again till their guts start to rumble. It *looks* like the thing has its own momentum from where you sit, but I'm telling you that our boys are still the ones that're keeping it going.'

'What kind of crap are you trying to hand me?' Fraden said. 'Can't you even *count*? The reports say there's something like ten thousand incidents a day planetwide. You expect me to believe that about a hundred groups of our boys are responsible for half of 'em? Come off it, man, come off it!'

Vanderling frowned hard, seemed deep in thought – Fraden sourly imagined that he could smell the wood burning. 'Er . . . so I exaggerated a bit . . .' Vanderling finally said. 'But it's . . . er, the competition . . . yeah, that's what you'd call it, *competition*. Look, I'm going from group to group in the outback, and I hear of a district where things are too quiet. The local yokums have made a big haul and they're just sitting around playing with themselves, right? So then I have our boys hit four, five, six times in the same area, real quick – boom! boom! boom! Dig? Then the local talent gets to figuring that if they don't start moving, someone else will knock over all the easy marks. We keep 'em on their toes. Sure, the yokums do most of the raiding, but we keep 'em at it. Leave 'em to themselves, and they get lazy.'

Fraden studied Vanderling dubiously. The whole thing smelled like an *ex post facto* cock-and-bull story. All reports indicated that Sangrans were really going ape, raiding everything in sight, wasting food like there was no tomorrow. The planet was full of Meatanimals running wild, half-eaten corpses, even dead Meatanimals that the bandits just let lay where they fell. So what was Willem's *real* reason?

'Okay . . .' Fraden said slowly. 'So we'll assume that

195

you're right. But that doesn't mean it has to tie *you* down.
Our raiders can handle that end of it by themselves. In
the meantime, we start stage three. You concentrate on
planning ambushes, get things moving. As you said yourself, even if we keep a couple thousand men on the
raiding campaign, you've still got six thousand to work
with.'

Vanderling frowned, scratched his bald skull. 'Look,'
he said, 'I'm telling you that the raids are what count
now. I've gotta keep my hand in, gotta keep the feel of it.
That's the way I run an operation like this. Maybe you
think those 'heads will keep their cool without me dropping in on each group every once in a while? Those babies
don't give a shit about your Revolution or tactics or
anything else except killing and herogyn. I give 'em a big
supply of herogyn when they go out and they stay stoned
the whole time. Give 'em *no* herogyn, and they'll go
utterly ape. This way, I hit every group a couple times a
month, and give 'em just enough to stretch out till the
next time I see 'em, and man, they *know* it. It's the only
way to keep 'em in line.'

'Okay, so we phase the 'heads out of the raiding
operation. We – '

'Goddam it, Bart, this is *my* line of evil, remember?'
Vanderling snapped churlishly. '*I'm* the tactician; you just
said so yourself. I don't tell you about over-all strategy,
don't tell me how to run things in the field! I say that I've
got to stick with the raiding programe, and you'll just
have to take my word for it. Or do you want to try
running *everything* yourself? Try it! Be my guest. See how
far you get!'

Fraden was taken aback by Vanderling's vehemence.
Besides, Willem had made some good points. And he had
always seemed to know what he was doing when it came

196

to running an army in the field. No point in stirring up trouble when you could avoid it . . .

'Okay,' Fraden said. 'So we compromise. You stay with the raiders another three weeks and phase out the 'heads. After that, I don't care *what* you think the tactical situation is, you handle the main force full time. Just remember that strategy dictates tactics and not the other way around. Dig?'

'I dig . . .' Vanderling said sullenly. He got up, headed for the doorway.

'Hey, you haven't eaten a thing!' Fraden called after him.

Vanderling turned, his face suddenly smiled. He seemed to be suppressing a snigger. 'Guess I just don't feel like bunny-food,' he said. Then he was gone.

As Fraden stared at the empty doorway, he felt Sophia's eyes on the back of his neck. He turned, saw that she was staring straight at him, sardonic amusement in her green eyes, a twisted, almost indulgent, smile on her lips. He stared back questioningly.

She continued to look silently at him, like a petulant Cheshire Cat.

'All right, all right!' he snapped. 'So what is it?'

'Far be it from me to interfere in the weighty and complex affairs of state . . .'

'Jesus Christ, Soph, spit it out, will you! Enough little mysteries for one day!'

'You mean you don't see it?' she said incredulously. 'You really don't see it? You're not putting me on?'

'See *what*, dammit?'

'Old Bullethead, what else? Why he's so dead set on going back to the woods with his trick-or-treat pals instead of staying here and playing general.'

197

Fraden sighed. Another tirade about Willem was about due anyway. Might as well get it over with.

'Okay, Sherlock,' he said, 'give with the brilliant deduction.'

'Good Lord, Bart, what's the matter with you? Are you so wrapped up in playing hero that you don't see what's happening with Chrome-dome? He's *digging* it! He's enjoying it; he's got his own planetwide pigpen to wallow round in and he doesn't want to give it up.'

'He's enjoying *what*?'

'What?' Sophia shouted. '*What! Running amok*, that's what! Ye gods, Bart, here we have old Bullethead on a special assignment – and what's his little chore but tearing up the countryside, killing and looting and behaving in general like the utter swine he is. He's wallowing in it. Killing and looting and god-knows-what . . . Do you know what? Do you really know what Chrome-dome and his goon squads are doing?'

'They've been ordered to raid small Killer outposts and storehouses and Meatanimal herds and distribute all but what they need for themselves to the villagers as an example. That's hardly – '

'Ordered, schmordered! Do you *know* that they've been following your orders? Do you have anything but Vanderling's word for it? You've been too busy with other things to check up on what they're really up to. I can imagine what's going on. I can just imagine! Fun and games! I notice that Bullethead looks mighty fat and healthy. You really think he's been eating the same rabbit food we're making do with? You think Bullethead and his cronies are about to live off grain and vegetables when you're not around, and when they've got all those nice fat little – '

'Not *Willem*! Fraden exclaimed. 'The Sangrans . . .

198

well, they're *Sangrans*, and you've got to make compromises here and there in a war like this, but *Willem* . . .'

'Oh sure, sure, dear sweet Bullethead. And wasn't he smirking like some dirty old man watching us eat this mung? Didn't you wonder what was going on in his shiny little head?'

'Now that you mention it . . .'

'Now that I mention it, he says!' Sophia shouted. 'Jesus H. Christ on a bicycle! I'll tell you what tickled his perverted funnybone – Bart Fraden choking down rice and vegetables while he's been dining on nice juicy meat for two months, and never mind that it's human meat. I'm sure that Chrome-dome is beyond such fine culinary distinctions at this point.'

'Aw, you're jumping to conclusions. Soph . . .' Fraden muttered without much conviction. Willem *did* look like he'd gained weight, and all that crap about momentum and competition *did* sound pretty damned phony . . .

'So I'm jumping to conclusions.' Sophia said with sudden sly calmness. 'Alrighty . . . So suppose you take the 'boat and have a look for yourself. Take some time. Ask some questions. The Animals will tell you the truth, won't they? You're the Big Hero, aren't you?'

'You may have a point,' Fraden admitted grudgingly. 'We're doing the liberator bit, we're not supposed to be carbon copies of the Brotherhood. If Willem's getting out of hand . . .'

Fraden gritted his teeth. If Willem was playing games behind his back, the time to stop it was now, before things went any further. It was all very well to throw away your sensibilities when you were fighting a revolution – war was no time for excessive scruples. But, hell, he thought, when we win, we'll have to *rule* this mudball. We can't

199

have everyone, including our own troops, going ape. If Willem . . .

'Okay, Soph,' he said. 'I'll leave in the morning. We'll soon see if there's anything to this.'

Sophia shrugged and went back to eating her rice and vegetables. 'Just don't holler when I say I told you so' she said between mouthfuls.

As he kept one eye on the lifeboat's viewscreen looking for a third Sangran village to case and conned the 'boat with the other, Bart Fraden felt a growing uneasiness. He had hit two villages at random so far, and superficially everything seemed to be swinging along according to plan. The fields of both villages had been lying fallow, with the local Brains having been killed by the usual guerrillas-dressed-as-Killers, they had both been half empty – the men were off in the jungle on raiding parties. Generally, all according to plan.

It was the specifics that bothered him. The women and children of both villages looked fatter and healthier than any Sangrans he had ever seen before, and the bones of Meatanimals littered both villages around burnt-out cook-fires. But then, what else could you expect when you encouraged a protein-starved populace to run wild? When the Revolution was over, and more conventional food animals could be introduced from off-planet, then it would be possible to deal with the rampant cannibalism with a heavier hand. No, that really wasn't what smelled so wrong . . . It was that story they told in the first village, about how the Killers who had killed their Brain had also killed seven villagers . . . And those *other* human bones in the second village, *adult* human bones, skulls with teeth filed to points – *Killers'* bones. They had taken prisoners and they had . . . they had eaten the Killers they cap-

200

tured. That was bad enough, but the story they told about it, about just happening to find two wounded Killers and being very hungry at the time . . . It just hadn't seemed like the whole truth . . .

Now Fraden saw another village in the viewscreen. Hey . . . what was that?

There seemed to be a big commotion in the centre of the village . . . people milling around, smoke rising from nearly a dozen fires . . .

Fraden gritted his teeth as he spiralled the 'boat down towards the village. It looked as if he was about to see exactly what they did do after a raid while they were doing it, and his curiosity was nearly outweighed by his apprehension.

He landed the 'boat in the centre of the village and, Hero of the Revolution or not, unshipped a snipgun before he stepped out of the airlock and into a grotesque carnival.

It was quite a sight. Ten big fires roared in the centre of the village, and a spitted Meatanimal was being turned above each fire by a Sangran woman. Other butchered carcasses, already spitted, were piled by the fires waiting their turn. The air was filled with the pungent odour of roasting meat, tormenting him, causing his mouth to water despite the essential horror of the situation. It had been so long since he had tasted well-cooked meat . . . About two hundred men, women, and children stood or sat around the fires, holding chunks of meat, whole joints of Meatanimal, drinking wine from clay jugs, and staring curiously in the direction of the 'boat as he emerged.

And as they saw him, they began to cheer, waving half-denuded bones, greasy bits of meat. Those who had been sitting sprang up, and the whole mob began to chant his name: 'BART! BART! BART! BART! BART!'

Fraden found himself being torn in all directions. The smell of the meat caused his digestive juices to flow, but the thought of what that meat was, the sight of the all-too-human-looking carcasses, turned his stomach. The sound of people chanting his name awakened old echoes, buoyed him, but the . . . the things they were waving as they cheered him edged the buoyant feeling with disgust. Still, this, after all, was what he had *known* was going on; it was all according to his own plan. But he had never seen and smelt it before, and the actual experience was viscerally nauseating.

The Sangrans formed a cheering, gesticulating welcoming mob as he reluctantly walked towards them: 'BART! BART! BART! BART! BART!'

'Long live the Free Republic!' Fraden shouted, trying to stop the chant, which, moment by moment, seemed to him to become more and more mocking. Sangrans clustered around him, shook his hands, slapped his back with fingers smeared with human fat, babbled, laughed, grunted, burbled with unholy glee.

Shouting, gesticulating men and women shoved jars of wine at him, thrust warm, fragrant pieces of crispy brown meat under his nose. He was disgusted, then tempted, then further disgusted, this time with himself, with his gut, which was greedily demanding that he take part in the ghastly feast.

They're *your* people, Fraden kept telling himself, you're their goddamned *hero*! But it took iron nerves to keep from shoving them aside, howling his loathing and disgust, and the snipgun seemed to grow warm and alive in his hands.

But they were his people, they were the citizens of his very own Free Republic of Sangre. They were the only people he had. He couldn't show what he felt. He couldn't even look unhappy.

He forced himself to smile genially, shake obscenely greased hands, mutter inane pleasantries while desperately holding back his gorge and fury.

He brushed aside the meat and wine, mumbled, 'Just ate in the last two villages . . . I'm stuffed t'the gills . . . Nice haul y'got here, keep at it! Take what y'want! Y'got the right idea here . . .'

God, what a nightmare!

It wasn't long before they began to drift away from him, back to the business at hand. Soon he was alone, watching the feasting and the drinking, mercifully ignored.

Sangrans lay sprawled on the ground by the dozens, in drunken stupors, wolfing down great chunks of seared human flesh or nibbling torpidly on half-bare bones. Laughter, gut-rumblings . . . the obscene sound of fat, human fat, dripping and sizzling on the fires. The smell of dirty bodies, spilt blood, sour wine, roasting meat all combined into a sickening ripe stench that reeked of decadence, obscenity, guilt, horror . . .

Fraden stood and numbly watched. Dreadful, nauseating, loathsome though it all was, there was nothing here that he could blame on Willem. It was all according to plan, all according to *his* plan. The phrase stuck in his mind, mocked him over and over again . . . all according to plan . . . *all according to plan* . . .

Then something hapened that emphatically was *not* according to plan.

A great shout went up from the far end of the clearing. Like small boys to a fire, the Sangrans ran to the far row of huts, laughing, shouting, waving their arms. In moments, they were a tight clot of squirming bodies, laughing, cursing and . . . and apparently kicking at someone or something in their midst.

Hesitantly, Fraden went closer to the stomping, mad-eyed mob. They parted for a moment and Fraden saw . . .

A thing that had once been a man, was still a man, what was left of him. Like some monstrous white worm, a naked human figure wriggled on its belly along the ground, futilely trying to escape the kicks and blows of the Sangrans. All his limbs were limp and grotesquely askew – broken in scores of places. His mouth was a bleeding red pulp: his teeth had all been yanked out. And as Fraden saw the face of the tormented man, the lean, hard face, the mad feral eyes, the receding brown hair, he knew why – the horribly mutilated creature was a Killer, his limbs smashed, his razor-sharp teeth pulled to make him harmless to the jeering, tormenting, stomping throng.

Like harrying dogs, the Sangrans drove the Killer towards the fires, kicking him, prodding him with rude spears and scythes till his body ran red with blood. Inching along on his belly, writhing like a decapitated snake, the Killer met his agony in the only way he knew how, the way that had been impressed on his genes before his birth: lashing out with his toothless, bleeding gums, snarling the battle chant, made ludicrous, pathetic by the circumstances – 'KILL! KILL! KILL! KILL!'

The Sangrans hooted and laughed. Then someone grabbed the helpless Killer, then another and another, and they dragged him to an empty fire, tied him to a spit and hoisted him out over the flames as he screamed and howled, more in hate than in fear.

Fraden averted his eyes as the flames began to lick the body of the Killer, as the 'KILL! KILL! KILL!' became a hideous shriek of pain.

Savagely, Fraden lashed out, grabbed the first Sangran that came to hand – an old, emaciated woman, her eyes mad with blood lust, her thin lips wet with drool. He held her firm by the arm, thrust the muzzle of the snipgun into her startled face.

'That Killer!' he roared inchoately. 'Who told you . . .? Who let you . . .? Where . . .? How . . .? WHERE DID YOU GET THAT KILLER FROM?'

'Y'People's Army!' the woman shrilled in fear. 'Was just here – y'Field Marshal gave y'Killer t'us! Y'friend, y'off-worlder!'

Fraden's grip loosened and she pulled away with a savage jerk.

Fraden felt fury pound through his arteries. Fury, disgust, rage, hate, all awash on an ocean of adrenalin as he stormed towards the lifeboat. Goddamn Willem, god-damn him! I'll –

A terrible shriek, worse than the rest, caused him involuntarily to turn his head back towards the fire.

A lean, redheaded man was holding a torch to the Killer's face. Hair, eyebrows, lashes, flared into flames.

But that was not what Fraden noticed, what made him ball his hands into fists so tightly that his nails drew blood from his own flesh. It was the tormenter with the torch that Fraden saw, not his victim.

For the redheaded man, his eyes blazing, his mouth an ugly smear, was Vanderling's pet herogyn-head, Colonel Lamar Gomez.

'Jeez, Bart, what the hell is all this about?' Willem Vanderling said as Olnay ushered him into Fraden's hut. 'There I was in the middle of nowhere and one of your sl—er, *agents* pops up and says you want to see me pronto. Man, to have found me at all, you must've had dozens of – '

Fraden motioned to Olnay, for the moment totally ignoring Vanderling, who stood in front of the table behind which he sat. 'That will be all, Colonel Olnay. See that Marshal Vanderling and I are not disturbed. For any reason. And I mean *any* reason, get that?'

Olnay nodded, seemed to feel the tension in the room to which Vanderling had so far been oblivious, withdrew uneasily.

'Okay, so now we're alone,' Vanderling said breezily. 'So what's the scoop?'

'*Siddown!*' Fraden roared, a sound like a shell impact. He slammed Vanderling into the chair in front of the table with his eyes, stood up as Vanderling sat down.

Now Vanderling's face went tense, questioning. The barked order, the fury on Fraden's face, the sudden reversal of positions, and all at once it was an interrogation session instead of a strategy meeting.

Fraden began to pace the small room, his eyes always on Vanderling who followed him with his own as a cobra watches a circling mongoose. Fraden searched for words, for the trenchant, biting thing to say, and came up dry.

Finally, as if in the middle of a long tirade: 'Brutality, I can understand! Stupidity, I can understand too! Perversion, sadism, cruelty, cannibalism, murder, torture – I've been on Sangre too long to be very surprised at any of 'em. But . . . but . . . but Christ, man, how in hell could you manage to tie *all of 'em* up into one neat bundle? Are you into your own stash of herogyn? Have you forgotten what we're supposed to be here for? WHAT THE FUCK IS THE MATTER WITH YOU?'

'Hey . . .' Vanderling crooned softly. 'What you got up *your* ass, Bart?'

'Don't Bart *me*, Willem! I know all about it, the game's up, finished, ended, kaput. I've been checking around. Torturing Killers for kicks, turning 'em over to the Animals, letting *them* torture 'em for kicks . . . *Eating* Killers, for chrissakes! I won't even bother to ask what *else* you and your wolf packs've been doing behind my back. I won't even bother to ask why you've gained weight, I won't ask what you've been dining on lately. I know, Willem, I know! All I'll ask is *why*, why, goddammit, why Willem, why?'

Vanderling's expression changed from bland incomprehension to a sneer of almost innocent cynicism. 'So that's what's stuck in your craw,' he said. 'Just because you're eating bunny-food, that means *I* have to? What the hell did you expect? You think human flesh tastes so bad? A little on the salty side, maybe, but you get used to that a lot easier than you get used to no meat at all.'

'You imbecile! You cretin!' Fraden roared. 'For all I care, you can eat shit! But what about torture? What about sadism? What about running amok? What about encouraging the villagers to act like . . . like . . . like the goddamned *Brothers*?'

'What's with you, Bart?' asked Vanderling, with genuine incomprehension. 'This was all *your* idea, remember? Stir 'em up, get 'em to raid, make 'em go ape, tie down the Killers. Well it's working, isn't it? The whole mother-jumping planet is going ape. The Killers *are* tied down, and they'll stay tied down. Isn't that what you wanted in the first place? I was just carrying out your own orders.'

'Thank you, Adolf Eichmann!' Fraden barked. 'Just carrying out orders, eh? I ordered you to eat the Meatanimals? I ordered you to torture Killers? I ordered you to encourage cannibalism and torture among the Animals? And I suppose I ordered you to put me on, too? "They won't do it themselves." "Have to keep my hand in or it loses momentum!" *Bullshit!* Sophia was right about you, she's been right all along. Don't try to shuck me any more, Willem; you did it for kicks. You *dig* torturing Killers, you *dig* eating human flesh, and not just because you're hungry. You dig *killing*, more than you dig winning, more than you dig ruling this crummy mudball. Did it ever dawn on you that someday we're gonna have to *rule* this planet? Did you ever stop to consider that when the war is over, we'll have to deal with the Animals, we'll have to clean up the messes we've made, we'll have to restore respect for order because *we'll* be the boys on top of the heap? Give the Sangrans a year or so of torturing and cannibalism and god-knows-what, and putting down the terrorism will make the Revolution look like a church social. You're not only a bloodthirsty sadist, you're a cretinous, blind, kill-crazy butcher!'

'Well, well, well,' Vanderling said coldly, calmly, smoothly. 'The gospel according to Saint Fraden. And of course, your hands are lily-white, aren't they? Butter wouldn't melt in your mouth, would it? It was someone else, wasn't it, who peddled Omnidrene to the Brotherhood, who had the Brains killed so the Animals would starve, who gave Moro the idea of torturing the whole planet out of its head and then bleeding the Animals dry? Not Bart Fraden. Bart Fraden's a regular pussycat, isn't he?'

Fraden flushed red-hot. What Willem was saying was true, but the way he said it made it a lie. He made it sound like it was all for kicks, like none of it had a purpose, like . . . like . . . like . . .

Vanderling laughed harshly. 'Who do you think you're conning?' he said. He put his right forefinger to his ear, his left to a tooth.

Fraden went cold.

'Yeah,' said Vanderling, 'you got a very short memory. "Bring forth the human animal." THUNK!' He brought his right hand down in a chopping motion. 'How's it feel to kill . . . what, a kid, a slave, maybe . . . maybe a *baby*?' He grinned, nodded his head, as Fraden's face contorted in anguish at the last word. 'So that was it, a baby . . . Boy! Let's just remember where it's at Bart. Let's forget the name-calling, eh? Two can play that game. Okay, Big Shot, you're still the boss; you know more about the revolution racket than I do, and we'll play things your way. So no more raiding parties and I start concentrating on wiping out the Killers. Cool. But don't get any funny ideas – just remember that every last one of the herogyn-heads is loyal to *me*, not you.'

'Don't threaten me!' Fraden shot back, grateful for a threat that could be dealt with with a counter-threat, grateful for something to grasp at, to deal with, to take his mind off . . . off . . .

'You're invisible, man,' he said. 'I'm the hero, remember? You've got a couple hundred 'heads, but I've got the whole planet. The Sangrans hardly know you from Adam. I need you, whether I like it or not, and there'll be no double-crosses on my part. But don't get too big for your britches. One word from me, *one word* to Olnay and into the rumour mill and you're a dead man. I can turn the whole planet into fifteen million executioners. What do you do then, go over to Moro? What kind of a reception do you think you'd get there? You're bound to me, Willem. I'm number one and you're number two, and don't you ever forget it. *That's* where it's at.'

Vanderling stared coldly at Fraden, and Fraden could all but hear the wheels turning. 'We understand each other,' Vanderling said evenly. 'We understand each other real well.'

Fraden studied Vanderling, felt the gaping emptiness, the wall of hate, the void of envy yawning between them. He felt very much alone. He realized now, only now, by the cold wind of its passing, that this man, whatever he was, had been his friend, the only friend he had in scores of light years. And now . . . now he would have to have eyes in the back of his head always.

Fraden sighed, slumped down into the chair opposite Vanderling. 'I think we do, Willem,' he said, suddenly abysmally weary. 'We had better get down to business. We've got a war to win, remember?'

Chapter 11

As he looked out across the bustling guerrilla camp, at three of the now standardized hundred-man companies resupplying themselves with ammunition and with men from the bottomless stream of replacements that was pouring into the People's Army at a rate as prodigious as the soaring casualty rate, at the agents coming and going at Olnay's hut, at the new barracks shacks, the row of armoury huts, the whole busily humming complex of men, buildings and supplies, Bart Fraden found wry amusement in the knowledge that all this was running on a kind of carefully calculated balance of desperation.

The desperation lay hidden below the surface, dormant but ready to be tapped when the moment ripened. The Killers, though they probably didn't realize it, though even Moro no doubt did not fully understand the import of his own orders, had in effect given up. Although Fraden was probably the only man on Sangre yet capable of deciphering the handwriting on the wall, the Brotherhood had lost the war. The People's Army had a good fifteen thousand men, could be pumped up to twenty thousand at short notice. The guerrilla casualty rate was admittedly hideous, but the Sangran countryside was now a massive reservoir of reserves, a reservoir in part created, ironically, by the Killers themselves.

For four months, the Killers had been bled dry by planetwide chaos, looting, banditry, pillaging; by ruinous ambushes of punitive expeditions against the bandits by regular guerrilla forces, by the impossibility of keeping the road network connecting Sade with the estates open; by having to fight two wars at once, one against the People's Army and another against the population at large. It was hard to tell just how many Killers were left, what with their being tied down in little groups all over the planet, but the count of captured weapons and extrapolation from guerrilla casualty figures made it pretty clear that the Killers had lost something like ten thousand men in the past four months. Since it took nearly twenty years from his conception to produce a battle-ready Killer, the replacement rate was, for all practical purposes, negligible, and the twenty thousand or so Killers that Moro had left would soon become outnumbered by the People's Army if the attrition rate continued at the present level. The Killers would be worn down to nothing in another year or so.

But Moro had not proved quite that stupid; he had had the wit to pull the Killers off the offensive. Now the Killers assigned to each district were holed up in one estate per district, several hundred men strong and heavily dug in. They had rounded up all remaining Meatanimals, confined them in great corrals surrounding the local fortified estates, where it would be suicidal for the bandits to attempt to seize them. The villagers were in desperate straits – the bandits had no more easy marks to live off, what Bugs that were left were useless, the peasants had no experience in growing their own food.

It was a deadly waiting game. The Killers, sitting tight in their defensive positions, had large but limited reserves of food, and the costs of wiping out such positions would be enormous. The peasantry was on the brink of starvation. Clearly, Moro's strategy was to wait it out until the desperate Animals turned on the Free Republic. If the peasants tried to grow crops, the Killers could sally forth in force and burn them. It was a game of desperate cats against equally desperate mice . . .

But desperation was a tool that Bart Fraden knew how to use. It was all a matter of timing . . .

Now what's *that*?

Olnay and two armed men were prodding someone towards him, a strangely slight, short figure in a Killer uniform. As they neared him, Fraden saw that the tightly trussed 'Killer' was no more than a boy, fifteen years old at the outside.

'Got us a Killer-cub,' Olnay said, shoving the boy before Fraden. Fraden studied the boy. He had the lean build of an adult Killer and his lank brown hair seemed to already be receding into the characteristic Killer hairline. His teeth were sharp needles. His fierce, burning eyes seemed strangely out of place in his smooth, beardless face.

'Where did you find him?' Fraden asked.

'Two truckloads of 'em 'bout seventy miles from here,' Olnay said. 'Bunch of our men wiped 'em out, but took this one prisoner. Wonder what y'Killer cubs are doing this far from Sade . . .?'

'Maybe our friend here can tell us,' Fraden said. It was more confirmation than information that he needed, though. This looked like what he had been waiting for. He looked at the boy kindly. 'You co-operate, and you'll be all right, son,' he said. 'We don't kill boys. Now suppose you tell us why you were sent out here?'

The boy stared back phlegmatically, fearlessly. 'A Killer does not provide information to the enemy,' he said.

'Well, you had better make an exception if you want to see tomorrow,' Fraden said quietly.

'A Killer does not fear death. To die at the hands of

213

the enemy is to die in combat. To die in combat is to die gloriously.'

Fraden tried a different tack. 'That's all very well for a *real* Killer,' he sneered. 'But you're just a snotty little kid! Since when does a puny little punk like you rate combat duty?'

The Killer cadet's jaws began to work. He flushed. 'A Killer is born a Killer,' he said thickly. 'A Killer is permitted the glory of fighting whenever the Prophet so decides. Save your breath to scream with when we destroy you, Animal!'

'You mean to tell me that you crummy little punks weren't along just for the ride, just to watch the big boys fight? Don't put me on – Moro wouldn't let little turds like you have a piece of the action!'

Something seemed to give way within the Killer cadet. His calmness evaporated, was burned away by mindless rage. He struggled against his bonds, bit his own lips cruelly. 'Cadets have already killed gloriously all over Sangre!' he screamed, his eyes blazing hate. 'We kill like all other Killers! To kill is glory! We will kill you all, Animal! Kill! Kill! Kill! Kill!'

He lunged at Fraden, kicked out, used his head as a ram. Fraden sidestepped as one of the guerrillas brought his rifle-butt down sharply on the back of the boy's head. The Killer cadet crumpled. The guerrilla caught him by the arm as he fell, the other guard caught the other arm, and the two of them held the unconscious Killer cadet limply upright.

'Okay, Olnay,' Fraden said. 'This is what we've been waiting for. Moro's getting so hard up that he's sending cadets into combat. Means they've got no reserves left, they've got their asses to the wall. It's time for the Big Push. Send out agents to all districts. I want as many bandit leaders as you can round up in camp a week from today. Tell 'em there's big news, tell 'em anything, but get 'em here. We've got the Killers where we want 'em, but now we need all the gun—, er, *troops* we can lay our hands on, and to hell with discipline.'

Olnay nodded. 'And what about y'Killer cub?' he said. 'We'd have t'guard him night and day, and we don't have no food t'spare . . .'

Fraden studied Olnay's expectant face, the grim grins of the two guards. He sighed unhappily as he realized that while he controlled the Sangrans, that control had its limits, that they would only follow him to the extent that he led where they wanted to go. A show of mercy would mean weakness to them. They did not understand mercy; they only understood power. He could not afford to be incomprehensible at this point.

'Shoot him,' Fraden said. Olnay nodded approvingly, motioned to the guards, and they began to drag the boy off.

'But make it quick and make it clean!' Fraden called after them, feeling sick to his stomach.

Fraden heard low murmurs go up from the crowd as Vanderling emerged from the hut. He paused a moment for dramatic effect, then stepped out into the hot red sunlight.

A roar went up, a roar that quickly became the familiar chant of 'BART! BART! BART!' Fraden let it go on for a while as he stood there, the red and green flag of the Free Republic waving from the hut behind him, flanked on either side by a long crescent of officers who stood silently facing the motley group of several hundred men who stood chanting before the hut. They were sure a sad-looking lot, these bandit leaders. Skinny, emaciated-

215

looking – and they were probably a lot better-fed than the men they led at that – mostly armed with captured rifles and morningstars – though their men largely had to make do with scythes and clubs and spears. They were desperate men, more desperate perhaps than even the men they led, for with the Meatanimals all concentrated under heavy guard, their bands were starving, and sooner or later (and probably sooner) starving men turn on their leaders. Yeah, they were up against it, all right, just desperate enough to let their men, if not themselves, be used as kamikazes . . .

'Long live the Free Republic!' Fraden shouted. The bandit leaders returned the salute somewhat perfunctorily, then quieted down.

'So y'got troubles,' Fraden said. 'Y'live by raiding, and all of a sudden, no more easy pickings. Y'men are getting mighty unhappy. Maybe they're starting t'think you're not such hot-shot leaders any more, eh?'

The bandits began to mutter among themselves. He had said what they were all afraid to admit to themselves, and they didn't like hearing their unvoiced fears out in the open.

'Well why don't y'raid the corrals? Plenty of Meatanimals there . . .'

Despite the presence of the snipgun-armed herogynheads, the bandits began to hoot and jeer and snarl. 'We could just slit our own throats, 'n'save the trouble!' a bandit shouted. 'Be dead before we started, 'gainst a couple hundred Killers!' another yelled.

'Y'dead right,' Fraden said. He paused, grinned. '*Alone*, that is,' he said. 'Of course, if you had well-armed regular troops with you on those raids . . . If you were part of the People's Army . . .'

The bandits went quiet. They had no eyes for fighting

for the Free Republic or anything else but loot, but he had painted them into a corner. Fight for the People's Republic – or do nothing and eventually be killed by their own men.

'Deal!' Fraden said, not giving them time to fully see the naked club he was holding over their heads. 'You put yourselves and your men under the command of the People's Army. You'll be led by experienced officers, backed up by well-armed troops. Together, no Killers can stop us. Our plan is short and sweet. With your men fighting with us, we can attack those estates, ten, twenty, fifty at a time, all over the planet. We can throw a thousand men against a couple hundred Killers every time. The Killers have no reserves – they're starting to use cadets as it is. Five or six to one is good odds, even against Killers. But you'll have to follow orders, no questions asked. What d'y'say?'

'What d'we get outa it?' someone shouted. There were strong mutters of agreement, but already they were edged with sullen resignation to the inevitable.

'Everything y'want!' Fraden said. 'Let's not put each other on. Y'People's Army is out t'kill Killers, and you're out for loot and plunder. Okay, you help us do what we want to, and we help you get what *you* want. You help us kill Killers, put yourselves under our orders – and it's all yours! Everything in the estates we sack except guns and ammunition – Meatanimals, grain supplies, women, *all of it*! All there for the taking! What d'y'say *now*?'

There was a long moment of silence. He had shown them the stick, the stick of starvation and eventual mutiny among the men they led, and now he had thrown them the carrot. There was no free choice for them to make; they could only bow to the inevitable.

'Long live the Free Republic!' someone shouted. The

217

cry spread, somewhat reluctantly at first. Then it picked up steam and they were all shouting it. They wanted in before it was too late. No doubt, they were already convincing themselves that *they* would be using the People's Army to do their dirty work and not the other way around. And for the ones who survived, it would indeed work out that way . . .

For the ones who survived . . . But there would be precious few of those. When the Revolution was won, these bandits would have to be crushed anyway. There would be no place for looting and pillaging in the Free Republic when Bart Fraden ruled Sangre. Agriculture would have to be re-established on a new basis, later industry. This was a time for tearing down; after the Revolution was won, it would be time for building up – and the last thing a successful government needed was a horde of bandits tearing up its property. This was *better* than killing two birds with one stone – the birds, the bandits, and the Killers, would end up killing each other!

'Field Marshal Vanderling will assign you and your men to units,' Fraden said. 'You'll be given your orders, and within ten days, you'll be sacking estates. Good hunting!'

Fraden retired to his hut, leaving the bandit leaders to Vanderling. I can't turn my back on Willem any more, he thought, but at least there's one thing I can still trust him to do – use up gunfodder to the best possible advantage!

Fraden huddled closer to Sophia, who slept lightly beside him. Better than three weeks had passed since he had commandeered the bandits into the People's Army, and dozens of fortified estates had already been sacked. It was going well, it was going very well indeed. Victory was no longer a vague, far-off goal – it was the culmination of a train of events that he had already set in motion, a

218

sequence he could trace in his mind's eye from beginning to end. Sangre would be his. The Revolution would be won, and in the easily foreseeable future.

So he wondered why he felt uneasy, tense, unsure. Unsure of *what*? What did he have to be unsure of? Not eventual victory. As sure as the woman sleeping beside him was his, he would have Sangre. His woman, his planet . . . What else was there to be unsure of? *What else was there?*

He found himself caressing Sophia's back, stroking her gently as if she were some talisman that could hold back . . . hold back *what*, dammit?

She stirred, rolled over, blinked, stared across the crude bed at him. 'What is it?' she mumbled.

'Huh?' he grunted, suddenly realizing that he was awakening her. 'I'm sorry . . . didn't mean to . . . I was just thinking . . .'

'With your *hands*?'

'I didn't mean to . . .' He looked across at her face, could dimly see that she was frowning, and all at once it came to him. She was all he had. There wasn't a human being on the planet that he could call friend. Worse, there wasn't a human being on Sangre that he could *want* to call friend. Except for Sophia, he was alone. He needed someone else, a specific someone else, and it scared him. He was dependent on another human being for something. It was a new experience, and he didn't like it.

'Soph . . .' he mumbled. 'Soph . . . I'm . . .'

She reached out, touched his cheek. 'I know,' she said. 'You're lonely and you don't like it. You've seen what Chrome-dome is, and here you are on a planetful of savages alone. Just you and me and no one else for a hundred light years.'

'How could you know how I – ?'

219

'Because it's the story of my life,' she said. 'What am I? I'm Bart Fraden's woman, and before that someone else's woman. What am I without a man, what would I be without you? On a planet like this . . . in a universe like this. Without a man like you, a woman like me's a slave, a thing, a nobody. I need you so bad . . . I need you just to stay *me*. And in a place like Sangre, you're finding out that maybe you need me to stay *you*. Just to stay sane. That's where it's at, Bart, isn't it, whether we like it or not – you and me against the field. We're bound together, stuck with each other, by something a lot stronger than love. You and me in here, and out *there* the wolves are howling.'

'Soph . . . are you trying to tell me you love me?'

She laughed, with perhaps a bit too much cynicism. 'If you want to call mutual parasitism love,' she said. 'I suppose it does sound cleaner . . .'

'Why . . . why haven't you said anything like this to me before?'

She put her arms around him. 'Because until now, you wouldn't have understood a word I said, Peerless Leader,' she said. 'You wouldn't have understood it because you didn't need it.'

'Soph, I . . .'

'Don't say it. Don't give me any I-love-you crap. You don't mean it. You don't love me, you just need me. Just need me as long as I need you. Deal?'

'Deal,' he said, holding her to him. 'Don't worry – where else on this miserable mudball am I going to find an innocent young thing like you?'

He felt her laugh against his chest, a constricted, perhaps forced spasm, and felt constrained by the unvoiced rules of some unnamed game to laugh back.

Nevertheless, they stayed in each other's arms for a long, long time.

'First wave – yo!' Willem Vanderling shouted crisply, dropping his snipgun smartly to waist level. For a moment nothing happened, and Vanderling looked irritably down into the shallow defile behind him and slightly below the level of the broad plain on which he and the estate compound about two hundred yards to the west stood. Hidden in this depression were three concentric crescents of about three hundred men each, and the tightly packed wedge of bandits nearest him, the first wave, armed with spears, clubs, knives, scythes, a few score rifles, a few dozen morningstars, was milling about sullenly instead of charging forward.

'Move 'em out!' Vanderling roared, and three herogyn-heads armed with snipguns and sandwiched in between the first and second wedges of bandits waved their weapons menacingly at their own troops. Now the rear ranks of the first wave of bandits bolted forward, pushed into their fellows, and the whole ragged bunch finally surged forward up out of the defile and on to the plain towards the compound.

Vanderling kept one eye on the bandits running rather raggedly towards the compound, prodded onward by the three 'heads, and the other on the rest of his men – another three hundred poorly armed, ill-disciplined bandits and a few more 'heads to make sure they moved on orders, and behind them three hundred regular, well-armed troops of the People's Army.

The first wave of bandits was moving well now, towards the walled compound. The compound was between the bandits and the great corrals filled with Meatanimals directly behind it – a good thing too, because the bandits were little more than a horde being herded forward by the 'heads like sheep, and there was no telling what would happen if they could get to the Meatanimals first. The bandits were the stupidest, most unreliable troops Vanderling had ever commanded.

However, in the past couple of months of fighting, Vanderling had evolved a simple, straightforward tactic for attacking estates which did not require the bandits to be anything more than pairs of feet heading more or less in the right direction – the maximum effort of which they were capable anyway. He had successfully sacked dozens of estates himself already, and he had reduced the method to such a simple formula that even his dumb herogyn-head officers had been able to use it independently. After all, he thought, when you've got five or ten to one superiority, who needs finesse?

Now Vanderling saw that the ragged mob of bandits was within a hundred yards of the compound gate. Would the Killers try to hold the gate against three hundred . . .? Nope, here they came!

The gate in the palisade opened, and black-clad Killers poured forth, fifty, eighty, a hundred, maybe two hundred or so of 'em, which figured to be almost the whole force holed up in the estate.

Vanderling noted with a kind of detached professional approval that the Killers seemed to at last have learned something. Instead of the usual blind, headlong charge at the attacking men, they quickly formed a tight, semicircular firing line, a cup to catch the charge, stood their ground, and opened up with their rifles. An interesting, if futile, variation . . .

Seventy yards from the Killers, the bandits ran into a solid wall of lead. The first rank went down like tenpins. Instantly, the mass of bandits began to break and turn tail

– and then charged right back into the buzz saw, as the herogyn-heads sliced down a dozen of their own tail-turning men with their snipguns.

It was pure panic, but a controlled panic, as the 'heads ruthlessly forced the bandits forward straight into the massed rifle fire. Fifty, forty, thirty yards to closing . . . Had to time this just right . . . Now!

'Second wave – yo!' Vanderling shouted, stepped aside as the herogyn-heads prodded the second wave of bandits forward towards the compound.

As the second wave charged across the plain, Vanderling saw that the remnants of the first wave – no more than a hundred and fifty men – had reached the Killers.

It was, of course, sheer slaughter. The Killer crescent locked its arms around the panic-stricken bandits, began clobbering them with morningstars, boots, gun butts, teeth. All that Vanderling could make out from where he stood was a tight, writhing pack of men in futile, mortal combat. Man, look at those Killers go to work! he thought. A few more minutes, and there'll be nothing left but dogmeat!

But the plan was working smoothly. The second wave of kamikazes was already halfway to the battle, and for every four or five bandits the Killers killed, they lost one of their own men. And, yup, they were obeying orders! The three 'heads who had herded the bandits forward were lying back, forty yards away, and were slicing into the mêlée with their snipguns, cutting down Killers and bandits indiscriminately.

And the beauty of the whole bit, Vanderling thought, is that it couldn't matter less. Both waves, all six hundred bandits, were dead men from the word go. The woods were full of gunfodder. Six hundred otherwise useless bandits were a small price to pay for the hundred or so Killers they would take with 'em.

Now the second wave of bandits ploughed mindlessly into the already waning battle. For a moment, the solid crush of bodies, clubs, and spears pushed the Killers back, threw them off balance.

But then, inevitably, the Killers recovered from their momentary confusion, and just as abruptly, the tide of battle turned again. They tore into the new wave of victims in a mad battle frenzy, splitting skulls, ripping limbs, morningstars against clubs and spears, fearless, bloodthirsty human killing machines against terror-crazed bandits. Now, keening above the cries of the stricken, Vanderling heard the Killers' terrible, massed battle-chant: 'KILL! KILL! KILL! KILL!'

Man, you can just about time it by the sound! Vanderling thought. When you hear 'em chanting loud and clear, louder than the screams, it's just about over, just about time to . . .

Vanderling motioned to the 'heads leading the three hundred regulars. The 'heads moved the troops into position just behind him. He took one last clear look at the battle. The bandits had about had it. The Killers were thrashing around in a heap of bodies, like cats in a garbage dump, cracking the skulls of supine bodies, stomping, milling about virtually at will, finishing off the wounded. It was hard to get a body count, but it seemed like the Killers had paid for their kicks according to plan – scores of black-clad bodies lay among the dead bandits, dozens of other Killers were minus arms or legs or both as the 'heads, lying prone in the tall grass, stood off and continued to take pot shots here and there with their snipguns.

It was time for the *pièce de résistance*.

Vanderling made his way to the rear of the long, thin

224

skirmish line spread out on the lip of the depression like a picket fence. 'Forward – yo!' he shouted.

The line of troops trotted quickly forward towards the waning battle. Vanderling trotted behind the screen of troops, clutching his snipgun. Fish in a goddamn barrel, he thought. Just like fish in a barrel . . .

The skirmish line, an open semicircle now, reached the position about forty yards from what was left of the battle, where six 'heads crouched in the grass, firing their snipguns. The line of men advanced another five yards, and the 'heads ducked behind it to Vanderling's side.

'Drop and fire!' Vanderling roared.

The semicircle of men dropped to one knee, opened up with their rifles. Vanderling and ten 'heads, all armed with snipguns, crouched behind the line in a tight group at the focus of the semicircle.

The first volley caught the battle-crazed, preoccupied Killers almost totally by surprise. Scores of them went down. Then the rest charged right at the massed fire.

There was a short moment or two of confusion, rapid gunfire, and death. The remnants of the Killer force charged, firing their rifles as they came, perhaps ninety or a hundred of them, determined to close with the guerrillas at all costs, madly confident of their superiority in hand-to-hand combat, no matter what the odds. Men fell on their faces all along the guerrilla line as bullets tore into them. Vanderling dived on his face, hid behind a body . . .

But the Killers were charging straight into the focus of a withering, shallow crossfire. Twenty yards away, fifteen, twelve, and Vanderling, peeping up over his human bulwark, saw that the screaming Killers, their lips flecked with blood-reddened foam, were going down like flies as they passed between the horns of the crescent, took volley after volley from three sides.

Then they were only ten yards away from the centre, maybe fifty of 'em, tossing aside their guns and unshipping morningstars, waving them above their heads, howling like the hounds of hell.

'NOW!' Vanderling shouted, rising to one knee, pressing the trigger of his snipgun, fanning it in narrow little arcs.

On either side of him, five herogyn-heads, eyes blazing, arose to firing position, fired their snipguns at point-blank range into the pack of screaming Killers.

It was over in an instant. One moment, fifty black-clad men charged forward, howling, waving morningstars. The next, they were fifty headless torsos that stumbled forward for a few steps, then fell among their still-rolling heads, like a flock of mad turkeys that had barrelled straight into the blade of an enormous knife.

Screaming wordlessly, his hands convulsed like claws around his snipgun, Vanderling kept firing, raking the twitching bodies, cutting them into chunks of bleeding meat, slicing the chunks into smaller pieces till all was an amorphous mass of featureless, bloody flesh.

A long minute later, he stood up, the warm flush of adrenalin filling him with a pleasant languor. Before him was a grotesque pile of loose arms, legs, chunks of bodies, heads, lying in a great pool of bright red blood. Two hundred or so soldiers of the People's Army stood up dazedly, then cheered. The bodies of scores of others did not move.

Fifty yards away was a mess that utterly dwarfed the carnage at his feet – a great garbage heap of bodies, pulped bleeding corpses, Killers and bandits alike at last united by an ocean of congealing blood. Here and there a body – Killer or bandit – twitched, screamed, or moaned and was stilled by a fusillade of shots from the watching soldiers.

Vanderling smiled, a deep smile of satisfaction, as he surveyed his handiwork. Another easy turkey shoot! The Killers were all washed up, they were losing thousands of men like this all over the planet. Soon, very soon, they would have to try a retreat, pull back to Sade with their tails between their legs.

Vanderling laughed. Then would come the best turkey shoot of all!

'War as a spectator sport,' Sophia O'Hara said as she eyed the scene in the lifeboat's viewscreen dubiously. 'What won't they think of next? Peanuts, anyone? Programme? Can't tell the good guys from the baddies without a programme . . .'

The viewscreen showed a thick column of trucks snaking across a wide plain towards the horizon, trucks filled with Killers, more Killers on foot, herding Meatanimals, prisoners, a gigantic convoy heading east towards Sade, as Fraden kept the 'boat circling high above the massive movement of men and machines, well out of rifle range.

'You didn't *have* to come along . . .' Fraden muttered, knowing that it was a half-lie, knowing that she could no longer bear being in the guerrilla camp alone, anywhere on the planet except by his side for more than a few hours. Knowing too, that he wanted her here, wanted her with him to share this moment of triumph.

'Wouldn't have missed it for the world,' she said drily. 'Nothing like a woman who shows some interest in her man's job, I always say. Or as Count Dracula put it to his somewhat reluctant progeny, "A family that preys together, stays together."'

Fraden made a choking sound, somewhere between a

laugh and a groan. 'I'm not sure you don't really mean that,' he said.

'Neither am I,' she answered. 'This planet seems to bring out the Transylvanian blood in everyone. Bullethead . . . I won't even mention him, we've just eaten. And you trading the lives of your own men for Killers as if they were marbles – six greens for a black. And here *I* am, getting my jollies out of watching . . . what did you call it, the Long Retreat? On top of everything else, you've developed a revolting penchant for speaking in capital letters.'

'Just a passing allusion to the great Chicom march to Yunan in one of those endless twentieth-century wars,' Fraden said somewhat archly. 'The circumstances are somewhat similar.' He pointed to the viewscreen. The road that wound across the plain, around hills, through patches of jungle, was black with Killers and trucks, virtually from horizon to horizon. Far away on the western horizon, a pall of smoke hung in the air over the jungle where one of the innumerable little harrying forces had hit the convoy. It had been a Long Retreat for the Killers, indeed, far longer, no doubt, than they had bargained for . . .

'There it is, Soph,' he said. 'The fruits of nearly a year on this lousy mudball! Every Killer on the planet in one big column hightailing it for Sade with their tails between their legs! It sure as hell took enough to send Moro the message. We must've knocked off better than a hundred estates, wiped out two or three thousand Killers before he finally got it through his fat head that if he tried to keep the Killers in the countryside, he'd have no men left at all in a few more months. And so we have – the Long Retreat.'

Although it made him uneasy to admit it, Fraden

realized that the retreat had been a lot more cleverly planned than he had anticipated. Instead of trying to pull the scattered Killer units back to Sade piecemeal, as he had hoped he would, Moro had made the calculated risk of sending a big relief column, better than fifteen hundred men and a thousand trucks, out into the countryside from Sade and had actually been smart enough to evacuate the Killers backwards. That is, the relief column had picked up the Killers holed up nearest Sade first, used those reinforcements to beef up the force as it moved deeper into guerrilla territory, growing ever larger and stronger as it got further from Sade, so that by the time it had reached the most isolated, most vulnerable Killer groups deep within the Free Republic, it was a huge force of nearly eight thousand men, heavily armed, well-motorized, and impossible to engage in a frontal battle.

It had been a big gamble – it meant, in effect, that most of the Killers had to make the long march twice: once out into the countryside and then back. But Moro had apparently realized that the game was worth the candle. The size and strength of the mobile force had enabled them to take back great quantities of grain, Meatanimals and prisoners with them, enough provisions for a long, long siege, if the bulk of the force got back to Sade intact.

And it looked like they just might pull it off. The column had been on the march back to Sade for a week now, and while Willem had been able to pick off perhaps as many as five hundred Killers in scores of little ambushes, there had been just no way to safely launch an all-out, crippling attack.

But now, with the column nearing Sade, there would be one lone opportunity to smash the huge convoy and forestall a long, uncertain stalemated siege of the city.

Fraden accelerated the 'boat to full speed, flew due east

until the outskirts of Sade were visible above the wide, level plain on which the city was built. Here, the road passed through a long, shallow canyon between two ridges before debouching upon the broad plain. It was the only spot on the whole route that was ideal for a really big ambush.

Fraden dropped a thousand feet, put the 'boat on hover above the canyon.

'Look down there, Soph,' he said, pointing to the ridges on either side of the road. Just beyond the crestlines, out of sight from the road, the far slopes of both flanking ridges were black with men. Six thousand on each side of the canyon, twelve thousand regulars, better than half of the People's Army. To reach the city, the long column would have to fight its way through that gauntlet; there was no way around for the trucks. It looked like a perfect, deadly trap.

But somehow, as he waited high above the trap, as the minutes ticked by, Fraden felt his confidence gradually evaporating. The trouble was that this was just *too* perfect a spot for an ambush. The Killers would *have* to anticipate it. Still, just what could they . . .?

'Look!' he shouted. 'Here they come!' A thin line of trucks and men on foot had emerged from the tangle of woods at the western end of the valley and were making their way along the road that led through the jaws of the trap towards Sade. A thin, vulnerable line that inched halfway through the valley, two-thirds . . . Willem's plan was to allow the forward salient of the column to actually reach the eastern mouth of the valley, then snap the jaws of the trap, forcing the bulk of the column to fight its way through a valley-long gauntlet of fire and plugging the entire valley with massive confusion . . .

But there was something wrong! The line of trucks and

230

men that even now was reaching the eastern mouth of the valley was too thin, was just a trickle, and . . .

Suddenly, the inner slopes of the defile all along the valley were filled with guerrillas, two solid waves of men converging on the roadway. The slopes blossomed in thousands of tiny pinpoints of fire and smoke. The Killers in the roadway began to go down; trucks exploded into flames as scores of bullets tore into their gastanks.

According to plan, Willem halted the guerrillas on the left side of the road which he commanded about fifty yards from the roadbed; Gomez's men on the right came to a somewhat more ragged halt at roughly the same distance from the road. The guerrillas formed two long parallel lines of fire all along the road, less than a hundred yards apart, with reserves backed up scores deep halfway up the hillsides.

The Killers caught in the valley did not even have time for one futile berserker charge at the two solid walls of men that lined the road. They were wiped out in seconds by two valley-long solid fists of lead. The gauntlet was set, the column would keep coming, and . . .

But Fraden saw that no more trucks or men were entering the valley. The firing was petering out in confusion. What – ?

'Oh no,' Fraden cried, for he realized what the Killers were doing even as it happened.

There was a terrible roar, a roar so loud that Fraden could feel it through the 'boat's hull, a thousand feet above the valley. A huge wall of Killers on foot erupted from the woods at the western end of the valley, a great wide front only a hundred men deep. The wall of Killers burst into the valley, filling the entire mouth, extending up both slopes clear to the ridgelines.

Like a vast piston, the wide, shallow wave of Killers

roared through the valley, enveloping it from crestline to crestline, a solid advancing wall of black bodies.

Fraden cursed as he realized that the Killers had fully anticipated Willem's tactic. They had sent in a column to spring the trap, force Willem to commit himself, but they had held their main force, nearly eight thousand men, back. Instead of trying to push trucks and men through the narrow defile past the guerrilla gauntlet, they had sent most of their force, at least six thousand men on foot, into the valley on a wide front, a front that was now flanking the guerrillas deployed lengthwise in the valley on both sides. Behind the screen of six thousand screaming Killers, the trucks, with their cargo of Meatanimals and supplies, were now advancing along the roadway.

'Pull back, you idiot, pull back!' Fraden yelled.

For the Killers, outnumbered two to one though they were, had in fact gained an irresistible advantage – they tore into the narrow, parallel lines of guerrillas in a great flanking front, smashed the lines into mindless confusion, flanked them, enveloped them on both sides, as they barrelled through the valley, a great, tightly packed piston of death.

On the right, Gomez's men were routed, fled mindlessly straight up the slope perpendicular to the Killers' charge, and perhaps fully a third of them, the third nearest the Killers, were overrun, split into hundreds of little vulnerable groups by the advancing right flank of the great Killer front, decimated as the Killers charged across the valley from ridge to ridge. They had reacted instinctively, fled up the slope where they were already outflanked, and their instincts had been disastrously wrong. Only the easternmost half of the long line managed to crest the ridge to safety before the Killers; the rest were hacked to bits.

On the left, Vanderling had somehow been able to maintain some semblance of order. His line of men was fleeing straight up the valley ahead of the Killers, a long, thin column retreating before the wide Killer front, and as they fled at top speed, the Killers were not gaining on them.

Vanderling was saving his men. The head of the guerrilla column reached the mouth of the valley, debouched on to the plain, rounded the edge of the ridge and doubled back down the next defile towards the eastern edge of the woods and safety, with the Killers now bursting out of the valley and on to the plain.

Fraden held his breath. Would they pursue the fleeing guerrillas, or . . .?

But the Killers, for once, were playing it safe. They fanned out on to the plain on both sides of the valley mouth, halted as the long stream of trucks passed between their now divided fronts and out on to the plain towards Sade.

When the last of the trucks had passed the valley mouth and was on the road across the plain to Sade, the Killers formed a wide, solid screen behind them, protecting their rear as they made for the city at top speed.

Numbly, silently, Fraden swooped the 'boat low over the valley, a valley littered with corpses – most of them guerrillas – and here and there a ruined truck.

He put the 'boat into a climb, then headed west, back towards the guerrilla camp. It was an utter disaster. Maybe two thousand Free Republic casualties – and for nothing. The Killer force, with its huge load of supplies, was now nearing Sade, virtually intact.

'Well, you can't win 'em all . . .' Sophia said wanly, saying anything to break the oppressive silence.

Fraden grunted. 'This is trouble,' he said grimly, 'big

trouble. It means a long siege of Sade. They've got enough men to make that damned Palace Compound impregnable, and they've got enough food for months. A waiting game . . . Christ, who wants to play a waiting game? How long can we wait 'em out with an army of goddamned bloodthirsty Sangrans and hopped-up hero-gyn-heads?'

Five goddamned weeks! Bart Fraden thought as he left his hut to survey the guerrilla camp, for lack of anything more positive to do. Five weeks of stalemate!

Moro was playing it cool, all right. He had eight thousand Killers holed up in the Palace Compound, and with that kind of garrison force, the damned thing was impregnable. He had enough Meatanimals within the walls to last the few thousand remaining Brothers and himself for three, four, maybe even five months. And then there was the mess in Sade. Moro, damn him, was playing the guerrilla game in Sade. He made no attempt to hold the city, an attempt which would tie down thousands of Killers. All he needed from Sade was Sadians themselves to feed the Killers, and every once in a while the Killers would venture into the city, seize some Sadians, and then hole up in the Palace Compound again and sit tight. There wasn't even any point in trying to take Sade – the city was a nightmare of starvation, a no-man's land of petty cannibalism, where the only rule was that of the jungle and the only guarantee of safe conduct a gun. With the usual flow of dead victims from the Palace cut off, the Sadians had taken to filling the Public Larder with their own numbers, with the old, the diseased, the weak, anyone they could grab. Guerrillas and Killers alike ventured into the city in armed squads, but although either side could take it, neither could hold it – and who would want to? Both sides were playing a waiting game.

234

Fraden was waiting for the Brotherhood to run out of food, and as he surveyed his base camp, he knew all too well what the Prophet of Pain was waiting for. Moro might not be the brightest guy in the Galaxy, but he knew the Sangran people all too well.

Fraden gazed around the guerrilla camp and saw men lounging idly everywhere, sleeping, muttering among themselves, cleaning their guns. The camp had a sullen, brooding feeling to it; a camp filled with idle men, an army hungry for action, an army that was now held together largely by promises and the threat of force. Yeah, Moro knew his Sangrans!

The Sangran peasants were still with him. He was in solid there – he was the Liberator, the Hero, he had driven the Killers from the countryside, given them circuses if precious little bread. They would be on his side to the end – they had no other place to go. He had got them started on farming, he had wiped out the last of the bandits who had taken to raiding villages once there was no more Brotherhood property left to loot.

But the People's Army, he knew, as he knew Moro knew, was another matter. They had no one to fight, and they had guns. They had guns and there were no Killers to stop them if they decided that maybe they'd do better as bandits themselves, and they knew it. Moro's game was clear. If he could hold out long enough, the People's Army would mutiny, perhaps kill the off-worlders, degenerate into dozens of separate bands, finally into a leaderless horde. At that point, against bandits instead of an army, those eight thousand Killers would look mighty big indeed, and he could simply send them forth methodically to repacify the countryside, district by district if need be.

As long as the Brotherhood enclave existed, Fraden knew he could not disband the bulk of the People's Army and leave a small remnant as a police force. If only there were some way to take the Palace Compound . . . An all-out attack combined with a general uprising in Sade? Easy enough to ignite an explosion in the city, but how to focus its wrath on the Palace, keep it from being just a citywide orgy of looting, killing and mass cannibalism . . .?

It was so damned tantalizing. Victory was only one step away. Wipe out the Palace, he thought, and you can disband most of the People's Army, reduce it to manageable size.

The volunteers would surrender their guns to the 'heads if ordered to at snipgun point, just as their fear of the Killer-like 'heads with their fearsome off-world weapons was just about all that was keeping them in line now.

Fraden grimaced. That was another piece of nastiness. He had been forced to let Vanderling addict another five hundred men. The couple of hundred snipguns were rotated among the 'heads to give the illusion that they all had 'em, and the yokums were scared silly of the herogyn-heads, and the Big Slice. The 'heads would be utterly loyal as long as the herogyn held out.

Loyal to *Willem*, that was the bitch!

Willem was all too transparent. Sure, the five hundred new 'heads were needed to keep the army in line, but Fraden was reasonably sure that Willem had other ideas of how they might be used if an opportunity presented itself.

But Willem couldn't see past his own nose. In any showdown situation, Fraden knew it would be child's play to turn the whole planet against Willem and his 'heads. Let him plot! He's harmless, and it keeps him off the streets!

And speaking of the devil, here comes Willem now,

looking about as happy as a basset hound with a tooth-ache. What now? Fraden wondered gloomily.

'Don't tell me,' Fraden sighed. 'The snipgun energizers are all on the fritz. The army's all come down with bubonic plague. You've got a dose of the clap.'

'Worse,' Vanderling said dourly, shaking his head. 'Much, much worse.'

'Well?' said Fraden. 'Let's hear the happy news. Things just can't get *that* much worse.'

'Oh no?' Vanderling said. 'I just came back from the ship with the next six weeks' supply of herogyn. How much herogyn you think we got on the ship now? Go ahead, take a guess.'

'How the hell should I know?' Fraden snapped. 'You've been keeping track of that. I'm hardly in the mood for twenty questions!'

'*Nada*,' said Vanderling. 'Zero. Cleaned out. With no action and an extra five hundred 'heads to keep stoned almost all of the time . . . You dig? We've got enough goddamned Omnidrene to turn on five million elephants and not a bag of herogyn left. When this six weeks' supply runs out . . .'

He ran his finger across his throat.

Fraden shuddered. When the herogyn ran out, the seven hundred herogyn-heads would go plain ape! They'd make the Killers look like Rebecca of Sunnybrook Farm! They'd attack everything that moved, they'd kill till they dropped, and with the 'heads running wild the guerrillas would probably . . . *brrr!*

'Well, genius, when do you pull the rabbit out of your hat?' Vanderling said, half-sourly, half-imploringly. 'It better be quick.'

'I'm working on it,' Fraden muttered. 'Bet your ass, I'm working on it! Of course . . . we could play it safe and knock off the herogyn-heads right now. It'd be easy – just slip 'em a massive overdose . . .'

Vanderling's eyes narrowed, and Fraden could read his thoughts: Willem was not about to give up what he fancied as his ace in the hole.

'And then what?' Vanderling said. 'Without the 'heads, what happens to the army?'

Of course, there was no real answer to that one. There it was, the time limit he had been subliminally dreading. Wipe out the Brotherhood and the Killers in the next six weeks, or you've had it, boy! And even if you do wipe out the Killers, what then? The herogyn still runs out, the 'heads still go ape, the army still . . .

But . . . *but why wipe out the Killers?* Why, *Brother Bart?* The Killers were bred and conditioned to obey anyone in a Brother's robe, in the absence of Moro. And if the Brotherhood was destroyed, 'Brother Bart' would be the closest thing to a Brother left on the planet. It just might work. He just might be able to arrange it so that he would inherit the only really disciplined force on the planet – the Killers . . . and they could have their uses. But first, the Brotherhood would have to be destroyed. How to break the circle . . .?

'Well, Bart?' Vanderling said, breaking into Fraden's reverie. 'Looks like something's cooking in that head of yours.'

'Ah . . . nothing yet, Willem. Just . . . er . . . wool-gathering. But I'll come up with something, don't worry. Always have. I'm thinking, Willem, I'm always thinking.'

'I'm thinking too,' Vanderling said coldly. The way he said it made Fraden's back itch; he could all but feel the knife.

'Don't think too hard, Willem,' he muttered. 'Brain-strain can be mighty unhealthy. In severe cases, it's even been known to be fatal.'

238

Chapter 12

Six weeks to zero, Willem Vanderling thought as he walked towards his hut. Six weeks for Ma Vanderling's kid to come out on top, or . . .

Yeah, Bart's got it pegged pretty good, he thought. I've got the 'heads in my hip pocket – for another six weeks anyway – but every other Animal on this miserable mudball is loyal to Bart, that is if you can call these cruds loyal. Well whatever you called 'em – and you sure as hell could call 'em plenty – the Sangrans'd come down one hundred per cent on Bart's side in a showdown, and all I'd have would be my seven hundred 'heads. I know it, Bart knows it, and he knows that I know, so he thinks he's got me right where he wants me, doing his dirty work for him and playing second fiddle to Napoleon Fraden.

Yeah, Bart has it just about pegged. *Just about* . . . But just about's not going to be good enough if Willem Vanderling has anything to say about it.

Vanderling entered his hut. Trussed up in one corner, with Gomez guarding him closely, was a Killer, a Major by his stars, pretty high brass as the Killer hierarchy went. Two weeks ago, anticipating the needs of this moment, Vanderling had quietly ordered his most trusted 'heads to get him one live Killer officer. He had expected a lieutenant, a captain maybe, but the Killers were scraping the bottom of the barrel, and after months of fighting, the pyramidal Killer command structure was top-heavy with ranking officers. With the situation in Sade – Killer patrols, Fraden's agents, People's Army patrols all mingling in a chaotic no man's land – it had been no sweat for Gomez and a small squad to grab this Killer away from the patrol he had been leading, just a matter of being willing to sacrifice a few men to do it.

And now it was time for some real action! Vanderling studied the tightly bound and gagged Killer. He doesn't know it yet, but he's a lucky man.

'Okay, Gomez,' Vanderling said. 'I want to be alone with this crud. Prop him up in that chair by the table and then split. I'll call you when I need you.'

Gomez did as he was told, but he did it in sullen silence. Trouble is, Vanderling thought, that when I'm trying to stretch the herogyn this thin, they're too edgy to trust anyone, even me. Well, what the hell . . .

He reached into a footlocker, pulled out a bottle of herogyn, poured out two blue pills. Gomez stared at the pills greedily, almost menancingly.

'Okay, Colonel,' Vanderling said, dropping the pills into Gomez's outstretched palm, 'have yourself a ball. But before you take 'em, go get Jonson and have him wait outside.'

'Yessir,' Gomez grunted, and he left, rolling the pills in his palm in anticipation, all traces of suspicion gone from his face. Vanderling laughed. Enjoy it while you can, man! he thought. You won't be enjoying *anything* very long.

Vanderling sat down across the table from the Killer. Gingerly he reached over, undid the gag, pulled it away with a quick flick of his wrist – and the Killer's sharp teeth snapped shut on the empty air where his hand had been a moment before, as he had expected.

'Naughty, naughty,' Vanderling said. 'Better play it cool, pal. You and me are gonna be friends. I can do plenty for you, and you're gonna do something for me.'

240

The Killer stared up at him laconically. 'If you wish, I will do one thing for you, Animal,' he said evenly. 'Release me, and I promise you a quick, honourable death in personal combat, a Killer's death. Why take the risk of dying like an Animal? Pain Day is but two weeks away, and all Animals captured between now and then are to die in the Pain Day Pageant – a death with no honour at all. Release me now and die with honour, my word as an officer of the Prophet.'

Vanderling laughed good-naturedly. 'Play your cards right,' he said, 'and I'll release you, all right, and I'll get you a nice promotion from your boss in the bargain. But let's not get gruesome about it.'

The Killer was quiet, puzzled. Vanderling grinned. *This*, you weren't expecting, eh? he thought. Well don't worry man, you'll have lots of company before too long. A lot of people are in for some unpleasant surprises.

'I've got a job for you to do,' Vanderling said. 'You're gonna take a message to Moro. You tell him that Marshal Vanderling is interested in talking turkey; we can do some business together. You tell him that I'll meet him at midnight five days from now in . ./. let's see . . . Yeah! The Public Larder in Sade. And no funny stuff – I'll have five men with me all armed with snipguns and more watching the approaches. I want a parley and no tricks.'

'Fool!' the Killer snarled, eyes suddenly blazing. 'To think that the Prophet is stupid enough to walk into such a trap! To think that I would be fool enough to carry such a message! I would be sent to the Stadium to die like an Animal on Pain Day for being part of your stupid scheme. Animal! Idiot!' The Killer seemed on the verge of flying into a mindless rage; his eyes rolled, his jaws began to work convulsively.

Vanderling cooled him with a quick slap across the

face. 'You shut up and listen!' he barked. 'It's no trap; it's all on the level. But you do have a point . . . Okay, here's the deal, safe for all concerned. Moro sends one Brother to meet me. He's allowed three Killers to keep him safe from those crazy Sadians, but no more. The Brother brings along a radio, see, and I deal direct with Moro that way. He's safe in his Palace. He's got nothing to lose by talking.'

The Killer Major seemed torn between contempt and curiosity. He eyes blazed hate, but they narrowed in thought.

'Why should Moro grant me an audience?' he snarled. 'Why should I bear your message and risk dying like an Animal? Why should the Prophet deal with you, even if I did give him your ridiculous message? Why – '

'Because you'll have *this*,' Vanderling said, reaching into a pocket and pulling out a small polybag of Omni-drene. 'Believe me, this'll get you an audience with the Big Cheese *muy pronto*. You tell him where you got it, and you tell him Marshal Vanderling can deliver a whole shipful of the stuff if he plays ball. I guarantee he'll be interested. And when the deal goes through, you'll be made a colonel . . . what the hell, I can afford to be generous – I'll make that part of my price: a colonelcy for you. What do you say to *that*?'

'What is in the bag?' the Killer said sharply.

'You know the stuff Brother Bart was passing out? The stuff your Brotherhood pals were busting themselves trying to make by torturing Animals till they're crazy and then bleeding 'em? The stuff they're dying for? Well, this is it . . . Omnidrene, and I'm offering Moro a mountain of the stuff, in return for . . . certain considerations.'

The Killer's eyes lit up, with hope this time, not rage. Yeah, he knew where Omnidrene was at, all right,

Vanderling thought. And who didn't want to live? And be a colonel? But the crud's still hesitating! Well, screw him!

'The clincher is,' he said evenly, 'that if you don't do as I say, I don't execute you, I drag you to the nearest village and turn you over to the Animals. You know what they've been doing to Killers, don't you? They're *mighty hungry* these days . . . How's *that* for an honourable death?'

The Killer's lips twitched, and he went pale. Even a Killer didn't feel so goddamned indifferent to being roasted alive and eaten. 'Very well,' the Killer Major said. 'I have no honourable choice. I will take your message to the Prophet.'

Vanderling stuffed the polybag into a pocket in the bound man's tunic.

Yessir, he thought, Bart has it all figured pretty well. But not well enough! The Sangrans'll back Bart against me all the way – as long as Bart's alive, that is.

But if Bart is killed, and killed by the Brotherhood at that . . . Well, the only candidate left for President of the Free Republic and Grand High Muckety-Muck will be yours truly, Willem Vanderling.

With Bart dead – and what a nice martyr *he'll* make – and the People's Army and the rest of the Animals behind me, I can knock off the 'heads before the herogyn runs out and still control the planet.

And the kicker is that the same bit that gets rid of Bart will also get rid of Moro and Company, leaving me as sole proprietor of this crummy mudball. Two tough birds killed with one stone – in fact, they'll be knocking off each other!

Maybe the thing to do is crown myself the new Prophet of Pain, Vanderling mused. Why not? Moro had a sweet setup going for himself till we showed up – do what you want, kill who you want, eat what you want, and have the whole goddamned planet sit still for it all because you were the little tin god. Why screw around, conning the yokums like Bart? Why not just lay it on the line – I'm the boss and anyone that looks at me cross-eyed gets a one-way trip to the arena?

Besides, it had a nice ring to it – Brother Willem, Prophet of Pain, and Lord High Poobah of Sangre! Yeah, it had real class!

Vanderling stuck his head out the doorway and yelled for Jonson.

'Take this bird to the outskirts of Sade and let him go.' Vanderling ordered.

Jonson blinked his hollow, bloodshot eyes in disbelief.

'Yeah, yeah, I know it sounds pretty weird,' Vanderling said. 'But don't strain your brain thinking. I got a nice little plan going here – final victory by Pain Day. There'll be a double dose of herogyn for you when you get back, so think of *that* and move your ass!'

Vanderling led his men through the nearly empty streets of Sade in semi-darkness. There were no electric lights in the Animal sections of Sade; the narrow, filthy streets were illuminated only by the stars in the moonless sky and the occasional flickering orange light of fires glowing through the doorways of the brooding wooden hovels.

Vanderling and his five herogyn-heads all carried snip-guns. He saw three near-naked Sandians stalking them across the shadowy street, four more about twenty yards behind. He raised his snipgun, catching a glint of firelight from a nearby hovel on its barrel, and the Sadians, now aware of the weapons carried by the men they were stalking, slinked hurriedly off down side streets.

Yeah, he thought with a grin, they still got enough

sense to leave armed men alone. Armed men were about the only things in Sade that weren't considered fair game. That was why the streets were so empty at night. Anyone out at night looking for a meal stood an even chance of ending up on some starved family's dinner table – a family, that is, if the old man hadn't gobbled up his wife and kiddies yet, as some of 'em already had.

Starving or not, a few lessons from snipguns had taught 'em to leave armed guerrillas alone. By now they knew that anyone who attacked a guerrilla would end up in the Public Larder himself.

Yeah, Vanderling thought as they walked through the silent, empty streets, their boots casting up harsh echoes, it's dog eat dog all right – or Animal eat Animal. The only place they kept their stinking hands off each other was the Public Larder. Anyone who died – with or without help – was dumped in the Larder, and it was all that kept the local yokums from complete starvation. They killed anyone who tried anything in the Larder out of self-preservation, so the place was the closest thing to a Sanctuary, and hence the logical place for this little negotiation.

Vanderling and his men rounded a corner, and a big, dirty, windowless barn of a building loomed across the street before them. It had one big open doorway, and the flickering orange light from within revealed the vague shapes of a few dozen Sadians inside. Vanderling heard muffled sawing sounds, dull thunks, men haggling shrilly – the Public Larder.

Vanderling gathered his men around him – Jonson, Gomez, three other herogyn-heads. 'Okay, Gomez,' he said. 'You go in and case the joint. Now remember, you guys, when we go in, you keep your mouths shut. This is a trick to kill the Brothers, and I'm gonna be telling some

245

mighty fancy lies. Some of 'em you won't like. Just remember, it's all a double-cross on Moro. Okay, Gomez, get going!'

They waited across the street as Gomez entered the Larder. For a moment, the voices within seemed to quiet, then the haggling resumed. After a few tense minutes, Gomez emerged, trotted back across the empty, offal-strewn street.

'Well?' Vanderling grunted.

'Brother, three of y'Killers, couple dozen Animals,' Gomez said.

'Good enough,' said Vanderling. 'We go in. Gomez, take two men and clear those Animals out of there. Then you and Jonson'll guard me while I parley with the Brother. Keep your snipguns ready and your eyes on those Killers. Rest of you'll guard the doorway – it's the only way in or out. You see anything move outside, you give a yell. Now let's go!'

Gomez and two other 'heads crossed the street, entered the Public Larder. Vanderling heard orders being barked inside, shouts of protest, ugly murmuring, more orders, even more harshly delivered. Then, in twos and threes, sullen, gaunt men began to troop out of the Larder, greedily clutching chunks of raw meat, bloody arms, legs. Eyes darting suspiciously at everything around them – Vanderling, their fellows, the flickering shadows that danced in the dark, brooding streets – they slunk off, disappeared one by one down side streets, alleys, choked with garbage, ordure, splintered white bones.

Vanderling waited till Gomez appeared in the doorway, gave him the all-clear signal. It wouldn't do at all for Animals to see Marshal Willem Vanderling, their next President, palavering with a Brother.

The interior of the Public Larder was one huge, foul-smelling room, lit by a circle of naked torches that ran around the wooden walls far below the shadowy high ceiling. Piled against the far wall was a large mound of human corpses, grey, naked, scarred, men, old women, children; limbs and torsos jammed together, intertwined, as if frozen in the midst of some unimaginable, obscene orgy.

Heavy, rough-hewn wooden tables were scattered over the grey stone floor of the Larder. Many of the tables held whole corpses, some with limbs already hacked away, some intact. Others were piled with raw arms, legs, unidentifiable cuts of meat – ghastly butcher shop displays. Bloody knives and cleavers lay on every table.

The tables, the floor, even the far wall clear up to the seven-foot level, were stained a deep, deep umber-brown with a thick crust of old dried blood.

Under a flickering torch along the left wall, four men sat on stools at one of the tables. A body lay sprawled on the stone floor directly by the table; the fresh blood had been wiped away, leaving a drying smear on the scarred wood of the table top, where a big bloody cleaver still lay next to a small radio transceiver.

Vanderling approached the table, Jonson and Gomez, snipguns at the ready, a pace behind him. He saw that three of the men were tense-looking Killers. The fourth was dressed in a black robe, and in the orange torchlight, Vanderling could see heavy wrinkles and folds in the loose flesh of his face, the old-elephant look of a fat man who has recently lost many pounds. His small blue eyes darted from focus to focus like those of a bird. Brother-whoever-he-was was in bad shape and scared stiff.

Vanderling glanced around at the pile of corpses, the half-butchered carcasses on the tables, the cleaver gleaming wetly on the table before the Brother.

He laughed. A goddamned butcher shop! Not a bad place to carve up a planet, he thought as he sat down facing the Brother as Gomez and Jonson stood flanking him.

'I'm Field Marshal Willem Vanderling, Commander in Chief of the People's Army of the Free Republic of Sangre,' he said with half-sardonic grave formality.

'You're a filthy ringleader of the stupid Animals,' the Brother shrilled, the fear on his face turning to disgusted scorn. 'Say whatever you came to say and be done with it. You will make no demands. You will state your wretched proposal to me and I will relay it to the Prophet. And be quick about it! The stink of the place oppresses me.'

'Screw you, Charlie!' Vanderling snapped. 'I'm running this show, and you'll do as you're told and like it, or . . .'

He gestured negligently, and Gomez and Jonson whipped their snipguns up to cover the Brother and his three Killers. The Killers started up off their stools, then slumped back. The Brother's bravado evaporated as he stared straight into the muzzles of two snipguns.

Vanderling smiled. 'Now that we've taken care of the formalities,' he said, 'suppose you get Fat Boy on that radio.'

'I – '

'Hop to it!' Vanderling roared. 'I've got the radio, and I'd just as soon add your carcass to that . . .' He pointed towards the contorted heap of bodies at the far wall.

The Brother went pale and began to fiddle with the radio. Crackles, sputters, hisses, then abruptly the heavy, oily voice of Moro came through loud and clear: 'Well, Brother Andrew, did the swine actually show up?'

Vanderling grabbed the radio, spoke into the microphone grid. 'This is the swine speaking, butterball. Suppose we leave personalities out of this. I don't like you and you don't like me, but there's someone else neither of us can take.'

'Which is?' Moro's voice said, echoing in the cavernous, empty room.

'Brother Bart,' Vanderling said. 'Bart Fraden.'

There was a long, pregnant silence. Vanderling wished the thing had a video hookup. Moro's face would be something to see now!

'Well, Moro?' Vanderling said. 'What happened to your big mouth?'

'It's your treachery, off-worlder,' Moro said. 'Obviously, like any Animal, you're quite willing to betray your own. Obviously, you want something from me, and just as obviously you fancy that you have something to offer in return. I'm waiting.'

'Beggars can't be choosy, eh, Moro?' Vanderling sneered. 'And don't bother trying to put *me* on, I know you're up against the wall – I put you there, remember? So here's the scoop. Fraden figures on getting rid of me as soon as he's finished you – which he will unless you play ball – and keeping the whole planet for his private playpen. Now I'm not the pig Bart is. I want the lion's share of this mudball, sure, but I'm willing to leave you with some turf of your own if you decide to co-operate – say, everything within a two-hundred-mile radius of Sade plus, maybe, a regular quota of slaves and Meatanimals.'

'You expect me to give you my planet?' Moro roared.

'Spread it on the ground and watch the flowers grow!' Vanderling said. 'You got no planet left to give and we both know it. What I'm offering you is ten times what you've got. You think you can double-cross me later and try to reconquer the rest of the planet, you're welcome to try. Call it a temporary truce – after we've got rid of Fraden, we can worry about settling things between us. But first things first. You follow me?'

'I'm still listening,' Moro said evenly. 'Your plan . . .?'

'Sweet and simple, man, sweet and simple! This Pain Day jazz I've been hearing about? What's all that?'

'Pain Day? I hardly see what Pain Day has to do with – ?'

'Of course you don't!' Vanderling said. 'But then, you're not too bright. Pain Day is like a national holiday, right? There's some kind of celebration in that Sadium, a pageant or something?'

'The great Pain Day Torture Pageant!' Moro said excitedly. 'The greatest day of the entire year – a masterful display of no less than a thousand subjects tortured to the ultimate. It is traditional to allow ten thousand Animals to share in the pleasure on this one day, a day of deep significance for all Sangre. Yes . . . we are looking forward to Pain Day, despite . . . despite the present unpleasantness.'

'Just what the doctor ordered,' Vanderling said. 'A perfect setup! You send a message to Fraden, tell him you're willing to surrender conditionally – safe passage off the planet for you and your Brothers. Then – '

'Never!' Moro roared, and the Brother and the Killers sat stunned. 'Unthinkable! We will never surrender! We – '

'Can it!' snapped Vanderling. 'Let me finish. You offer to surrender, see, but you insist on making a big production of it. You'll only surrender publicly, on Pain Day, in the Stadium, and Fraden must be there to accept your surrender personally. And then when we've got Fraden in the Stadium . . .'

'I see,' said Moro, and the Brother's face cracked a wan

250

smile. 'But even an Animal like Fraden couldn't be stupid enough to walk right into such an obvious trap.'

''Course not,' Vanderling said. 'Not unless he thought he had an edge. So we hand him the edge. You demand as a token of good faith that Bart must supply a couple thousand victims for the Torture Pageant, right? So Bart figures that's his edge – he'll double-cross you and those two thousand men will be armed guerrillas.'

'You expect me to allow two thousand armed hostile troops within the Palace Compound!' Moro screamed.

'Hold your horses!' Vanderling said. 'Number one, you've got more than enough Killers to pack the Stadium and take good care of any two thousand troops. Just keep most of 'em out of uniform so it won't look obvious. Number two, you search 'em before you let 'em in – I'm the military commander, remember, and I'll make sure their weapons are empty. You can check on it. Besides, six, seven thousand Killers against two thousand of our boys . . . Come to think of it, they can't very well smuggle in guns anyway; it'll have to be knives. You afraid of a couple thousand Animals with knives with all those Killers around? Bart'll take the chance; he's a gambler, and he'll figure surprise is on his side. So you get Fraden, and two thousand of my men as a bonus. It's a piece of cake, Moro, a piece of cake.'

'It should work . . .' Moro muttered, 'but why should I trust you?'

'Don't you dig? I'm setting it up so you don't *have* to trust me. Six thousand Killers with guns and two thousand guerrillas with knives. And I'll be right there, where you can get at me. What can you possibly lose?'

Of course it looks like I'll have to trust *you*, Fat Boy, Vanderling thought. But don't sweat that . . .

'I find it hard to trust an enemy who seems to trust me,' Moro said shrewdly.

'I got no choice,' Vanderling said. 'I get rid of Fraden or Fraden gets rid of me. Besides, I got some pretty good insurance of my own . . . Or are you forgetting that little present I sent you?'

'*The Omnidrene!*' Moro cried shrilly. Across the table, Vanderling could see the Brother's little eyes light up greedily. 'There really is more Omnidrene? I thought it merely a trick to – '

'Hundreds of pounds of the stuff,' Vanderling said. 'More than you can use in five lifetimes. And that's my insurance, 'cause you don't get one ounce till Fraden's dead and I'm safely in the outback. Then you get it *all*. What do you say? Deal?'

After only a short pause the voice on the radio said, 'Why not? You seem to have . . . thought of everything. We complete the transaction, and then . . . then perhaps we deal with each other.'

'Fair enough,' Vanderling said. 'We work together till Pain Day. Get your end rolling, and I'll . . . work on mine. Out.'

Without a word to the bemused Brother, Vanderling arose, motioned to his men, and walked swiftly to the doorway, with Gomez and Jonson trailing him with stunned uncomprehending looks on their faces. Vanderling bit his lower lip as he walked past corpse-laden tables and skirted puddles of half-dried blood. His upper torso was shaking convulsively.

Finally, when he and Gomez and Jonson and the sentries he had stationed at the doorway were alone in the dark, silent street, Vanderling broke into gales of laughter.

'Moron!' he roared. 'Oh, what a schmuck! Hook, line and Omnidrene!'

Yeah, the Prophet of Pain thought he had pulled a fast one, didn't he! Sure, go along till Bart was kaput, then grab me, torture me to get the Omnidrene, kill me, and back to business as usual. What a dumb greaseball!

He saw that the 'heads were staring at him, muttering among themselves, fingering their snipguns uncertainly.

'Stow it, boys!' he said, still half-laughing. 'You don't get the picture? Six thousand Killers in the Stadium to wipe out Bart and the victims? So how many does that leave guarding the Compound wall? Gomez, you're gonna have the whole bloody People's Army waiting on Pain Day. Nearly twenty thousand men! While most of the Killers are tied up in the Stadium, you'll storm the front gate, get our men inside, knock off whatever's guarding the outside of the Stadium, bust in, and . . .'

'Kill y'Killers!' Gomez cried. 'Kill y'Brothers! Kill y'Prophet! Kill – '

'You got it!' Vanderling said. 'Save your yelling for Pain Day.'

Of course, there was still one more angle to this neat little triple-cross, he thought. While our boys are wiping out the Killers, there'll be enough confusion for me to take care of Bart – maybe toss him to the Killers. That would touch all the bases, all right. Bart Fraden, the Liberator of Sangre, fell today in the final battle. Hearts and flowers, folks, hearts and flowers! The President is dead – long live the President!

And there was only one little loose end left to tie up.

'Come on boys, back to camp,' he said. 'Gotta let our Peerless Leader in on our little scheme, right?'

Too much, man! Vanderling thought gleefully. It was all just too damned much!

Chapter 13

When Vanderling had finally finished, Sophia was shaking her head in a combination of disbelief, anger, and so it seemed to Bart Fraden, no little amusement. As she opened her mouth to let fly some verbal barrage at Vanderling, who sat across the table from both of them with his coarse, tough face a ludicrous mask of small-boy innocence and satisfaction, Fraden shot her a quick, definitive 'cool' look, then turned to face Vanderling again, shook his head slowly.

'I hear it, Willem,' he said, 'but I just don't believe it. Tell me again, once over lightly.'

'What's so hard to dig?' Vanderling said earnestly. 'It's a perfect setup. I got Moro thinking I'm double-crossing you, which sets us up to double-cross *him*. The two thousand victims you're supposed to supply will all be armed, dig?'

Fraden moaned. 'As a conspirator, Willem,' he said, 'you leave much to be desired. Do you really suppose that *Moro* trusts *you*? How in blazes do you expect to smuggle rifles, or anything else into the Stadium on semi-naked Sangrans?'

'You don't get it, man,' Vanderling said. 'Sure Moro don't trust me. Sure we couldn't really smuggle weapons in. But I foxed *Moro* into taking care of that. I told him that the only way you would fall for *our* double-cross was if you thought *you* were doing the double-crossing. Remember, he doesn't know that I'm really working with *you*. He thinks that you'll think you'll have the element

254

of surprise, so he's gonna *let you* smuggle knives in on the victims to suck you in – because *his* surprise is that the Stadium is gonna be packed with six thousand or so Killers in mufti. He thinks that will take care of you and the Animals with the knives easy enough, and then he can double-cross *me* by capturing me and torturing me into bringing down the ship with the Omnidrene. It's a gas – he's so busy double-crossing both of us that he doesn't see that we're pulling a fast one on *him*. Sure, the Killers will take care of the boys with the knives, but most of 'em will have to be inside the Stadium to do it, and it'll make for plenty of confusion. If we time it right, we have the whole damned People's Army attack the skeleton force guarding the Compound while it's all going on – and goodbye Killers, goodbye Moro, goodbye Brotherhood.'

Fraden leaned back torpidly, suppressed a laugh. How many of the holes in this juvenile scheme are Willem's ridiculous attempt to put over on me? he wondered. And how many are just sheer stupidity? Still, if you gave clowns like Willem and Moro enough rope, they'd be sure to strangle each other . . . This mess had possibilities.

'And goodbye us!' Fraden said. 'Okay, so all this hugger-mugger just may let us bust into the Stadium with the whole army. So the Killers will be completely occupied with what's going on inside the Stadium . . . But what *is* going on inside? What's to prevent all those Killers from just bumping the both of us off on the spot?'

Vanderling's jaw fell. 'Uh . . . er . . .' he spluttered.

Well, well, well, Fraden thought. So *that* part of it *was* sheer stupidity, after all. The idiot's so busy double-crossing everyone in sight that he was going to walk into the most obvious trap of all himself – and that's what always happens when a man steps out beyond his depth. Three blind mice . . . see how they run!

'I see you weren't thinking that far,' Fraden said. 'Well maybe we can make this half-assed scheme of yours work anyway. It's all a matter of timing. We need a margin of safety between the time the fun starts in the Stadium and the time our boys break in and take control of the situation. Five, ten minutes at the very most . . .'

'Yeah . . .' Vanderling muttered, befuddled at having lost the initiative. 'That'd do it. But how . . .?'

'Even Moro couldn't expect me to walk into something like that without some kind of personal bodyguard. A hundred men or so wouldn't put him up tight – he's not thinking in terms of an outside attack, so he'll figure his six thousand Killers will have all the time in the world to do us in. So why should he object to a hundred-man bodyguard that could only keep us from being killed for ten or fifteen minutes?'

'Hey, yeah!' Vanderling exclaimed. 'A hundred 'heads would do it! I mean we should use 'heads, because they're the most disciplined men we've got, right?'

Oh, brother! Fraden thought. A mind as deep as a saucer of milk. *Your* 'heads, eh, Willem? *They all ran after the farmer's wife . . .*

'Why not?' Fraden said. *She cut off their tails with a carving knife . . .*

'Then we'll go ahead and do it?'

'If I can talk Moro into granting us the bodyguard,' Fraden said. 'Start the preparations anyway.'

'Right,' Vanderling said, rising, heading for the door. 'Long live the Free Republic, eh?' he said, grinning over his shoulder. *Did you ever see such a sight in your life . . .?* 'Long live . . . the President,' Vanderling said, and was gone.

'*As three blind mice,*' Fraden muttered under his breath.

As soon as Vanderling was out of earshot, Sophia O'Hara exploded. 'Bart, you can't be serious! You can't be so – '

'Ye gods and little fishes!' Fraden interrupted, laughing. 'Give me credit for being a *little* smarter than the average baboon, Soph! Of course, he's planning a double-cross – or a triple-cross, if you want to get technical, since he's double-crossing Moro too. So, of course, we quadruple-cross him!'

'Double-cross . . . triple-cross . . . quadruple-cross! Gak! You've lost me, oh Peerless Leader. What the hell's going on in that warped little mind of yours?'

'Shall we unravel it one double-cross at a time?' Fraden said jauntily. 'Moro and Willem cooked up a plan to double-cross me, kill me, and somehow split the planet between them. So far a piece of treachery of classic simplicity. So of course double-cross number two – Moro's – is to kill Willem as well as me and come out on top. Follow so far?'

'Even old Bullethead seems to have seen through *that* one . . .' Sophia said. 'But . . . oh, I get it! Chrome-dome figured on that double-cross and double-crossed Moro by telling you and setting up the attack on the Compound!'

'You'll make a Machiavelli yet!' Fraden said approvingly. 'So far, it's as simple as a game of three-dimensional chess. But now comes the finesse, or so Willem fancies it. Because he's set up a triple-cross – he double-crosses Moro, using me, wipes out the Killers and the Brotherhood, and then, in the confusion, somehow gets rid of me. Our little bodyguard will be *his* herogyn-heads. Dig? He figures that after the dust clears, everyone's dead but him.'

'I'm getting a headache,' Sophia said. '*Won't* all this come out his way?'

Fraden laughed. 'You're forgetting the quadruple-cross,' he said. 'Sometimes the easiest thing to do is let your enemies concoct the plot and then just pull a couple of aces out of your sleeve at the last moment. Saves brain-strain. And I've got *two* aces in the hole. First of all, with all the Brothers dead, and me technically a Brother, I may just be able to use whatever Killers are left . . .'

'That's a pretty long shot to gamble your life on!' Sophia said, her lower lip quivering. 'I couldn't stand it if . . . Er, after all, it's probably *my* life too . . .'

'Two aces,' Fraden said, holding up two fingers. 'Count 'em, *two*.'

'And just what is this second strategic gem? A pocket fusion bomb? A bulletproof vest? Clean living?'

Fraden laughed. 'Nothing so esoteric as . . . *clean living*,' he said. 'It's nothing any more arcane than the good citizens of Sade themselves!'

Fraden stared across the table, past the radio transceiver, at the sallow, half-smiling Brother and his four nervous-looking Killers. Apparently Brother Andrew was in on it all, he thought, but these Killers aren't. No wonder they're uptight. Here they are in the middle of the enemy camp, and they've just heard their little tin god offer to surrender!

'Well?' Moro's voice boomed, impatiently, over the radio.

'Now let's see if I've got all this straight,' Fraden said into the microphone grid. 'You'll surrender on condition that I grant you and your Brothers safe passage off the planet and send for the necessary ships? But I've got to formally accept your surrender in the Stadium on Pain Day. That sounds just fine and dandy to me, but what's

258

this business about me supplying two thousand victims for this Torture Pageant thing?'

'We shall seal the treaty with the greatest Pain Day Torture Pageant in all history!' Moro said. 'Since it shall be the last Torture Pageant that the Brotherhood will enjoy, we will go all out to make it the best ever. I promise you that on this Pain Day, the art shall reach its zenith! Do not forget that the Animals, no matter what the . . . situation, expect a great treat on Pain Day – it is the only opportunity they have to stand on the other side of the Great Choice, to give Pain and receive Pleasure. If you plan to rule Sangre, it would not be wise to disappoint them on the first day of your rule. Besides, think of your own pleasure! I promise you an exhibition the like of which – '

Fraden fought hard to suppress his mirth. Moro had it all ass-backwards! I'm supposed to need those 'victims' there, not him! I should be talking *him* into it. But the swine is so hot to have a big torture-party that he's forgetting why he's supposed to 'let' me supply the victims in the first place. Some plotter!

'Okay, Moro,' he said. 'It sounds like so much fun that you've talked me into it. It's a deal. Just one minor detail – as President of the Free Republic, I should of course be permitted an . . . er, honour guard. Four, five hundred men should do nicely.'

'What! Out of the question!'

'I don't get it, Moro,' Fraden said slowly. 'Why not? You're not planning some trick, are you? After all, you've got nothing to worry about – it's all on your turf. Unless you're pulling a fast one, you've got no reason to refuse me – '

'Er . . . perhaps a token number,' Moro broke in hurriedly. 'I have no objection to, say, fifty men.'

Fraden was having trouble deciding who was more transparent, Moro or Vanderling.

'A full hundred men or no deal,' he said. 'After all, I'm the President of the Free Republic of Sangre. Without at least a modest hundred-man honour guard, I'd look like a piker.'

'Very well,' Moro said grudgingly. 'I'll not quibble.'

'Very sensible,' Fraden said. 'See you on Pain Day. Out.'

Brother Andrew got up, led his Killers out of the hut with the look of a hungry cat about to devour a particularly dull canary.

My, my, my! Fraden thought when he had left. I'm surrounded by sharpies and assassins! Everyone's out to take advantage of poor little old me. And the old Romans used to throw lions to Christians!

Yessir, all *does* come to him who sits and waits. Willem and Moro have busted themselves conniving a whole series of Byzantine plots. Sure saves me a lot of effort. All I have to do now is make one little minor adjustment in the whole can of worms, and by the time Pain Day's over, Willem and Moro will have neatly connived themselves into oblivion, and I'll be in the catbird seat.

He laughed aloud. With enemies like *these,* he thought, who needs friends?

The deep red Sangran sunset seemed to be like some heavy liquid, bathing the grubby huts, the filthy, narrow streets of Sade in dark venous blood, transmuting the streets and hovels and alleyways into a grotesque landscape of burgundy highlights and long, brooding black shadows. In the waning red light, the scuttling shapes of the occasional scrawny Sadians in the half-deserted streets seemed like furtive, shy vermin of the night, figures of cowardly, ghoulish menace.

Bart Fraden shivered, despite the omnipresent heat, glanced to either side of him at the six guerrillas guarding him with snipguns, and cursed his over-active imagination.

But as he loped hurriedly down the offal-strewn streets, past the open doorways of hovels where lemur-eyed women, tight-lipped men, hollow-chested children with hunger-bloated stomachs stared half-threateningly at him and his armed guard, he knew that the foreboding appearance of the city was more than a mere trick of the light. Sade was like some great festering pustule building up pressure for an explosion. His agents had told him this, before he had seen it with his own eyes, and he had temporized for more than a week, fed into the rumour mill the promise of some vague Armageddon on the impending Pain Day, but knowing all the while that if Pain Day was to be a victory instead of a disaster, he would have to go into the city, focus the ominous rumours he was spreading into a carefully timed moment of calculated mass action. To do that, to have a properly primed mob in the right place at just the right time, hundreds of Sadians would have to be given the word directly from the horse's mouth, to ensure sufficient redundancy so that the word that would finally be spread through the city would be spread accurately.

And with the city a jungle of starvation and solitary cannibalism, the only place he could find a crowd to speak to was the Public Larder.

It was not fear that Fraden felt as he moved past hovels, piles of garbage, lumps of ordure, grisly little heaps of cracked bones painted pale red by the twilight. There was little to fear – the Sadians were too cowardly to attack

261

armed men, and besides, the rumour mill had spread his mystique even to the city. And with Moro fully expecting to have his head three days hence, they would not be bothered by Killer patrols.

Yet still the city filled him with dread and loathing. The omnipresent filth, the odour of decay, the scattered people on the streets scuttling through the city like carrion-crabs in a boneyard, the tension that hung over the place so heavy you could taste it . . . And the horrid centre of it all, the bowels and stomach and cloaca of Sade – *the Public Larder*.

They reached the street on which the large, windowless building squatted, dark and gross in the twilight, and Fraden's stomach fell as he heard the sounds of many shrill voices haggling like fishwives' from within, the sounds of sawing bones, heavy blades on flesh and wood. His nerves stretched piano-wire thin as he saw dozens of scuttling figures silhouetted in the orange light streaming through the open doorway. As the rotten stench drifted across the street to him, he thought for one insane moment of giving the whole thing up, anything but going in *there* . . .

Don't be an imbecile! he told himself. You gonna throw away a whole planet over an upset stomach?

Gritting his teeth, with his guards surrounding him, Fraden loped quickly forward, and he was inside the Public Larder.

The place assailed him like a mailed fist; an avalanche of monstrosity engulfing him through all his senses. The cavernous, smoky room was filled with milling people, hundreds of them, and they all seemed to be screaming at each other at once. Heaped crazily against the far wall was an enormous pile of intertwined, naked human corpses, fish-eyes staring mockingly in all directions. A great pool of congealing blood oozed out from under the mound of bodies, dry and crusty at its periphery, scabbing the grey stone floor. Like a horde of ants, a steady stream of men were dragging corpses from the pile, diffidently unravelling the maze of intertwined, stiffening limbs, hauling the bodies over to great wooden tables where others proceeded to hack them to pieces with cleavers – Thunk! Thunk! *Thunk!* Knives sawed through bones with a horrible grating sound that set his teeth on edge. A sound that mingled with hundreds of raucous voices, all arguing over human arms, legs, choice cuts of meat, as each table was the centre of a wildly gesticulating clot of Sadians, many holding limbs and chunks of meat in one hand while grabbing for more with the other.

And the stink of the place! The rank odour of filthy sweating bodies, old blood, meat already beinning to go bad, a sickly, rotten stench that mingled with the smoke of the flickering torches to form a visible miasma of decay and loathsomeness.

Fraden felt acid vomit sting the back of his throat, choked it back with a terrific convulsion of his throat muscles. Fighting for control, he made his way behind his screen of guards to a table roughly in the centre of the room as curious Sadians clutched at him, jostled him, followed in his wake.

'Make way f'y'President!' one of his men shouted as they reached the table where, amidst a hollow-eyed little mob, a sallow-skinned Sadian was phlegmatically sawing the arm off the body of a withered old woman.

'Clear y'table!' the guerrilla ordered, and a dozen Sadians clawed at the corpse, pulled it away to disappear into the large, tightly packed crowd that was beginning to coalesce around the table.

Shaking, weak-kneed, Fraden scrabbled to the table

263

top, stood in a shallow smear of blood, looked out over the sullen-eyed crowd, the tables littered with butchered and half-butchered bodies, the great pile of grey corpses . . .

He felt the spasms rising in his gut, closed his eyes tightly, trying to fight it off . . .

And in that moment, the murmurs of the crowd ceased, became a guttural, echoing chant: 'BART! BART! BART! BART!'

Fraden felt a moment of abysmal self-disgust, then steeled himself, consciously, purposefully, eyes still tightly shut, and gave himself forceably over to the chanting, the sound of his own name shouted by his people. He grabbed for the sound, clutched at it, slipped, and then he was riding it, above the offal, above the blood, above his own nausea, above all save the visceral, mindless glory of *his* name being chanted by *his* people on *his* planet in the universe of which *he* was the centre . . . Mine! Mine! Mine!

'BART! BART! BART! BART! BART! BART! BART!'

'He opened his eyes, and yes, it was all a vague haze! All of it – the bodies and the blood and the stink. He looked down, saw a sea of eager, waiting, chanting faces. He kept his eyes tunnel-visioned on that sea of anonymous faces, not daring to look at anything else, and at last he felt his nausea burn finally away, evaporated by the animal heat of *his* people pulsing up at him.

He held up his hand for silence and he spoke.

'Y'know what day is three days from today?'

'PAIN DAY! PAIN DAY! PAIN DAY!' the Sadians howled, and there was a terrible, wolfish frenzy in the sound that he did not understand, that curdled his blood.

'Pain Day! Pain Day!' Fraden screamed, shouting

above the voice of the crowd. 'But not just any Pain Day – Death Day! Death Day for the Prophet and the whole Brotherhood of Pain!'

Now the Sadians were quiet. They looked up at him eagerly, expectantly. He had to be careful now. He wanted a mob on Pain Day, a mob that would listen only to his voice, a mob he could command like an army – not an uncontrollable horde.

He lowered his voice, spoke almost softly. 'Pain Day will be the day of final victory,' he said. 'And there'll be a place for *you* in that victory. On Pain Day, you and I and the People's Army will kill the Prophet and the whole Brotherhood!'

They began to shout, scream, chant: 'Long Live the Free Republic! Kill y'Brotherhood! BART! BART! BART!'

'Wait!' Fraden roared. 'Wait! Wait! There's more!'

After a few minutes of continued tumult, he had relative silence again.

'I can't tell you the whole plan,' he said. 'We need secrecy. But I can tell you what to do and when to do it. You'll hear strange sounds in the Stadium on Pain Day – the sounds of gunfire. And that's the signal! When you hear the sounds of gunfire in the Stadium, all of you, every single man, woman and child in Sade, storm the Stadium! Don't worry about the Killers – they'll be taken care of. Don't worry about getting into the Palace Compound – the gate will be smashed open. When you hear gunfire, storm the Palace Compound, break into the Stadium! And when you get there, I'll be there to tell you what to do. Me! You'll get the word straight from me! And I promise you, that word will mean freedom for all Sangre and death to the Brotherhood, death to the Killers, death to – '

His voice was drowned out by a great roar. 'Death t'y'Killers! Death t'the Brotherhood! KILL! KILL! KILL! KILL! KILL!'

Futilely, Fraden tried to call for silence, to remind them to spread the word. But it was no use; they were beyond listening to anything.

The Public Larder had become a churning chaos of gesticulating, twitching, jumping, madmen, working themselves up into a mindless frenzy, screaming 'KILL! KILL! KILL! KILL!' over and over and over again in one voice, the voice of a single, blood-crazed carnivore.

Fraden got down from his table, hesitated, then stepped into the maelstrom, tightly surrounded by his armed guards.

They'd spread the word, all right, he knew. Three days from now, the whole city would be ready to tear the Stadium apart with their fingernails if he gave the word. The trap was set.

Moro and his Brotherhood would be killed, and when Willem thought he was in control, when the army had broken in, when the 'heads surrounded them and Willem tried whatever he was going to try . . . The whole city would burst in on them, loyal only to *him*, to their Hero, to their President, to the man who was giving them their ghastly treat, ready to do his bidding, eager to rip to pieces anyone he pointed his finger at.

Three days from now, Sangre will be mine, all mine!

Now, in their screaming frenzy, the Sadians were yanking corpses from the tables, swarming over the great pile of bodies at the far wall like a maddened nest of termites. Bare hands tore off limbs, brandished them as banners. Here a man ripped a gobbet of flesh from a mutilated corpse with his teeth, screaming and slavering all the while. They began to pummel the corpses, kick

266

them, toss them about like beanbags, tear at them, claw them, rip them to shreds as if the pathetic bodies were live, hated Brothers, as if, somehow, this moment were the climax of the Pain Day to come. And all the while, the shrill 'KILL! KILL! KILL!' echoed from the high, smoke-obscured ceiling as the flickering torchlight illuminated a scene that seemed wrenched from the nether bowels of hell.

Fraden felt the nausea welling up again, stronger now, well-nigh irresistible. He pushed his guards forward, faster and faster.

'Come on, come on,' he grunted through constricting throat muscles. 'Let's get the hell out of here!'

Savagely, almost gleefully, the guards cleared a path through the screaming frenzied Sadians with the butts of their guns.

And at last they were outside, and the riot in the Larder was an ululating echo at the far end of the dark street, the offal stink a bad memory in the back of Fraden's nose. The comparatively fresh air of the city hit Fraden's gut like a pile driver.

He lurched away from his men, retched, began to vomit. He looked down, saw that he was adding his own gorge to an awful mound of amorphous slop out of which a human skull projected whitely. Utterly sickened, he vomited again, and it splattered wetly off the naked bone.

He retched and sobbed and couldn't tell one from the other. It's worth it! his mind screamed into the darkness. It's worth it! It's worth it! It's worth it! A whole bloody planet!

The spasms finally stopped, and he looked up into the cold black sky. Stars stared back at him unmercifully, icy pinpoints of light in the big, big nothing.

'Damn you!' he muttered in defiance of he-knew-not-what. 'It's *got* to be worth it!'

The guerrilla camp was dark, quiet, somnolent as the crimson Sangran sun set behind the western mountains on the eve of Pain Day. The waning light etched a pitiless black and burgundy chiaroscuro of empty barracks, stripped armoury huts gaping useless and empty, patches of earth burned dead-black by countless cookfires, bits of debris scattered unthinkingly about the area – the portrait of a place used up and now freshly abandoned, Bart Fraden thought as he stood near the doorway of his hut, looking out over the nearly empty camp.

The People's Army, virtually the entire force, had already been moved into position in the hills that rimmed the plain on which Sade stood, ready to move quickly into the city in captured trucks, less than twenty minutes away from the Palace Compound itself. With the army were the two thousand 'victims' that Moro had called for – ordinary Animals or bandits mostly – being armed with small locally made knives, concealing the knives in their loin-cloths, being told only that they were part of a compli-cated battle-plan, and being convinced of it by the sight of the entire People's Army encamped on the margin of the Sadian plain, ready to roll.

The guerrilla camp was indeed deserted, save for Fraden, Sophia, Vanderling sleeping across the clearing in his hut near the herogyn-head barracks where a hundred 'heads, who would be the so-called honour guard were sleeping off their last big herogyn-binge, and twenty trucks, gassed up and ready to go, sitting dark and silent near the margin of the jungle, where a roadway had been hacked from the camp to the nearest spur-road.

Bart Fraden, looking out over the empty camp, over

the jungle base which had been his home for months that now seemed like years, saw the empty armoury huts, the deserted barracks, and realized that no matter what happened when the sun rose, he would never see it set on this place again. This place was done with, a hand of cards that had already been played out. It was a hand that he had played well. Less than a year ago, this place had been emptier than it was tonight, and he had built it into the centre of an army, a revolution, that tomorrow would either place him in Sade, the President of the Free Republic of Sangre secure in his capital, or . . .

Or I'll simply be dead, Fraden told himself bluntly. All or nothing, that was the name of the game, the game of Pain Day, the game of revolution, the game of his life. Idly, he looked up at the stars, cold white fires in the deepening blackness of the Sangran sky . . .

Suddenly, he found his eyes drawn to something that shone wanly in the starlight a dozen yards to his left, a smooth, greyish rock jutting up out of the earth, whitened by the pale starlight.

Fraden shuddered, without, for a moment, knowing why. He felt his guts suddenly contract, felt something rising in the back of his throat, felt a soul-deep twinge of . . . horror? Dread? Remorse? Fear?

Even as the pang went through him, he realized its source. For that instant before his eyes had shown him the rock shining in the starlight for what it was, he had seen something else, a wraith, a vision caused by the trick of light – something else white and naked in the starlight of another night: a ruined human skull in the street in Sade, shining obscenely as he puked his gorge upon it. The illusion passed like a ghost in the night, but the pang within him called into being by the *déjà vu* refused to pass.

Fraden laughed aloud, trying to exorcize the demon.

Guilt, at this late date? he thought. Ridiculous! What do you have to feel guilty about? You did what you had to do, you're no Moro, no Willem.

The nameless feeling stayed, mocked him. Again Fraden forced a laugh. Okay, okay, he told himself. Shades of Father Freud! So you're uptight about killing that baby, that's where it's at, Bart, isn't it? He forced himself to relive that dreadful moment . . . the scream, the feel of flesh yielding under his axe, the thrill shooting up his arm as the blade buried itself in the wood beneath the flesh . . .

'Lord . . .' he whispered hoarsely, for what he felt was . . . *nothing*. He felt no guilt at all; he was blameless, he had done what he had been forced by circumstance to do, and now, looking back past months of war, past tens of thousands of deaths, calculated deaths, deaths he had knowingly, willingly caused and just as knowingly used, at a moment which had been the most horrible of his life, he felt nothing at all.

And then he knew that cold pang for what it was, not a pang of guilt, but one of *fear*. He knew that it was not fear of the future, of the danger he would face in the morning, but the fear of the *past*. *Something had been done to him.*

All his life, Fraden had been in control, had bent situations, conditions, people, to his own will, used them, shaped them, manoeuvred them for his own purposes. *He* was constant, and the universe around him was malleable. Events swirled around him, but like a rock in the sea, he had stood hard, untouched and immobile in the heart of the maelstrom, reaching out to move men and events into line with his needs, but never changed by them, the unmoved mover. He had been booted out of Great New

270

York, and it had not changed him, he had taken and lost the Belt, and he was still the same Bart Fraden.

But on Sangre . . . *something had been done to him*. He had been moved, deeply moved, by that one personal act of murder. He had been moved enough to seek more than merely another fief to replace the lost Belt Free State – he had wanted revenge. He had felt guilt for the first time, and the guilt had bred hate, hate for himself instantly transmuted into hate for the Brotherhood. Somehow, he had made the mistake of becoming *involved* in the Revolution, of subtly being seduced, raped, into seeing it as more than a means to a rational, sanely selfish end. Guilt had led to hate, hate had led to the lust for revenge, revenge was not a rational end, it was an *emotion*. It had led to more emotion, it had made the Sangrans themselves more than pawns in a cold game, it had made him *care* about becoming a hero, it had made the sound of his own name being chanted by his people something more than merely a sign that his techniques were working. And now . . . now the one moment of horror that had triggered the sequence meant . . . *nothing*!

He had been changed, tampered with. Unwittingly, he had committed the one sin his personal code allowed: he had blown his cool.

For the first time in his life, Bart Fraden felt himself moved by forces beyond his conscious control, a plaything of fate. *Something had been done to him*. He had changed Sangre – or had he? Had he changed the planet . . . or had the planet changed him? Was he really remoulding Sangre in his own image, or was the planet slyly changing him into the only kind of man it would let rule it – a Moro? A man who craved power for its own sake, not for the comfort and security that that power could bring?

Fraden felt an internal uncertainty – the only brand of fear he could ever know. Despite all he had ever done, he had always been able to consider himself as essentially *good* – a man who caused no unnecessary pain. Was it now a lie? Was Sangre making a monster of him by his own definition? Had he copped out? Was this what Sophia had been trying to tell him?

Soph . . . Had she seen it all along? Did she know more about him than he knew about himself? It was a strange new thought – that there could be someone who knew more about him than he knew about himself. He had always known himself through and through . . . he had prided himself on that self-knowledge. Was it merely a cop-out? Did Sophia *know* that it was a cop-out? She now seemed to know so much . . .

The real cop-out was lying to a woman like that! Before he had killed that baby, he had never lied to her; he had never felt the need. And now . . .

Fraden cursed, slammed a fist into a palm. Torn by doubts, one certainty asserted itself. Sophia deserved the truth. If he told her the truth, perhaps . . . perhaps it would dispel all this nonsense, all this stupid doubt. Don't just stand here, idiot, he told himself. When in trouble, when in doubt, flap your arms, scream and shout . . . the old saw went through his mind. And that was just what he needed now – someone to flap his arms at.

He turned sharply, stepped inside the hut.

Sophia stood just inside the doorway. She looked at him, and her eyes went wide, her mouth opened almost imperceptibly, and Fraden found himself wondering what his own face looked like at that moment, how much of what he was feeling he was giving away . . .

He cursed himself inwardly. Had lying to her become *that* much of a habit? What had happened to him?

'Soph . . .?' he said. 'Have I changed?'

'Changed?' she said, a sound as devoid of semantic content as the voice of an Animal. He studied her smooth face, her big, green, intelligent eyes, and for the first time he wondered what *really* went on behind that mask of flesh. For the first time, it really seemed to matter to him. He had never really looked at her before.

'Soph . . .' he stammered. 'Do I look like . . . like a murderer?'

She laughed, looked at him peculiarly. 'I've never seen anyone who looked less like a murderer,' she said. 'You look like you've seen a ghost – murderers don't see ghosts, and I know because I once lived with one. And a murderer would never ask that question. Bullethead's a murderer – can you picture *him* asking such a question?'

Fraden looked at her in wonder. She was right; she was dead right. He had to tell her the truth – somehow, from the way she stood, the way she cocked her head at him, the way she almost seemed to be waiting to hear what he had to say, *somehow* he simply *knew* that, for better or worse, she would understand.

'I've been lying to you,' he said. 'I've been lying all along. Know who gave Moro the idea of torturing the Sangrans into madness to bleed 'em for Omnidrene? *I* told him that fairy story because the Animals weren't desperate enough for my purposes!' He found himself speaking defiantly, almost daring her to condemn him. 'And it was *my* idea to kill the Brains and starve the villagers. My idea! You think I didn't really know what Willem was becoming? The hell I didn't! I needed someone to play monster. I used him!'

'Why are you telling me all this?' she said abruptly. 'Why are you telling me all this stuff I already know?'

'You already . . .?' he stared at her transfixedly.

273

'Who do you think you're talking to?' she said. 'Do you think I'm utterly blind? Ye gods, Bart, what've I been telling you all these months? And I'll bet I can tell you the next thing you're going to say. That Initiation Ceremony – you killed a human being, didn't you? I know men – it was written all over you.'

Fraden felt as if an immense weight had been lifted from his shoulders. And yet, now there was something else, something inexplicable . . .

'Just like that?' he said 'You knew I was lying, you knew what I was doing, and . . . and *nothing*! All that talk about Willem, and you knew I was a murderer, you saw me being sucked in by this lousy mudball, and you slept with me, said nothing, and . . .'

'What am I, Rebecca of Sunnybrook Farm?' Sophia snapped. 'Am I some kind of father confessor, say three Hail Marys and drop a Confedollar in the collection plate? One thing is certain and the rest is lies – you can't tell anyone anything he doesn't want to hear. And don't put me on, Bart Fraden! You look ludicrous beating your breast and howling *mea culpa*. You wouldn't know guilt from your own rectum with a roadmap! You're afraid, that's what you are. Wasn't it you who told me, "Never look behind; something may be gaining on you"? So you've finally looked behind you, and you don't like what you see. Welcome to the club, Peerless Leader! Welcome to the human race!'

'You mean you knew all along, and you still . . . still . . .'

'Still *what*?' she cried. 'Don't go putting words into my mouth! Don't get sloppy on *me*. I've lived with murderers and thieves, I've sold my body for a meal. Who am I to judge you? We've got a business arrangement, Bart Fraden! I need you and you need me. We're trophies on

274

each other's mantelpieces. We both live in the same jungle – if you're a monster, what does that make me? You knew what I was when you latched on to me – a chick who needed a man who could stay on top. And I knew what you were – a man who would claw his way to the top of the mountain one way or another, and stay there, one way or another! Just because I knew you had killed and still . . .' Her voice broke. 'Just because I stayed with you even though . . . Just because we're the same breed of monster . . . Just because you're the only man I ever met who I . . . *Bart* . . . ' The last was a tiny, whimpering sound.

'Now who's lying?' he said. 'Sophia O'Hara, tough as nails! You phony bitch, you! I love you, you little liar! God, help me, I'm in love . . . Who needs it? But I can't help it, I'm so alone here, so alone . . . All of a sudden, I don't know anything any more. Except that I love you, and if I lost you . . . You can hurt me, Soph. For the first time in my life, someone can hurt me . . .'

Suddenly, she flung herself at him, threw her arms around him, buried her face in his chest. 'Hurt you?' she said. 'You idiot! I couldn't hurt you if you came at me slavering with a knife! I'm such a goddamned cop-out, such a stupid cretin! Here we had such a nice little business arrangement, and I have to get myself hung-up over you! Not over what I need from you like any sensible woman, but over a lot of stupid trivia, like some moon-struck yokum. Your body . . . and the way you walk . . . and your goddamned delicate gut . . . Trivia! Nothing! Nothing! Nothing! A first-class man for a first-class woman! First, shmirst! We could be two monsters, and it wouldn't be different. You could be a leper, and I wouldn't be able to leave you. I can't care what you are or what you've done or what you'll do. I've got to stick by

275

you as long as you'll have me. I hope that's what you'll always need, because that's all I have to give. And I'll always have to give it.'

'Soph, what're you trying to – ?'

'I'm telling you I love you, you moron!' she sobbed. 'What a loathsome word! I hate it! I hate it! But I can't help it, I love you, I love you, I love you . . . Hasn't anyone said it to you before?'

Fraden found himself looking at her through misty eyes. He felt young and alive, he felt old and used up. He lifted her face, looked at it like some strange jewel. She was crying. He had never seen her cry before. No one had ever cried for him before. He felt bound to her and did not want to feel it and knew that what he wanted to feel was totally beside the point.

He carried her to the bed, and as he had a thousand times before, he made love to her. But now, he could not stop himself from thinking of it in those terms. *I'm making love to her*, he thought, even as he undressed her, entered, found himself swept away by an act that he had always felt as a moment of pure, selfish pleasure. But it was that no longer and could never be so again.

He found himself shepherding her tenderly towards fulfilment, half against his own will, found himself lost in the world of her body, aquiver from each little shudder of delight he felt beneath him, transported by each small moan of pleasure, his own body and ego something tiny and remote, fading away into another universe, and when the moment of fulfilment came, they reached it together, and for a timeless instant he felt himself merge with her, drawing unthinkable pleasure from her own ecstasy, drinking up her cresting passion, giving of his own, and the mad, somehow fearful, explosion of feral, uncomplicated joy was a thing apart from him, neither his nor hers but a blinding flash of mortal pleasure as vivid as the most terrible pain that united them as one, and was *theirs*, theirs together.

And that night, for the first time in his life, Bart Fraden slept in a lover's arms.

Chapter 14

Quiet . . . it was too damned quiet! Bart Fraden looked back over the tailgate of the truck at the long truck convoy behind, the last of the trucks, the last of nearly a hundred, now finally passing through the final defile and out on to the broad plain on which Sade stood. Two thousand men in those trucks, men from nearly a hundred different villages, armed only with the knives concealed in their loincloths, the knives that Moro would *let* them smuggle in, a strange cargo indeed for the People's Army to be trucking towards Sade on Pain Day – yet all along the route, the road had been empty.

For the last three miles, they had passed hundreds of trucks waiting on the shoulders of the road, the trucks that would begin to bear nearly twenty thousand guerrillas to the city as soon as the convoy entered Sade. The hills on the western rim of the plain were filled with guerrilla bivouacs – yet there were no crowds of curious Sangrans turning out to watch either the People's Army or the President's convoy, even though all the Killers were safely buttoned up in the Palace Compound. Fraden didn't like it. It just didn't smell right. Had the word he had spread in Sade only three days ago leaked out to the countryside? Did all the Animals know that this was to be something more than an ordinary Pain Day? And what would they do about it if they did know?

Fraden turned to face Sophia, who was sitting on the slab bench jutting out from the side of the truck beside him. He reached out, touched her hand – an unfamiliar

278

gesture – and she smiled at him wanly, took his hand in hers.

Willem Vanderling, sitting on the bench across from them, cradling his snipgun in his arms, seemed to notice the byplay as the corners of his mouth turned upward in a minute smirk.

Fraden smirked back, and Vanderling, misreading it as a grin of masculine camaraderie, smiled at him insincerely.

Poor Willem, Fraden thought. He thinks he's got it made, and even his goddamned snipgun will punk out on him in the end. Fraden glanced forward over the cab of the truck at the five trucks filled with herogyn-heads armed with rifles. That had been a little game of Willem's too – arming the 'heads with rifles instead of snipguns. Snipguns would look too threatening, Willem had said. It had all been so transparent – with the 'heads carrying rifles instead of snipguns, Willem's own snipgun would be a badge of authority, making it that much easier for him to order the 'heads to turn on Fraden when the time came. No doubt he was counting on that little extra bit of leverage. But he didn't know that it would be working *against* him, that his own snipgun had a dead energy-pack, slipped in while he had been making a final inspection of the 'heads back in camp.

To hell with Willem, and to hell with the Animals! Fraden thought. I've thought of everything. He glanced down at the paper-wrapped bundle at his feet – his Brother's robe. It wasn't essential to the plan, but if he could pull it off, if the Killers really would obey orders from a live 'Brother Bart' rather than their dead masters when the final hand was played, it would be a nice final touch – a mob hanging on his word and the only disciplined army on the planet obeying his orders. Poor Willem!

Now the lead trucks were approaching Sade. The road entered the city through the Animal section, and as the truck in which they were riding began to roll along one of the main side streets towards the avenue leading to the Palace Compound, past empty hovels grimed with dust and old smoke, Willem Vanderling grimaced, clutched tighter at his snipgun.

'I don't like this . . .' he said. 'It's so goddamned quiet. And where are they all?'

Indeed, the streets were all but empty. Fraden could make out men and women staring at the trucks as they rolled by towards the Palace from within the hundreds of shacks. Here and there a man or woman was clearly visible in a doorway, nodding knowingly as the trucks passed by, holding a club or a knife, or a rag-wrapped stick that could become a torch. A small, thin child, his bones visible through the taut skin of his naked chest, darted out from behind a shack, stood on the street watching silently for a moment, picked up a femur that was lying on the ground, ran behind the shack again.

'Maybe it's this Pain Day thing . . .' Sophia said. 'I don't like the sound of that at all . . .' Fraden squeezed her hand. He had thought of telling her of the whole plan, but it would only worry her. No one could understand that a mob could be used in a planned, controlled fashion until he had actually felt such a mob under the sway of his own voice . . .

'Probably you're right,' he said, speaking more for Vanderling's benefit than hers. 'From what I was able to pump out of Olnay, the Animals take this Pain Day thing as seriously as the Brothers do. A nice piece of psychology on the Brotherhood's part. Give the Animals a big torture-show one day a year, let 'em dig the same things the Brotherhood does to 'em all year, and instead of thinking that Moro and Company are monsters, they get to feeling that the Brothers are just like them, only luckier. If they get a little taste of sadistic kicks and dig it, it makes 'em believe in the so-called Natural Order all the stronger. Reminds me of the one about the three guys talking about how often they have women. First guy says, "Once a week," and doesn't look too happy. Second guy says, "Once a day," and he looks jaded. Third guy says, "Once a year," but he looks like the cat that ate the canary. When they ask him what in hell he's so happy about, he says, "Ah, but *tonight's the night!*"'

Vanderling grunted.

'*Very* funny,' Sophia said.

The trucks swung on to the main avenue of Sade, past the gleaming, gaudy false front of the fetid Sangran capital, the façade of synthmarble, wood and metal buildings that belied the miles of stinking makeshift warrens behind it.

They reached the hill on which the Palace Compound stood, came to a halt at the main gate beneath the heavy concrete walls. Fraden saw that the guntowers spaced along the walls were manned, but the galleries that ran around the top of the walls, which could hold thousands of armed men, were empty.

The gate swung open, and the trucks rolled forward between two lines of perhaps fifty Killers each, and they were inside the Palace Compound. Vanderling nodded, grinned at Fraden, and Fraden grinned back. Only a hundred Killers guarding the gate. The wide courtyard was jammed with wooden corrals packed tight with fat, naked little moronic children. There were perhaps a hundred Killers patrolling the corrals that held thousands of Meatanimals, and that was it. Two hundred Killers to hold the gate against twenty thousand troops!

'A setup,' Vanderling muttered *sotto voce*. 'Sweetest little setup I ever saw.'

The trucks rolled past the Palace itself, and Fraden saw perhaps another dozen or two Killers positioned by the steps leading up to the main entrance. The trucks rounded the corner of the Palace, and the black Stadium loomed before them.

About two hundred Killers were waiting for them by the main gate. A Killer captain led a small squad up to the lead trucks, waved them towards the main gate. Another officer led the rest of the Killers to the rear of Fraden's truck. They cordoned off the trucks carrying the two thousand victims, led them around the back of the Stadium to the arena entrance, where they would ostensibly be searched for weapons, then led up through the bowels of the Stadium and up on to the arena floor through the ground-level arena gate.

The trucks carrying the bodyguard parked in a semi-circle between Fraden's truck and the Stadium. The hundred herogyn-heads jumped down, quickly formed up into two lines of fifty men each to the right of Fraden's truck.

'Well, here goes nothing,' Fraden said, and, carrying his bundle, he vaulted over the tailgate of the truck. Vanderling lowered the tailgate, and he and Sophia scrambled after Fraden. The three of them positioned themselves between two lines of troops, the Killer captain led his men to the head of the formation, and Fraden ordered: 'Let's go!'

Silently, the Killers led them through the main gate and down a long, dank passageway that finally became an upward-curving ramp. At the end of the ramp, an open portal lit the dark passageway with a blaze of red sunlight. Vanderling made a hand signal, and the 'heads trotted ahead of them out into the sunlight behind the Killers. Fraden could dimly see them fanning out in the stands, forming a protective cup surrounding the entrance. Vanderling strode briskly out behind them.

Fraden glanced quickly at Sophia, she squeezed his hand for a moment, then let go. He took a deep breath, and then led her out into the glaring noon heat of the Stadium.

For a moment, as his eyes adjusted from the gloom of the passageway to the bright light of the Stadium, all seemed a piebald blur to Fraden. Then the blur resolved itself into a sea, a great tiered cliff of faces and bodies.

They were standing about halfway up the stands in the section of the Stadium farthest from the Pavilion – well out of snipgun range, from the point of view of the Brotherhood. A narrow strip of benches had been cleared immediately in front of and behind them, stretching from the top lip of the Stadium to the fence separating the stands from the arena floor, and about twenty seats wide.

The rest of the Stadium, every inch of bench space, was jammed.

From where Fraden stood, facing the roofed Pavilion across the entire width of the Stadium, two great sections of seats filled with Sadians arced away on either side of the small empty area towards the Pavilion. From the upper lip of the Stadium to the fence at the bottom of the stands, the two huge semicircular sections were packed tight with Sadians, at least ten thousand of them, emaciated, semi-nude bodies, pressed tightly against each other on the backless benches. Fraden saw that an unusual proportion of them were old men and women, occasional

283

cripples – a great rarity on Sangre. He waved to the stands, and a murmur swept through them. Fraden grinned. They weren't about to start any ruckus here with all these Killers around, but they *know*, he thought. Old folks and cripples . . . It was a good sign, it meant that all the more able-bodied Sadians were preparing to take a more active part in the events of this Pain Day . . .

Fraden squinted, peered across the arena towards the Pavilion. The Pavilion itself was all decked out in gold and black bunting, and it was packed with thousands of Brothers – every remaining Brother on Sangre – and their slaves and women, the thousands of black robes contrasting grimly with the colourful tables of fruit, roasts, jugs of wine, with the naked tanned flesh of the slaves and the finely formed houris. Like vultures at a parrots' convention! Fraden thought.

In the front and centre of the Pavilion, he could make out Moro, black-robed like the rest and if anything grosser than before, sitting atop his raised throne with an electric bullhorn hanging loosely from one hand like a sceptre.

Above, below, and on both sides of the Pavilion, the stands were black with uniformed Killers, perhaps as many as two thousand of them, sunlight glinting redly off thousands of rifles.

Flanking the Killers on both sides were two great sections of loincloth-clad men, perhaps two thousand on each side. Fraden grinned. They were got up as Animals, but even at this distance, he could see the healthy muscles of their chests instead of the ribs-through-leather look of the Sangran Animals. He didn't have to see their teeth to know that they were filed to points, he didn't have to pick out the rifles hidden in the forest of feet to know they were there. You couldn't hide a mink among rabbits, and you couldn't hide Killers among Animals. The trap was set, and the trap within that trap, and the final trap . . .

Suddenly, he felt a hand grab his – Sophia's. Silently, she nodded towards the arena floor, her teeth clamped over her lower lip, her eyes wide.

He followed her gaze and swallowed hard, for only now did he see that the entire arena floor was a forest. A forest of crude wooden crosses jammed into the packed earth, thousands of them, row after row, and the base of each cross was heaped high with faggots. Here and there a brazier of oil blazed, and the braziers held long-handled iron dippers, and unlit torches were stacked in piles beside them. Piles of torches, and heaps of big iron nails. A couple of hundred Killers stood scattered among the crosses, waiting, gripping large, heavy-looking hammers.

With Sophia holding his hand tightly, Fraden led her and Vanderling to the centre of the cleared area in the stands. As they seated themselves, and as Fraden carefully positioned the paper-wrapped Brother's robe beneath his seat, the herogyn-heads filled in the stands all around them, forming a protective wall of flesh about them, a square of seated armed men, with Fraden, Sophia, and Vanderling at the centre.

Fraden surveyed the stands, the Brothers in the Pavillion: drinking, wolfing down great gobbets of flesh, toying with their houris, being toyed with; the Animals tense and silent, most of them staring his way with feral anticipation in their eyes; the Killers in uniform with their hands on their guns; the ludicrously disguised tiers of Killers, their hands hidden in their laps, near their concealed weapons . . . He felt a terrible tension hanging over the Stadium, a wave waiting to crest, as each group waited for the moment when the waiting would be over, when the dreadful events of this penultimate Pain Day would at last begin.

Then Moro rose ponderously to his feet, raised the bullhorn to his lips, and the air was shattered by a great, hollow voice.

'Pain Day!' Moro bellowed, and the echoes reverberated from the bowl of the Stadium. 'Pain Day! Pain Day! Pain Day!' The amplified chant melted with its own echoes, formed a huge, shattering, shimmering cascade of sound.

The Brothers picked it up, began to chant, thousands of voices drowning out Moro's amplified shouting in a guttural, staccato roar. 'PAIN DAY! PAIN DAY! PAIN DAY! PAIN DAY!'

The vast sections of Killers were chanting it, and finally the Animals, and the whole Stadium shook with the sound of twenty thousand voices chanting: 'PAIN DAY! PAIN DAY! PAIN DAY! PAIN DAY! PAIN DAY!'

The Brothers tossed aside haunches of meat, jugs of wine, women; began to roll their heads madly and clap rhythmically. The Killers caught the beat and began to pound the concrete with their boots and rifle butts. The Animals began to clap too, stomp bare feet on hard concrete, and it was a sound like distant thunder, a sound like guns: 'BOOM-da-da-BOOM-BOOM! BOOM-da-da-BOOM-BOOM! BOOM-da-da-BOOM-BOOM!'

And a counterpoint above it, the chant, working itself up into a huge snarl of frenzy – 'PAIN DAY! PAIN DAY! PAIN DAY!'

'PAIN DAY! PAIN DAY! BOOM-da-da-BOOM-BOOM! PAIN DAY! PAIN DAY! BOOM-da-da-BOOM-BOOM!'

The sound assailed Fraden's ears. Through the concrete of the quivering Stadium, through the soles of his feet and up his leg bones, the vibrations jellied his guts, rattled his teeth, set the short hairs on the back of his neck on end. Sophia's hand was a constricted claw around his, her face was ashen, her jaws clamped shut like a vice.

'PAIN DAY! PAIN DAY! PAIN DAY! PAIN DAY! PAIN DAY!'

The clapping, the boot and foot stomping were dying out now, and the entire Stadium was screaming, the chant became a wild, blood-curdling, shrill, ululating cry: 'PAINDAYPAINDAYPAINDAYPAINDAYPAINDAY!'

Across the arena, the Pavilion was a serpentine tangle of writhing bodies, as the Brothers tore flesh from roasted human limbs, screaming all the while, spitting greasy fragments as they howled, biting off more meat, screaming, spitting, pummelling and kneading naked women with cruel and brutal abandon, a ghastly riot in a vast churning pit of vipers.

And now the disguised Killers were all too apparent even to the Animals, as they chewed madly on their own foaming lips, bathing their lower faces in beards of blood-red spittle.

The Animals too became lost in the frenzy, screaming, pummelling, clawing madly at each other, old women's claws raking the scarred flesh of cripples, wizened, bent men beating unthinkingly on the heaving backs of crones . . .

Even the damned herogyn-heads who were supposed to be guarding them were howling in frenzy, their hollow eyes the eyes of kill-crazed wolves.

Fraden felt it coming up at him, down on him, penetrating into his guts – the concentrated animal fury of twenty thousand human beings giving themselves over utterly to the darkest urges within them, a mindless, bottomless, shoreless sea of horror, an inchoate wave, a great tide of liberated berserker blood lust.

He teetered on the brink of engulfment, felt the yawning jaws of the beast reach out to take him, this beast that lurked within every man, this giant carnivore, this kill-crazy, primeval thing. He felt the beast without call to the beast within, the beast that pounded in his blood in a great unbidden surge of adrenalin. His mind strained against the mindless, primal call of the jungle, of the raging carnivore within him so long denied . . .

Desperately, he grabbed for Sophia, clung to her, sucked at her softness, her warmth, her womanness. She buried her face against his chest, sobbed uncontrollably.

'PAINDAYPAINDAYPAINDAYPAINDAYPAINDAY!'

Out of the corner of one eye, incredulously, he saw Willem Vanderling beside him. Vanderling howling, Vanderling, his face a contorted, reddened devil-mask, a huge purple vein distended and pounding atop his bald skull.

'God, god, god, god, god . . .' Fraden muttered, half-praying.

And then, abruptly, it crested. There was a final, terrible, roar, and then a sudden silence, a deep loud silence more terrible than the screaming, the ominous, clammy silence of the tomb.

Below them, on the arena floor, the big gate had swung open, and a knot of bound men, and then another and another and another were being ushered out into the blood-red sunlight by small squads of Killers. Then more men and more Killers, and more and more . . .

The victims were being led to the slaughter.

Utter silence reigned in the Stadium as the squads of armed Killers herded the two thousand bound men, naked to their waists, out of the bowels of the Stadium on to the dirt floor of the arena, dispersed them among the great forest of upright wooden crosses, one man to a cross, one Killer, armed with rifle and morningstar, to each four crosses. The victims, their hands bound behind them, daggers hidden uselessly in their loincloths, looked up at the stands, at the silent, waiting Animals, at the Killers, their mouths oiled with bloody foam, at the Brothers in the Pavilion, gnawing distractedly on human limbs, swilling wine from clay jugs, and all the while staring down at them, red-eyed and grinning.

And the bound men looked up at Vanderling and Fraden, beseeching, waiting for a sign, for the deliverance that had been promised them. Fraden could not meet their eyes, for the timing was too coarse to save these men. Even now, the People's Army must be approaching the Palace Compound, but before they could break in . . .

The Killers on the arena floor holding the great hammers raised them over their heads in a grotesque salute. Moro held the bullhorn to his lips.

'Give Pain, receive Pleasure!' Moro shouted. 'Give Death, receive Life! Let the ceremonies begin! In the name of the Brotherhood of Pain and the Natural Order, let all share in the Pleasure of giving Pain – Kill! Kill! Kill!'

The oppressive silence was sheared by a shrill, animal cry from twenty thousand throats as Animals, Brothers and Killers began to chant, 'KILL! KILL! KILL! KILL! KILL!'

The chant quickened in tempo, lost its rhythm, became an endless, wordless, mindless scream like the sonic pulse of a siren: 'KILLKILLKILLKILLKILLKILLKILL!'

Fraden, his arm around Sophia's waist holding her to one side now, willed himself cold, banished all emotion, commanded himself to become a juiceless calculating machine. Beside him, Vanderling was staring down into the arena, his lips working silently, mutely forming the syllable 'kill'.

Savagely, Fraden drove his elbow into Vanderling's ribs. 'Snap out of it!' he shouted in Vanderling's ear. 'This is it! Get your goddamned 'heads into position!'

Vanderling started, shook his head like a man emerging from a dream, barked orders to the seated herogyn-heads. The 'heads snapped to their feet, rifles at the ready, formed a solid shield of flesh and guns all around them.

Fraden forced himself to estimate coldly. By now, the army should have reached the Compound; perhaps they were already breaking in. It was impossible to hear anything over the endless, shattering scream.

He craned his neck, trying to see over the human wall in front of him. He let go of Sophia, climbed up on the bench, looked down over the shield of men to the arena floor. Killers and victims alike seemed frozen, transfixed. The Killers stood immobile, listening to their own battle chant being howled by twenty thousand throats. The bound men stared up at the tiered stands filled with creatures howling for their blood, their faces white with fear, their eyes great saucers of shock and anguish.

Unbidden, a great spasm of self-loathing tore through Bart Fraden. For these men would not be saved, and he had planned it that way. Their slaughter was to keep the Killers preoccupied while the guerrillas broke in, and Fraden-the-calculating-machine hoped for panic. Fraden the man was disgusted. Both watched and waited.

He did not have long to wait.

Suddenly, as if on signal, each armed Killer grabbed a victim, dragged him to a cross. The Killers with the hammers grabbed up fistfuls of nails from the piles by the

290

braziers, and each ran to a cross where a Killer held a writhing, bound victim. Near the centre of the forest of crosses, two Killers made the first move. One ripped away the struggling man's bonds, shoved him up against the cross, spread-eagled him on the crossbar, while the other leapt to the top of the heaped faggots, drove nails through the victim's palms and deep into the rough wood. The man screamed as blood spurted from his ruined hands, and then all hell broke loose.

Instantly, hundreds of other teams of Killers were ripping away bonds, crucifying victims. But some were not quick enough. Here a man's bonds were ripped away – and he pulled loose from the Killer's hands, reached into his lioncloth, pulled out a dagger, and without pausing thrust it into the heart of the startled Killer, grabbed the dying man's morningstar, smashed the skull of the Killer with the hammer before he could move, took the hammer in his free hand, and swinging hammer and morningstar attacked the Killers by the next cross. Scores of Sangrans hung screaming from their crosses, but scores more had broken free, stabbed their tormenters, were freeing other men, grabbing the weapons of the fallen, lashing out blindly in all directions.

The organized slaughter became a boiling chaos, as the outnumbered Killers reacted, unshipped morningstars, began dispatching still-bound Sangrans, fought off men wielding knives and captured morningstars and hammers. Braziers were overturned, spilling boiling oil on Killers and Animals alike, crosses were toppled, some still bearing their bleeding victims. The arena floor was a great mêlée of furious, formless combat, a tangle of bodies and weapons and flowing oil, a writhing pit of hundreds, thousands of disjointed individual slaughters.

In the stands, Animals were howling with glee,

Brothers were staring down wide-eyed in silent shock, and the Killers . . .

Killers, in uniforms and mufti alike, bolted to their feet, rifles in hand, their battle chant on their foaming lips. The two great sections of black-clad and semi-naked Killers surrounding the Pavilion were on their feet screaming. Then Fraden heard a single shot ring out.

Instantly, the entire far end of the Stadium came alive in thousands of flashes of gunfire. The roar was deafening as the Killers in the stands began to fire volley after furious volley down into the chaos on the arena floor.

Below, scores of bodies, Killers and Animals, were blasted off their feet by a tremendous hail of bullets. A great cloud of dust went up as bullets ripped into the packed earth that formed the arena floor. The air became filled with splinters as thousands of errant shots smashed into the forest of wooden crosses.

The Killers kept firing. The gunfire became a single, earth-shaking roar, a peal of continuous staccato thunder; a great pall of acrid smoke hung over the far end of the Stadium. Volley after volley struck the men on the arena floor, a continuous storm of death, a cloudburst of lead. Killers and Animals were no longer fighting each other – they were milling about crazily, trying to find cover behind the twitching bodies that were falling all around them . . .

Fraden could see Moro, obscured by the gunsmoke, bellowing something through his bullhorn. But the Killers were beyond his control now, beyond anyone's control, not even Moro could stop them from –

Then Fraden saw what Moro was doing. He could not stop the Killers, but he could direct some of their fury. The sections of Killers nearest the Pavilion were turning, bringing their guns to bear in his direction . . .

He grabbed Sophia, pulled her down under him, dived behind the screen of herogyn-heads, rolled the two of them half-under the bench, saw Vanderling hit the floor beside him, crawl back under the bench, clutching his snipgun futilely.

Bullets began to whine overhead, ping off the concrete of the Stadium, tear into the standing herogyn-heads who began to go down, firing wildly across the breadth of the arena at the Killers. Bodies fell in front of them, behind, to all sides . . .

Moro had made his move. While the bulk of the Killers were still firing madly down into the arena, he had gained enough control of some of them to order them to slaughter the 'heads and the hated men they guarded.

Fraden glanced at Vanderling, prone beside him.

'Any minute now,' Vanderling muttered. 'Any minute . . .' A bullet whistled off the conrete inches from his head, a herogyn-head behind him screamed as he caught the ricochet. Where in hell are our men? Fraden wondered. How much longer – ?

A great roar went up, a roar that could be heard above the massed gunfire. The direction of the rifle shots seemed to change; they were no longer whining overhead, and there seemed to be a new concentration of gunfire directly below. The 'heads were no longer falling all around them; they were screaming, cheering.

Cautiously, Fraden stood up and looked down into the arena.

The big arena gate had been smashed from its moorings. Below him, the near end of the arena was a solid mass of men in green loincloths and sweatbands, soldiers of the People's Army pouring into the arena, firing their rifles as they came, an irresistible tide of men surging across the packed earth towards the Pavilion-end of the

Stadium, smashing down row after row of crosses with the sheer weight of their bodies as they advanced, pushing Killers and Animals towards the far end of the arena before them.

And still they came, pouring forth in a packed crush of flesh from the arena gate, and in moments the arena floor was half-filled with them. More surged into the arena, more and more and more, twenty thousand men filling the entire arena, firing up at the sections of Killers, wall after wall after wall of deadly lead.

The Animals in the stands were chanting again, wildly, shrilly, but now it was a new litany, *their* litany: 'BART! BART! BART! BART! BART!'

The Killers in the stands were still on their feet, firing down into the arena, volley after volley, even as the bullets tore into them. The whole forward front of guerrillas, thousands of men, went down. But the rest kept firing. It wasn't a battle; it was a mutual slaughter as two great solid masses of Killers and guerrillas, firing at point-blank range, lacking the barest semblance of cover, stood their ground and mauled each other, decimated each other's ranks, trading volley for unthinkably deadly volley. But the outcome was never in doubt. Killers and guerrillas went down by the thousands, but for every guerrilla that fell, three more burst into the arena through the broken gate, an endless tide of men.

There was mindless panic in the Pavilion, as thousands of Brothers, women, slaves rushed for the single exit all at once. The Pavilion was a clawing, kicking, turgid mass of screaming, terrified humanity, a feral dogfight for the exit that let no one escape, a choked, self-destructive, monstrous clot of fighting bodies that sealed the doom of the Brotherhood of Pain.

For now, even under the fearsome fire that rained on

them from the Killers in the stands, the herogyn-heads among the guerrillas had marshalled some small semblance of control, and hundreds, thousands of soldiers began firing straight into the Pavilion itself, volley after volley.

At any moment, hundreds of guerrillas were hit and fell, but still they poured into the arena, a massive jam of armed men firing furiously into the tightly packed Pavilion. Now they were all firing into the Pavilion, thousands of bullets a second.

Bodies flew into the air like flopping fish, burst apart in gouts of blood, as wave after wave of bullets tore into them, terrible fists of lead smashing into flesh, wood, concrete, at supersonic speed. The air above was a maelstrom of flying concrete chips, wood splinters, fragments of bone, bloody pieces of flesh. In seconds, the Pavilion was a garbage heap of broken bodies, shattered tables, clay shards. Even as the ceaseless, continuous rain of bullets ripped them to shreds, the Brothers, and their retainers tore at each other, slaughtered their own fellows in a fruitless fight for the body-clogged exit. The Brotherhood of Pain was dying as it had lived, a clawing, murderous tangle of human beasts.

It was over in moments. The Pavilion was a vast abattoir, an offal-heap of inert shattered bodies, cracked concrete, splintered furniture, and all was covered with a thick, congealing patina of bright red blood. Here and there a ruined thing twitched, sending droplets of red flying, was slammed black by a hail of bullets.

Fraden gagged, even as he realized that it was over, that every Brother had died, that now the planet was his . . .

Then he saw a figure, a lone, gross figure moving in the Pavilion, scuttling like a crab on its belly from body to pulped body, swimming in blood, using the corpses as cover, zigzagging towards the exit.

It was Moro. Moro, his face a mask of bleeding meat, a steady river of blood leaking out from under his tattered black robe.

Moro crawled from behind a body, and a bullet caught him in the shoulder. He reared up slightly in pain, and more bullets hit him. He screamed, a sound lost in the gunfire, threw up his arms in anguish. Scores of bullets tattooed his exposed arms, a tremendous fusillade that flipped him upward and backward, like a thumb flipping a card, exposing his back.

The bullets that hit his back lifted him clear off his feet like a monstrous metallic fist. His body seemed to float in space for a moment, borne aloft on a wall of lead.

Then the Prophet of Pain tumbled backwards, a ruined doll, flopped over on his belly, and was still.

The Animals in the stands began to jump up and down, writhe convulsively like crazed marionettes. And the Killers in the stands, seeing their masters gone, all discipline, the last vestige of their sanity gone with them, surged down out of the stands, smashing the fence enclosing the arena to flinders with the crush of their bodies, guns flung aside, morningstars waving, thousands of voices screaming 'KILL! KILL! KILL! KILL!' through bleeding, foaming lips.

The Killers charged straight into a barrage of bullets, a fire so concentrated that the entire first wave of them was thrown backwards into the stands, bleeding pulps. But the thousands of Killers higher in the stands threw the bodies back as missiles, pushed forward, an avalanche of flesh against a wall of bullets. Killers tumbled into the arena already packed to bursting with guerrillas, dead Killers, maimed Killers, fighting Killers.

Swinging morningstars, kicking, biting, the Killers half-ran, half-fell into the great mass of guerrillas. But like animalcules enveloped by some great amoeba, the remnants of the Killers of Sangre were engulfed by the great horde of guerrillas in the arena. Pushing the bodies of fallen comrades before them like so much driftwood, they tore into the guerrillas with morningstars, boots, teeth.

But it was like fighting the sea. Of the six thousand Killers who had been in the stands, not two thousand had survived those first furious minutes of carnage, not a thousand reached the arena floor alive. Those who reached the enemy to tear at him in mindless, fearless fury were outnumbered ten or twenty to one.

They disappeared like raindrops into the sea, and all that was visible were hundreds of clots of writhing guerrillas pulling down Killers by the sheer weight of their bodies, here and there a morningstar raised above the mêlée coated with red blood and grey, pulpy brains. Though the fighting would go on till the last Killer was a bloody smear on the arena floor, the battle was over. The Killers were finished.

Fraden hugged Sophia to him, nauseated, exhilarated, victorious, disgusted, all at once as the battle, now decided, continued to rage below him.

'End of the line, Bart!' the voice of Willem Vanderling said behind him.

Fraden whirled, found himself staring into the muzzle of Vanderling's snipgun. Vanderling grinned. Herogynheads turned to face them, brought their rifles around uncertainly.

'Hero!' Vanderling crowed. 'Genius! Thanks for the free ride, Bart. Thanks for the planet. It's my planet, now, *mine*!' He gestured down towards the arena floor.

'Down there, Bart,' he said. 'That's where you're going.

297

Let the Killers rip you to pieces, or maybe our own slobs. Either way, you'll make a nice martyr, you and Little Miss Bigmouth. Your choice, Bart, down there or I slice you to bits on the spot!'

Fraden stared straight at Vanderling. Poor Willem! he thought. A twinge of pity went through him. Enough killing for one day!

'Don't be a fool,' he said. 'Give it up. Forget it. I can still use you. I don't want to kill you, Willem.'

Vanderling laughed. 'You've got it a little ass-backwards, haven't you?' he said.

Fraden smiled, a slow, confident smile as Vanderling moved the muzzle of the snipgun closer to his gut, the muzzle of the deactivated snipgun. Another minute or so, he thought, and the mob'll be here, *my* mob. Willem's harmless whether he knows it or not, but I've got to stall those 'heads.

Fraden sighed, spoke to the 'heads. 'Arrest Marshal Vanderling,' he said. 'He's a traitor.'

'Cool it, boys,' Vanderling said. 'I'm in charge now, and that means unlimited herogyn for all!'

The herogyn-heads cheered, trained their rifles on Fraden.

Any second now . . . Fraden thought.

'Try anything,' he said, 'and you're all dead men.' He laughed. 'Play it safe. Let Willem do his own dirty work. Better forget it, Willem, while you have the chance. That thing you're holding's got a dead energy-pack.'

Vanderling's face fell. 'You're not conning me that easy . . .' he said uncertainly.

Fraden laughed. 'Even *you* can't be so stupid as to think I'd gamble my life on trusting a snake like you,' he said.

'Shoot him!' Vanderling screamed. 'Shoot him!'

The 'heads trained their guns on Fraden's belly, their fingers tightened on the triggers. Yet they hesitated.

Fraden stared them down, read their eyes. They were Willem's creatures, all right, but they knew who it was they were about to kill. If there was any foul-up, if the Animals in the stands clearly saw them kill Fraden, Fraden the Hero, Fraden the President, they would be torn to pieces. Why didn't the off-worlder use his terrible weapon? Why was the President smiling? What did he know that made him laugh in the face of death?

'Shoot him! Shoot him!' Vanderling repeated shrilly.

The herogyn-heads hesitated.

They hesitated just long enough.

Chapter 15

Abruptly, as if some fault deep within the earth below had suddenly slipped, the entire Stadium began to quiver. Drowning out the screams from the waning battle in the arena, the howls of the Animals in the stands, came a sound like the sea, storm-tossed, pounding a great cliff of unyielding metal, millions of tons of wind-whipped water rhythmically slapping a great wall of steel: 'BART! BART! BART! BART! BART! BART!' A deep sound, a sharp sound, a sound so powerful that its shock wave could all but be felt by the skin.

In the stands across the arena from where Fraden stood, the focus of a circle of guns, a huge explosion seemed to take place. An explosion of people. From every entrance portal, they erupted, a tide of Sadians so tremendous that the crush of their bodies tore away the concrete frames of the portals like so much rotten balsa wood. Thousands upon thousands of men, women, small children, brandishing knives, cleavers, clubs, spears, torches burst into the stands like some piebald chemical foam released suddenly from under extreme pressure, filling the far section of the stands in moments, so many that the Stadium shook, that concrete and steel beams seemed to creak under their weight.

And more Sadians surged through the broken arena gate, a solid tide of men, women and children that ripped the entire section of fence by the gate aside like matchsticks, pushed the churning mêlée of Killers and guerrillas towards the far end of the arena, casually irresistibly, like a breaker washing driftwood and old seaweed before it on a mountain of heaving foam. The Sadians who had entered through the stands poured down the aisles, over the benches, across the bodies of the less swift and down into the arena, until the whole near half of the Stadium was covered with a carpet of human beings from upper lip to arena floor like some wretched beast being eaten alive by a horde of soldier ants. And every one of them, tens upon tens of thousands, screaming 'BART! BART! BART! BART! BART! BART!'

Vanderling's jaw fell, his eyes went wide with terror, he stared around hopelessly like a rat in a trap.

In that instant of utter shock, Bart Fraden moved. As Vanderling took his eyes off him for the briefest of moments, Fraden lunged forward, drove his right fist deep into Vanderling's gut with the weight of his entire body behind the blow.

Vanderling grunted, doubled over, clutched at his stomach, dropped the snipgun. Fraden grabbed it, slapped Vanderling erect with the back of his left hand, jammed the muzzle of the snipgun into his gut.

'Want to bet your life that I *wasn't* lying?' he said to Vanderling. He turned to face the armed circle of hero-gyn-heads.

'Drop your guns and run!' he barked. 'Those are *my* people! Listen to 'em! Run or you're all dead men! Drop your guns and get out of here, or I turn you over to them and they eat you alive!'

The 'heads glanced around at the sea of chanting Sadians below, at the tide of people waving knives and clubs and torches and spears converging on them from the left, shouting Fraden's name as they poured towards them across the splintering benches. To a man, they broke and ran for the exit, some flinging their rifles aside, others still clutching them grimly.

Fraden scooped up a rifle, discarded the useless snip-gun, planted the point of the rifle in Vanderling's back. 'Wrong guess again!' he shouted at Vanderling, then half-turned to face the arena.

Killers, the few that remained, were scrabbling up over the railing of the Pavilion before a solid wall of screaming Sadians who now all but filled the arena floor. The Sadians threw knives, cleavers, spears at the fleeing Killers, and scores fell back into the mob, blades, spearshafts sticking out of their backs, to be torn to pieces by hands and teeth and nails. The Sadians filled the arena now, waving knives, shards of shattered crosses, flaming torches, blood-dripping limbs still festooned with shreds of black cloth.

'God!' Fraden muttered, scarcely believing his eyes. They were going totally ape! But it was all over! The Brotherhood was finished, Willem was helpless – they had to be stopped!

For the Sadians were attacking everything that moved. Killers and guerrillas alike were being torn to bloody fragments by cleavers and nails and teeth, and all the while, like one crazed organism, tens of thousands of throats were chanting his name with one mighty voice.

Fraden pulled Sophia to him with one hand, kept the rifle at Vanderling's back with the other, jumped to the top of the bench, elevated the rifle to cover Vanderling's head, put his free arm on Sophia's shoulder as she stood ashen-faced to the left and below him.

He fired four quick shots into the air – and Vanderling winced as the gun went off inches from his head.

Fraden stared down into the boiling sea of mad, feral faces. Thousands of them, a small fraction but thousands, had heard the shots, were looking up at him, nudging their neighbours, and in a minute or two the fighting died out, the chanting waned, as tens of thousands of Sadians stared up at their Liberator, while thousands more continued to pour into the Stadium in a never-ending stream.

Still covering Vanderling, Fraden raised his left arm, cupped his hand to his mouth. The chanting became a guttural, low, powerful rumble, the closest possible thing to silence in that crazed sea of humanity as they saw their hero trying to speak to them.

'It's over!' Fraden screamed, straining his lungs but still barely audible even to himself over the gargantuan murmuring. 'It's over! We've won!'

Mindlessly, the mob began to roar, and they took up the chant again, 'BART! BART! BART! BART! BART! BART!' And Fraden's voice was washed away like a zephyr in a hurricane. The great, all-enveloping carpet of Sadians began to jump and writhe madly, and Fraden could see whole bodies, limbs, severed heads being tossed above them like beach balls. The Sadians began to attack guerrillas still trapped in the arena, scattered Killers, even each other.

Got to stop 'em! Fraden thought desperately. But there was no way of . . . *Unless* . . .

He raised the rifle, pointed it dramatically towards the Pavilion, the Pavilion, which was a hideous heap of shattered bodies soaked in a great congealing puddle of red-umber blood.

Below, eyes followed the point of the rifle, saw the charnel heap of bodies, the bodies of the Brotherhood of Pain which had ruled Sangre with a fist of iron for three hundred years, the bodies of the hated enemy, the broken ruined bodies of the Brothers lying inert and bleeding in the red Sangran sunlight.

303

The fighting stopped again. The chanting stopped, and this time there was no great murmuring, but a silence, an ominous, pregnant silence as a hundred thousand eyes gazed in disbelief and wonder at the raw, bloody meat that was the last remnant of the Brotherhood of Pain.

With all the power of his lungs, feeling capillaries bursting in the back of his throat, Bart Fraden shouted into that terrible aural vacuum: 'FREEDOM! FREEDOM! THE BROTHERHOOD IS DEAD! LONG LIVE THE FREE REPUBLIC! GO BACK TO YOUR –'

Then everything seemed to happen at once.

Vanderling jumped up and backwards, reaching for the rifle of the distracted Fraden, twisting around to face him as he leapt, his face a crimson mask of rage and hate.

As Vanderling's fingers brushed the rifle, about to snatch it from Fraden's startled grasp, he suddenly screamed, doubled over, stumbling against Fraden.

Fraden saw Sophia had leapt up to the bench, had driven her knee into Vanderling's groin.

Even as the Stadium erupted in an explosion of screamed warnings, Fraden recovered, caught the doubled over Vanderling on the point of his jaw with the rifle butt.

Vanderling tumbled backwards, twisted half around, and Fraden caught him flush in the rear with a tremendous, savage kick. Vanderling rolled crazily down the steeply sloped stands, smashed through the shattered railing separating the stands from the arena, disappeared in a maelstrom of churning bodies, arms, legs, spears, torches, clubs.

It had all happened in an instant – the pointing to the Pavilion, the silence, Vanderling's attack, Sophia's blow, the screams of the Sadians, Vanderling's tumble into the crowd. In an instant, like neutrons bombarding an unstable nucleus from all directions at once, and in the next instant, the unstable mass exploded with a terrible, primal fury.

Freedom! The Brotherhood was gone! Freedom! The knowledge swept through the great packed crowd in the Stadium like a firestorm, setting every drop of blood in every wretched body ablaze with release, release from three centuries of a tyranny so gross it had all but implanted itself in their genes. Freedom!

But this was Sangre, planet of opposites, of blacks and whites graven into the souls of men by an absolute despotism that adored Pleasure as a god but worshipped the devil of Pain, that knew no middle ground. To be a slave was to be an Animal. To be a Brother was to be free. Not freedom *from*, but freedom *to* – freedom to murder, to torture, to consume living flesh, to answer the call of every twisted whim that festered in the nether regions of the human soul, to pile a mountain of corpses to the sky in order to scratch the most ephemeral, sordid itch. Brothers were . . . *Free!*

But the Brotherhood was dead, gone forever! Now the Animals of Sangre were Free! They were all Brothers of Pain now.

The entire Stadium erupted into a bestial orgy of cruelty, murder, and senseless horror. Man turned on woman, woman on man, children on parents, sires on offspring. The Sadians fell on each other with knives and clubs, with spears and cleavers, with teeth and claws and bloody severed limbs wielded as clubs. The Stadium rocked and heaved as the entire packed arena and the far half of the Stadium tiered with writhing humanity above and beyond it became one solid mass of ripping, slashing, stomping murderous beasts. Men and women embraced, an embrace of death, as nails tore away faces, as hands ripped away hair by the bloody roots. Children went down under stomping feet, knives, spears sticking from their ruined backs, sank their teeth into bare feet and thighs, hung on by their mouths like snapping turtles in their death throes. Limbs were ripped off by scores of hands, sent skipping over the heads of the mob as the still-living bodies were pulled down, disappeared gushing blood in a forest of kicking feet, snapping and biting as they died.

The far wall of the Stadium burst into flame, casting a lurid, flickering orange light on the madness below. Like reverse after-images burned into the retina of a blinded eye, emotions, drives, hungers turned inside out, became their opposites. Love was hate, pleasure was pain, sex was cruelty, murder was mercy, life was death, death was life as three centuries of victimized frustrations burst forth in an endless explosion like a huge, inflamed pustule lanced at last.

And every throat that was still connected to a pair of functioning lungs was screaming a hideous, mocking chant:

'BART! BART! BART! BART! BART! BART! BART! BART!'

As Fraden watched mindless, rooted to the concrete on which he stood, the great mass of packed, crazed, tortured humanity surged against the stands to the left of the great sheet of flame, battered against the wood and steel and concrete with the weight of thousands upon thousands of bodies, hundreds of tons of infuriated, seething flesh. Like an irresistible ram, the entire mob began to press against the grandstand. The Stadium groaned and creaked and sighed like a living thing in agony, and finally, weakened by the adjacent conflagration, stressed beyond endurance by the solid mass of insane humanity, with a terrible crack like the sky splitting open, the entire section of grandstand gave way, crumbled, fell, bearing the thousands upon it to their deaths, burying the vanguard of the mob in an avalanche of bodies, splintered steel girders, great jagged chunks of concrete.

But the great mass of the mob surged forward, the outer wall gave way, and, amidst the falling concrete chunks and girders, a great canyon opened up, splitting the far end of the Stadium, a clear line of sight and march to the shattered Compound wall and the city beyond.

Between the Stadium and the city proper, all but obscuring the ruined Compound wall with their bodies, was a sea of people, a sea that seemed to reach clear to the buildings of the city, a sea upon which bobbed a thousand torches; and beyond, the city was engulfed in a great pillar of fire below a huge cloud of heavy black smoke as thousands of wooden shacks were put to the torch.

And then Fraden saw Willem Vanderling.

Like a cork tossed up by a wind-whipped sea, Vanderling, his visage bloodied, his right leg twisted grotesquely like that of a ruined doll, seemed to pop up above the mass of humanity still packing the arena floor, bounced crazily above the Animals as they tore at him with a thousand hands.

By his churning arms, his tortured convulsions, it was clear that Vanderling was still very much alive. Then one of the uprooted crosses was raised erect, high above the heads of the mob by scores of hands. It dipped, disappeared from view into the human whirlpool. Then hands pulled Vanderling down and he too disappeared, a man sucked into living quicksand.

But a minute later, both the cross and Vanderling

reappeared, united now, held erect and aloft above the blood-crazed throng like some monstrous tribal totem.

They had nailed Vanderling to the cross, cruel spikes through his wrists, his forearms awash in his own blood. Yet Vanderling, his head snapping back and forth in agony like that of a bat nailed to a barn door, his body writing in torment, was still alive.

Like moths drawn to a candle, the Animals in the Stadium surged through the great rent towards the grisly funeral pyre of their city, their world, snapping at each other's entrails like a pack of rabid dogs, still slaughtering each other as they ran forward to wreak their will upon the planet.

And in their vanguard, as if some mystic icon, as their battle-flag as they poured forth to sack and pillage and rape their planet, to plunge all Sangre into a long, long night of savagery and murder and cannibalism, which seemed as if it could not end until the last rabid mouth had torn the last shred of flesh from the last splintered bone, they bore the cross, with Vanderling impaled upon it. And as they bore this living totem before them, men, women leapt up, snapped at Vanderling's body with their teeth, climbing halfway up the wood and tortured flesh, before falling back or being torn down by others, with shreds of skin and gobbets of warm living flesh still clinging to their fingernails and teeth.

While the cross bobbed away and out of sight towards the city, while the Stadium emptied through the jagged rent, their voices cried out, a great, horrifying, mocking chant, a paean of sickening, soul-searing adoration:

'BART! BART! BART! BART! BART! BART! BART! BART! BART! BART! BART! BART! BART! BART! BART! BART!'

'Willem! Willem!' Fraden wailed, a lost frail sound in

the hurricane of obscene chanting. 'I didn't know! How could I know . . .?'

Willem was a thug, a killer, everything that was crude and vicious and wrong in a man. Willem had tried to kill him twice in the past few minutes. But they had fought side by side in two wars, crossed light-years together, talked, eaten, cursed, argued, shared victory and defeat together. Whatever else he had been, traitor, killer, liar, Willem Vanderling was, after all, a real human being. To see him like this, the broken plaything of a mob of rabid beasts, this man who had been *real*, a real friend, a real enemy . . .

Fraden tore at himself with his fingernails, trying to make himself feel something, anything – hate, guilt, loathing, even pain. But he felt nothing. He knew that what had happened, what was still happening, was real, but he could not feel it. The horror was too much to comprehend, too abysmal to feel; his capacity for guilt, hate, loathing had been whited-out, overloaded. *It's not real!* his mind screamed. It can't be real!

But it was! It was! Willem, broken and dying, was real! Sangre was real! The universe was real! It was real, and it was a bottomless, infinite black pit out of which things spewed before which the mind of man, his very soul, was a poor lost thing whining in everlasting darkness.

The centre of the universe, the mind in control! That was the lie he had lived by, the lie that had let him stand strong, and unafraid and proud. But existence had no centre, and no man could control or comprehend it and it was a void of infinite possibility, infinite horror, in which a man was but a cruel, sick joke of fate, a ship tossed by monstrous, fell forces. And it was real, all real, and only the Bart Fraden he had known all his life was unreal, a lie, a cipher, a pathetic, powerless nothing. Fraden was drained, sucked dry, overcome, powerless, unable even to care . . .

Like the will-less creature he had become, he looked down, saw that Sophia, on her knees, was clinging to him, tears streaming down her face, her body wracked with sobs.

'Bart, Bart, Bart, . . .' she moaned. 'Get me out of here! Please, please, please get me out of here!'

His heart went out to her, one poor nothing crying in vain to another in a black void that felt nothing, cared not whether they lived or died. Some small dying ember still glowed hot, deep within him. She would not die here, not like this! It was all absurdity, action or inaction, but he would choose his own absurdity – at least nothing could deny him *that*.

He jerked her to her feet, looked around narrow-eyed like an animal at bay. The Stadium was rapidly emptying through the great wound in its side, but the arena was still a maelstrom of horror. He looked at the stands above him, empty now, ruined. He saw a clot of perhaps two dozen Killers, clothes tattered shreds, eyes wild with fright, standing uncertainly, abandoned by their dead masters, near an exit portal. Poor lost creatures like . . . *Act!* he told himself. Enough thinking! Act! Act!

He scrabbled beneath the bench, pounced on the paper-wrapped bundle, catlike, ripped away the wrapping, threw the black Brother's robe about his shoulders.

Pulling Sophia behind him, he ran up the stands, confronted the Killers.

'You!' he roared. 'Form a circle around us! Now! In the name of the Brotherhood of Pain, I order you to obey me! Jump to it! Move!'

The Killers stared woodenly for a moment at this wild-eyed, roaring demon. A Brother! Orders! Merciful orders! The Killers formed a rough circle around them, rifles pointed outward.

Down through the bowels of the ruined, burning Stadium they ran, through passageways choked with smoke. Empty, all dead and empty. They emerged into the sunlight between the Stadium and the Palace, by the circle of parked trucks. The Palace was burning, huge orange flames lighting up the sky, the heat searing Fraden's flesh.

Fraden shoved Sophia before him, half-lifted her into the cab of a truck, jumped up behind the wheel beside her.

He turned the ignition, jabbed the accelerator, and the engine sputtered and caught. He tore off the Brother's robe like an unclean thing, flung it down at the startled Killers, gunned the motor and the truck lurched away from the Stadium in a cloud of dust and rubber.

The truck screeched around the corner of the burning Palace, and Fraden saw that the mob was fast receding towards the city. Every outbuilding had been smashed to flinders. The Compound walls were breached, broken, piles of loose rubble, in dozens of places. The makeshift corrals that had filled the courtyard were gone, a million wooden splinters, and the entire courtyard was filled with the pulped, bleeding bodies of the Meatanimals – the pathetic corpses of thousands of naked children. To the west, Sade was a pillar of fire, a great consuming firestorm, towards which, like a living carpet of insects, the Sadians swarmed, bearing ten thousand tiny, bobbing torches.

Fraden floored the accelerator, steered the truck towards a rubble-strewn gap in the eastern wall. The truck jolted through the rent with a piercing scream of metal on concrete, sending a shower of sparks flying.

Fraden's foot on the accelerator was jammed against

the floorboard. The truck careened madly down the grassy hill on which the Palace Compound stood, reached the broad empty plain.

South, south, across the empty plain, Sophia staring woodenly ahead, not speaking, not looking at him. Perhaps fifteen miles south of the city, Fraden turned the truck to the northwest. The truck jounced cruelly across the plain, and each bump seemed to mock him, another blow inflicted by an uncaring fate, yet at the same time caused by his own hand.

Finally, they reached the road that led west across the plain towards the guerrilla camp. Fraden steered the truck up on to the roadway, drove west towards the camp and the lifeboat.

Escape! Escape! he told himself as they reached the canyon that funnelled the road west off the plain, the canyon littered with the refuse of that last, terrible battle now seemed a thousand years in the past.

For hours they drove on in silence, Sophia a frozen mannequin, Fraden but a pair of hands on the wheel, a foot on the accelerator, connected by a mind that scrabbled for purchase, a place to stand, any place to stand. They drove through jungle, across clearing, here and there past a village, all burning, burning, as the madness spread cancerlike and swift from the crazed thing that was Sade.

Escape! Escape! Vagrant thoughts tormented him. He remembered another flight, less than a year ago, the flight from the Belt Free State. What had happened to the man who had fled the Solar System, cool, calm, calculating, with a smile on his lips? Where had he been lost? How had he become this thing that had plunged a whole world into darkness, step by step, blind, utterly blind, moved like a pawn by an invisible demon hand to the brink of the final pit?

Finally, they reached the guerrilla camp. Fraden brought the truck to a halt beside one of the shiny, antiseptic-looking lifeboats. Wordlessly, he got down, helped Sophia from the cab. He went over to the 'boat, pressed the airlock door stud. The outer airlock door slid smoothly upward, and the interior of the 'boat beckoned. Beckoned to *what*?

He looked behind him at the empty camp, the silent huts, the dregs of dozens of cookfires. Far in the distance, a wisp of smoke curled above the treetops, and another, and another. It seemed as if the planet were one vast decomposing corpse, and he was dissolving with it. Where would he go? What would he do?

He thought of the first moment he had set foot on Sangre, the stranger who had landed on an unknown planet to make it his own. A wave of unbearable nostalgia and loss inundated him as he remembered that man who had stood so jauntily under an alien sun, who had seemed to hold existence in the palm of his hand, the Hero, the centre of the universe, the Man Who . . . It all seemed so long ago and far away. Could he find that man again? Could he go back? Was there any *other* place he could go?

He turned to Sophia. Her eyes were red, her cheeks stained with dried tears, her long red hair a tangled heap. His mouth worked soundlessly for a moment.

'You know what I've got to do?' he finally said.

She stood there looking up at him, still as a corpse, her face an immobile, stricken mask.

'I've got to go back,' he said. 'Back to Sol, back to the Belt, back to Earth. Where . . . where else is there? I can't go find another planet, start another . . . another

Sangre. Lord only knows what they'll do to me . . . I suppose I'm a war criminal or something.' He laughed, a bitter, whining sound. 'Who cares?' he said. 'What's the difference? I'm finished anyway, empty, used up. I never was what I thought I was in the first place. It's all . . . it's all just too big for me, for anyone. I feel like a bug, like a bug who thought his wet rock was the universe, till someone came along and flipped it over . . .'

'Bart . . .' she murmured, touched her hand to his cheek. He jerked his head away.

'How can you stand to touch me?' he cried. 'Look at me! Look at what I am, remember what I've done! I'll put you off on Mars – I've still got connections there. You'll be all right, no one will be after you. I owe you that much. You'll be safe, and someday you'll look back on all this like it was a bad dream. You won't even be able to believe that it happened. I hardly can, even now. You'll forget all about me. You won't even remember how much you hate me now.'

'H-hate you?' she stammered. Some of the old fire crept back into her eyes. '*Hate you*'? she shouted. 'You utter imbecile! You stupid, self-centred swine! Haven't you ever been kicked in the ass before? You think life is one success after another? Sure life is full of horror and wretchedness and miserable filth! Sure we all do things we can't bear, things we want to puke every time we remember them! Sure we're grubby little worms scrabbling in a garbage-dump! I knew all that before I was sixteen years old. Welcome to the club, Bart, welcome to where it's at. Is that any reason to whine like a kicked puppy? Maybe it is . . . But are you going to give *it*, all the stupidity, horror and sheer banality of life, the goddamned satisfaction? That's not the Bart Fraden *I've* been sleeping with! The Bart Fraden I know would have the balls to fight back. My Bart would roll it all into a tight wad and shove it down existence's puerile throat!'

Blazing fury, her eyes rheumy and bloodshot, her face smeared with dried tears and dirt, her mouth a snarl – he had never seen anything so beautiful in his life.

'Soph . . .'

She flung herself at him, buried her face against his neck. 'You're not getting rid of me that easy,' she said, her voice a breaking, quavering parody of cynical toughness. 'You made me love you, you bastard, and you're stuck with me whether you like it or not. Whither thou goest . . . my Peerless Leader!'

'Soph . . .'

Arm in arm, they went into the lifeboat.

An hour later, they sat side by side in the control room of the starship as the lights of the computopilot console one by one went green, completing the automatic checkout cycle, and in the viewscreen, Sangre was a calm, benign globe of peaceful browns and greens and blues.

Bart Fraden stared at that image, and wondered at what he felt. For what he felt was nothing. Somehow, he had bounced. Perhaps, he was able to wanly tell himself, perhaps somewhere there is a something that laughs knowingly and takes care of its own.

He looked at Sophia, at the strange new softness in her eyes, and he knew that whatever he had lost, he had also gained something. Life was worth living after all. And even if it wasn't, it was still the only game in town.

The last light went green and, deep within the ship, the automatics were about to begin the long journey back to Sol, back to uncertainty, back to . . .

Screw 'em all! Fraden thought, If I survived Sangre, I can survive anything! He smiled.

'What're you smiling about?' Sophia said softly.

Fraden laughed. 'I was just thinking about the mess we're going back to . . .' he said. 'I wonder how Great China and the Atlantic Union and the GSU are holding the Confederation together, with the Uranium Bodies to squabble about. Now *there's* an unstable triangle! Hmmm . . . you know, I never formally renounced my AU citizenship. Now if I popped up and claimed that I was still *de jure* ruler of the Belt, and offered to apply for admission directly to the Atlantic Union, that would give the AU a legal claim to sole possession of the Uranium Bodies . . . China and the GSU would scream bloody murder, but with a prize like that, the AU might just decide to play ball with me . . . It has its possibilities . . . Who knows, I might even be able to get hold of Ah Ming again . . .'

Sophia O'Hara laughed, the old, old laugh. She squeezed his hand, kissed him.

'Sackcloth and ashes never did become you,' she said with a wry, knowing smile as the ship lurched, began to break orbit. 'Back to business as usual, eh, Peerless Leader? Fun and games! *Fun and games!*'

The world's greatest science fiction authors
now available in paperback from Grafton Books

Samuel R Delaney

Stars in My Pocket Like Grains of Sand	£2.95	☐

William Gibson

Neuromancer	£2.95	☐

Sterling E Lanier

Menace Under Marswood	£1.95	☐
The Unforsaken Hiero	£2.50	☐
Hiero's Journey	£2.50	☐

Ian Watson

Chekhov's Journey	£1.95	☐
The Book of Being	£1.95	☐
The Book of the River	£1.95	☐
The Book of the Stars	£2.50	☐

Kevin O'Donnell Jr

Ora:cle	£2.95	☐

Robert Sheckley

Mindswap	£1.95	☐
Dimension of Miracles	£2.50	☐
Options	£2.50	☐

To order direct from the publisher just tick the titles you want
and fill in the order form.   **SF1382**

The world's greatest science fiction authors
now available in paperback from Grafton Books

Philip José Farmer
The Riverworld Saga

To Your Scattered Bodies Go	£2.50	☐
The Fabulous Riverboat	£1.95	☐
The Dark Design	£2.95	☐
The Magic Labyrinth	£2.95	☐
Riverworld	£2.50	☐
Gods of Riverworld	£2.50	☐

Other Titles

Dayworld	£2.50	☐
Dark is the Sun	£1.95	☐
Jesus on Mars	£1.50	☐
Riverworld and other stories	£2.50	☐
The Stone God Awakens	£1.50	☐
Time's Last Gift	£1.50	☐
Strange Relations	£1.95	☐
The Unreasoning Mask	£1.95	☐
The Book of Philip José Farmer	£1.95	☐
The Image of the Beast	£1.95	☐
Blown	£1.95	☐

To order direct from the publisher just tick the titles you want
and fill in the order form.

All these books are available at your local bookshop or newsagent, or can be ordered direct from the publisher.

To order direct from the publishers just tick the titles you want and fill in the form below.

Name _____

Address _____

_____

Send to:
Grafton Cash Sales
PO Box 11, Falmouth, Cornwall TR10 9EN.

Please enclose remittance to the value of the cover price plus:

UK 60p for the first book, 25p for the second book plus 15p per copy for each additional book ordered to a maximum charge of £1.90.

BFPO 60p for the first book, 25p for the second book plus 15p per copy for the next 7 books, thereafter 9p per book.

Overseas including Eire £1.25 for the first book, 75p for second book and 28p for each additional book.

Grafton Books reserve the right to show new retail prices on covers, which may differ from those previously advertised in the text or elsewhere.